Dear Joan & David,
    I much appreciate your
interest in my novel,

THE WIDOW'S

PARAMOUR

and hope you will
find enjoyment in reading
it. With sincere best
wishes, I remain,
    yours sincerely

THE WIDOW'S PARAMOUR

*Murder and Sexual
Indiscretion Plague
a 1962 Church*

A. C. HELDMAN

To order additional copies of this book, contact:
Xlibris Corporation
1-888-795-4274
www.Xlibris.com
Orders@Xlibris.com
18776

Contents

ACKNOWLEDGEMENT 11
MAP: CATHEDRAL AND GROUNDS OF FIRST
    PRESBYTERIAN CHURCH 12
PROLOGUE: MONDAY BEFORE DAWN—
    JANUARY 22, 1962 13

PART ONE: FIRST HEAT WAVE

CHAPTER 1: MURDER'S LEGACY 19
CHAPTER 2: LOOKING FOR LOVE 42
CHAPTER 3: NIGHTMARE YEARS 62
CHAPTER 4: "A DREADFUL MAN" 98
CHAPTER 5: DAY OF REST 116
CHAPTER 6: SLEEPLESS NIGHT 140
CHAPTER 7: TEMPERATURE RISING 161
CHAPTER 8: THE BURDEN OF SECRETS 181
CHAPTER 9: EXPOSURES 198
CHAPTER 10: DISCOVERIES 223
CHAPTER 11: IDLE INSIGHTS 251
CHAPTER 12: LONESOME TONIGHT 286
CHAPTER 13: LOST MOMENTS 314
CHAPTER 14: COMPLICATING CIRCUMSTANCES 343
CHAPTER 15: DRIVEN 356
CHAPTER 16: SINNERS OR SAINTS? 377

CHAPTER 17: A DEATH IN THE FAMILY 408
CHAPTER 18: FLIGHT TO MIDNIGHT 418

PART II: YEAR'S END, 1962

CHAPTER 19: LOOKING BACK,
  LOOKING FORWARD 435
CHAPTER 20: TO MURDER AGAIN 462
CHAPTER 21: LOVE ME! 488

To Betty Lou, wife and friend these many years.

"A solemn consideration, when I enter a great city by night, that every one of those darkly clustered houses encloses its own secret . . . that every beating heart in the hundreds of thousands of breasts there, is, in some of its imaginings, a secret to the heart nearest it."

—Charles Dickens
A TALE OF TWO CITIES

ACKNOWLEDGEMENT

I wish to thank all those in my literary discussion groups who bore with me in the making of this novel. Without their critiques and suggestions, I dare say the task would have withered long ago. I am especially grateful to Claude Campbell ("Abou and the Angel Cohen, *Bridge Works*), who read the novel in full during its early development. His insight and critical eye egged me on. In the end, one must write as he sees and feels his characters. And while I could wish for a shorter story, this time I gave it my all.

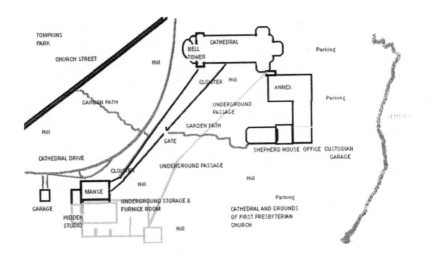

Cathedral and Grounds of First Presbyterian Church

PROLOGUE

MONDAY BEFORE DAWN
JANUARY 22, 1962

The cathedral at First Presbyterian Church appeared ghostly in its ornament of snow-crusted ice, an artifact of useless praise as its great bell began a five o'clock toll into the cold breath of morning darkness. Towering above Tompkinsville's only hill, the gray stone structure seemed apart from surrounding city streets and country lanes adrift in a foot of snow, left there by a blizzard passing northeast on New Jersey's southern plains. Now changed to icy residue, the tempest fell with renewed vigor, streaming through the lancet arches of the cloister that connected the minister's residence and the cathedral, thus, deterring the forward approach of Rhonda Maefield.

She planned to go no farther than Shepherd House, her husband's study, which stood midway between the two church buildings. She wished the lighting was better, for she had to make do beneath decorative lamps, recessed every twelve feet in the vaulted ceiling. Any more illumination would ruin the "old-world" charm, church traditionalists had told her, a "stupidity," she scoffed, thinking how impractical to install the lamps if not to benefit the safety of parishioners. But her mind was mostly on her husband, the Reverend Doctor Daniel Maefield, who often remained at Shepherd House from dusk to dawn. She mused how much he enjoyed nights like this when he could build a fire in the fireplace, exchange his shoes for velvet slippers and, from the comfort of his chair, read, sip English sherry, and predictably fall into a restful sleep. He relied on her visit to awaken him. After idle chat, even on bad weather mornings like this, they would go out to breakfast at an all-night diner, a walker's mile from the church. In recent years, this had become their best time together.

Before that thought had left her mind, the tower bell struck its fifth note, followed by a loud crash of metal. Startled, she stopped and searched the darkness where a moving figure appeared to cross her path. In that moment, needles of sleet pelted her face, forcing her to remove her glasses. Looking again, she concluded she had seen nothing more than a stirring of shadows cast by outlying flood lamps onto branches of blowing cedar trees. Numb with cold, she pulled tightly on the belt of her coat and drew her muffler over her head. Bowing to the wind, she moved on to the iron gate guarding access to Shepherd House, but now swinging on its hinges, awaiting a new force of wind to crash it another time against the cloister wall.

"Why is the gate open? It should be latched," she protested. "He has become more neglectful of his safety, too trusting, careless and forgetful. *"Du Frommer* (Pious fool)" she complained, using her favorite phrase of ridicule from her native German.

Shuffling through the opening, she latched the gate behind her. Hanging on the stair rail, she supported her way down ice-coated steps to the garden landing where she made her way over rutted snow to the shielded entrance of Shepherd House. She did not have a key and he would have to let her in. She reached to ring the bell, an old brass fixture that operated by turning a crank. She noticed then that the oak door hung slightly open.

"First the gate, now this," she hissed. Her voice gruff with irritation, she shouted into the open way, "Daniel, are you there? Daniel!"

Seconds passed. She barked louder. "Daniel!"

Again, she waited. A terrible fear, born long ago, stole her boldness. She cranked the bell. A loud, harsh ring overrode the wailing wind.

"He may be in another building. Perhaps he went to the cathedral," she explained to herself and once more, she turned the crank, this time longer and more insistently.

Her gentle push swung the door into semi darkness. She stepped over the threshold, and poked her head around the corner. Opposing the stillness, she pounded her feet on the entrance mat, knocking bits of packed snow from her storm boots. Her fastidious style required leaving shoes at the door. But she would not do that here, not now, not while sensing something eerily forbidding in this place of treasured books and old furnishings.

"Daniel, where are you?" she called, her voice grave and pleading.

She stepped ahead of his cluttered desk and lingered for a moment, listened for some indication of his presence, some answer to the stale silence. Her glasses fogged, she removed her gloves to get at the tissue in her pocket. Wiping them clean, in the low light before her, she observed the jagged stones of the fireplace, the heavy oak mantle, the helmet-rose shade of the Tiffany lamp as it sparkled above his empty chair. She saw embers glowing red in the fireplace, smelt the mild smoke rising from the smoldering wood and heard the last remnants of the fire spit and crackle. All seemed peaceful until she saw red splattering on the glass doors of bookshelves, and the ottoman upended and moved forward.

"Daniel?" she asked in a chilling tone.

Sharp fear ignited her nerves and hesitant steps moved her forward. Denying instinct to turn away, she moved past the oval conference table to peer over the ottoman. And there she saw him on the floor, rigid, on his back, his legs wide apart, his arms at his sides, his head unnaturally positioned on his neck.

Her mind strained to believe the gruesome scene her eyes saw. But she spoke as if to a living being. "Why is blood on your face? Your clerical collar? Your jacket? Your shirt torn in so many places? Where are your glasses?" she demanded.

Of course, she knew the folly of such questions. She knew he was dead. She knew she was looking into lifeless eyes in a body that had fed the rug on which it rested all of its lost blood.

PART ONE

FIRST HEAT WAVE

June 5-13, 1962

CHAPTER 1

MURDER'S LEGACY

Tuesday Morning, June 5, 1962

Jerry Flynn had the road to himself. Straight and narrow, the highway cut through lush farmland watered by a better-than-normal wet spring and sleeping under a cool morning mist. He marveled at the beauty of the landscape rushing toward him and thought that nothing could delay the rapid growth of these fertile fields of fruits and vegetables. Yet, if weather forecasters had their way, these massive gardens would soon wilt under the weight of the region's first heat wave.

He had left his campus apartment at Princeton Seminary by the first light of dawn to drive south by a web of highways through New Jersey's central plains. His route avoided toll and other high traffic roads and, in no hurry, these county blacktops gave him a view of the land he found both comforting and exciting. His destination was the heart of the "Garden State's" truck-farming industry, the city of Tompkinsville, almost equal in distance as the crow flies from Philadelphia northwest and Atlantic City northeast. In less than two weeks, he would become pastor of the city's First Presbyterian Church.

*   *   *

Founded in 1760 by refugees from Scotland's last failed war of independence from England, the congregation of Presbyterians had ever since owned the hill, a topographical oddity amid flatland that sloped on a gradual plain east to the sea. Here they had grounded succeeding houses of worship until just after the Civil War, when they had built their towering cathedral. Now numbering over fifteen hundred members, post war growth had come rapidly as new housing developments sprung up in and around Tompkinsville. Church endowments numbered in the millions of dollars. Its buildings fit a gothic image as durable as a French original. A connoisseur of church architecture, writing in "The American Architectural Review," had assessed the hundred-year-old First Church as among the ten most beautiful church developments in the United States, and had judged the cathedral as *unequaled in its inspiring representation of God's presence.*

But if some folks saw this grand cathedral an idyllic paradise, most knew better. Jerry Flynn would take over after the headline murder of his sixty-three-year-old predecessor, Daniel Maefield, a crime that remained unsolved. And even absent this murderous event, First Church had a history of ministries that had ended more ruinous than the one that had preceded it. During the last twenty-five years, one minister, less than three years at his post, married and father of four children, had resigned when his affair with the church secretary became common knowledge. The man who followed had despaired over personal criticism so much that he hanged himself from a tree in the backyard of his residence. The next minister, accused of embezzling church funds, resigned less than two years into his pastorate. The search committee took its time to find a replacement and finally recommended a man they considered a saint. He appeared in excellent health, but six months into his "call," at age forty-three, in the middle of his Sunday sermon, he fell over, dead of a heart attack. His successor resigned when he lost in a power struggle with the Board of Trustees. Conflict among the church's lay leadership had gotten so out-of-hand, Presbytery (the name for the denomination's

regional governing body) had to appoint an outside commission
to run the church. And, unable to decide on an agreeable
candidate for the pulpit, the church was without a permanent
minister for nearly three years.

Then Doctor Daniel Maefield, a world-renowned New
Testament scholar and professor at Columbia University, came to
First Church. A graduate of Scotland's Edinburgh University and
then Princeton, at the time of his call to First Church, he was
writing biblical commentaries and teaching Renaissance History.
Wearing two hats, he served with distinction as pastor of a non-
denominational church in Harlem. Soft spoken and meek by
disposition, he seemed the perfect match for the hard-working
farmer folks on these Jersey plains. But if God had called a lamb
to lie down with a lion, they were not at peace in First Church.
From Dr. Maefield's opening days to his death, old and young
lions alike roared against his social activism, found fault with his
theology and complained about his liberal interpretation of the
Bible.

Removing him was no easy task. Installed for life, without
moral or legal grounds to send him packing, his adversaries had
no option but to accept this "peculiar" lamb. Nor was Maefield
without followers. An excellent preacher, and, while few listeners
agreed with his social agenda, most respected his views and
enjoyed his colorful and dramatic pulpit parlance. Ironically, his
hottest critics applauded his administrative style, which he
conveyed through a passive nature and hands-off management
policy. Free to study, write, preach, pastor and travel as he saw
fit, he simply ignored how the church's trustees administered the
buildings and interest income. He never attended their meetings.
And while required to moderate sessions of the church's elected
elders, he called "The Session" to order infrequently, usually
only to listen politely as elders complained at what he referred to
as "inconsequential matters."

But if Maefield had been derelict in his polity, his Scottish
brogue and old-way demeanor had made up for it. Scotland was
after all the cradle of Presbyterianism and as Jerry saw from the

records of former ministers, a majority had degrees from its Edinburgh University.

And here he was, as totally different from them as a shamrock in a barrel of oranges. Born and raised Roman Catholic, four years ago he had not a thimble full of knowledge about what Presbyterians believed. He had grown up in an Irish neighborhood of Philadelphia, his mother the widow of a city cop killed in the line of duty, his stepfather a former Catholic priest.

How well he recalled that night when Father O'Flanagan, the police chaplain, brought news of his father's death. Jerry would never forget his mother's shrill cry as she screamed his name, a wail surely heard at heaven's gate. Once more, she folded into "Father O's" arms when word arrived that his oldest brother, Matthew, was among Pearl Harbor's fallen sailors. And again, when news arrived that Joe, the next oldest, had his legs blown off on Guam. Father's comfort continued when news arrived about his sister, Mary, an army nurse, stationed in the Philippines, who became a prisoner of war when General Wainright surrendered Corregidor. They called the Flynn house a house of heroes, but to Jerry, it was a house of grief.

Today, Joe would enter Walter Reed Hospital to have his stumps refitted with new prostheses. A fighter, Joe had superior patience and courage to match. What a marvel he could walk so well on artificial limbs. If anyone, who did not know better, asked Joe about his slow and awkward progress, he would comment on his arthritis or make a joke about the weather getting into his joints.

General Macarthur was Mary's hero. The only time she met him, which was at a hospital in Manila after the war, she kissed his West Point ring in a way a Catholic kisses the ring of the Holy Father. "Mary still weeps for the dead," Jerry said into the wind whipping through his open window. "She weeps for all those she couldn't save in that dark, rotting prison hospital where the Japanese interred her." That feeling had led Mary to take vows as a nun and to join an order dedicated to the care of the terminally ill. As Jerry thought about Mary, he saw a person of infinite compassion, forgiveness and kindness. "When I see the face of my sister," he said, his eyes glued to the road, his mind far away, "I see the face of Christ."

Jerry believed that out of such grieving family experiences, his own life had found purpose and strength. You have to build on the ashes, he told himself. You have to take a positive view of people and circumstances and, as the prayer of St Francis of Assisi prescribes, concentrate on changing those things that you can change.

He guessed he would be the first in his family to try that as a Protestant, a change that had occurred not out of personal rebellion or even theological conflict. He had known too little about those Catholic things for them to have made a difference. Rather he explained it as something like marooned at sea without the slightest idea of where you are or where you are headed, then, awaking one morning to hands reaching out and pulling you in. The rescuers feed you, care for your wounds, cloth you and love you. Had saving hands come from Mohammad, Jerry understood, he could have become a mullah.

At age thirty, he would become the youngest minister ever elected to serve First Church and the only one unmarried. For his undergraduate education, he had attended a state teachers' college, paid for from an ROTC grant, which had in turn made him the product of the U.S. Army for three years. Seminary at a Presbyterian institution, he owed to an army chaplain, by denomination a Presbyterian, who had turned his life around, had rescued him.

All things considered, Jerry thought it unlikely that his first parish would be Tompkinsville.

But the Nominating Committee had liked him from the start and had evaluated his preaching as superior to some of the most experienced men they had heard. They had counted his three years as a commissioned Lieutenant in the U.S. Army as part of his working experience. They had seen him as eager and ready to assert vigorous leadership where there had been none. The majority had no kinship to Scotland and could care less whether doctoral stripes emboldened their pastor's academic gown. As for his age, they had reasoned that if Jesus could begin his ministry as young as thirty, why not any minister who came to First Church. And when assessing the value of marriage, marriage was a man's prerogative and they would not make it a requirement of employment. In recommending him, the committee spoke of Jerry Flynn as their church's best hope in a youthful and growing community.

*   *   *

The straight emptiness of the highway and ease of acceleration built into Flynn's 1957 Chrysler Crown Imperial made speed effortless. Driving into the rising sun, he reached to pull down the visor. Simultaneously, a flatbed truck raced from a field and turned sharply in front of him. Loaded high with crates of fresh-picked produce and four farm workers holding on to flimsy side panels, the truck strained to pick up speed and outdistance him. He could not pass because of a car coming toward him. His only option was to hit the brakes hard, and he did so as he leaned on the horn. The Imperial struggled to stop. Its wheels screeching, tires skidding, the big car began sliding into the hulking vehicle. Jerry's face froze in death. He braced for the crush. With seconds and inches separating truck and car from impact, the flatbed lurched forward and drove on to the crusty shoulder. The Imperial straightened and stopped unscathed. A stroke of anger followed a stretch of silence and immobility to catch his breath. Moving quickly, he drove up on the truck's cab and shouted out his down-turned window, "Hey, you crazy cowboy! You almost killed us!"

But the driver merely shrugged, a broad grin lighting his Latino face. He tipped his broad hat and, with a wave, he turned off the shoulder onto a dirt road. Jerry watched in his mirror as the truck disappeared in a haze of dust and smoke amongst more vegetable fields.

"Jerk! He never looked to see me coming. No excuse . . . I shouldn't have lost my temper. What the hell . . . " he sighed, "the man's right! Why get annoyed at what you can't change?" Farm workers as much as owned these rural roads, he thought to himself. This is their busy season—planting and harvesting, tilling and fertilizing, weighing and packing. Those boys probably picked that truckload in the first crack of light, and have more to do before the noonday sun shuts them down.

Ten miles farther, he slowed as he approached a crossroad where a dozen Mexican farm workers waited for transportation to the fields they would work today.

"I doubt those *campesino* would have much appreciation for me as a worker," Jerry blurted for his own edification. For them, work is bending all day; lifting heavy equipment, walking a mile or more just to begin labor. Work is tilling with a hoe and digging with a shovel. You don't do work writing at a desk, reading in a chair, preaching from a pulpit, visiting at a hospital. But work is what it is. "I hope I'm ready, as the liturgy says *'to serve in the way a shepherd cares for his sheep'.*" Jerry frowned. The analogy gave him goose bumps. He grimaced as he remembered the book of Genesis, where the farmer, Cain, killed the shepherd. The murder of Abel was committed out of jealousy of a shepherd's easy and, Cain believed, God-favored life. The man who worked with his hands and broke his back, so to speak, laboring under a boiling sun, never recognized the value of the lounging idealist, poet and dreamer. Caring for sheep was no work. After spilling the shepherd's blood, Cain had only derision in his voice. "*Am I my brother's keeper?*" he enquired when asked about his brother's whereabouts. Jerry saw the story in parallel with Jesus' death. People who misunderstood Jesus' shepherd's crown murdered him. "How can any mortal take on that 'Good Shepherd' role? How can I?" he shouted into the rising sun. Then, annoyed by his self-doubts, he answered himself, quoting a verse of scripture. "*With God, all things are possible.*" He smiled at this subtle rejoinder. For every negative, he believed a positive followed. His logic had set his mind on solid ground again.

Several miles north of Tompkinsville, he spotted the spire of what folks in this area called The Presbyterian Cathedral, a misnomer, he believed, a designation for a church building more suitable to Lutherans, Episcopalians and Roman Catholics. In Presbyterian circles, there was no tradition of a bishop governing the church domain from a "cathedral" that called attention to his ecclesiastical wealth and authority.

"I'd have to dress in petticoats," Jerry said, a smirk replacing the broad smile on his face. He laughed at the image—ministers in lace dresses and fancy hats, pageantry from his childhood he had never understood and he now saw as foolish.

As he sped into the outskirts of Tompkinsville, he caught a clear view of the high-standing cathedral. Right or wrong, he had to admit the building had all the markings of a gothic edifice born in the fourteenth century. From this vantage, he recalled his travels in Europe, where grand churches in rural settings were common. Surrounded by endless rows of grape arbors, guarded by walled cities and tall castles, village cathedrals stood as places of peace and refuge. In that way, First Church seemed tranquil, even romantic.

All that changed as he passed lines of low unsightly warehouses. Crushed cardboard boxes and wooden vegetable crates reached the roofs. Among the warehouses stood food-processing factories. Here tomato soup flowed like a molten river and string beans came out chopped, steamed and preserved as if forever in vacuum-packed tin cans. And dispersed amid the ugly buildings, waiting to service the wakeful city, used-car lots, farm-equipment show rooms, agriculture-supply stores, gas stations, motels, bars and restaurants lined the traffic-clogged highway.

A minute later, he drove into the city's business district. He slowed to take in its small-town urban features—a Woolworth's, a bank and a Sears and Roebuck. Across the street was a Penny's and next to it stood a storefront public library. Turning on to Main Street, he passed Engine Company 2 Volunteer Fire Station, an Acme Super Market and a corner bar with black plate-glass windows. Soon he reached Tompkins City Park triangle, a busy intersection separating Main, Tompkins and Church Street.

It was rush hour and a single line of cars, bumper to bumper, followed his sluggish progress. He continued through the green light, crossed the westbound lanes of Main Street, when his engine coughed and cut off. The car rolled to a complete stop in front of the Revolutionary War statue of Colonel Samuel Tompkins. Behind him, he heard a horn honk and then another and another. He was holding up traffic. But what could he do other than sit and wait a minute? He had had this problem before. If he couldn't get the car started after one try, he would ask for a push. His hand out the window, he motioned those behind to pass, but oncoming traffic blocked the single west lane. So, he drew in his hand and turned his head to face the musket-ready sentinel. He tried to read the inscription, something about bravery on Long Island. He raised his hand in a sharp, military salute. By now, some blocked motorists had become livid and several vehicles, honking all the way, sped around him. He pushed the gas pedal to the floor and turned the ignition. The engine burst to life. He had less than a mile to drive. Halfway past Tompkins City Park, he signaled right and turned through the opened gates on the shaded grounds of the cathedral at First Presbyterian Church.

There, in front of him, in bold letters on the church message board, he saw—**Welcome! THE REV. JEREMIAH COVENTRY FLYNN.**

*　　*　　*

Madge Todd held her temper, but the driver in front had her doing a slow burn. Although tempted, she did not join others who blew their car horns in anger and frustration when he stopped dead center at the Revolutionary War statue guarding Tompkins Park. "What is he doing there?" she questioned as she scanned her left-side-view mirror, but then cars coming toward her gave no chance to get around. "And why does he choose now to salute the statue?" She saw an opportunity and signaled her intention to pass, but just as she started to move, the black Imperial edged forward. Once more, she had to run close to his bumper. When he turned into the drive at First Church, she felt relief. Finally, he was out of everyone's way.

As she charged on, it occurred to her that the driver might be the new minister. She had heard he would arrive today. "If it is Reverend Flynn, let's hope he loses his tourist wings real soon. And thank you, God," she uttered in a pious aside, "for keeping me from beeping my horn at him. After such rudeness, how could I face him?" she exclaimed and, as quickly as her blushing smile had begun, it receded. How silly, she thought, becoming overburdened with stress about something as incidental as having shown a little impertinence at the minister. Yet, she knew she had only been kidding herself. The action of First Church calling a pastor close to her age excited her. The church needed a man with new ideas, someone interested in meeting the needs of the hundreds of kids in their Sunday school and youth programs. Three housing projects had sprung up in the last six months alone. With young families moving into every home, the church required energetic leadership. "He'll be a refreshing change," she purred.

Madge had met Jerry Flynn seven weeks ago at a reception following his election. One member among a room-full congratulating him, she wondered if he would remember her. She could not forget him. Tall, handsome, friendly, humorous and articulate, she had liked him right away. "If only things were different," she sighed.

That Madge yearned for things different would have surprised people who knew the thirty-two-year-old beauty, mother of two, as a graduate of Cornell Agriculture College, Personnel Manager and Vice President of Marketing for T&T Produce Company (daughter of the company founder, wife of the president), active in PTA, Grange, 4-H, Sunday-school teacher and President of the Women's Guild of First Church. She appeared to have it all. To friends who knew her since grade school by her nickname, *Sweetpea*, she had remained simply that—loveable, pretty and bright. None of those things would she want changed. What lay beneath the surface was another story—those dark urges, those matters that manifested themselves in relationships she questioned and could not reconcile, those actions that bothered her conscience and which, should they become known, would destroy her life.

"Why think about such things now?" she berated herself as she turned sharply onto the south entrance ramp of the Garden State Parkway. Like fire inside a mountain that randomly rises to the surface, she could feel her dark memories erupting from the pit of her stomach, eroding her peace and destroying her normal composure. Putting her hand on the rear view mirror, she adjusted it to her eyes. Only, what she glimpsed was a mirrored image of naked shame. "O God, no!" she moaned. "Won't you ever go away?" she screamed. "Why are you rising to taunt me?" she demanded. In that instant, her face turned red, her eyes burned and filled with tears. She had trouble seeing the road. Her hands grew numb. She jerked the wheel to avoid a bridge abutment. And beyond it, she had to swerve right, missing the guardrail by seconds. She swallowed hard to keep down a surge of vomit.

She spotted a roadside rest area and pulled in. She parked far away from other cars. Without turning off the ignition, the air conditioner running on high, she rested her head against the steering wheel. She thought about the sleeping pills she carried in her purse. With the windows rolled up, the engine running, how long will it take to die?

But suicide was not her way and she had known that all along. She had her children and parents to consider. She had a job where people depended on her. Let the moment pass, she told herself. She shivered until reason reassured her and the dark feelings subsided. As her stomach settled and her tears stopped flowing, she straightened up and switched off the ignition. She rolled down the window to a mild breeze and wiped perspiration off her face and hands with a beach towel she kept on the front seat. Compact in hand, she applied fresh makeup and combed out her damp hair. She had errands to run and people to see. She drove off.

*   *   *

"Little bastards," Everett Wheeler grumbled as he inspected the flooded floor in the men's locker room, complaining about the mess left there by a group of junior highs last night. Using a wire coat hanger, he warily fished a jockstrap out of a toilet bowel. "I'll tan their hides," he lamented as he dropped the elasticized fabric into a trashcan. And he would get his retribution, for he had a way of identifying the culprits, a matter he would attend to before this day ended. After mopping up the mess, he left the floor to dry and went back to moving chairs and tables into the gym in preparation for a Girl Scout banquet Saturday afternoon.

Everett had become chief custodian at First Church fifteen years ago. Although this was a fulltime job and included supervision of other maintenance people, Everett also worked as a portrait-and-wedding photographer, doing most of that work in people's homes and in area churches. The only heir of truck-farmer parents, he had sold the family farm several years ago to low-income-housing developers for more than he and his wife, Marie, would ever need to maintain their comfortable life. Some people wondered why, therefore, he kept his church job. Everett, however, never asked. He was master of his domain. Whether managing his investments, running his photography business, or keeping First Church in order, he tolerated no interference. "The little punks. They'll pay for their hour of mischief," he scowled, as he unfolded a heavy table and dropped it soundly into position.

*   *   *

Jerry Flynn had no prospect of marriage. At his age, some people thought this wasn't normal. Unmarried ministers were the exception in the Presbyterian denomination. And once married, he agreed that infidelity was inexcusable. Keeping that commitment was another matter. On the celibacy issue alone, he doubted he could have made it as a Catholic priest. He could not imagine spending the rest of his life without a woman for sex and companionship. And when he thought about the Presbyterian community, he wondered what the "Fathers and Brethren" (their formal order of address) would do if they knew about his carnal dalliance? As expected, his ordination examiners had not asked. Among seminarians, examiners assumed chastity in singleness or faithfulness in marriage. No one dug into a candidate's personal life. Such questions were considered impolite and intrusions on a man's privacy. Only after ordination, if a sexual problem surfaced, was there hell to pay. For now, Jerry contented himself that his carnal indulgences were far less "sinful"—if indeed judged as such—as a single male than as a married one.

He thought about his date over the Memorial Day weekend, an outing with a woman friend long ago promised in marriage by her parents to a person of her orthodox faith. She had no regrets regarding her future. Neither friendship nor sex with him would come between "the promises" made for her. Doing right by her parents and her religion were all that mattered. *"It was great knowing you, Jerry,"* he recalled her saying as he dropped her off at her college dorm. They had camped on the Maryland shore, had spent chilly nights in sleeping bags they had zipped together to cover their naked bodies. *"Lots of luck in your 'calling',"* she had added as she picked her bag and other personal things out of the trunk, then turned one last time to kiss him goodbye, this time not on his lips. Of course, he had known their parting was coming. They had talked about it more times than he could count. If she had believed he would pursue her, he had shown no such willingness.

He had to admit he levitated toward those kinds of relationships. He coveted single women who shied away from marriage, or because of ethnic origin or religion, they retreated from marriage to him as quickly as he did from them. But with ordination, he realized that had to change. He promised himself to look for a serious mate. He wished for affection and fidelity in the way the marriage service liturgy said: *until death do us part*. He wanted a loving relationship with children, whose births coincided with his and his wife's circumstances. He thought about this as he toured the castlelike minister's residence the church called a "manse" and paused to look into the large bedroom that would be his. With its high, ornate ceiling, and mahogany-framed oriel windows looking out over the church gardens and Tompkins Park beyond, even empty of furniture, the room conveyed a message of quiet pleasure. He examined the closets, glimpsed into the adjoining bathroom and a small apartment next to it, a nursery room, he guessed, and snickered at the thought of it.

Again, at the bedroom window, he looked down on his 1957 Crown Imperial in the driveway. The luxury limousine, built by Chrysler, was the last automobile of his Uncle Arthur and Aunt Jessica. They had driven it over a hundred thousand miles before life-threatening illnesses had put the car beyond their use. Uncle Arthur had cared for the Imperial as if stabling a thoroughbred racehorse. He had a vivid memory of the meticulous man washing and polishing the vehicle after little more than a drive to the store to fetch a loaf of bread. In 1956, the couple had paid twelve thousand dollars for this limited model. Chrysler had built only six hundred of the gadget-jammed cars.

Fifteen months ago, Jerry's mother, as executor and principal heir of her late-widowed brother's estate, sold the Imperial to Jerry. He paid her one dollar to take title. Age, wear, and salted roads had by then eroded its luster. His use brought its further deterioration. Last summer, he drove the car to California for his internship at a Los Angeles church. In the inner city of Watts, the car became an instant success. He had used it like a Greyhound bus. He remembered crowding as many as ten kids inside for day trips. He laughed as he thought back to the noisy, happy excitement of the children who had poured in and out of the car for almost three months. Uncle Arthur would have had a fit had he seen those kids dribbling ice cream and dropping potato chips as they crowded on to the seats.

Lately, there were problems starting the car. And more often, without provocation, the engine went dead, as it had this morning. He knew "the monster" needed a tune-up. He made a mental note to get it in for service.

He left the window to examine the rest of the magnificent house.

Tomorrow a moving van would bring furniture and half a dozen boxes of books, his complete library, from his boyhood home. And taking up most of the truck space would be antique furniture, fine linen, dishes, rugs, wall hangings, lamps, clocks—all of it left to him in Uncle Arthur's will. His uncle and aunt had traveled North America collecting household items all their married life. His mother had said the antiques alone were worth a quarter million dollars and they could only increase in value over time. Jerry had no reason to question her appraisal. "Well, they'll fit nicely into this house," he exclaimed. Tomorrow, his mother and his stepfather, the former priest he still called "Father O," would arrange all the furniture in the right places. They were due in just ahead of the moving van.

As he descended the broad, circular staircase to the foyer, he turned his thoughts to Shepherd House where he would do his work. At the landing to his right was a small sitting room connecting the foyer and kitchen. From here, he opened a century-old door that led him outside to the cloister with its slender pillars and wide arches of stone running as a walkway on a slight incline past Shepherd House to the cathedral.

It seemed to him that the architect had shown uncertainty as to which in-vogue style to impose, and, perhaps, as a compromise to discordant directions from the church board, had blended Gothic Revival and Victorian popularity. With no rivals in this town, nor Jerry guessed anywhere else, the building results had taken on an essential heir of acceptability and, over the years, respectability. Even so, the gray fieldstone, ashen with age, which veneered each building frame, had retreated to a visual impression that made them cold and distant. "Thank goodness," he murmured, "for the well-tended lawns and flower gardens. They lend softness to the place." He admired too the American elm, cedar, spruce and a variety of maple trees that filled the rise separating the church complex from the surrounding city, and which continued into Tompkins Park, a triangular block flanking the church grounds, and south into low-rolling country where the church cemetery rested.

Of course, when they designed, built and planted all this, no one anticipated motorized traffic. In time, the church had to tear down its backyard horse and buggy stables, as well as a portion of its forested acres on the cemetery side, to carve out a parking lot. In 1952, they built the annex. This two-story building provided a regulation basketball court (used also as a banquet hall), locker-shower rooms, modern kitchen, multiple classrooms, office, library and parlor. Esthetically, the annex in no way matched the gothic beauty and style of the cathedral, Shepherd House, or the manse. For that reason, many church members disliked it. Approval had come only after a bitter fight. Ten years later, the rift lingered. But Jerry could not understand the fuss. Because the annex sat in lowland, unless you drove around back, you would never know it was there. True, its L-box shape, constructed of concrete blocks, veneered in red brick (rather than gray fieldstone), and covered with a flat roof, was plain and simple. But to Jerry, these compromises to economy were less important than that the building met the more youthful needs and interests of the growing post-war congregation.

Midway along the south wall of the cloister, Jerry unlatched and swung open a heavy iron gate. He descended slate stairs through a terraced garden and stopped to admire colorful flowers and hearty shrubbery in full bloom. A practiced hand had tended every plant and bush and had kept the church lawns and gardens healthy and free of weeds. To his right, he followed a gravel path to a sheltered entrance that avoided the reception area and secretary's office on the parking lot side. Here he grasped the handle and thumb latch on Shepherd Door, a high panel of arched oak with a foot-square window. As he started to press down, behind the glass, a movement, a lightening interruption creased the inside darkness. On the side post, waist high, he saw a crank to turn a brass bell. Reasoning that someone was watching and waiting on the other side, he did the polite thing. He cranked the bell. In spite of the thick wall of wood and stone, he heard its shrill sound. He waited. After a half minute, he held down on the thumb latch and pushed on the handle. The door opened. He marveled at the ease and silence by which the heavy portal swung on its tailored hinges. He entered behind a wide desk in a long room paneled in American Black Walnut. In spite of sunlight streaming from stained glass above, the room accommodated more darkness than light. Reminiscent of earlier times, Shepherd House drew attention to days when ministers were among the few highly educated people in an agricultural community. The facing walls held floor-to-ceiling shelving behind glass doors. No doubt, the architect had recognized the value of books and had thought of them, in the pastor's study, as of such superior knowledge, they needed protection from dust and light, or perhaps the touch of unwashed hands. This shelving divided to make room for a stone fireplace with a hearth that rose two feet above the floor. To its left was a door into a washroom with a sink and toilet. To its right, another corner door opened to the office of Miss Blatty, the church secretary.

Jerry remembered Miss Blatty was due back from vacation tomorrow. He had met her seven weeks ago when he had come to First Church to preach and to attend the congregation's meeting that elected him their pastor. Miss Blatty came with the job. He understood she had been church secretary for some twenty-five years. Sixty years old, never married, loved by all, she had immediately impressed him. *"I'm here to make your work as easy as possible,"* she had said. By all accounts, she meant it. Miss Blatty had a reputation for efficiency, typing excellence and, best of all, she knew everyone. He walked farther into her area. Miss Blatty's office was actually part of the 'new' annex. It had its own easy access from the second floor, or from an outside stairway that lead down to the parking lot. The office was modern, neat and well equipped. It was airy, colorful and unpretentious. It contained a comfortable reception hall, a little kitchenette, a large walk-in storage closet with shelves filled by reams of mimeograph paper as well as other print materials. In back stood another restroom facility.

He returned to Shepherd House, where he estimated its overall dimensions at thirty-by-forty feet and its height at its open peak as high as its width. He appreciated how much time went into keeping the oak floor and the dark walnut paneling in meticulous condition. The scent of varnish and furniture oil was fresh in the air. He had always called it the church smell and even now, he recalled its familiarity when he was a boy and a student at St. Denis Catholic School. He smiled at the memory as he focused his eyes on the Persian rugs, one stretching under his desk and another beneath a central, oval, conference table. They looked new, though he understood they were at least a hundred years old. He shifted his eyes above. Ten feet over his desk, the wall opened to one of the few windows admitted to the room, a stained glass portraying a life-size Jesus as the Good Shepherd. The figure of Christ held a lamb in his arms, its artistic brilliance shown brightly from the sunlight. As in the past, when he had sighted this view of Christ, he wondered why the artist had drawn such sad eyes for what should have been a happy moment. He turned around to face the center of the room and an oval table, which held a sculptured stone vase filled with a torrent of colorful spring flowers. The floral setting testified to a florist's artistry. Like other room furnishings, the oval table on which the flower vase rested was made of oak. Twelve cushioned chairs were neatly set around it and a thirteenth chair—with a little more comfort upholstered into it—stood at the far end. Jerry guessed with a smile that that must be his chair.

Above the table, the ceiling rose through the thirty-foot vertex. Twelve stained-glass windows circled its barrel-shaped base, each in the form of a crusader's shield set in blue glass containing a mixed-colored-glass symbol remembering an apostle. With few exceptions, the symbols recalled the horror by which the apostle had met his death: the upside down cross on which Peter was crucified, the saw with which pagans decapitated the head from the body of James the Less, the flaying knives used to skin the flesh of Bartholomew, and other gruesome reminders of violent killings. Whenever Jerry saw these symbols, he considered how sadistic and murderous the church began. Perhaps that explains the sadness in Jesus' eyes, he thought as he lowered his face to focus on more pleasant sites in the room.

To the side of the fireplace stood a reading chair, ottoman, and a floor lamp with a colored-glass shade. Jerry examined it to assure himself that it was an authentic Tiffany. He pulled the brass chain to admire the dazzling leaded glass over light. He settled into the reading chair, put his feet up on the ottoman and swiveled around to gaze admiringly at the whole room. His eyes came to rest on the center table, or more precisely on its center vase with its abundance of spring flowers. Their placement must be recent, he thought. He left the fireplace chair in exchange for one at the head of the table, so he could smell the rich aroma from the flowers. He faced his desk and the Good Shepherd Window, his back to the fireplace and the outer offices. He looked up again at the sad Jesus figure cuddling a lost sheep in his arms. A tingling chill raced up his spine.

"I see you found the heart of the place," he heard from behind him. The voice was high-pitched and he recognized it before he turned to see the face

"Mr. Tompkins. How good of you to come by."

While Jerry's face had shown no alarm, he had winced at the quiescent ease by which the man had entered his study. For he had heard neither the crack of a door or the step of a foot.

"Son, I hope I didn't startle you. But I did see the car in the drive and thought I should check it out. Can't be too careful these days, lad. Happy to see you."

Walter Tompkins had an unkempt and stiff appearance. Tall, angular and a head crowned by a thick mass of snow-white hair, with his dark-grooved eyes highlighting a long, thin face, Jerry thought he could just as well be looking at an Old Testament prophet. He wore brown bib overalls that must have seen the ringer a thousand times. His blue work shirt, from cuffs to shoulders, showed grease and soil. His hand held an equally stained, green baseball cap advertising the John Deere Tractor Company. No one would guess that this man was Tompkinsville's richest produce farmer. His company employed hundreds of seasonal workers to pick lettuce, strawberries, blueberries, tomatoes, beans and whatever. His canning factories hired as many as a thousand local people year round. He worked on the farm for the sheer love of work. An expert mechanic, he kept machinery purring long after its useful life. Appropriately, it was with an oil-blemished hand that he reached out for Jerry.

"Sir, it is my pleasure," Jerry said, rising to his feet, extending his hand to Walter, whose powerful grip closed around it. "I should have called to let you know I'd arrived."

"No need to do that. This is your abode. Like it?"

"Oh, I'll say. However, I'll never fill all these bookshelves. My whole library will fit on one rack."

"Yes, well, you remind me now that Reverend Maefield's library was boxed up after his death and moved into storage in the church basement. His widow wants you to have it. She told me, any book you don't want, you can discard! Frankly, we didn't know what to do with the lot, and for the longest time, I don't think she did either. I can't tell you how many volumes, but they once overflowed these shelves. Maefield was a prolific reader. When Mrs. Maefield heard that a young man right out of seminary would be our new minister, she graciously offered Daniel's entire library."

"That's very generous of her. I'll call and thank her for thinking of me."

"You should. I know she would appreciate hearing from you. You can get her phone number from Miss Blatty tomorrow. She would have Mrs. Maefield's new phone number in Manhattan."

Walter paused and then walked to the great fireplace. Jerry followed behind.

"That's where he fell," he pointed, indicating the floor area in front of the raised hearth. "Right here!" Walter said, stamping his foot in a space where the varnished oak floor was pale by comparison to the shinny area surrounding it.

Nothing had ever troubled the city more than that cold January morning when it awoke to sirens and the screech of police and emergency vehicles at the cathedral grounds. Word of the brutal murder of Daniel Maefield, age sixty-two, got around fast. His body—showing multiple stab wounds, his neck slashed and his head branded by a coal shovel from the fireplace—had drawn its last breath sometime between eleven thirty Sunday night and one o'clock Monday morning.

"Who found him?" Jerry asked.

What Jerry knew about the murder had come from news clippings and what little information officials of his denomination had conveyed. He had not heard anything from church members. He sensed most people did not want to talk about the murder and he would not press the issue. Yet, he had to learn the basic facts if only to help people deal with their grief. More crucial, until police made an arrest, Jerry would have to cope with those who remained frightened about their own safety in the buildings and with those who, by virtue of this heartless crime, were experiencing a crisis of faith.

"Rhonda Maefield found him," Tompkins replied.

Clearly, Walter Tompkins was one person who could talk about it.

"Blood was all over this area. They had to remove the rug on which his body rested; they needed it for evidence. We told them we didn't want it back. Imagine, they insisted we should have it cleaned to look like new. We said, 'throw it away! We'll get another one.' God knows we don't want that reminder hereabout now, do we?"

Walter was silent for a moment and kept his head bowed. Painfully, it seemed, he looked up at Jerry, gently placed his hand on his arm.

"Reverend, I apologize. You don't need to hear these things today. Everything in its time." He paused again. "Now, you will come to dinner tonight!" It was not a question. "We'll be looking for you at six."

"Thank you, Walter. I'd love to."

"You can't miss the house. Go out to the triangle and right on to Main Street, drive five miles east of Tompkins Park. When you come to the Texaco Station, turn left, go three miles north to the first farmhouse on the east side of the road. The house is a half mile back. The fields in front are planted with tomatoes."

"One other thing before you leave, Walter. Who can I thank for the beautiful flower arrangement?" he asked, gesturing toward the oval table.

"Oh, that would be Madge, my daughter," he replied with pride. "She loves her flowers, you know! Twice a week she comes in with a fresh armful from her garden. She's done that since the Forsythia and the Rhododendron bloomed. About that time, the police gave this room back to us."

"Well, they're lovely. She has an expert's touch."

"Yes, Madge is like that with everything she does; she's a very sensitive and talented girl. I would say that even if she wasn't my daughter," he added, all smiles.

Jerry accompanied Walter into the reception hall, where they exited to the outside and ambled down the stairs to the parking lot.

"Some people haven't forgiven me for opposing this new monstrosity," Walter said as they paused by the annex. "A few more bucks and we could've matched the other buildings and added a trussed roof. It's not that we're a deprived church and couldn't afford it. This building takes away from the old-world decorum. And, you know that flat roof leaks. I'm no spendthrift, Pastor, but I do like things done right and I respect the past. This new building cheapens things. What do you think?"

"I'm glad we have the annex, Walter. I can't imagine this church without Sunday school facilities and all the other conveniences. I know you agree with that. But you're right! It would have looked nicer matching the old."

Walter smiled. "I'm happy you understand. I hope you'll be at home here. Tonight we'll talk about getting you settled in."

Jerry watched Walter climb into the cab of his flatbed produce truck and waved politely as the farmer drove off the church grounds. He started back to Shepherd House when he heard a grinding noise. Looking to his right, he saw a brown pickup truck backing out of the maintenance garage under the church office complex. He recognized the driver as Everett Wheeler, Walter's nephew and the church's head custodian. They had met briefly at the congregation's meeting. Everett beeped in acknowledgement of Jerry as he used a remote device to lower the garage door. Jerry wanted keys from him, especially those for the manse, but the man ignored him and, in a hurry, he raced out the east exit of the parking lot.

"I guess he didn't want to talk to me," Jerry mumbled to himself, a confident grin passing over his face. He would catch him later, or else he'd have to leave the manse unlocked while he went out for supper.

Minutes later, Jerry welcomed the cool interior of Shepherd House, the only building with air conditioning, a refreshing luxury in this early June humidity. Sitting behind his desk in a comfortable swivel chair, he now viewed Shepherd House with a sense of dread and detachment. "How long will this room hide its secrets of brutality and death by murder?" he asked of no one, though, in his heart he believed he had asked it of God. Just then, the phone rang, his first call, he thought, in what he believed would be a long and productive career.

CHAPTER 2

LOOKING FOR LOVE

Tuesday Afternoon-Evening, June 5, 1962

Charlene Cunningham sat at her desk in the offices of Jason, Dolby and Herzfeld, a Philadelphia law firm that represented major insurance companies before they paid off large claims. She looked out of place in this company where women were secretaries and men were bosses. She worked out of a private office and had a female secretary. Charlene was, so to speak, one of the boys. But a boy she certainly was not. Twenty-five, blond, sea blue eyes, unblemished fair complexion, and suggestive in dressing her picture-perfect body, she appeared as every woman's envy and every man's desire.

During her college years, she had actively pursued the idea of modeling and with some success. She knew, however, that she was too short for the standards of fashion modeling. And neither was she prepared to pose nude, not even to the waist, which seemed the other option, an offer she had turned down in her senior year. Her decision about nudity had less to do with modesty and more to do with career goals. Such exhibitionism would deny her what she really wanted to do. For Charlene, since a child of eight years old, this was police work. In that vocation, she believed a woman could rise to levels of excellence yet untested. And if having an attractive body improved her chances of professional success, all the better. People, however, learned that beneath her looks, there was an intelligent, perceptive and diligent adversary. She knew how to use her wits to succeed in her career as a private investigator.

As for her future, she aspired to the Federal Bureau of Investigation. Friends said the FBI would never give women equal status with men. They said that the Bureau was like the priesthood in Roman Catholicism and J. Edgar Hoover its Pope. But Charlene believed times were changing. And while right now she could not expect an FBI appointment, other investigative opportunities in the federal government's Justice Department were opening to women. That was her foot in the door. She had passed the physical and done well on all the written tests. She had an outstanding record of accomplishment with her present employer. They could still flag her out, but who knows?

In her time at Jason, Dolby and Herzfeld, usually working incognito, the partnership of lawyers had paid her well to dig up useful information, often of the kind that could cast aspersions on the character of a claimant, thus, softening their appeal for a larger-than-reasonable settlement. Uncovering insurance fraud was her other specialty. Today, she began to pour over background material of a claim by Rhonda Maefield, widow of the Reverend Daniel Maefield.

Twenty years ago, the minister had purchased a half-million-dollar life insurance policy naming his wife sole beneficiary. The policy included a double indemnity clause in case of accidental death, which included murder. With the crime still under investigation, the insurance company had legitimate reason to delay paying its obligation to the widow. But that was about to run out. After reading case-background material, Charlene Cunningham had seen nothing to cast doubt on Rhonda Maefield's innocence or to question her character. The prosecutor's office had stopped inquiries and ordered the return of all her husband's personal property. The insurance company's own investigation had judged Mrs. Maefield an upstanding citizen of good moral character and a loving wife. Their research showed she had independent wealth and promise of lucrative future employment. There was nothing to suggest insurance fraud. Still, Charlene would do her job. Principally, she would try to uncover sensitive information on Rhonda Maefield, listen to gossip, turn up any secrets that might darken the reputation of the lady, probe for offhand news that could coincidentally connect her to her husband's untimely death. And she would look into Reverend Maefield's and his wife's social history. As she saw it, she had until the end of June to recommend the claim or to advise more delay.

She decided to start at the place of the murder. Her information showed that Jerry Flynn, the church's newly elected minister, might be at the church today, so she telephoned to ask for an appointment. Already knowledgeable of his age, education, military service, Philadelphia roots and single status, she saw him as an open window to view the church buildings and grounds. Using her cover as a freelance magazine writer from Philadelphia working on a story on how Tompkinsville folks were handling the aftermath of the minister's death, she inquired in a decidedly sympathetic tone if it would be all right to come by his office tomorrow morning. She wanted his advice and recommendation on people she could interview.

Jerry discouraged her, saying this was only his first day on the job. "Honestly, I don't know much about the murder, Mrs. Cunningham!"

"I'm not married!" she politely corrected, a slight giggle attached to her soft voice. Then with sweetness that tops a cake, she added, "I'm just a hard working girl, trying to do her job. Getting my article published may depend on anything you, as Reverend Maefield's successor, can contribute. You're very important."

"Well, I appreciate your confidence, but I might be more helpful a month from now!"

"Oh, but that will be too late, Reverend Flynn," she exclaimed, her voice barely shielding her disappointment. "I have a deadline to meet. You're the only one who can explain the nature of Reverend Maefield's work. I know so little about the Presbyterian Church. I'm sure you can contribute that without knowing a thing about the murder. And, you can show me his office and home, which are essential to writing background material. Also, I need your suggestion of people in your congregation and on your church staff. I would not want to interview them without your permission."

After a pause, he asked her to hold. Someone was at his door. The phone clanked on a hard surface and she could hear muffled voices. As she waited for him to come back on the line, she hoped she hadn't sounded too accommodating. One way or another, with or without his permission, she planned on talking to significant people at First Church. She drummed her fingers until she heard his voice.

"I apologize for the interruption," he said, then, as if there had been none, he caught her by surprise with his answer. "How can I refuse to meet someone from my hometown?" She laughed with him after he had said this. Hey, whatever makes it easy for you, she thought. "If you want to stop by," he added in a casual manner, "I'll be in my study at Shepherd House for most of the morning."

She did not like fill-in-the-blank appointments. "Let's make the time ten o'clock, Reverend. If your plans change, you can telephone me." She read him the telephone number for her answering service as well as The Green Onion Inn, a motel midway between Tompkinsville and the turnpike exit. He said he looked forward to greeting her and hung up. It occurred to her then that he had sounded nothing like what she had expected, but youthful and full of play. His voice had held a strong and friendly quality and she wondered if he was like that in person. For the briefest of moments, she wondered what it would be like to date a bachelor clergyman. She just as quickly laughed at the idea, but in her appointment book, next to his name, she drew a question mark and a heart as a smiley face.

*   *   *

Walter and Greta Tompkins were parents of three daughters. Their youngest, Barbara, was sixteen, going on seventeen, and finishing her second year in high school. Their second, Leslie, engaged to be married a year from now, was twenty-five and living away from home in her second year at medical school. Their oldest daughter, Madge, had turned thirty-two a week ago. Madge had married her high school sweetheart, Michael Todd and they had two sons: Michael, Jr., who they had knick named Chip, age nine, and Dudley, age four.

Several years ago, Walter Tompkins and Michael's father, Jessie Todd, formed a corporation that united family farms and canning factory operations under single management, known corporately as T&T Produce Company. Then, a few years later, Jessie, with 39 percent of assets, and Walter with 61, transferred entitlement of the company to their married son and daughter. Under that agreement, Michael assumed ownership of all his father's shares and Madge took title to 20 of her father's sixty-one shares. Walter retained the balance—inheritance for his other two daughters—and, in the event Michael and Madge disagreed, he had the deciding vote. To augment their decisions, Michael, Madge and Walter relied on an advisory board, people from both families (wives, daughters, brothers, sisters), who stood to benefit from a percentage of company profits.

Leaving the produce business to the "children," had freed Walter to do what he enjoyed most: overseeing his real estate holdings. Two to three days a week, dressed in a gray business suit, he drove his late model white Cadillac up and down the New Jersey coast collecting rent money and arranging new land deals. Scuttlebutt had it that Walter Tompkins owned prime property in and around Atlantic City. If casino gambling came to the ailing boardwalk city, he stood to make millions more.

*   *   *

Jerry Flynn arrived at the home of Walter Tompkins and his wife Greta a little before six o'clock. The house sat on a patch of manicured lawn surrounded by flowerbeds and tall shade trees, all of this encircled by acres and acres of planted fields. Its white sideboard looked freshly painted. And, clearly, over many years, the house had grown by several additions, including a broad porch that rambled across the entire front as well as the long south side. Here were several rocking chairs and, close to the front door, an ornate bench swing with a padded seat.

He rapped on the screen door. He waited almost two minutes before Greta Tompkins appeared, admonishing him that there was no need to stand there. "Walk right in anytime!" she said in a way that let him know she really meant it. Tall, lean and dark haired, Greta's beauty had not been set aside by her age. She appeared the perfect hostess, neat and fashionable in dress, well spoken yet folksy. Certainly, she was not the picture Jerry had had of a farmer's wife, a stereotype left over from children's books he needed to dissolve. Gracious and friendly, Greta immediately took Jerry's hand and ushered him into the parlor where Walter rose from his chair, set down the evening paper, and warmly greeted him.

The room stretched across half the front of the house and was dark and cool with the shades drawn against the evening sun. Old furniture and a stone fireplace that filled the entire wall at the far end made the room comfortable and cozy. Walter pointed out that this section of the house was the original Samuel Tompkins homestead. As best they could tell, construction took place in 1765.

A Labrador retriever with a black shiny coat had found a cool place on the stones in front of the fireplace. He looked up but made no effort to greet Jerry.

"Some watch dog," Jerry remarked, bending low to pet him on the head.

Walter laughed. "This is Max. He's too old to worry anymore. He once ruled this place with an iron paw, like me," he said, "but it appears those days are in the past."

Walter laughed again after saying this and Jerry laughed along with him. But, Jerry believed the truth drifted in a different direction. Walter did not appear to him as a man who would lie down like an old dog.

As Jerry chatted with Walter, other family members sauntered into the parlor. Greta interrupted to introduce Jerry to her young brother, Tom, who waited like a shy giant next to her. Jerry estimated his height at six feet seven inches and that he weighed maybe three hundred pounds. With Greta close behind him, Tom moved toward Jerry with both hands outstretched. His slow awkwardness and Greta's coaching gave away his retarded condition.

"Tom is the most handsome man on the farm," Greta said proudly.

With soft eyes, a broad smile and a childlike manner, he accepted her complement and paused to smooth back his silver hair. Walter praised him as his best produce packer.

"He puts the hired help to shame," were Walter's words. Tom beamed as he vigorously shook Jerry's hands.

Burt and Louise Grimm came in next. Greta and Louise were sisters. They were not at all alike in appearance. Stout and gray haired, Louise was older and more in conformity with Jerry's farm-wife stereotype. Appearances are however deceptive. After retiring three years ago from teaching positions at the county agriculture college, each with doctoral degrees in earth science, Burt and Louise Grimm had taken over as managers of T&T Farm Emporium, the largest and most versatile of T&T roadside produce stores.

"They sell only the freshest vegetables," Walter said proudly as Burt and Louise Grimm took turns shaking Jerry's hand. "Whatever you need, Jerry, you go to these people. They're members of our church and you'll find them among your most reliable volunteers."

"Hey, I like them already," Jerry replied, his face glowing in a warm smile.

As Louise turned and pecked Walter on the cheek, he kidded her. "And, Louise is the best kisser in town." Playfully, she pushed him away.

From behind, another voice added to the hilarity. "Now, now, Walter, you said the same thing about me just yesterday," a full-bodied, bright-smiling, older woman butted in.

"This is Aunt Pat, Louise and Greta's aunt; she's one of the many pretty ladies on this old folks' farm." Walter roared with contagious laughter. He reached over to hug her close and kiss her on the forehead.

"Reverend, this man is the biggest flirt ever filled a pair of overalls," Aunt Pat admonished. "You just remember," she said looking around her before focusing all on Jerry, "that I'm the only woman single and available in this room."

Everyone laughed except Aunt Pat. She took Jerry's arm.

"We bachelors have to stick together, Reverend Flynn," Pat said as she escorted Jerry into the adjoining dining room and showed him a place at the table. "You sit next to me, Reverend."

Already seated opposite across the broad table was John Tompkins, a younger brother of Walter. Greta explained how John had his own farm ten miles east. Widowed several years ago and with no children, John was another tenant at the Walter Tompkins house. A man of shy composure and few words, John, tall and gangly like his older brother, rose awkwardly to politely lean across the table, catching Jerry's outstretched hand. Like Walter, Uncle John presented a crushing handshake. Jerry grinned and bore it.

Slowly, everyone gathered around the table. Jerry had just pulled in close when, above the dull roar of conversation he heard, "Hi, everybody!"

Madge Todd and her two boys trooped into the dining room. Against her smiling protests, the entire group immediately got to their feet to crowd around her. Greetings were warm and affectionate—laughs and smiles, hugs and kisses. Jerry stepped to the side and watched. He knew her right away from the church reception, though, until now, he had not known that the cheery beauty, with coal black hair, wearing a fashionable white suit that day, was Walter Tompkins' married daughter.

She had styled her hair in the popular Cleopatra-look, and he thought it made her wickedly attractive. Only for Madge, the hairstyle accommodated an endearing face, one with soft blue eyes set off by long, black lashes and dark perfectly arched brows, a slightly upturned nose and valentine-red lips opening to a poster child's white teeth. She had an easy smile, the kind that would reassure you even as the day turned to night. She stood bare foot in sandals—her toenails painted the same shade as her lips— and wearing black shorts capping her long legs just above her knees. An oversized man's white shirt covered her torso. Buttoned just above where her breasts divided, the shirt tails banded and knotted in front, thus, opening a thin line of flesh for viewing. She had rolled the cuffs above her elbows as a card player might do, revealing her dark-tanned arms and a silver and topaz bracelet on her right wrist.

Jerry watched as she stood on tiptoes in an effort to hear Tom, a hand embracing his arm, her head tilted slightly, her face disciplined to show interest and amusement at the same time. In that pose and arresting smile, Jerry perceived a mix of shy innocence, incredible sensuality and magnetic beauty.

A few minutes passed before uncles and aunts sauntered back to their table places. Greta continued talking. Then, as if suddenly reminded of Jerry's presence, she stopped in mid sentence and, holding Madge's hand, she stepped toward Jerry. "This is our daughter, Madge, Reverend Flynn and our grandchildren, Chip and Dudley."

Jerry reached for Madge's hand. Concurrently, their eyes met. If looks could power electricity, that was how charged Jerry felt. She drew him in. He lost touch with himself, as her eyes held him there. Then, he felt a tug on his pants' leg and, reluctant, nevertheless, he looked down to see Dudley competing for attention. Jerry bent his knees to take Dudley's little hand. When he straightened, Madge's sparkling eyes met him again.

"Thank you for the flowers in Shepherd House," he said, the sound of his voice moderated by the excitement he felt.

"Oh, I'm happy you like them. I do it to bring new joy to an old, sad room," she said, a hint of nervous laughter in her voice. "As long as it's all right with you, I'll keep them fresh."

"Won't you stay for supper?" her mother asked, anxious to remind them, Jerry thought, that everyone was waiting on them.

Madge replied that they had only stopped by to say hello and to pick up fresh-picked strawberries. She had to beat it home to get dinner for her tribe. Michael was president of Grange, she explained, and he would want his cream and berries before running off to his meeting.

"It was nice meeting you, Reverend," she said, again closing the distance between them. And then, as if lost for anything better to say, she said, "Our prayers are with you!" In that moment, she gently patted him on his shoulder and slid her hand down his arm to take his hand as if for a final handshake. But the grasp fell around his fingers and lingered perhaps longer than was necessary. Then, as if reality had come to separate them, in the next motion, she turned slightly and, releasing his hand, she bent to pick up Dudley, who had reached up for her. The little boy was too heavy to lift onto her hip, but she did it anyway, appeasing his restlessness for several seconds before setting him on his feet.

Jerry did not miss a move, and once more, their eyes met. It was as if time and sound had disappeared and they were the only ones in the room. The intensity of the dual gaze could have gone on without end had not Greta come between them. "Dinner is served!" Talk and laughter at the dinner table finally overcame them. Madge took Dudley's hand and, with Chip following, they all waved goodbye, but with one last look before passing out of sight. Only then did Jerry dicker with his emotions. She's married, he lectured himself, with two children. I have no right feeling like this. What is going on in my head?

Greta summoned everyone to sit. Jerry realized then that two field hands had entered the dinning room. Walter introduced them as Manuel Lopez and Jorge Garcia, his field bosses. Manuel, who spoke guarded English, looked about forty years old. Jorge, the more talkative of the two, and in complete command of his adopted language, looked older. Jerry would learn to his surprise that Jorge had just celebrated his sixty-first birthday and had worked for Walter as his labor manager for the last twenty-five years. They were big, wide shouldered, muscled men—Manuel tall, and Jorge short, with a barrel chest and powerful arms. Their bronzed faces brought instant smiles when Walter, speaking to them in Spanish, told them Jerry was the Tompkins' new family padre.

Jerry thought, what's a little white lie at a time like this? He realized, too, Walter had forgotten he knew enough Spanish to figure out what he had said; or, maybe Walter had not forgotten.

"Pastor, will you offer thanks for our meal?" Walter asked.

Jerry prayed and the "amen" was hardly out of his mouth before mashed potatoes, roast beef and brown gravy started rounding the huge dining table. Four hot dishes of garden vegetables, sauces, bread and butter, pitchers of milk and plates of salad greens quickly followed. A robust woman named Maria assisted Greta. Jerry later learned Maria was Jorge's wife. A young Mexican woman, whose name he did not hear, also helped get the meal on the table before taking a place next to Manuel. After servings of deep-dish apple pie, decked with double dips of vanilla ice cream, and hot coffee, conversation turned to business.

At first, talk was pleasant and interesting. Michael Todd had recently put a new irrigation system into use. This had included water cannons that spray the equal of three-fourths an inch of water in 250-diameter circles, a total of 420 gallons of water per minute for four consecutive hours. The machines cool the plants and soil as well as provide water to the root system. Delighted with the results, Walter was considering approval of more of the same machinery to supplement the cheaper motorized mobiles that run along furrows in the fields. He asked what the others thought and all agreed if they got into another summer drought situation, the units would pay for themselves in no time.

As talk became more technical, people began leaving the table. Jorge and Manuel remained. Jerry thought he too should leave. Walter, however, told him there was no need to and he had church things to discuss with him. He then turned back to Jorge and Manuel.

Jorge, who managed the field workers, said he needed more hands. Their best quality strawberries were late maturing.

Normally, this wouldn't be a problem. However, lettuce, snap beans, early peas, and summer squash were all ahead of schedule and the overlap had brought havoc to the labor market. Ten strawberry acres, reserved for commercial sale and frozen packaging, would be ready for picking Thursday. If the weather stayed hot through the weekend and into next week, another ten acres of strawberries would be ready for harvest.

Walter explained for Jerry's benefit how the delicate strawberry crop, picked by hand, required backbreaking labor. In hot weather, they had at most a few days to sift the ripe fields. There was no mechanized equipment to do it.

Jorge reported Michael had already sent a bus to Delaware for another crew; they should arrive here early tomorrow. Walter expressed concern that housing twenty more workers would be the big problem. Jorge did not agree. He replied that extra help would only be for two weeks and he could double up the men's dorm as well as several families. Walter smiled at that, a knowing smile, followed by: "We'll have to keep an eye out for state inspectors with all their damn regulations."

"That won't be a problem," Jorge said.

Jerry wanted to ask why. But he kept his mouth shut. Still, he imagined, either Jorge knew how to bribe or had ways to deceive New Jersey labor officials. The conversation continued along the same line.

They talked about California, where a farm labor leader named Cesar Chavez had held a large-scale meeting with grape pickers to organize an association. "Bad news!" Walter declared. "It's all part of a communist plot to take over this country."

"The threat of farm-worker strikes in California and a national boycott of table grapes are very real," Jorge responded. "It may not happen this year or the next, but it'll come."

Clearly, this was not something Walter or his field management team relished. Jorge showed little sympathy for his Mexican underlings and, speaking now in Spanish, assured Walter he could handle any discontented workers. "There will be no farm unions here," Jorge said in Spanish, pounding his hand on the table.

Walter, as if suddenly remembering Jerry understood what they were discussing, abruptly ended the discussion. Their conversation completed, Jorge and Manuel excused themselves and left the table. Walter turned to Jerry.

After inquiring about Jerry's ordination plans, Walter asked about the manse. There had been discussion once of Jerry's mother and stepfather moving in with him. Jerry said that had changed.

"As you may have heard, my stepfather was once a Catholic priest."

"Yes, I did know that, Jerry."

"My father was shot and killed while on duty as a Philadelphia policeman. I was just six years old. Father O' Flannigan was Police Chaplain at the time and, well, after many years of being like a father to me anyway, he married my mother. Of course, the Catholic Church has no place for married priests and defrocked him. Since then he has taught high school English in Philadelphia public schools and will be retired at the end of this month. I thought he and my mom would enjoy a year or so in the manse. But, after considering it, they decided to buy a place in Florida and plan on moving to Boca Raton in the fall."

"I see . . . well, the offer stands . . . anytime they want to move in with you, Jerry. We had thought it would be nice to see you all together there."

"Thank you. We appreciate the church's offer. I'm sure they'll visit often."

"I was going to suggest, regardless of their plans, Jerry, that you hire a housekeeper."

Walter went on to explain that there was a lady named Rosa, who would be perfect. Her seventy-three-year-old husband had died of a heart attack while picking tomatoes a year ago. Rosa was too old to work in the canary anymore, he explained. She needed a place to keep house, cook and sleep. Walter would take her in himself, but thought of Jerry first.

"You could pay her fifteen dollars a week and with free room and board she'd be pleased," Walter said. "I'll even keep her on my factory payroll so she'll have medical benefits."

The employment arrangement Walter suggested surprised him. He wondered why the church couldn't pay medical premiums for its own employees. There were enough of them, and even he had to pay his own. He did not, however, want to get into such matters now. He said he would consider it. He would like to meet Rosa.

"Well, I can tell you," Walter grumbled, "she's a Christian lady with high standards."

"I'm sure she is," Jerry answered and at once perceived that Walter's concern might have more to do with his bachelor status than with his pallet or pad. "Let's talk about it after I get settled in."

As there was no furniture at the manse, Walter insisted Jerry stay overnight and any night needed hereafter. The large farmhouse had plenty of guest rooms, and bedding down the preacher would never be an inconvenience. Jerry graciously accepted.

Almost three hours had passed since Jerry's arrival. He needed exercise and fresh air. He excused himself to take a walk. The light of day had disappeared but the night was radiant. A full moon was rising and he had no trouble seeing his way. The air was cool and clear and the night sky exhibited a billion stars. He extolled the heavens as he followed a dirt road that ran through the freshly planted fields north and then east from the house.

A mile from the main house, Jerry walked toward a clearing where a long row of cottages stood, a low light glowing from some of their windows. It took a while to realize the light came from candles and kerosene lanterns. These cottages had no electricity. Each one had a front porch where two or more people sat silent on the steps, or relaxed in aluminum folding chairs. Here and there, he saw workers in old rocking chairs, moving, it seemed, in time with the slow breeze that blew in off the wide, open fields.

Jerry could feel all eyes upon him as he approached. He heard a baby's cry and a plea for quiet by the mother who rocked the little one close to her breast. Children scurried to their mothers, who held them as if now safe from the dangerous stranger who walked in their midst.

Jerry waved and said "Hello!" He heard some weak acknowledgment.

A delinquent odor that transcended the area caught his attention. Why the smell of excrement and urine? Then he understood these tiny houses did not have toilets. A string of outhouses stood ten feet back from the road.

He wished he had gifts for the children. He hated to think they were seeing him as an enemy. Again, he waved and this time said "Hello!" and "Good evening!" in Spanish. For now, this was all he could do. Tonight he could offer no relief from meager wages, unsanitary and crowded houses. Most of these people were here today and gone tomorrow. Few stayed in one place for more than a month. There were those who followed the strawberry crops as they ripened from Georgia to New England. Another group would show up in late summer to harvest blueberries, others for cabbage in the fall.

Jerry followed the dirt road that turned back across the field to the Tompkins house. With its lights shinning brightly, he could see the house on the far distant field. What do you say to truck farm owners like this? What preaching will change their view of laborers in the field? How would owners respond when he preached on Jesus' parable about farm workers and generous wages? Walter's remark at the table—that he was the family padre—troubled him. Is that how he sees me? Am I? Jerry knew he would return to this row of houses. He saw his ministry as much caring for poor folk in dilapidated gray shanties as rich folk in big white houses.

Fifteen minutes later, he completed his circle and hiked out of the field road on to the spongy lawn of the big house. As he drew close to the porch steps, he saw in the lighted background a slight female figure rocking in the swing. She was less shy than he was.

"Hi, you must be the new pastor. I'm Barbara, but please call me Bob; everyone else does."

She pushed over to the far end of the swing to make room. Jerry accepted her warm hospitality and moved on to the suspended bench.

"Thank you. I'm pleased to meet you?" he replied and fell in with her swinging motion.

"How was your trip down here?" she asked and before he answered one question she had another one ready for him.

At first look, it would be hard to recognize Barbara as Madge's kid sister. Barbara had long blond hair. She was, however, no less pretty. Then in her sparkling dark eyes and friendly face, Jerry saw her resemblance to Madge.

"And how was your date?" he asked for conversation and because he wanted to show an interest in her. He thought he would repeat what he had heard at the dinner table. "I heard—" He never had to say "*tall, dark, and handsome . . .* "

"A drag," Barbara cut in, "that's why I'm home already—really, such a bore."

"Well, I'm sorry to hear that," Jerry said, sympathizing with her obvious frustration.

"Boys are so unpleasant at my age. They don't know how to carry on an intelligent conversation. Everything out of their mouths is fresh."

A pleasant smile lit her face. Whatever she was thinking at that instant, she decided to keep it to herself. In the second of hesitation, she slapped her arm.

"Mosquitoes are biting. It's time we moved indoors."

She took Jerry's hand and sprung from the swing, pulling him towards her.

"I hear you'll be staying with us tonight," she said as he towered above her.

"Wow, news sure travels fast down on the farm."

"Would you like to play a hand of Gin? That's something you'll find out about us . . . card sharks! We're cutthroat players."

"Gee, Barbara, I really would like to, but . . . " He looked at his watch.

"But not, and it's Bob! You can say it. You know I am the last from my mother. There won't be another. Daddy thought for sure I would be a boy. When I wasn't, well, he accepted me, or at least he pretends that I'm all right. He does love me, I know that, but, after all, in this family, no boy. Therefore, it's Bob."

"Okay, Bob it is! One game, and then you have to let me run my head to the pillow."

They entered a house that was quiet except for a distant sound of a television. Bob mentioned that her dad and mom retired after the news and everyone else was off to their separate rooms. "Early to bed, early to rise," she laughed without completing the popular quote.

She and Jerry played five hands of gin rummy at the kitchen table. She beat him four times. All the while, she chatted about boys, her love for animals, her teachers and women's basketball, which she hated, because girls could not play by the same rules as boys.

"It's so dull," she lamented. "No body contact. No running. It's absolutely stupid!"

"Well, some things are bound to change," Jerry insisted.

Finally, Bob conceded that it was time for bed. Two more weeks of school and this week was all review for exams. She guessed she better be bright and cheerful. Her gabby girlfriends would want to know all about her "horrible date."

As she jabbered, they climbed the stairs to a third-story landing. "You're at the end of the hall," she laughed. "With the windows open, it's cooler up here than anywhere else." She opened the door to a small, comfortably decorated bedroom and showed him the bathroom across the hall. "Mom has put out towels and washcloth. Look, here's a new toothbrush and—"

"Thank you, Bob. I'll find my way from here," he smiled and stepped around her to the doorframe of the bedroom.

"I feel more like you're my big brother than the new 'Rev'," she said.

"Bob, that's a nice compliment. I enjoyed your company. Maybe I'll see you in church Sunday. I'm going to look for you."

"Oh, I'll be there, the whole family will. We never miss Sunday. Well . . . Goodnight!," she beamed, and stood on tiptoes bringing her tender face, so grown up for one so young, close to his. She kissed him on the cheek, turned and walked away.

"Sleep well, Bob!" he called as she disappeared down the stairs.

Minutes later, he was in bed with only stars and moon, visible in the open window, lighting his eyes. Certain things about the evening kept him awake. For one, Bob's manner gave him cause to wonder. Her friendly, easy familiarity had seemed flirtatious. But when he compared her with other family members, particularly the women, he saw a natural inclination to friendliness, a desire to bond with someone immediately liked. And maybe that was all he had seen in Madge, a natural instinct to welcome him in the same way she would welcome any dinner guest in her parents' home.

Nor could he dismiss his own indulgent attraction to beautiful women. Hadn't he learned by now that because a pretty woman smiled at him, even looked him in the eyes, that she had fallen for him the way of husband and wife? Yet, Madge showed such powerful appeal tonight, he could not dismiss her signals as mere reflections of a friendly personality. Beneath the smile, the look and the touch, he read a desire for sexual contact and more. "Don't tread there," he exclaimed. "God, why can't I get sexual thoughts out of my mind?" he said and, after several more minutes thinking about her, he closed his eyes to the stars and the night air and the long day that had preceded them.

*   *   *

Madge Todd treated herself to the luxury of a scented bath and chose nightclothes of brief blue panties and a matching semi-transparent gown, complete with spaghetti straps over the shoulders and mid-thigh length. She saw it as an appropriate choice for this warm night and, while she had not dressed for sexual appeal, as she stood before her full-length mirror combing out her damp hair, she had to concur with that message. But for whom had she dressed? Her husband? He would prefer to find her naked and that was how she would be if she wanted him? The face of Jerry Flynn came to mind and she paused to think about him. She had dropped in at Mom and Dad's for the sole purpose of seeing him and now she could not dissolve the pleasing way he had looked at her. The feelings he had generated had provoked her libido and still made her blush. "I thought his eyes would swallow me, and he must have gotten the same impression from me. If he was thinking as I was, how dangerous?" She turned away from the mirror, admonishing herself. "I'm certainly not going to have an affair with the minister," she mused as she switched off the light and climbed into bed. "But would that be more or less shameful than what I've already done?" she questioned. Affection is such a dangerous pleasure, she thought; it can drive you crazy or set you free and either way, it can kill you. Exhausted from her long day, sleep overcame adversity and her worries fell silent to its comforting darkness.

Less than two hours passed before Michael turned on the nightstand lamp and abruptly rolled Madge onto her back. She opened her eyes to see him naked and crawling above her. As he positioned his knees astride her hips, she smelt rose-scented powder and stale beer. And as he bent to kiss her, she saw his bloodshot eyes, flushed cheeks and smelt the stink of his sour breath. This way of approaching her for sex had become more common. She had learned that to resist only prolonged her fright, better to let him get it out of his system and done with it. So, she said nothing and remained passive, even as abrasively he took away her gown, tore down her panties, and drove into her. She held her breath until her pain disappeared and his movements died. But then, as he stayed on top of her, his heavy torso crushing her chest, and gave no hint to withdraw, she perceived he may have passed out. So, she shouted angrily for him to get off her and beat on his back. Like a resting goat that had smothered a lamb, weary and grumbling, he rose up and pulled away. And, without saying a discernable word, he left her for the bathroom to shower.

For several minutes, she sat on the side of the bed waiting for her nerves to calm. At her feet, she saw his discarded clothes and knelt on the floor to inspect them. On his undershirt, she saw a residue of facial powder. From his trouser pockets, she took out packaging from a condom, as well as "Big Red" chewing gum, and a match pack advertising an Atlantic City striptease club. "How considerate he was for his prostitute . . . ," she said out loud, "but me, he hasn't the courtesy to awaken politely."

Suddenly, unusual rage seized her. Bundling his clothes in her arms, she walked into the bathroom, opened the shower door and threw pants and all at his feet.

"Wash your own fucking clothes!" she screamed.

Her uncommon use of that word caught him by surprise. She saw a look of protest flash across his face. She heard him shout at her as she slammed the shower door. He wanted to explain, but she about faced and ran across the hall to the children's bedroom where she used a key she kept over the doorframe to lock herself in. He tried to get her to come out. He knocked softly for her, but she ignored him. He threatened to break through to her, but she knew he would not do that. Michael would respect the children, if not her. Soon enough he stopped. She heard him leave the house and watched from the window as he drove wildly off to some midnight destination. She dropped into the upholstered rocking chair in which she had often sung her babies to sleep. But there would be no more sleep for her tonight, only harmful memories that made her hate herself and fear that with every passing day her life came closer to the edge.

CHAPTER 3

NIGHTMARE YEARS

Wednesday Morning, June 6

Rhonda Maefield awoke before dawn, a cold sweat covering her body, her hands trembling. Her recurring nightmare had done it to her. While silent now, only seconds ago she had screamed amid an imagery of Nazi atrocity followed by the murdered appearance of her dead husband. "How crazy!" she exclaimed, always inclined to pass off this dark dream. "What does one have to do with the other? How the mind plays tricks!"

She switched on the lamp at her bedside and left her bed for the kitchen where she made coffee before she showered and put on a summery blue cotton dress with a wide neckline and short sleeves. Too early to take her morning stroll, holding a mug of scalding black coffee, she advanced to the living room, opened the drapes and, using a pillow behind her back, propped herself up on the window seat. Carefully, she positioned the mug on the wide sill beside her.

Her eighth floor Manhattan apartment provided a spectacular view. Turning her head, and looking north, she could see the lights of the George Washington Bridge and below, like a chain of sparkling diamonds, the Henry Hudson Parkway as it meandered south along the Hudson River and New York Central

Railroad tracks into the narrower depths of Manhattan. The scene facing her all looked so beautiful and peaceful.

She considered herself lucky to have acquired this spacious two-bedroom apartment in a turn of the century building of the city's affluent west side. She loved the building's old world white granite fronting, its gilded gold leaf and marble entry parlor with twelve-foot walls of beveled mirrors. Reminding her of structures in pre-war Berlin, the building was one of several remaining on this block reflecting the wealth and style of a bygone Morningside Heights community. With Columbia University expanding rapidly, she guessed, in a matter of a few years, this valuable property would yield to the wrecking ball and the need for new dormitory space.

"Enjoy it while you can," she told herself.

Especially important to Rhonda were the intellectual and religious institutions that surrounded her. Within throwing distance stood the Interchurch Center, national headquarters of several Protestant denominations. Next to this office-building rose Riverside Church, with its carillon bell tower and ornate cathedral, a near replica of the cathedral she had left in Tompkinsville. Within a short walk were Barnard College and Columbia University campuses, Union Theological Seminary, Jewish Theological Seminary, St. John the Divine Cathedral, and St. Luke's Hospital. She could cross Riverside Drive to catch a bus, or five minutes away on Broadway, she could ride the subway into downtown Manhattan—theaters, museums, fine department stores, Greenwich Village and Soho coffee houses, the New York theater district. This was a familiar city, one filled with pleasant memories. Here she had friends and, best of all, here she believed she could begin life free of the nightmare past.

She had moved in two months ago. Some of the furniture she had brought from Tompkinsville, but most of that, she had considered "junk" and given to the Salvation Army.

Besides a well-equipped kitchen and two tiled baths, her Riverside residence included a stylish, large living room and two bedrooms, one of which she used as an office, but by installing a Simmons' Hide-A-Bed, which she placed along the wall as a sofa, the office doubled as a guest bedroom. She had decorated the living room windows with rose-colored lace curtains and heavy matching drapes, which she often closed in daylight. This she justified by saying that a darkened room saves the furniture from fading in the late afternoon sun, but her reasoning was also personal. Rhonda preferred to sit and read in a darkened, artificially lit room. The soft and massive furniture, consisting in part of two sofas and two lounge chairs, recently reupholstered to match the drapes, provided comfort in the palatial room. Off to one side, close to the open kitchen and foyer, she had set up a modest-size dining area with a round table and four matching high-back dining chairs. A glass-fronted hutch housing her parents' crystal and china that had miraculously survived the ravage of war in her Berlin home stood along the east wall.

Oriental rugs crisscross the floor. None of them matched. But this made no difference in a room of startling contrasts, nine-foot ceilings and dark oak floors. Renaissance prints adorned the white walls—favorites from her husband's collection, all expertly framed with gold-painted wood molding. She had also hung a few valuable paintings by modernist artists. Her husband had called them "bloody scandalous," one of his favorite expressions. She had to admit they were eye-catching for their outlandish and complex integration of colors and figures.

Rhonda revealed more of her dark side in the way she had decorated her bedroom. Everything there she had bought new to her since moving in. The room allowed only shades of black and stark white. Gray carpet covered the floor. The high, wide, bed frame, constructed of heavy wrought iron, encased a snow-white comforter and fat, overdone pillows. For decoration and story effect, perched vultures looked down with disdain from the top of massive iron bedposts. A copy of Henrie Matisse's *La Dance*, a circle of nudes, their pink skin providing the room its only color, hung above the bed. On the opposite wall, above a black leather bench, was a wrought-iron weld that complemented the vultures on the bedposts. Only here, each frightening bird held a naked girl or boy in its talons, lifting their comely youth—it would seem—to a place of pleasure, or perhaps destruction. She had purchased the bed frame and wall decorations from a dusty furniture store in Chinatown. The owner had told her the pieces were ancient and imported from Hong Kong a half-century ago. He claimed they had once decorated the palace bedroom of an emperor. Rhonda did not doubt their origin and had easily paid a price that few emperors would have thought wise. The single window in this room supported a fire escape and admitted a view of apartment windows across an ally less than twenty feet away. A thin lace curtain carelessly diffused the stark urban view.

Rhonda's coffee had cooled and she began to sip it slowly. Unlike American brews, this was syrupy and harsh, a quality she believed only a born European could appreciate. Enjoying its taste, she stared out the window at the river and the city park below. She remembered twenty-three years ago when hand in hand she and Daniel had taken long morning walks along Riverside Drive or used the paths through the adjoining park. Experientially romantic and full of conversation, they enjoyed each other's company. They used to stop for breakfast at a Russian bistro on Broadway and 139th Street. She remembered it as the only place about that served coffee like hers. She wondered if the place was still there.

* * *

The son of Scottish missionaries, Daniel Maefield was educated in English boarding schools and the University at Edinburgh in Scotland. In 1926, he came to America where he graduated from Princeton Seminary before earning a Ph.D. in medieval art and literature at Princeton University. While pursuing his doctorate, he published two books, the first a commentary on the Gospel of John and the second a history of Jesus, entitled, *The Life and Loves of Jesus.*

The second book was immediately controversial because Daniel proposed that Jesus had married Mary Magdalene and that John Mark was their biological son. In conservative religious circles, leaders considered the book's contents so preposterous and radical they banned it. But no one with an ounce of a scholar's curiosity could doubt Daniel's ability, or question the scholarship he had applied to his conclusions. The book was reverent and-in no way suggesting illicit behavior—it won high critical praise: *Worth the time of serious New Testament scholars,* reported the religion editor of the New York Times.

That remark alone put Daniel in the spotlight. At age thirty-one, he accepted a professorship in classical studies at Columbia. That employment gave him the opportunity to become pastor of a church in the Harlem neighborhood that adjoined the university. Daniel now lived in the two worlds of university professor and inner city minister. If that were not enough, just up the street stood Union Theological Seminary and its Presbyterian bedfellow, Auburn Seminary. At these centers of religious education and theology, Daniel became a frequent guest lecturer.

Cynical, humorous, never shirking from an honest answer if he had one, whether lecturing at Columbia or Union, Daniel's classes were always full. And in the pulpit of his Harlem church, his sermons were sharp and stirring, crammed with colorful word pictures of human dilemmas and conflicts with sin. A follower of Christian Socialism, Daniel Maefield used his pulpit to sound the battle cry in the fight for racial equality and social justice.

Perhaps no neighborhood felt the Great Depression more than the one in which he ministered. Yet, everyday—somehow—Daniel Maefield's church managed to feed hundreds of people soup and sandwiches and on Sundays a full-course dinner. He found ways to get many of his people employed in urban development aid programs. He fought and usually with success to save families from evictions. He was an outspoken member of the Democratic Party and called Franklin Delano Roosevelt an Apostle of Jesus Christ. For that and other remarks of a socialist nature, criticism was widespread. When his enemies called him a communist, he got into more hot water. "Better that than calling me a bloody Republican," he fired back, a cynicism that did not help his popularity among more than a majority of the Columbia faculty. Yet, clearly, Daniel Maefield was above all such names. The Reverend Professor was an outstanding intellect, a man in love with knowledge and totally dedicated to the premise that he must be free to share his knowledge with all those wishing to hear it from him.

*   *   *

The first time Rhonda saw Daniel, he was lecturing on the economic implications of the European Renaissance. From the last row of the packed lecture hall, she thought he looked handsome in his dark double-breasted suit. Up close, however, she did not quite know what to make of him. She saw wrinkles in his suit and its frayed cuffs. His pants, drawn up too high on his lanky body, exposed one black sock and the other definitely dark green. Nor would she ever forget his multicolored tie, hanging irregularly over his lapel, showing signs of age and how many meals she could not count. If anything was obvious, Doctor Maefield needed someone to dress him. Maybe his pitiful state made her want him.

But there was much more to it than that.

She found Daniel Maefield intellectually stimulating. His critical evaluation of history fascinated her. It helped too that he encouraged her to follow her dream and pursue law as a career. For those qualities, she needed him in her life.

That he was close to nineteen years older and had little experience in dating were irrelevant to her. At the time, such opposites were probably what attracted them to each other. They needed what each one had, and love—with its accompanying intimacy—was then far less important than intellectual security.

Their courting began one evening after an event of his sponsorship brought her to tears.

Professor Maefield held an open off-campus seminar every Monday afternoon at a place called Shulster's, a Jewish eat-in bakery on 118th, east of Morningside Park. Maefield had a standing reserved room in back. With robust coffee and delicious cakes and pastries, students would sit with him for hours discussing in depth the world of politics, art, ballet, music, but mostly politics. On this particular afternoon, the reverend professor was especially upset. The American Nazi Party had held another rally and parade just across the East River on Long Island. Actually, the event had taken place at a park near Lake Ronkonkoma in Suffolk County, a three-to-four-hour drive east of the city, but for Maefield, who had little appreciation of American geography, it was just across the East River.

"The evil bastards," Maefield scolded, and smashed his fist against a newspaper he held up that included a photograph of men with swastika bands on their arms saluting a portrait of Adolph Hitler.

"Look here 'et the politicians hugging up to the lot o' that filth. Don't they know the hatred that lies in their hearts? It's a sin; worse, it's hell on earth. They think they can reason with these pigs. Hitler's stolen Czechoslovakia, he 'as Chamberlain looking like an inflated dove and he'll be knocking on France's door before the next full moon. Be forewarned, England will stand—alone! We ought to lockup the lot of this American brand of Hitler scum now and throw the key into the deepest pool of the ocean."

"Yes, professor, but you can't miss the good Hitler's done for Germany where there's virtually no unemployment, very little crime, free education, industry booming! There seems nothing they don't excel in." Johnny Murphy had gotten into it with Daniel.

"Murphy, they've got beer in their bellies and that's all those Krauts really have. Their economy is a lie, because that tyrant has stolen, bribed, and frightened Germany's aristocrats to accept phony notes. They build tanks and battleships while we twiddle our thumbs. The politicians and generals thought they could outsmart the Austrian corporal. Instead, he pulled down their bloody pants and aroused their inclination to blame the Jews for their troubles. A sickness that lives on the same side as hell.

Mark my words; soon, there won't be jobs, there won't be beer, because the free world, us included, will have to fight 'm to the death."

"You think the United States will be drawn into war with your 'Limey' cousins, Dan?" Murphy asked.

"Murphy, your wicked Irish streak is showing. You had better pray tonight that the British alliance with France does not fail. If Hitler marches his maniacs into Poland, the whole of central Europe will catch fire. And our islands will be in jeopardy. Hitler won't stop in London or Dublin. Nor will he be satisfied 'till he roots up every potato in your spoiled, sacred soil. And when he starts sinking American shipping, it'll be a world war again."

Then Rhonda spoke up for the first time. She was not the only woman present, but she was one who had a definite opinion about central Europe. She had reasons.

"There are horrors in Germany others cannot imagine."

"What do you know about it, Rhonda?"

"I know my father is dead because of the Nazis."

There was surprise and amazement. She was quiet for an instant, but tears filled her eyes and seemed to say it all.

"I am sorry, I should remain silent. I know nothing."

"Please, you are among friends," Daniel said softly.

He wished to console her, yet, he was just as anxious to press her for more news. This young, noble woman, with her deep German accent, was a mystery to him. Since the beginning of the term, she had attended two classes he taught. What's more, he had seen her in the congregation at his church several times. And, here at Shulster's, he delighted in her presence. He knew she was brilliant. A reading of one of her class papers was proof of that. He had encouraged her as he had all his Barnard women students to rebel against the politics that kept women second-class citizens. She often stayed after class when students pelted him with additional questions and he argued his personal views.

Flattered by her interest in him, Maefield had to admit he found her alluring and he looked for her in every opportunity.

Indeed, he saw her as different from any woman with whom he had personal contact. Now, as she sat across from him and tears flowed from her eyes, he knew he had met a woman about whom he cared.

"My father was pastor in Berlin. The Nazis executed him because he used his pulpit to protest the treatment of Jews. He preached that National Socialism and the Devil are the same. He called Hitler the anti-Christ. Suddenly they arrested my father. On the Sunday before, he taught about a loving God. On Monday, my father was in the hands of the Gestapo, men who know nothing except hate. Yes, one night he went to bed with his wife at his side and the next day he was a prisoner with no hope of survival. They moved him to Berlin's Plotzensee Prison. Do you know what the Nazis do in Plotzensee? As we meet here today, they torture respectful, loving German citizens, neighbors you shopped with and went to church with, lawyers, teachers, shop keepers, soldiers, anyone who speaks against the evil, who tries to rally public opinion to defend the powerless. The Nazis have no tolerance for debate. They take swift measures to suppress free thought. Nothing like what we do here is possible. If you don't conform to the politics of Hitler, a Nazi street leader, a bully, interrogates you. At Plotzensee, they hung my father on a meat hook. They burned holes into his body with branding irons, then, they beheaded him. Everyone in Germany knows this. That is the secret of Nazi power—inform the neighbors of what happens to those who do not conform, who do not cheer or believe the propaganda. You will end up like your beloved pastor. And you know what? When people are afraid, and they know what happened to their kind, loving pastor, they become indifferent. That is when they do not know why thousands of law-abiding Jewish merchants are suddenly absent from their shops or their houses, or why Jewish children no longer come out to play in the street. That is when German citizens do as told . . . No one is safe. Today, I do not know if my mother is alive or dead. If she is not dead, she soon will be. This is as much because she was born Jewish as because she became a Christian."

Rhonda could say no more. She arose and left the room. A long, respectful silence followed. Daniel Maefield, who had taken a seat while Rhonda spoke, rose.

"I think we should call it a day, friends," Daniel announced. "We'll meet here again next week. I have a special guest. I hope Rhonda will be all right to join us. She should hear this man. He is Deitrich Bonhoeffer, a German pastor, theologian, and a guest in our country lecturing at Union Seminary. He is an accomplished theologian and teacher. He has just left Germany where he is director of a seminary of the Confessing Church at Finkenwald. The Confessing Church is constantly under siege by the Gestapo. In spite of the danger, these German Christians have joined in preparing a new Confession of Faith at Barmann. I am sure that my friend, Professor Bonhoeffer, can throw light on the terror that has grown up in his country. Until then, thank you all for coming."

The group shook hands all around. Rhonda stood by the door. She knew about Bonhoeffer and already felt better. He was one of the leaders in the German underground church. So far, he had succeeded where others had failed, or at least thus far, arrest and torture had eluded him. However, Bonhoeffer should not return to Germany as he has promised. (Deitrich Bonhoeffer was executed by an SS firing squad in 1945.)

Rhonda waited in the doorframe as students passed her, gesturing with eyes and slight waves of the hands that they felt bad for her. Some reached out to enclose her in a friendly hug. Even the Irishman, Murphy, grumbled, "I'm sorry," in her ear. Just then, Daniel Maefield threw an arm over her shoulders and escorted her out of Shulster's.

"Come on, Rhonda, I'll walk you to your flat."

They were married three months later.

*　　*　　*

All that seemed like such a long time ago and yet so very near. Rhonda gulped the last of the bitter, now cold, liquid from her coffee mug. The first rays of sunlight were striking the tops of the Palisades across the river. Light was flooding the bridge and in less than ten minutes, the sun would glide into the concrete canyons of the city. She got off the window seat. It was time for her walk, time to begin a new day.

*   *   *

Jerry Flynn left the Tompkins' house just as the sun rose above the flat, misty fields. On his way out, he heard movement in the kitchen. He knew the family would welcome him for breakfast, but he didn't want to take the time. He preferred to stop at Tommy's Place, a local diner on the other side of Tompkins Park from the church, a block from City Hall.

He parked across the street at curbside. He figured he would hang out at Tommy's a lot. Its convenience and reputation for good food made it attractive. He liked the idea of meeting friends and neighbors there. Inside, he was immediately pleased that the waitress pushed a cup of coffee under his nose without him asking. She instructed him on where to find the morning paper and took his order for "two eggs over light, bacon and a double order of toast."

He heard other patrons call her Millie, sensed that she already knew his name and probably a lot more about him. A new minister at First Church became major news and Jerry perceived such information flowed freely in and out of Tommy's Place. Jerry guessed Millie at around fifty. Tall and busty, she carried herself well and moved with nervous energy from one customer to another. Her long, peroxide-blond hair, tied in a youth-oriented plaid bow, hung straight. She spoke in harsh, loud, fast tones, a sound and phrasing heard in much of the New York metro area. Millie took no guff from anyone and never—he would learn—confused an order.

Jerry was not past the front page when Millie brought him breakfast. She filled his coffee cup for the second time. When he finished eating, he left a tip. Before paying his tab at the register, Millie was next to him.

"Reverend, I don't take no tip from you." she said slipping the coins into his breast shirt pocket. And Tommy don't take a dime for feeding you. We thank you for coming and we're j'st happy to serve a man of God."

When Jerry started to protest, she retorted, "We don't charge Father Joe and we don't charge you. If my Rabbi ate in here—he won't because he's kosher—we would say the same. Have a nice day, Reverend."

There was no arguing with Millie. Jerry returned his wallet to his pocket and thanked them all. This is a friendly town, these are good people, he told himself as he started walking in the direction of his car. A busy day ahead of him, he had many things on his mind. Yesterday, he had committed himself to meet with a woman journalist who had convinced him she needed his help writing a human-interest story about how people about town and church were coping with Reverend Maefield's murder. He had matters more pressing on his mind than a journalist's deadline. He had agreed to see her at ten. That would be about the same time his parents and the moving van were due to arrive.

He thought about these things as he stepped off the curb and passed between parked cars to cross Main Street. On the run, he looked left and dodged a passing westbound car. I wonder if Charlene Cunningham is as pretty as she sounded, he asked of himself while paying no attention, not looking, to eastbound traffic on his right.

A loud horn blared sharply. He spun right to see the broad front of a bus with green markings coming at him. He stepped back, out of its path. Another blast of a horn westbound frightened him more and he inched forward toward the bus while the car passed behind. The bus screeched to a stop, its side-view mirror less than a foot from his ear. A dozen heads protruded from open windows, eyes staring at him, hands waving, voices shouting. As the bus idled before grinding gears and starting to move again, he heard: "Watch it, gringo! You asshole! Stay out e' the way!" But others, concerned for his safety, looked relieved. "God bless you, friend," one man called and did the sign of the cross. "You, okay, Mister!" a woman with a kerchief tied over her head yelled and gave him a V for victory gesture. As Jerry stood his ground, he waved and smiled. Most of the window gazers waved and smiled in return. Only one man, with black wavy hair, mustached and unshaven, hanging out the back window, continued to harangue him. As the bus gathered speed, this fellow pounded the flat of his hand against the side while he yelled in English, "Next time, we get you, you half-ass gringo!" and gave Jerry the finger as the bus moved away.

Jerry could not easily dismiss the man at the back of the bus. Written all over his face, he had read hatred and animosity.

In his bedroom, he opened his suitcase and took out underwear he would change into. He had already thought ahead to hang up a casual short sleeve shirt and slacks. He had no intention of getting too formal with tie and starched collar, or worse, clerical garb, on these hot, humid days. He did, however, like things neat, especially his clothes, crisply ironed, and his shoes with a bright shine.

In the shower, he enjoyed the heavy steaming spray and lost himself in thoughts of yesteryear.

*   *   *

When nine years old, at the urging of Father O'Flanagan, "before he gets corrupted," Jerry passed to the holy domain, and enrolled and boarded at St. Dennis School. Of course, St. Dennis served as a womb for holy orders in the church. Without explanation or permission, the nuns and priests of St. Dennis began grooming him for the priesthood.

He could look back now and laugh at the strictness. It was not so funny then. He had not been the only boy to piss in his pants at the rough disciplines handed out by his superiors. He recalled Sister Grace in particular, who had a severe habit of mauling boys between their legs. It was nothing sexual. He had laughed with others that Sister Grace was not a part of any animal species. No, she went for the balls because she knew where guys hurt, and no boy, regardless of his age or muscle, had the courage to lie, cheat, steel, curse, smoke, spit or jerk-off while she was on duty for fear she'd surely know and drop him to the floor.

"Had I remained at St Dennis, how different my life would be today," Jerry reflected.

But all that changed one warm day in May when he was just twelve years old.

Sister Grace, an unusual smile parting her dry, lifeless lips, escorted him to the rectory next to the school. In his mind, this could only mean painful family news. After waiting alone for an hour in one of the plush sitting areas, the door opened to reveal his mother—fresh and more beautiful, he thought, than he had ever seen her. Smiling, colorfully dressed, she held the arm of Father O'Flanagan. Only "Father O" looked much different and Jerry almost did not recognize him without his starched white collar and black suit. Had Jerry come of age or had he lived in surroundings more in tune with romantic things, the corsage pinned on his mother's dress would have said it all. After a long pause, his mother started to say the obvious. *"Jerry . . . Father . . . a . . . Paul . . . "* But it was Father O, who once more came to her aid. *"We've been married, son!"* Perhaps nothing could have prepared him for such news. Never, even in his fondest fantasy, had he connected his mother and her priest as husband and wife. *"Can I still call you Father O?"* Jerry remembered asking.

* * *

How strange life is, Jerry thought as he came out of the shower. Today I begin where God left me off, different in scope, redirected, but no less the person I was then. Time will tell," he sighed and began dressing.

* * *

At the Green Onion Motel, Charlene Cunningham dressed for her day. Buttoning her satin, sleeveless blouse, she thought perhaps she should choose something more modest. After all, if someone was looking for it, her blouse did leave the contours of her black bra viewable. The thought however was only fleeting and quickly she zipped up her black leatherlike skirt, admiring how neat it hung three inches above her knees. Stockings with elastic tops were her safety valves, she conceded, freeing her from garter belts and "all that other leg gadgetry" she so hated. Seeing herself one last time in the full-length mirror, she tipped her head appreciably. Confident and pleased, she left the room for the parking lot.

Summer heat has come early this year, she thought, as she pushed inside the steaming confines of her sports car, an MG Midget. She wanted to drive with the roof collapsed, but a threat of rain discouraged her, especially considering how she had struggled to get it in position yesterday and had had to tie it closed with banding wire. That aside, like her choice of clothes, Charlene loved style. To her, the froglike look of the "Midget," with its "perky" engine and its parrot green color, meant everything. She needed, however, to get the car in for service. If only she had more time for "stupid" things like that, she thought. If only she had more patience with things that don't work, she chided. She really hated it when her plans went wrong. If she had a fault, it was adjusting to the unexpected and making amends with herself for lost opportunities.

*　　*　　*

Roberto Ramous liked sitting in the back of the farm-worker bus, the windows open and the breeze whipping his unordinary long hair. "That stupid gringo! We sure as hell scared the shit out of him!" he jabbered after pulling his long body inside and flopping down in the double seat shared with a short Mexican man sporting a white cowboy hat. Playfully removing the man's hat, Roberto put it on his own head, the Mexican laughing as Ramous pretended to be a distinguished gentleman by tipping his hat at women the bus passed in its slow movement through Tompkinsville morning traffic. Once out of town, he returned the hat to his seat companion, crushing it on the little man's head and chuckling at how it fit at the bridge of his nose.

*   *   *

Unlike most farm workers on the bus, Roberto Ramous was born in the United States. In 1941, his Mexican, turned American parents moved from El Paso, Texas to Mississippi, where they hired themselves out in the cotton fields. Work was plentiful during the war years, but after that—with new machines and more laborers than needed—there was little work and little pay. Mexicans soon found themselves as segregated and as impoverished as the Negroes with whom they competed for jobs. In 1951, sixteen years old, Roberto left home.

His reason for doing so had more to do with his own safety than the poor economic condition of his family. Roberto feared his father more than he feared other men. His theft of five dollars from the family savings meant a brutal beating. He had, of course, believed he could replace the cash before anyone would notice it missing. When that didn't happen, he believed his life depended on getting away.

One advantage he had, Roberto looked much older than his sixteen years. He was tall and muscled, had a heavy head of black hair and already sported a mustache. His older look and willingness to work hard got him a job aboard a fishing boat out of Biloxi. The owner let him sleep nights on the boat and the boy managed to hold his own for two months. After that, the fisherman paid him what he owed and Roberto bought a bus ticket to St. Louis, Missouri.

In the Woolworth store across the street from the bus station, the store manager caught him with a pocket full of candy bars, a shirt still in its wrapping stuffed down his pants, and—the real clincher—another customer's wallet, which he had snatched from her open purse while she looked the other way.

Had Roberto told the truth about his identity and age, he would have gotten off as a juvenile first offender. That would have meant sending him home, but he so feared his father, he told the arresting officer that he was nineteen and an unemployed fisherman. With no missing-person report or outstanding criminal warrants on him, the police-booking sergeant accepted his ruse without question and typed—**Name: Roberto Ramous; Date of Birth: December 2, 1932, Place of Birth: El Paso, Texas; Sex: Male; Nationality: Mexican descent; Address: None; Occupation: Unemployed fisherman; Comments: Illiterate, Drifter.**

Like his father, Roberto had a mean and bullying disposition and that night in the holding pen of the city jail, he got into a fight with another prisoner, which required medical attention for both him and the man he assaulted. The next day he badmouthed the judge. Roberto had a problem with authority figures. The judge decided to teach him respect and sentenced him to nine months in the county jail. Roberto's public defender made no effort to appeal this harsh sentence, which jailhouse lawyers told him shouldn't have exceeded thirty days. But Roberto did not complain. In the county jail, he was dry, clean, better fed than ever in his life and he had made a friend.

His name was Mike and Mike was Roberto's cellmate. Older by fifteen years and street-wise, Mike played the part of big brother, teacher and protector. He coached Roberto to better English, taught him how to write his name and soon had him reading and writing English at a fifth grade level. Best of all, Mike promised to give Roberto a job upon completion of his sentence. When Mike got out of jail three weeks ahead of Roberto, he left him his telephone number. After his own release, Roberto promptly telephoned and a half-hour later Mike came by the jail in a new, shinning 1953 Buick. He drove Roberto to his place, a rooming house in an ethnically Mexican neighborhood of urban St. Louis.

Mike now looked like a successful businessman. He wore an expensive suit, had plenty of cash in his pocket and ate out every night at a different restaurant. Mike paid for Roberto's room next to his and for all his meals. He bought him new clothes and his first pair of fancy shoes. He showed Roberto around the city and took him to see a Browns-Yankees baseball game. Roberto had never known a happier time.

On the fourth day into Roberto's time out of jail, after a hearty lunch and several beers, while listening to rollicking music from a jukebox in a neighborhood bar, Mike put his hands on Roberto's shoulders and looked at him straight-faced. "Roberto, it's time you got laid!" Mike let out a belly laugh and slapped his friend gently on his cheek. "This is the day, Roberto. You go'n out, man. You fuck'n a whore today."

Roberto should have expected it. Jail talk had revolved around two subjects, injustice and the anatomy of all things sexual. Nor had Roberto spoken wisely when he let on that he had never so much as kissed a girl, a matter of amusement among his caged compatriots. For such an admission was unheard of in the conversations of jailed men. But Mike had recognized the boy beneath this made-up man and had treated him as a "brother." And now he meant to direct him to—as Mike called it—"coming into manhood."

"Today's the day," Mike repeated and promptly escorted Roberto to an apartment house a few blocks from the bar.

Mike rang the bell, listened to a voice through an outside speaker ask who was calling and, upon identifying himself, was buzzed inside. Two flights up, Mike knocked on one of three doors facing the hall. The door cracked the width of the security chain and coal-black eyes stared through.

Mike said, "Ginger, meet my friend, Roberto; he's virgin!"

He handed through a wad of bills. "Give 'm the works. I'll be next door at Kitty's."

The space narrowed to release the chain. The door opened wide to reveal a woman Roberto guessed as more than twice his age. Mike gave Roberto a shove and, before another word passed, the door closed and latched behind him.

Short and stocky, Ginger had dark, reddish, straight hair

that loosely hung over her shoulders. She had brightened her face with rouge, a thick coat of lipstick and a lot of purple eye shadow. She had painted her eyebrows black. She wore a black slip that left a V between her ample breasts and fell short of her knees. Her feet and legs were bare.

"You ever see a naked lady, sonny?" Ginger giggled while reaching for his hand.

"My sisters, I guess," he replied.

Ginger's giggle became jovial and she moved in close. He could smell her overdone perfume as she took his hands in hers and placed them on the solid peeks of her covered breasts.

"How you like them suckers, sonny? Now don't tell me they feel like your sisters'," she laughed, this time loud and guttural, the vibration of her chuckle shaking her mounds. Applying more pressure, he felt through the silk material and felt their ripeness beneath her brassiere. "You like to kiss my 'beauties,' sonny? . . . Good! . . . Mama give you your wish."

Ginger stepped back to let down the straps from her slip. She pushed the silky fabric to her waist and lowered the left cup of her brazier, exposing the nipple and its saucerlike dark aureole. Roberto reached too late; Ginger had unexpectedly turned her back on him. "Undo the little hooks, sonny," she said in a low voice, pointing her fingers to the metal clip of her brazier. He thought how much the elastic strap sunk into her fat, leaving red marks where it had rubbed. Nervous and fumbling, he undid the coupling. As the elastic catch sprung away, Ginger spun around to face him. Smiling, but the laughter gone, she teasingly lowered her bra off her breasts. Their size stunned him. He would have thought of her as a creature from another planet had she not grabbed his hands quickly and held them to her naked bosom. "Stay with the teacher, Roberto," she asserted, mechanically releasing his right hand so she could lift her own breast to her mouth. She watched Roberto's eyes as beads of perspiration dropped off his chin. "Just like a lollipop, sonny, only much sweeter. You do it! Suck mama's tit! Nothing makes a woman fuck better," she prompted, "than sucking her tits." Shyly he did her bidding. She laughed at his awkwardness. But when she tried backing off, his hands reached behind and forced her to remain. Suddenly, this shy boy had turned aggressive and she became alarmed. She poked his stomach. "Take it slow, sonny," she admonished in a low, wilting tone. "You don't want to hurt mama." Desperate to detach him, she got her hands up, wrenched free, slapped his face and drove him an arms length away. "You overdo," she lectured and for a second she feared he would hit her with his clenched fist. This man might be a virgin, she thought, but he has a manly mean disposition. "Let's go to bed," she said, hoping to appease him and pushed her slip past her broad hips to the floor. Naked except for waist-high bloomers, she signaled him to follow her into the adjoining bedroom. "We just starting, man . . . no need to rush," she cooed, but fright was in her voice and on her face. "Don't run away from me," he shouted and, suspecting she might lock him out, he grabbed her wrist and held her tightly. Maybe she should jerk him off where he stood, she thought. Get him over quick and be done with him. But professional she was, instead she opened her arms and hugged him close.

"I feel you hard, sonny. That's good!"

The gesture calmed him. Expertly, she undid his belt and let down his pants. She reached into his underpants to hold his penis.

He would not let her have him so easily and slapped her arm, forcing her hand away. Once again, he grabbed her wrist, turned her roughly and locked her arm behind her back. He used his free hand to play with her breasts. "You goanna do me," he shouted in her ear and moved her arm higher.

"Easy! Easy does it, sonny!" she squealed. "Mama take care of you."

He dropped her arm and shoved her through the doorway into the bedroom.

"No need to get angry, sonny," she exclaimed.

"You don't call me, sonny, no more!" he shouted and turned her to face him.

"What I call you? Big man? You, big man now?" she shouted back.

"Roberto! Roberto!" he screamed. He raised his hand, ready to slap her.

"RO-BER-TO!" she spit out the name, mimicking him, over pronouncing each syllable.

She went to him then, kissed him hungrily on the mouth and cuddled him to her chest. The embrace played well for several minutes. She would have to take him fast, she thought and stepped back to finish undressing him, then, slowly she pushed down her bloomers. With him naked and erect, she reached into a table drawer next to the bed and took out a condom. "Don't want you getting me pregnant," she kidded, laughing loudly as she opened it and unfolded it over his penis. "You got nice 'Big Joe' there Ramous. Always make the girls happy with that," she sniggered. And, taking his hand, she pulled him with her onto the unmade, filthy bed, straddling him as he lay on to his back. With experienced casualness, she took his hard penis inside her and rode him to completion. When spent, she started to remove herself, but he held her breasts and demanded other sex acts. She said she didn't do such things for what she was paid and besides his time was up. She started to get off him but his strong arms now on her shoulders held her in place. She exploded in a fit of anger and connected hard with a fist on his midsection. He had no time to recover, when, as if by magic, a pocket automatic pistol was in her hand, its three-and-half-inch barrel resting below his nose. She must have had the tiny handgun snarled in the bed linen, he thought, because he had never seen it coming.

"Move your hands and you dead!" she asserted.

Only his deep breathing moved him as she dismounted, the gun now pointing at his vitals. He followed her cold, black eyes where the bullet would fly. She got off the bed and, keeping her distance, her eyes never leaving him while he found his clothes and dressed. Only when they were in the front room and she had unlatched the door, did she relax her aim.

"You not a nice man, Roberto!" she said as he opened the

door. "You control your temper, sonny, or some girl going to scratch your eyes out, or cut off your balls. You come here again and I shoot your brains through your asshole."

"Next time I beat your fat ass raw!" he bellowed as he backed out of the room. The door slammed behind him.

He turned to see Mike, who leaned against the opposite wall, a devilish grin on his face. "You man now, Roberto! The boys don't laugh at you no more! You tough fucker, man!"

Roberto smiled broadly, his head high like a peacock, his tall frame taller.

That night Mike said it was payback time and he needed Roberto to help him "whack some gas stations." They drove west across the state to the outskirts of Kansas City. In the three nights that followed, using a rural motel as their headquarters, they stuck up two gas stations.

On the fourth night, planning to make this their last heist, they waited in the station kiosk while the clerk filled the Buick's tank. When the attendant came in to open the cash register to get change for a ten-dollar bill, Mike put his arm around his neck and the snub-nose of his revolver against his temple. Roberto rifled the drawer, spilling cash into a paper bag. Suddenly, he stopped to grab bags of potato chips off the counter. Mike angrily shouted at him to finish cleaning the register. Roberto retorted he would do what he pleased and the men began exchanging angry words. That was when the attendant saw his opportunity. From his belt, hidden by his long shirt, he drew out a Remington Automatic, home engineered for rapid fire. Wrestling free, he fired three shots with the sound of almost one into Mike's heart. Roberto ran for the door, the attendant following, firing, hitting Roberto in the left leg, bringing him down before he reached the Buick. Looking up, Roberto saw the clerk aiming at his head. The man would have killed him had he not already emptied his automatic. Bleeding and hurting, Roberto waited for an ambulance and his arrest.

Convicted of aggravated robbery, the court sentenced Roberto Ramous to the Missouri state penitentiary for twelve years. This was hard time and Roberto suffered every indecency imaginable. There was no Mike to rescue him here and, with no friends or family on the outside, he lived as a forgotten number. But after serving seven years, a spree of prison reform laws commuted his sentence to four years probation. Best of all, the state found him a factory job.

But going straight was not his desire. Six months into life on the outside, Roberto became a suspect in a string of rapes and burglaries. He counted himself lucky when they let him go after appearing in a lineup. The victim—her eyes swollen and her face bruised from the beating she had endured—could not make a positive identification. Fearing she might change her mind, within hours, Roberto bought a bus ticket to Philadelphia, where— a year ago at a Latino hiring hall—he signed onto a no-questions-asked job to pick strawberries in the "Garden State."

Now he was back. After all, he surmised, he had managed a whole year of freedom on the migrant farm circuit. And in Tompkinsville, a man owed him a hundred dollars. He now meant to get his money. He smiled at the thought of doing the guy in when he least expected.

The T&T bus bounced over the rutted, dry, dirt road between fields of late harvest asparagus. When it reached weathered-gray worker houses and packing barns at the far end of a tomato field, it stopped. As passengers piled out, Jorge waited at a table shaded by a red beach umbrella to take names and assign numbers. Standing behind him, Manuel scrutinized each worker as he or she came forward.

"Name?" Jorge asked gruffly, ready to write it down and give the man his number.

"Antonio Lopez," Roberto Ramous bellowed, but he need not have lied. Neither Manuel nor Jorge remembered names. A face, however, Manuel never forgot and he immediately recognized Roberto's face.

"You pick here last spring?" Manuel commanded.

Roberto nodded and smiled appreciably, hiding his distaste for the tall Mexican charged with keeping order among workers.

The Widow's Paramour

Murder and Sexual Indiscretion Plague a 1962 Church

A. C. HELDMAN

and put a check next to where Jorge
erto knew he had a problem.
use?" Jorge asked looking up.
to produce identity papers, Roberto

' he timidly added.
who?"
zen."
f, but wrote the new information next

el interjected, his face lit in a sardonic
ad temper. Any fights, Lopez, and you
is!"
dred seventeen! Don't forget it! Move

ace by himself and waited for the
had reason to worry. There had been
ey wanted to, Manuel and Jorge could
Manuel referred to came during a poker
nd knives had stung flesh. Manuel had
the bunkhouse. When allowed back in,
e table was gone. When Ramous asked
ld him to "fuck off!" Not wanting more
d his bitterness. Strangely, he had hoped
eless, a good sign, he had spoken in his
anuel wanted to, he could have turned
, he watched the man with bitter eyes.
e new men to bunkhouses. The few women
nily cottages, where they would have to
quarters inside the men's lodging reeked
e and body odor. Bunk beds were stacked
three feet between them. Roberto dropped
ed. If another man claimed his place, he
s a wanted man, he would keep his peace
at could lead to questions, fingerprinting
He located the latrine out back and then

assembled with the other new arrivals. Once more, everyone boarded the white and green bus for the ride to strawberry fields five miles north. Roberto's seatmate, the same little Mexican who had accompanied him earlier, loaned him a spare baseball cap.

"Use this 'til you get your own," he said. "Broad rim, like mine, is best."

As they embarked from the bus, Jorge handed each picker ten one quart grocery-store-ready baskets. When a picker filled them, he or she would get a credit marked by their name and number. At today's eleven cents a quart, the field worker got credited a $1.10 for every ten baskets turned in. Jorge explained if he found any mashed, over ripe, or undersize fruits, he would reduce the piece value by two cents. He would check baskets at random. He explained, too, "Full baskets better not weigh much more or less than sixteen ounces." A scale was available to check basket weight. Jorge also announced the quota for today at one hundred. Most pickers would gather more than the expected quota of a hundred quarts. For every container above quota, their value increased to thirteen cents. Pickers had to watch closely that their tally matched the field-boss's record, though disputes rarely favored the picker. Whether gathering strawberries, iceberg lettuce, string beans or another vegetable, owners paid field workers by the quart, bushel, peck, crate, whatever unit of measurement or weight fitted the produce. Fieldworker quantity pay was set in accordance with ripeness of the fields and by how the grower valued the produce market price for that day.

"We got ten acres to pick," Jorge shouted in Spanish. "Get to work!"

Roberto and the little Mexican staked out their rows and bent their backs to the task side by side. Up to now, the little man had remained quiet. Now he complained about T&T farm conditions and the little pay for such hard labor.

"We don't even make minimum wage," he said, "a dollar fifteen an hour they have to pay in the canning factory. And they sit on their ass watching string beans poured into acid. We worth more than that. We got to organize the people of the fields," he roared as if speaking at a rally of workers. "Where do you stand?" he said as he paused to look at Roberto. "Are you with your brothers and sisters who want to organize a union?"

"No way, man! I don't fuck with no union. Pay me today so I can go somewhere else tomorrow. That's all I care. And you better keep your mouth shut about that union shit. You see these hands, little man?"

Roberto held up his strawberry red hands.

"Jorge hear you talk union, you be out o' here with your brown ass this color and faster you can spit a sour fruit."

After that, Roberto distanced himself from the Mexican in the white cowboy hat. He did not return the man's baseball cap.

*   *   *

Jerry Flynn entered the church-office complex from the parking lot. While exchanging pleasantries with Miss Blatty, she smiled and handed him a note: **Ten o'clock appointment / Miss Cunningham / in study.**

Arriving ten minutes before her scheduled time, Miss Blatty had shown Charlene into Shepherd House.

She sat straight up in a cushioned wingback chair cater-corner to his desk and he smelled her perfume before he crossed the long room, his hand extended to greet her. She stood, appeared almost to curtsy in the way Catholic schoolgirls do when meeting a priest or Mother Superior, but elected instead to take his hand and present a confident smile. Perhaps the informality of his dress and his relaxed manner had stopped her, he thought.

"Welcome to First Presbyterian," Jerry said happily.

"Thank you, Reverend Flynn," she said, her smile breaking into adorable cuteness.

"Please, I'm Jerry! And is it all right to call you Charlene?

"Of course," she said, her look seeming to applaud his easy manner.

He was already disposed to her as an artist would to a model. In that way, he scanned her silver blouse and accepted its invitation to look into its loose opening, the top of her black brassiere discretely visible. Passing on, he eyed blond curls that framed a youthful face, kept that way it seemed by dark, sparkling blue eyes, a doll-like nose and lips that broadened instantly to smile, as if to invite you in for a moment of pleasure. Adorable, Jerry thought. But when her smile lifted from sensual to curious, he wondered what in his makeup she had found humorous.

His moment of insecurity passed as he escaped behind his desk. He waited as she eased into the chair and crossed her legs, her short skirt riding precariously over her thighs, though no further than borderline modesty would allow. Only then did he take his own seat. It always amazed him how much a woman could show without really showing anything. Charlene Cunningham was all so simple and yet so real.

"Thank you for meeting with me today," she began. "I understand how busy you are, but it is important I learn as much as I can about your predecessor. In my magazine article, I want to do justice to his name and reputation. So much can be learned by seeing his home and place of work."

"Doctor Maefield did most of his writing in this room," he replied. "These empty shelves," he said, looking up and gesturing, "once held an immense personal library. The professor was a world-renowned author, a New Testament scholar. On the night of his death, he came here to work on a commentary of the Gospel of Mark. He wrote for several religious journals and, besides maintaining the busy life of a pastor, he lectured extensively in the United States and in Europe. As if this were not enough, he taught Renaissance History on Mondays at Columbia in Manhattan."

As Jerry spoke, Charlene took notes on a pad supported by a black leather binding she balanced on her raised knee. Attentive to detail, she frequently stopped him to ask for explanations of things she did not understand. She seldom looked up from her note taking, but when she did, she looked straight at him with serious eyes. They talked for close to half an hour. There were moments when both were distracted with bits and pieces about unrelated things, especially when they learned they had graduated from rival Philadelphia high schools. Clearly, Jerry wanted to learn more about her. She remained, however, persistent in the reason for her visit.

After exhausting what little Jerry Flynn knew about the death of Reverend Maefield, Charlene turned him in another direction.

"What can you tell me about Mrs. Maefield?"

"Well, really, much less than I know about him. I've never met her and I don't know that I will anytime soon. It's all very vague, but right after her husband's death, Mrs. Maefield stayed with friends in New York. About two months ago, she moved into her own apartment on Riverside Drive. It's near Columbia in uptown Manhattan, not far from the Harlem church where she and her husband resided before coming to Tompkinsville. Just prior to Reverend Maefield's demise, Mrs. Maefield graduated from Columbia Law School and passed her New York bar exams. I understand she currently works for a law firm giving special attention to women's rights in the workplace."

"Wow! We could certainly use some legal advice," Charlene commented without looking up from her notebook. "What are Mrs. Maefield's address and phone number?" she asked, ready to write them out, things she already knew but her cover demanded she ask him.

"I'll have to get that from my secretary," he replied. "I'm sure she has them on file."

"Maybe I'll drop by this afternoon and get them myself."

Charlene looked up now, caught Jerry's eyes. "With your permission, I'd like to interview Miss Blatty."

"Yes, if anyone could help you, she would be Miss Blatty. She worked for Reverend Maefield the whole time he was here."

Charlene focused once more on her pad and wrote out the new information.

Jerry folded his hands on top of his desk and leaned forward. It was a chance to glimpse her nicely bundled legs. In turn, she set down her notebook, uncrossed and stretched to look up at the high ceiling, admiring the stately beauty of the stained glass window above him.

"This must be an inspiring place for a minister to work," she said.

She rose out of her chair, turned and walked to the large conference table, to stand in the sunlight streaming through the twelve-disciple windows above.

Jerry stood. His eyes focused on her. He strolled around the desk.

"Yes, the room is inspiring. But you must also see the cathedral and the manse."

"Come again?"

"The manse—where I live. Manse is the name for the family residence of a Presbyterian minister. Catholics call it a rectory, Methodists, a parsonage . . . "

"Yes, I see . . . " she smiled.

"All three buildings go together. Manse, Shepherd House and the cathedral are in proportion and in harmony."

"Can you show me it all?" she asked. "I would love if you could take me on a grand tour. I'd like to see the manse, the cathedral . . . "

"I'll tell you what; you're going to be in the area for a few days. Right now is a busy time for me. My parents are due to arrive with a truckload of furniture this very hour. We'll be getting the house—manse—ready. Right now, it's a barren shell. Why not come back Sunday and we'll explore every little corner? This is an immense building complex and I haven't begun to see it all myself."

"Sounds good to me," Charlene agreed. "What time?"

He had to make a decision, whether to set the time while his parents were still here—for they would leave about mid afternoon—or meet her alone.

"Can you come at five? I'll be free by then and I can rustle us up something for supper."

"That's very nice of you. I'd like that." She looked at her watch. Her smile turned into a childlike pout. "I can't believe an hour has passed. If, however, you can spare me just a few more minutes, will you show me the cathedral, just the dime tour?"

"Got a dime?" he kidded, holding out his hand.

Charlene playfully slapped it. "I'll have to owe you. No change!"

"Fair enough! This way," Jerry said.

He led her out of Shepherd House, up the garden steps, and on to the cloister path.

Charlene enjoyed how he kidded her. His easy manner and humor were qualities she liked in a man. His polite habits, opening each door for her to pass through before following, and then rushing ahead to the next door, flattered her. It bothered her that many women her age rebelled against what they considered male chauvinist behavior. But Charlene welcomed this kind of attention and never objected.

They entered a side door from the cloister.

Jerry extended his arm to steady her in her high heels as they climbed the six stairs that led to the landing in front of another door. The windowless stairway would be as dark as night if not for wall scones that lit the area but left dark shadows. She gladly accepted his arm. Her soft skin against his, moistened in the humid air, enhanced his already idyllic mood. They had known each other less than an hour, had made a date—kind of—and were now arm in arm. On the last step, he dropped her arm to take her hand. He did not release it as he pushed the swinging door and led her across the narthex, then through double swinging doors into the nave of the great cathedral. Brilliant hues of light and massive arched pillars loomed before them.

They gazed at the high cathedral windows. Their blazing colors, captured by the rich daylight, related twenty-four epic stories, twelve on each side, from Old and New Testaments. Above the high altar, a more massive trinity of leaded stained glass remembered Jesus' baptism, crucifixion and resurrection. The high altar itself, an unusual furnishing in a Presbyterian Church, held a large, three step brass Latin cross, and twin candleholders. An old, opened, very large bible rested against the foot of the cross. In front of this stood a massive empty table used for the celebration of Holy Communion.

They started down the center aisle. In that moment, they heard the great bell from the tower begin peeling toward the eleventh hour. Though shielded by stone, timber and the height from which it struck, they could hear it clearly and sense its vibration. Already Jerry had grown used to this and loved the bell's sound and feel. Charlene, as if awakened to something new, stopped to listen, narrowed her eyes, counted out each toll and smiled respectfully as she checked her watch.

"It's always on time." Jerry assured her. "It works off an electric clock."

They resumed their walk toward the Crossing and the Choir beyond it. Jerry was about to explain the meaning behind the sights when they heard someone shout.

"Reverend Flynn! Is there anything I can do for you?"

Jerry dropped Charlene's hand. Startled and mystified by where the voice was coming from, he looked around him.

"I'm here Mr. Flynn, up here!"

Jerry followed the voice to a man seventy or more feet above the nave, where he stood on a narrow ledge built along the wall just below the clerestory windows. There was a waist-high, thin, iron hand rail to guide his way. He held a long pole with a gadget attached to its end with which he could reach the chandeliers suspended on ornate chains from the arched ceiling.

"Oh my God," Charlene muttered, her breath quickening at his perilous location.

For the first time, her smile vanished and Jerry saw fear expressed on her face.

Jerry said, "He's our church custodian, Everett Wheeler."

"You think it's hot down there," Everett laughed. "If hell is heat its all up here. Who's your lady friend?" he hollered as he leaned over the rail and stared at them.

"A visitor," Jerry shouted. "She would like to meet you— coming down?"

"I've had a look, Reverend, and I'm pleased to tell you I'll be down for a closer one. You keep her prisoner for me. I have one more bulb to change."

They watched as the large, agile man carefully retracted a light bulb from its socket above and a few feet to his left. Using the same pole, he replaced it with one in a sack tied around his waist. Charlene gasped as he turned toward them, walked the ledge to where he disappeared through a door above the balcony. A minute later, he emerged on the balcony, waved, and disappeared again. Then he reappeared out of the narthex by the same door Jerry and Charlene had used.

Perspiration flowed off his body. His t-shirt appeared glued to his back. Everett was a tall, muscular, heavily built man in his mid forties. His red hair, beginning to show signs of gray, hung straight past his ears, reminding Jerry of a Franciscan monk, especially the way a bald spot shown on his crown. Either too lazy to get a haircut or perfecting a rare style, Jerry assessed Everett's hairstyle as rather comical.

Everett reached out to greet them with a large, clammy hand that was also rough, callused and powerful. When it left his for Charlene's, it swallowed her hand and did not let go.

"This is Charlene Cunningham," Jerry said, "she's a magazine feature writer and plans to author an article on how people are coping after the death of Reverend Maefield. Charlene, Everett probably knew Doctor Maefield as well as anyone."

"Indeed, I did and not a better man ever graced God's meadows," he said, finally releasing her hand. "But I've told everything I know to the police, the district attorney, nosy reporters, and lots of ordinary folks. To tell you the truth, ma'am," he looked to Jerry now, as if wishing he had not come down so quickly for a better look, "I'm tired of talking about him. Can't we just let the holy man rest now in his Father's bosom?"

Charlene decided not to press. She perceived that Everett had overdramatized his situation, perhaps to impress the pastor. She wanted more time with Everett. She needed to hear what he knew about the murder. The police report had put him on the scene early that morning. But it was getting late and she had to be on her way.

"Thank you. I understand," she said. "Actually, I came here today to see your beautiful church. I have heard so much about it."

Everett's eyes brightened. His red cheeks got redder. He relished the opportunity to speak on a subject he was truly interested in and one that he knew a great deal about.

"Yes, First Church is one of the finest copies of fourteenth-century church architectures in the United States. Like many gothic cathedrals in this country, they built this one on the model of a French cathedral. But they did do some cheating here," Everett grinned in a fool's way, "because, instead of stone on stone, they form fit concrete over steel and hung the ceiling from flat timbers that crisscross the attic above what you see there."

Everett pointed above the ledge where he had just been walking.

"That made construction very fast, three years in all, and it was finished, not like St. John the Divine in New York, which began ten years after this and is still incomplete. I don't mean to say that this building is anything like St. John the Divine. If you've been there, you know that church is much larger. We're one-third its size. Actually, Riverside Church in upper Manhattan, which they completed in nineteen thirty, is more like this. It too has a single bell tower above the vestibule and is similar in many other ways.

"Well, at least you don't have to paint the ceiling," Jerry said, laughing a little, trying to get Everett to see that he was humoring him. Instead, Everett showed disdain, made no reply and went on with his history lesson.

"They laid the cornerstone for this cathedral on January 1, 1869 and went on to build Shepherd House and finally the manse. The cloister connecting the buildings was an afterthought and built to commemorate the turn of the century. Isn't it a wonder what money can buy?" Everett asked, smiling like a child, who had suddenly learned the worth of a ten-dollar bill. "Some of my ancestors were benefactors, though the man who gave the real money for all this was no Tompkins. He was a Philadelphia banker born in France named Henry LaSalle. He gave ninety percent of the cost in memory of his wife and children, who drowned while in transit from Liverpool to the United States. It seems that their ship went down in an Atlantic storm with no survivors. Henry LaSalle was a Huguenot, that's a French Presbyterian."

Jerry thought, well, not exactly, but he wasn't about to correct Everett's entrenched view of French history.

"When LaSalle heard about plans to build a new Presbyterian Church on land that reminded him of his native France, he asked the elders if they would agree to his specifications. Well, of course, those old Scots and Swedes around here at the time agreed. Henry did the rest. He hired the architect, the builders, supervised the construction and paid the bills. But he did much more. He endowed the finished buildings with three million dollars. LaSalle's endowment is now worth ten times that, and that's after the stock market crash when our stock lost half its value. The interest pays for the maintenance and preservation of all the buildings and grounds. Of course, we never use that much money," he laughed, "so it gets reinvested. It's restricted, you see," he said staring now at Flynn. "You can't use a penny for 'jungle bunny' schemes," he cooed derisively, "or send a dollar to those communist causes our national church supports."

"And are you in charge of all the buildings?" Charlene asked, her mind blocking a political discussion.

"That I am and a lot more," Everett replied proudly. "I employ three full-time assistants. The four of us cover this building fourteen hours a day, every day of the week. In addition, another man takes care of the grounds, mows the lawns and tends the flowerbeds and trees. By the way, Reverend, did you see that little Jap when you came in?"

Everett's sharp ethnic epitaph startled Jerry.

"I saw a Japanese man. I believe his name is Mr. Inoko. He was clipping hedges on the north side of the manse."

"Yes, yes, the little Jap is exactly where I left him. That's good, shows he can follow directions. You can call him Mister if you like, Reverend, but he works for me and I call the 'slant-eye' whatever I want."

Everett was emphatic. There was no missing his racist perspective.

"I have to be on my way," Charlene cut in. "Thank you for the tour, Reverend Flynn, and for the history lesson, Mr. Wheeler. I'd like to hear more. Perhaps we can find a convenient time." Without offering her hand again, she backed away. "I can find my way out. I will get in touch with you, Mr. Wheeler. I do want to hear what you have to say about Reverend Maefield. You can tell me about all the good things he did here." She smiled graciously and started to move in the direction she had come into the building.

"Go this way, Miss," Everett chimed in. He attached his hand to her arm and led her toward the pulpit and chancel area, "There's an exit and stairway behind the south transept, one flight down and follow the hall in the annex to the parking lot exit. It's closer to your car."

Obviously, Everett had seen her arrive, Jerry thought. He watched as Everett held her by the arm and escorted her to the end of the isle, then led her behind the choir. He followed to watch as Everett stood in the narrow doorway of the sacristy, purposely forcing her to brush against him as she passed through. She appeared flushed by the inappropriate move and, after a quick step back, she made eye contact with Jerry, flashed a smile, waved and, without acknowledging Everett, walked away. Everett watched her disappear down the stairwell.

"That was some cookie, Reverend!" he said as the door swished behind him. "Wow! Watch out for that one!"

Jerry let the comment pass. He was pleased Charlene had not given away their date. He wondered, though, if there could be any secrets here. Everett's manner had embarrassed him. He was boiling mad just thinking about the man's "Jap" remarks. But this was not the time or place to confront him. Jerry had other things to do. He headed up the aisle toward the narthex.

"Take care, Reverend!" Everett let out, his voice comical and sarcastic.

"Yes, I'll do that."

"And if you see that little Mister What's-His-Name," he said, enjoying his ridicule, "you tell 'm the Marines are coming, so get his . . . just tell him to meet me in the parking lot at one o'clock!"

Jerry stopped his flight and turned. Everett remained poised at the steps to the upper chancel, so Jerry had to shout the length of the isle. "You tell him yourself, Everett! By the way, I'll need you at the manse about that time. Bring a hand truck. I want you to move Reverend Maefield's boxes of books into Shepherd House. I understand they're stored in the manse basement."

Jerry did not wait for a reply. He moved through the swinging doors and out of the cathedral. There was no mistaking his deepening dislike for Everett Wheeler.

CHAPTER 4

"A DREADFUL MAN"

Wednesday Afternoon, June 6

After a brief stop at Shepherd House to visit Miss Blatty, Jerry Flynn continued on home where Father O and his mother were busy directing the moving men on the placement of furnishings. His mother marveled at how the period pieces fit into the Presbyterian mansion. If ever these antiques were to have perfect settings this was it. Everything from Neoclassicism to Victorian Renaissance furniture came to rest in the numerous rooms of the vintage dwelling. Some pieces were recreations of earlier designs. Yet, by virtue of their age and significance, they were all antiques of fine quality. A grandfather clock, said to have chimed uncontrollably the hour Abraham Lincoln was shot, found its place in the long foyer that opened to the front door. A Gothic Revival bedstead, incorporating lancet arches and crockets went into Jerry's bedroom. Jerry was glad that a modern box spring and comfortable full size mattress accompanied the fancy pieces of carved wood. A matching chest of drawers, tables, lamps and wardrobe closet took places in the same room. Under the careful supervision of the O' Flannigans, the moving men maneuvered the heavy furniture through doorways and many times up the circular stairway.

Just as Jerry entered the kitchen, Madge Todd arrived as the vanguard of a committee of churchwomen to help in getting the manse ready. Jerry held open the screen door and—at the same time—reached to take a cardboard box out of her hands.

"That's okay. I've got it. It's not as heavy as it looks,"

She set the carton on the kitchen counter and without pause went back out the door. Jerry started emptying it—fresh-baked bread, pickles, plates of sliced deli meats and cheeses, bowls of homemade salads, cartons of fresh-picked strawberries and lettuce. On a second trip from her station wagon, Madge put down giant jugs of ice tea.

"Look at all this!" Jerry said, "You people do so much. There's enough here to feed an army."

"It's only lunch," Madge corrected him and lightly pushed in front to take over.

"What? No child on the hip today?" he joked.

"Oh that's why I'm here. I took the day off from work and Mom has Dudley all morning. She'll be here with the afternoon crew. And you're excused, Reverend Flynn." She smiled her beautiful smile but only as a pretense. Her body language said something else. Hands on hips, shoulders slightly leaning, legs spread, she dramatized no further help would be welcome. "Listen, the tradition is that when a new minister arrives, the church fills the fridge and the cupboards. But you arrived on the scene before we got our act together. Mom will be bringing a whole grocery list." Madge turned away to open the refrigerator door, "Ugh, this looks like it hasn't seen the light of day in years."

Before Jerry could offer a word, Madge was pulling out the racks. "See if you can find some Clorox!" It came as an order, not as a question.

Then she was on her hands and knees opening cabinets under the countertop. "This is terrible. Look here, a half-empty jar of jelly, an opened box of spaghetti. You can see the mice have been sampling this." She tossed each item into a trashcan by her feet. "This place sure needs work."

"Well, you don't have to excuse me. I can squeeze a mop as well as the next man. Just tell me what to do."

Madge looked at him quizzically. "What to do?" The expression on her face was one of amusement. "You can begin by getting out of the way," she laughed. "The guild ladies will be here momentarily. And while they would love to see a man do housework, I don't think any of them will tolerate a man in the kitchen. Out, Mr. Flynn!" There was a knock at the kitchen door. "There they are. That's what you can do. Let the ladies in."

He did not get there in time. The knock was a warning to stand clear, for suddenly the kitchen was crowded—Janice Henry and Wilma Drew, both in their seventies, he guessed; Alice Carlson, a large, middle-aged woman with a Swedish accent. Behind her came Madeline Winston. Madeline brought in enough cleaning supplies to do a hospital ward. Introductions followed but only politely. These women were all business.

Jerry stood by stone faced as Madeline opened and climbed a stepladder to begin cleaning the over-counter cupboards. She was tall, slim, a few years older than Madge and, like Madge she dressed in trendy men's dungarees and a flannel shirt that hung below her waist.

"I don't believe this," Madeline said as she brought her dampened cloth to the surface. "Behold Adam's dust."

Jerry laughed at the expression, but no one paid him any mind.

"Yes, well, Rhonda wasn't here much in the last four years. Apparently the housekeeper they hired didn't bother with the little things," Wilma said as she began assembling gadgets onto a vacuum cleaner. "Mrs. Maefield was so meticulous about the rest of the house, but not the kitchen, that's for sure."

"I know she didn't like cooking much," Madge offered. "With her in New York most of the time, Mom often dropped off a meal for the pastor. He was a frequent guest for Sunday dinner. When Rhonda was home, they ate out. I don't think Reverend Maefield knew how to boil an egg."

"Well, the way I heard it," Madeline chimed in, "Rhonda cooked now and then and you were lucky if you missed it both times." Snickers and outright laughter broke out among all those who heard her. "Just watch out!"

"Remember the covered-dish supper," the Swedish lady broke in, "after which so many people got sick? I would swear it was Rhonda's tuna-something. I was smart enough to keep myself and children away from it, but my husband . . . you know he has to sample every dish on the table, well . . . he was the only one sick in our family that night."

"Girls, let's not pick on Rhonda," Madge suggested in a soft, steady voice. "None of us would want to trade places with her. Better we leave the past where it is."

Her plea silenced the room. When she raised her head from what she was doing, she stared into Jerry's eyes. He felt uncomfortable at her catching him, yet he did not look away. She smiled, but seemed also embarrassed. Shyly, she lowered her eyes to her work. He turned to take his leave, then, looked back; again, they caught each other's stare. Meekly, he waved and she waved in return. As he left the kitchen, the vacuum cleaner roared.

He took his time wandering through the spacious house. He was pleased with everything his mother and stepfather were doing. They had expert, artistic touches. He checked the master bedroom again. His mother was measuring the windows for curtains and drapes. There were three smaller bedrooms and another bath on this floor. Jerry looked in on their old, restful furnishings. Who would use them? He had no answer. He galloped down the back stairway to the alcove. He thought again about the idea of a live-in housekeeper. He needed to get Rosa's address and phone number from Walter Tompkins. Jerry knew it would be in his best interests. He peered into the separate maid's quarters by the kitchen. It occurred to him then that Maefield had lived as a bachelor for his last four years. The housekeeper the ladies had referred to was a one-day-a-week employee of a cleaning service. Why should he feel required to do otherwise?

"Pretty nice set up for the right person," he conceded while looking into the two rooms and bath set aside for such a person. He worried that he might not always find time to keep the manse looking fit. Yet, for one person, how bad can it get? "Even if I hire Rosa, entertain friends and family, how can I justify this whole house only for myself?" he said to no one. He peered into the living room just as the movers set a Queen Anne desk and bookcase in place, something from Revolutionary War times.

In the back of Jerry's mind, he had revolutionary ideas about how best to use First Church property. He would not dare suggest it yet, but in the not-too-distant future he wanted to propose turning the manse into a ministers' retreat house and conference center and using Shepherd House as a library and reading room open to clergy and lay teachers of all faiths. He could rent an apartment for himself in town and convert a small room in the annex into his pastor's study. That way, First Church would have a wider spiritual and educational use. There had to be a more generous way for the congregation to serve the public.

Also part of his hidden agenda: He intended to propose a weekday child-care center. With so many mothers joining the work force, finding good baby-sitting for their children had become a big problem. He thought too about migrants. Many women workers took their babies into the fields with them because they had no other choice. First Church had the facilities and money to lead the way in caring for infants, toddlers, family counseling and a whole host of other social services. What a waste, he thought, all those rooms in the annex sitting vacant six days a week. He returned downstairs by the back stairway where he heard Everett Wheeler's booming voice. Everett had deposited himself in the doorway to the kitchen to joke, banter, and mostly ogle the women working there.

"Oh there you are, Reverend. I've been looking high and low for you. I'm here as ordered to move them there books for you. Now will you first take a moment and have a look at these sweet bees fashioning your nest? What service you reverends get! I can see I just got into the wrong profession."

Jerry ignored his teasing remark. "I said to meet me at one."

"Yes, but I thought I'd show you where they are first. And maybe I'd like to get started. It's a lot of work, you know!"

Everett blocked the door. Madge, wanting to get through,

waited for him to move. Suddenly, he took her arm and playfully swung her against him. "Now have you met my little cousin, Sweetpea?" he cooed.

This was news to Jerry.

"Yes-sir-ee," he cackled, "a finer and prettier lady you won't find," he said, trying to draw her closer.

Madge quickly pulled away, her face showing annoyance.

"My mother and her daddy, sister and brother," Everett continued, a hearty smile pinned to his lips as he finally let her go.

"Everett, do you ever shut your mouth?" she scolded.

"Well now Mrs. Todd, I don't know I should answer that question . . . ," he retorted as Madge scurried past and out of earshot.

"If you'll show me the way, Everett." Jerry injected loudly.

Everett took the lead by opening a door in the hallway and descending a lighted stairwell. Jerry followed him into a paneled room that housed the laundry machines, then into a cool, damp, adjoining room, where stone foundation walls accommodated empty bottle racks.

"This is where Maefield stored his liquor," Everett explained. "The old man collected wine and spirits from all over the world. After his death, the little missus divided what she didn't want among people in the church and her New York friends. She should 'a gotten rid of his books as easily," he chuckled. "I'm taking you the long way, Reverend, so you can see how big this place is."

Everett showed Jerry into the furnace room. Half a dozen light bulbs dangled on cords from the ceiling, not nearly enough for such a large area. Dividing the huge space were several foundation walls, which rose in waves to support the ceiling.

"This part of the basement has six feet of rock and dirt over its concrete ceiling and sits under the back lawn of the manse. They once burned coal to heat the church buildings," Everett explained, pointing to the blackened walls. "That's what this underground was, a huge coal bin. In those days, they delivered coal through chutes built into the ceiling. You can see up there," he pointed to clean patches, "where they used to drop it."

Three monster boilers stood midway between the back wall and the old coal area. A fourth smaller unit stood close by.

"The furnaces produce steam heat. That's why they're so large and when running make a hell of a racket. The furnace on our right produces hot water and comes on when you take a hot bath Saturday night," he laughed. "We had these babies converted to oil when we built the annex. This furnace here," he said, slapping the side, wasn't part of the conversion and incinerates papers and trash. We buried the oil tanks outside. Before oil, me and my old man came down here every day in winter. We had to keep the fires burning, 'cause it would take too long to get them cooking again. We couldn't let the cathedral dry out, even in warmer weather, 'cause of the pipe organ—talk about a temperamental lady!" he whistled. "I check once a week to see that the water boxes are full under the old girl. Anyway, on Sundays me and my old man did double duty getting here at five in the morning so that the place would be warm as toast by worship. Once a year, we had to clean the grates, rake out the ash—a real filthy job. But when I was a kid, this was a fun place. Me and the preacher' kids used to play here. There are more spaces to hide in this cellar than anyone will ever know. Very spooky! That steel door in the corner opens to a passageway that runs to the annex and cathedral. I have a shop and maintenance garage under the secretary's office. That's where you saw me backing out yesterday, a nice convenience. I'll show it to you sometime. Whenever you've got a door that needs unlocking, you come to me. I hold all the keys. That keeps people from nosing where they got no business."

"I don't agree with your policy, Everett. I want my own keys to the manse and, as much as I appreciate your lockup service, I want keys to the rest of the buildings as well."

Everett became silent as a stone and stared down at his shoes. Seconds passed.

"I'll see what I can do," he said and looked up at Jerry. "You know, you can feel safe leaving the manse open during the day.

At least one member of my staff is here from eight in the morning until late at night. You don't need keys 'cause we'll be happy to assist you. But, okay, you should have your own keys to the manse and Shepherd House. I'll grant you that."

"Why not give me your manse keys right now, Everett? I don't know of any reason for you or members of your staff to come into the house unless I'm there."

"Can't do that! Church owns the manse and I got permission to go in to check that the plumbing is functioning, turn off lights you leave on, make repairs. I can go in that house anytime I damn well please! That's how we do things. If you're not comfortable with that arrangement, speak to the Trustees. They make the rules!" he said, walking away. "The books are through here, Reverend," he asserted and briskly led Jerry in the opposite direction.

His answer was unacceptable. As things stood, Jerry couldn't get into the cathedral without calling on Everett.

"If you leave me no choice, Everett, I will talk to the Board of Trustees,"

"Yah," Everett sneered, "and while you're at it, ask them to raise my salary!"

He led Jerry into a darker portion of the area. He unlocked a door and reached in to turn on the lights. At first, long fluorescents flickered from the ceiling.

"You have to fool with this switch a couple of times," Everett said and the lights blinked on again, this time without any flashing or appearing to be dead.

"Maybe they need new starters," Jerry suggested.

"Nah, don't fool with them. They work, just flick the switch!" he commanded.

The room had a raised wood floor, a finished plaster ceiling and paneled walls. In addition to stacks of folded banquet tables and metal chairs, the room held hundreds of old bed parts and mattresses of varying sizes and weight piled on top of each other almost to the ceiling. Several leaned on their sides against the walls. Because of all the clutter, it was hard to estimate the size of the area, but it seemed endless in length.

"What are these bed parts doing here?" Jerry asked.

"Some of it is from the war years. Many mattresses are recent acquisitions. They're hotel quality, no army barracks junk here," he laughed. "In case of a bombing up north, the church becomes part of a statewide civil defense plan. I don't believe it, but they tell me this basement is as secure as a modern bomb shelter. Shit! . . . that don't say much for bomb shelters. During the war, we had air-raid drills here. Air-raid wardens set up this room for make-believe evacuees. My mom and other ladies came down here in their starched Red Cross uniforms and played nurse. I guess we stayed on a government list after the war. So every time the government approves a new standard of comfort, someone sends us a new compliment of beds. They sit here with the old stock and gather dust. Ha! Maefield wanted to give this good stuff to Uncle Walter for his niggers and spics, but old Walter, he said, 'no!' The boys do better sleeping on the barracks junk. Don't want 'm getting too comfortable, you know.' Ha! Ha! Those boxes over there are Maefield's books, his 'children' he called 'm."

Along the back wall, boxes on top of boxes were stacked in three irregular rows. Jerry followed Everett to within a few feet.

"The police dicks said they went through every book, as if one held a clue to Maefield's killer. A lie! The idiots! Most of those guys never read a book in their shit-filled lives 'less it was a dirty book. Why the cop in charge thought the assholes would know what to look for is beyond me? Nothing in these books but heaven talk. And they weigh a fucking ton. I thought I'd break my back carrying all this shit down here. Now you want 'm back where they came from, right? I told Mrs. Maefield to let me burn 'm in the incinerator, but she saw too much of that in the old country. Imagine, she considers it's a sin to burn a book. You plan to read 'm, Reverend?"

"Right! That's what books are for, Everett. I doubt I'll read them all, but I'll pick out what I want."

"You know how much these boxes weigh, Reverend?"

"Yes, you already told me: 'a fucking ton!'"

If Everett heard Jerry's ridicule, he never showed it. His face looked pained as he kicked the boxes. "It's a lot of bull shit, if you ask me," he said.

"Listen, Everett, I'm sorry for the inconvenience, but try to understand their value. I know they're heavy. However, they can't remain here. It's too damp and they'll rot. I want them moved up to Shepherd House. No need to put them on the shelves. I'll sort and arrange them according to my needs." As Jerry spoke, he saw Everett's temperature rising on every word. "If you want I'll call for volunteers to give you a hand."

"No need of that. I got Billy and the Jap. We can handle it."

"Everett, I really wish you wouldn't use that name for Ikeda Inoko. It's not funny."

"I don't mean it to be funny, Mr. Reverend. I don't like Japs. I seen too many of 'm in Jap-land after the war and they still make my blood curdle."

"We don't judge a man's value on—"

"I don't need no sermon here!" Everett glared. "Maefield got the Jap hired without asking me. And I don't need no fucking, draft-dodging minister to tell me I got 'a love Japs. He likes doing gardens so I keep him. That's all there is to it . . . " He started to walk away.

Jerry had heard enough. He rushed Everett to turn him before he could take another step. The move surprised him, but Jerry's angry reply surprised him more.

"For one thing, Everett, I'm not a draft dodger. I'll be happy to show you my discharge papers. Also, for your information, my oldest brother died at Pearl, my surviving brother is a paraplegic with a silver star won on Guam and my sister was a prisoner of war because she and thousands of other Americans stayed on Corregidor. So, if anyone has reason to hate a race, I ought to qualify."

He gave Everett a shove. The big man hardly flinched. Still, Jerry showed no sign of retreat, a matter that both humored and dissatisfied Everett.

"But all that's water over the dam. I don't want to hear you use bigoted names again! I don't care who you are, or how long you've been a member in this church or that your 'old man' and you shoveled coal here for twenty years. I hear another racist remark and it will be your last day. You understand?"

Jerry was in his face. He was red with rage. He was ready to throw a punch, but Everett backed away, raised his hands in surrender, turned and walked toward the exit. Jerry feared this was only the beginning of a long struggle. He'd best prepare himself, he sighed. He left Everett in the storage room, and ran upstairs, where lunch was on the dining room table. Places were set and everyone was beginning to gather.

"Reverend, we've been waiting for you," said Madge Todd.

Jerry was still shaking, but he knew he had to hide it.

"Look at this spread," Father O said. "Come on everyone, let's enjoy this wonderful meal."

They crowded into the formal dining room around a huge pedestal table—the guild ladies, Jerry's parents, the moving men.

"Let's join hands," Madge said as she took Jerry's hand and reached for his mom. To Jerry, she whispered, "Is anything wrong?"

"No, everything's fine."

"Then why is your hand shaking so?" she whispered.

Father O asked Jerry to return thanks. Madge held his hand a little tighter. He took the hand of the guild lady on his right.

"Now, now, don't you lovelies eat without me," Everett pleaded as he broke between Madge and Jerry, gently taking her hand and squeezing Jerry's in a crushing grip. "Say it, Reverend Flynn, say thank you to the good Lord above for these beautiful ladies and for the grub they've been fix'n to share with us," he boomed.

"Yes, I'll do that, Mr. Wheeler . . . Let us pray. Lord, we give you thanks for the harvest that provides strength for our work and for the good people gathered here . . . " he began. All the while, his hand burned in Everett's grip. "And we entreat you, Lord, to hold us out of harm's way. This we pray in Jesus' name. Amen."

Everett let go. Jerry dropped his hand to his side. He knew he could not beat this man at his own game. He hoped no one had noticed him as he had endured the pain Everett had inflicted. But Madge, perceiving that Everett and Jerry had had a disagreement, stepped around to sit between them.

*   *   *

Rhonda Maefield had taken a cab from her Park Avenue law office and entered her Riverside Drive apartment at three in the afternoon. After depositing her briefcase in her office, she sauntered into her bedroom. With meticulous care, she removed her blue cotton dress and hung it in the closet. She dropped her underclothes in the clothes hamper. She pulled a silk pajama robe off a hanger and put her arms into its wide sleeves. Leaving it hang open, she walked into the living room where she looked into the liquor cabinet and set out a bottle of blackberry brandy. Filling a cocktail glass with ice cubes from the compact refrigerator of the convenience bar, she poured on the brandy and added a wedge of fresh lemon. She took a first sip before taking the glass with her to the window seat, where she positioned herself to look north toward the George Washington Bridge. Using her index finger, she stirred the liquor, then, sucked on her finger before tasting again from the glass.

She was in a dark mood. Every time she inhaled a breath of fresh air, her old wounds bled. Her teen years in Nazi Germany flooded her mind. "My memories provide so much pain and pleasure all at the same time," she said, speaking as if someone were listening.

She had always lived as two persons. Last week she had visited the Metropolitan Museum of Art for an exhibit of artwork by Pablo Picasso. If she had gone there looking for inner peace, she had made a mistake. Picasso's paintings troubled her deeply. Their grotesque and disemboweled presentment of life had shown her too much of herself. One painting in particular had caught her attention—*Portrait of Dora Maar*. Picasso had painted his mistress many times, but in this one, actually begun by another artist, he had taken less colorful liberties. Staring fixedly at Dora Maar's dark hair, long face and antiquated appearance, she thought she was looking at herself. As usual, Picasso had probed the inner self, looked behind the mask of normalcy, and painted the complexity of a human soul. And clearly, Rhonda saw two selves. In the left side of the model, Picasso had portrayed a woman under stress, fear and depression. The face hid anger and knowledge of betrayal. Rhonda saw her as a fallen woman who suffered because men knew she could not resist them. When Rhonda looked only at the heart side of Dora Maar, she felt equal distress. Here she saw her own usual decorum, a woman withdrawn, distrustful and yet superior. Dora Maar saw depravity, but it did not shock her. Her eyes saw violence, but it did not frighten her. She saw unclean bodies, but they did not make her want to wash them. "And that is both sides of me," Rhonda said loudly as she undid her hair, letting the black silklike strands fall beneath her neck and below her shoulders. She opened her robe to her nakedness and raised the window. Folding her arms on the upraised window, the warm river breeze brushed and pleased her exposed breasts. Now she felt lighthearted and free, and the idea of gliding on the wind as a gull was not beyond her spectrum of pleasure.

The telephone rang, interrupting her thoughts. She wrapped her robe securely around her. It was as if she would now be on display. She fled to the bedroom where she picked up the bedside extension on the sixth ring.

"Hello, how can I help you?" she asked, her German accent unmasked.

"Mrs. Maefield, this is Jerry Flynn. I'm the new pastor at First Church and I'm calling to thank you for the books you left here. That was very generous of you."

In less than a second, she had made the connection. "Yes, I know who you are. I'm glad you can use them, Reverend Flynn. My husband would be pleased. And thank you for thinking of me. I know how busy you must be."

"Everyone is busy around me, Mrs. Maefield. My mother and stepfather are here at the manse directing the moving men and arranging furniture. Several women from the church dropped in to help and fix us all lunch. Madge Todd just left. She had your telephone number handy, so I decided to call. She asked me to remember her to you. She sends you her love."

"Madge is a beautiful girl, Reverend. We are good friends. You remind me that I owe her a letter. When you see her next time, tell her . . . "

Silence reigned. She cuffed her hand over the receiver. She looked away, as if someone could see her tearing eyes and her face. She coughed to hide the emotion in her voice.

"Mrs. Maefield, are you on the line?" she heard Jerry Flynn ask.

"Yes, I'm here, Reverend Flynn," she said, her words slow and her tone poised. "Tell Madge Todd that I will write soon. You are kind to call Reverend Flynn. Enjoy the library. I must go now. I have someone waiting for me. *Lebewohl*, Reverend! I wish you the very best."

She heard him say goodbye. She placed the telephone in its cradle. She returned to the window. Since leaving this view to answer the phone, the sun had passed behind a formation of clouds and stormy darkness now filled the afternoon sky. She saw lightning strikes in the distance. Thunder reverberated along the Palisades, north of the bridge. Powerful winds blew the curtains. She lowered the window quickly, bringing it crashing on its sill just as heavy raindrops pelted the pane. She watched below as people rushed from Riverside Park to flag cabs or find shelter.

The real picture in her mind, however, was of that summer morning in Berlin when the Gestapo arrested her father. It was raining then. She heard pounding on the door of their apartment, gruff voices, curses, her mother arguing with the man in charge, her father trying to assure her mother that he would be all right. She remembered running upstairs to her bedroom window and looking through the heavy rain to the traffic-ridden street below. She watched as people passed with raised umbrellas and rushed for cover. She saw her father for the last time. He looked up at her and waved as his tormentors pushed him across the street and into their waiting car. She watched them drive away. She heard her mother crying.

Why was her life so damned? How could she ever give love or receive forgiveness?

*   *   *

Chief Inspector, John Burroughs of homicide had just come on the four-to-midnight shift. He did not hurry to answer the ring of the telephone. Removing his jacket, he hung it over the back of his desk chair and sat down. He lifted his black fedora off his sweating brow and slung it into the wooden chair facing him. He picked up on the seventh ring.

"Burroughs here! Homicide!" he commanded in a raspy, but not unwelcoming voice.

The woman's tone at the other end was polite, cheerful and soothing. As he listened, his sour face broadened to a warm grin. After identifying herself as Charlene Cunningham, a freelance writer, his caller explained her news feature on how people in Tompkinsville were coping with the murder of the Reverend Daniel Maefield. "As the investigator in charge of the case, your observations are crucial to my story," he heard her say, and then ask for "a little of your time."

Burroughs replied that he would only speak off the record. He didn't care to have his name in print as long as the killer was at large. He would share what he could only as an anonymous police spokesman. Cunningham agreed, but due to Burroughs's vacation time, the earliest he could see her was next Monday morning at ten. He hung up.

*   *   *

John Burroughs had joined the Tompkinsville P. D. in 1936. Bad eyesight had always plagued him and only after his third try at qualifying, the department decided to give him an opportunity. That was a wise decision. Burroughs constantly amazed his superiors with his brilliant police work. The day after Pearl Harbor, Burroughs tried to enlist. His age was already against him. And when the army doctor examined his eyes, he laughed as he told him only major league umpires had worse vision. Then, on a serious note, he hoped Burroughs would never have to use his service revolver to defend himself. "You may have made it as a cop," the examiner said skeptically and stamped his papers, "but as a soldier, the U.S. Army rejects you."

That policy changed as need for experienced police officers in military service increased. In 1944, the army overlooked Burroughs' optical deficiency and, after three months training, commissioned him a lieutenant in the Military Police, then assigned him duty in the Philippines.

Of course, John Burroughs had always compensated for his bad vision by wearing extra thick glasses. His heavy bifocals were adequate up close; however, things began to blur forty feet away. Blessed with intuitive intelligence, dogged persistence and uncanny patience, he had advanced quickly to detective grade where he excelled in the homicide division. Police work was in his soul. And nothing challenged him more than a nasty murder. At all times, he proceeded with decorum and dispatch. He readily admitted that the victim became his brother or sister and he could not rest until he had done everything possible to resolve the criminal imposed death.

Every day since the murder of Maefield, he reviewed the file. He laid it out now and browsed its contents. He had a **NEW EVIDENCE** folder open and read with interest a report by a detective he had assigned to research the background of Everett Wheeler.

"A dreadful man," he said under his breath as he laid the latest report on top of the rest of the Maefield papers. "All I need is motive, and if not for his wife corroborating he was in bed with her from eleven to five that morning, I'd sink his ass."

Burroughs had reason for his suspicion.

Wheeler had served in Japan in the US Occupation Forces, where—within a month of their dispersal—the army discharged him. The detective suspected the reason had to do with a sex crime against a Japanese citizen. His own military police experience had shown him many such cases where the army simply got the man out of the country and out of the army as quickly as possible. Burroughs believed Wheeler was such a man. Brash, bullying, profane, three times investigated for crimes against women, he fit the sex crime picture.

He recalled his interview with Wheeler the day after the crime, how he had described a drifter with snow-white hair and beard— "Santa Clause," Wheeler had laughed, "true as I'm standing here." Wheeler reported the man hanging around the church, "one of Maefield's charity cases . . . I waited until Friday to chase him off." But Burroughs was unable to substantiate the description. Someone looking like that would be hard to miss and no one else, not the cop on the beat or the dispatcher at the bus station recalled seeing a person of Wheeler's description. Still, he had to use it, the only lead he had. And, at the time, he had no reason to doubt Wheeler's sincerity. That changed when he began to investigate Wheeler's background. There was the matter of Wheeler as a prime suspect four years ago in a shooting incident in downtown Tompkinsville. Late one night, shotgun blasts decimated the plate glass windows of Siegel's Pharmacy. At a city council meeting a few weeks before, Siegel, a Jew, had formally presented his intention to prevent the use of Tompkins Park for a Christmas concert and scene for a crèche. Siegel argued such use of public property violated the separation of church and state in the United States Constitution and promised to take his case all the way to the U. S. Supreme Court. Wheeler was one among many Siegel hate mongers. More than one person had heard him threaten to "blow the Jew to kingdom come." But there was no clear evidence that Wheeler fired the shots and again, he had Marie Wheeler's signed affidavit that her husband was in bed with her at the time of the incident. The most interesting side in the case, Siegel's chief ally and spokesman was The Reverend Daniel Maefield. *"No liberal cause the clergyman sponsored before or since brought him as much hatred in his church,"* Burroughs read from the detective's handwriting, *"than his support of Siegel against Christmas programs in the city's park.* But who among those haters had so much animosity that they could plunge a knife forty times into the man's flesh?" Burroughs asked as he closed the file. "Wheeler?"

CHAPTER 5

DAY OF REST

Sunday Afternoon, June 10

All T&T farm and factory enterprises shut down Sundays. The Calvinist owners permitted no work in their fields or factories. Laborers were encouraged to attend church and the green and white busses of T&T Produce ran all day and early evening freely transporting *campesino* men and women to churches around town. Most Mexican laborers attended early mass at St. Joseph's Roman Catholic Parish, but there were exceptions—Pentecostals, Baptists, some Methodists and here and there a few Presbyterians.

Shortly after twelve, the Tompkins house became the scene of the most abundant meal of the week. All Walter and Greta Tompkins's relations, farm-staff families and invited guests attended a feast made up of no less than three kinds of meat, a half dozen or more vegetable dishes, fruits, homemade breads, desserts and beverages. How this all got on the table within minutes of everyone walking in the door after church was due to Greta's week-long preparations and the able assistance of several Mexican women who did the cooking and serving.

But cleanup was something else and for this, Sunday after Sunday, since Madge could remember, the task had fallen to females who were Tompkinses by birth or marriage. While Madge hated this sexist activity with a passion, she obediently did more than her share. Like so many other unpleasant roles she played, she was afraid to show her true feelings and rarely complained.

Instead, she smiled as men, children and guests left the Sunday dinner table to enjoy their afternoon of leisure and she, and four other "sisters and mothers" (their distinguishing marks), stormed the kitchen to dip hands in blistering water filled with harsh detergent or to scour pots and pans. Today, they had fed twenty-six people. Considering the hot and humid weather, cleanup appeared an especially trying task. But order and worker harmony made the job relatively easy and two hours later Madge alone remained kitchen bound.

With Michael out of town on business and the boys off to the river with grandpa and others at the old family swimming hole, she had no reason to rush putting things in their proper place. In reality, she was thinking how she might extend her time by shining the silver-plated coffee urn when she heard a loud knock at the front door. Since no one who knew any better ever knocked before walking in at the Tompkins home, she expected to see a stranger.

Looking down the long hall through the front screen door, Madge made out the figure of a female wearing white shorts that curved over her bare thighs hardly an inch below her crotch and a blue pull-over tank top that covered her chest as if pasted there. Madge thought she could be one of Bob's immodest dressed teen-age friends. Closer up, a more mature woman came into view. Untying her apron and throwing it onto a bench close by, Madge pushed out on the screen door.

Jostled blond curls, sky-blue eyes, a smiling face with magnifying cuteness and an engaging body presented themselves. Making an instant comparison with herself, Madge estimated she could exchange clothes with the woman for a perfect fit and, while the blond appeared an inch shorter and younger, no one would notice. But similarity ended there. Madge saw attire like this as inappropriate, especially on Sunday. Why, even her bellybutton was on view.

"Can I help you?" she asked in an unfriendly tone of voice.

Charlene Cunningham identified herself, said she was a

freelance writer and, after politely apologizing for intruding on the family day of rest, inquired if she could please speak to Mr. Walter Tompkins?

Madge had needed no introduction. She had heard tongues wag at church this morning about the "pretty"—though some said "scandalously"—dressed, blond, female reporter in town since last Wednesday asking questions about Reverend Maefield's murder. More than once, Madge had heard her father's feelings about "snooping reporters." So, she knew for sure he would not talk to one, especially on Sunday.

Madge told Charlene her father was away for the afternoon and suggested she should call for "an appointment" the next time. Miss Cunningham agreed, explained why she had taken a chance, then asked, bright and cheerful, "Maybe you can help me? I'd like to speak to anyone with personal knowledge of Reverend Maefield."

Madge was about to offer an excuse and retreat back to the kitchen. "What about you, Miss Tompkins?" the blond asked. "Can you tell me what qualities endeared Reverend Maefield to you? I'll only take a moment of your time."

"It's Madge, and I'm a Todd, the married daughter," Madge replied. She realized she had been curt, that she had allowed this woman's sensuality intimidate her. In less than a moment's pause, her accommodating nature took over. "But, okay, I guess I can talk to you, Miss Cunningham," she said, stepping out on the porch.

"Good! I am grateful and please, first names only," Charlene added.

They sat next to each other on the porch swing. In spite of their gentle rocking, Charlene managed to take notes in a hardback notebook. As it turned out, Madge found it easy to talk to Charlene. The woman asked thoughtful questions and Madge began to enjoy the interview. Madge volunteered that she was one of Reverend Maefield's fans.

"If you can call people who supported his liberal agenda half the time that. I respected him for his sincerity and commitment to unpopular causes, even if I didn't always agree with him. He was a nice man and very accommodating."

"Did you ever go to him for counseling?" Charlene quizzed.

The question caught Madge off guard. She wanted to say no and move away from personal things. She wondered, too, why the question? What motivated it? Was it a shot in the dark or did Charlene have information? After a few seconds pause and looking away, she replied, "Yes. I suppose you can say I did. I saw him every-so-often for personal problems."

Charlene recognized a streak of nervousness in Madge. She decided not to pursue at this time and asked how her father felt about Reverend Maefield. Madge hedged. She didn't want to speak for her father. She offered, however, that although the two men had seldom seen eye to eye on politics or religion, they had stayed friends. The Reverend had occasionally taken his evening meal at their house and often came for Sunday dinner. She related she could still hear her dad and Maefield arguing politics and racial things. Even so, when her father learned of Reverend Maefield's murder, he had grieved more than most men. He told her the death of Maefield was like the death of his brother. "For a man who had lost two brothers to American wars, the comparison was in itself painful."

Charlene switched from Doctor Maefield to Mrs. Maefield.

Madge hoped her nervousness didn't show as she described how Rhonda was not the friendly type. "The reason wasn't so much that people didn't like her; they just never knew her on a personal level. But that was how Rhonda wanted it. She did not encourage friendship. She gave the impression that she didn't care a 'hoots-holler' about anybody."

Charlene asked Madge how well she knew Rhonda Maefield. Madge turned to look at Charlene. Their eyes met, their smiles depleted. Madge knew her face was turning red. She chided herself, thinking if only she could hide her emotions. She realized by now that Charlene was a very perceptive listener and no airhead, that she had known her married name before she introduced herself at the door. Madge thought, no doubt, someone in the church has already told Charlene, *"Madge Todd is the only woman here who befriended the pastor's wife."* Charlene waited in silence. Several seconds passed. Madge turned her head and vaguely stared at the distant fields.

"I know Rhonda Maefield well enough to call her by her first name. No one else around here does that to her face," Madge said, hoping Charlene would drop the subject.

"And why is that? I mean, why are you able to feel that close?"

Madge kept her eyes steady on the fields. "I don't know . . . Maybe because we see eye to eye on the importance of education for women. I think she admired me as a businesswoman, educated even beyond college, things like that. We appreciated each other's professional significance."

"Did you happen to see her the Sunday before the murder?"

Madge cringed. Her feet touched the floor and the porch swing came to a standstill. She held her hands together real tight; they turned white and numb. No one had asked her that question. No policeman had called investigating visitors to the manse the afternoon before the murder. Months ago, she had concluded no one knew. Now Charlene wants to know. Has she spoken to someone who saw her? Madge hated the truth, the odd feelings memory of that day generated. She looked down, measured Charlene's legs to her own, the color of Charlene's toenail polish with her own. She wanted to dig a hole and bury herself in it.

"Yes, I saw her that afternoon," she said with a strain of uneasiness in her voice. "I returned some books her husband had loaned me. We met at the manse and chatted awhile."

There . . . she had said it . . . finally had said it, for the first time. Then she added, to explain her hesitancy and her tear-filled eyes: "I'm sorry . . . Reverend Maefield's death is still hard on me. I was one of the last people to see him alive."

There was no sympathy in Charlene's voice as she asked, "You saw Reverend Maefield with Rhonda that afternoon?"

"Yes, just as I was leaving, but only for a few minutes. He was concerned about me driving home in the snowstorm. I was okay. It wasn't so bad and I left."

Charlene reacted without changing her expression, her pen poised to write an answer. "And what time was that Madge?"

"Oh, I think about five. I know it was turning dark."

"So, you were with Mrs. Maefield how long?"

"Maybe two hours!"

"And, how would you describe Mrs. Maefield during those hours?"

"Ordinary, looking like she always did. She dressed old and ugly. What more can I say to describe her appearance? Colorless, flat, untouchable!"

Charlene's eyes lit up on the last word. She stopped writing, waiting for more details. When they didn't come, she was moved to ask, "But you liked Rhonda?"

"Well, yes, but that doesn't mean you can't find fault, does it?"

"Well, no. I think your use of the word 'untouchable' to describe her is what caught me."

"I meant it as the way she dressed, that's all. She just didn't have a welcoming look about her."

Charlene added the comment to her notes and then asked her favorite question about Rhonda Maefield. "Do you believe that Rhonda puts on a facade; that behind the hard, unpleasant-looking exterior people talk about, there is a soft, personable, attractive woman?"

Madge hesitated again. She had already said too much and feared false interpretations of her remarks. She replied, "Soft and personable would stretch it. Maybe she had moments, I guess. Attractive?" Madge became silent as she contemplated what to say. She turned her head and stared at Charlene. "Charlene, haven't there been times when you, as an attractive woman, wanted to build an ugly wall around yourself?"

Charlene smiled politely at that. "Yes, I suppose I have! So, I gather you're telling me Rhonda's ugly demeanor is her way of defending her privacy, perhaps guarding her more appealing self."

Madge nodded. She focused again on the fields and said, "Yes, I believe that."

Now it was Charlene's turn to stare at the fields as she contemplated that something disquieting, perhaps threatening, occupied Madge's mind. And, she wondered if the police knew about Madge's Sunday visit at the manse. But she changed course again and asked Madge how the congregation understood the death of their pastor.

Madge, glad to get away from personal items, readily responded, "I think most people believe a great evil invaded our sanctuary. They're frightened and some of them ask why God stood by while a good man died?" she replied. "Many people, and I'm one of them, believe the murder reflects the violence in our human condition and what can happen when love of God is absent from the human spirit. Wasn't that how it was when Jesus was crucified?" She didn't wait for Charlene to reply. "Of course, we're all hoping that with Reverend Flynn's arrival we'll stop looking to the unpleasant past for answers and focus on today and the future. Reverend Flynn made it clear in today's sermon that love alone will bring us together and we have to let Christ's love heal our anger and overcome our revulsion."

"Wow! What a perceptive way to say it," Charlene commented as she wrote it all down. Then she looked up from her writing pad and spoke about how much Reverend Flynn had impressed her when she had met him last Wednesday. Madge lost her smile as Charlene went on to make a personal reference to his good looks and likable personality.

If Charlene had meant to lighten their conversation, she got the reverse reaction.

Madge perceived her remarks as flirtatious and too familiar. Now she realized why she found Charlene so intimidating. She tried hiding her edginess, but Charlene's next element of talk made her burn. For with much enthusiasm, she told Madge how much she looked forward to meeting "Jerry" late this afternoon for supper and how he planned to take her on a tour of the church buildings. "I'm so flattered he asked me," Charlene giggled as a teenager would. "He's so unlike any minister I've ever seen or heard."

Madge immediately looked down and had nothing more to say. She wished her hurt did not show, but she couldn't avoid how she felt.

For the moment, Charlene joined Madge in silence and drifted with her in the gentle movement of the porch swing. She was not, however, one to endure too long and as if to reassure her enough had been said, she placed her hand on Madge's knee. "Well, I best be on my way," she said getting to her feet. Still silent, Madge walked her to her MG. Charlene commented on the unusual hot, humid weather this early in June. Madge smiled and nodded agreement, though, had Charlene seen Madge's true feelings, she may not have waved her typically friendly goodbye.

*   *   *

Charlene drove downtown to keep an appointment with Everett Wheeler. They had agreed to meet last night. In their telephone conversation, Everett had suggested a tavern twenty miles east, boasting he would be worth the ride. She knew a set-up and said no. She insisted on Tommy's Place or "never mind!"

"Since you put it that way, little doll, how can I refuse?" she recalled his words.

She arrived five minutes ahead of him and took a seat in a booth toward the front, facing the entrance. Everett walked into the diner in the manner of a flamboyant politician campaigning to stay in office. Shaking hands and laughing heartily with patrons, he whispered and shouted. He out-performed all takers. He knew everybody and loudly announced himself as "the guest of the mysterious, beautiful blond in the third booth." Then, with obvious relish, he fell heavily onto the bench opposite her. His large hands immediately covered hers. He held them tightly and kept them from returning to her lap.

"I am at your service my pretty woman," he told her. "Little girl, you and I could have such pleasure. Some fatherly advice, though," he said, getting very serious by lowering his voice. She prepared herself for something wicked. "I warn you, don't fool around with the preacher; there's hell to pay for one gone bad."

She laughed at his remark, but recognized he had not made it to be humorous. There was a high degree of possessiveness in Everett's voice. She knew his style. She could feel it in her bones. Given the least encouragement, he would take her forcefully, yet, claim his attack was her fault. Then, too, he would be the devil himself to ward off any other suitor, real or imaginary. If he could not have you, no one else should. Everett was like other men Charlene had known and she both hated and feared their presence. Detest him as she did, she could not let that persuade her to stay away. He was an important person in her investigation. She had come here today to learn more about the murder and so she had little patience with his flirting and boasting.

"Can I ask you some questions, Mr. Wheeler?"

"Oh, come on now, don't be formal. Please, call me by my God-given Christian name. It's Everett. Or, you can call me Mr. Sweets, if you like. I do have that reputation, you know!"

"All right, Everett!" she responded, hoping this would pacify an indulgent manner that was already annoying her. "Please! I need to take notes."

Reluctantly, he released her hands. She reached into her shoulder bag for her notebook and pen.

"What do you want to know?" he said, altering his posture to straight up like a schoolboy.

"How long have you been custodian at First Church?"

He told her how the trustees had hired him fifteen years ago. But he was a son of the church since his baptism. "I was confirmed and married there and both my parents, lifetime members, were carried out of First Church for their funerals."

He remembered previous ministers, none of whom got good marks on his critical report card. He loathed clergymen. "Snobs," he called them, "men who make out they are better than anyone else." "High and Mighty" was another term he used often. He especially liked the name "Preacher," and used it derisively throughout their conversation. He told her why a preacher twenty-five years ago had to leave the church. "He was humping the church secretary," Everett said, "a little 'extra' on the side," he smiled, seemingly to bait her into dirty talk. "After that, they hired Miss Blatty." He roared with laughter when he said her name. "No one's going to run off with that old battle-ax. Ha! One thing for sure, they never better hire you. Preachers would be waiting on line to chase you around the office. Ha!"

It was hard to keep Everett focused. He constantly got up to converse in low tones to one patron after another. He made a big thing of teasing the women, some of them in their late teens, she guessed, others older, in their thirties or more. Fat or skinny, he greeted them affectionately, made them giggle or laugh. But one young, attractive woman, with flaming red hair, did not look smitten by his rush to her side. Charlene supposed he whispered something vulgar in her ear, because she showed offense and angrily started to move away. But Everett grabbed her wrist, his face abruptly serious and scowling. He held the redhead close, this time to whisper more troubling words. As he kept her wrist in his big hand, preventing her from moving off, she looked coldly at Charlene, smacked Everett in the ribs. Whereupon, he let her go, turned his back, shrugged his shoulders and walked back to the booth, his mood sullen and scary. When she saw him crowd into the booth and face Charlene, she ran out of the diner.

"I don't think she liked what you said," Charlene commented.

"Little bitch!" he cursed. "Irish white trash is all!" His face was red, his eyes were angry.

Charlene returned him to the subject at hand.

"What was your opinion of Reverend Maefield?"

"Well, actually, I considered him one of the better reverends we've ever had. We did not agree on most things, but he was always decent to me, poor soul. He visited my wife when she had a miscarriage six months into her pregnancy, our only try at dropping one. That was a dreary day. Marie never wanted sex after that. She don't want to abort a second time, she says. Anyway, Maefield took a kind interest in her. My wife's an alcoholic and for a while the Reverend Doctor had her on the straight and narrow, though, ever since Maefield's death, Marie's drinking has become worse."

Everett kept looking away from Charlene as he reported this. He had shown no sadness when he spoke about these personal matters. It was as if these were incidents of no consequence. While he talked he tapped his fingers, turned his head out the window or toward the counter, snickered, or cursed.

"You have heard I'm sure how brilliant Doctor Maefield was," he said, quickly changing the subject. "The good man spoke six languages. He was the one person I could never win over in an argument. The trouble with him . . . he was always taking up for niggers and spics. He went down there to Albany, Georgia, last year to march in one of those nigger walks. The locals arrested him with a bunch of niggers when they wouldn't give up their seats in a whites-only restaurant. They called him a white-nigger and threw his ass in the same clinker with his restaurant pals. After the Presbyterian head-honcho, Eugene Carson Blake, another 'pinko' preacher, bailed him out, you'd think he'd of learned his lesson. But, no, a month later, he catches a bus to Mississippi. Now all this is on church time. We're pay'n his salary, mind you. This time, however, he meets more than his match. He almost gets lynched by a gang of Confederates . . . defend'n their turf, you know."

Suddenly Everett hit the table with his fist, his eyes flashing with anger.

"Why should those southern boys have to put up with reds and black-Yankees, a limey-Yankee at that, telling 'm how to treat their niggers? Reverend Maefield stuck his nose into someone else's business, his chief fault, and nearly got his neck stretched from a high tree branch. Some FBI men rescued him. Stupid! You know, sometimes the more brains you got, the stupider you are." Then, just as suddenly, Everett turned away from her again, lightly swatted the behind of one of the waitresses passing too close to their booth. "But he was okay. Whoever did him shouldn't have. He didn't deserve to die like that. Me and my crew had just started shoveling the walks when the cops arrived that morning. Mrs. Maefield had locked the door to Shepherd House after she discovered his body, so I had to let the cops in. I saw him dead. Hell, the murderer cut his throat from ear to ear. Because of where he lay, I couldn't tell, but I understand, had the knife gone an inch deeper, it would have separated his head from his body. The blood around him was a red lake, much of it already dry and stinking. He looked like he been machine-gunned, he had so many holes in him. I never saw such a gory mess, man or animal. I hope they catch the prick that did him and he fries! I'd volunteer to pull the switch!"

Charlene decided this was about as much remorse as Everett could show. He had sounded sincere and she accepted his words for their underlying value.

She quizzed Everett about his perception of Rhonda Maefield. "I don't know her that well," he began. "I think she took a bad rap in the church. Folks around here saw her as unfriendly and unappealing. She was the blunt of a lot of jokes and ridicule, though never to her face." Charlene kept her head down as she scribbled his remarks. "Of course, Mrs. Maefield was always nice to me, but then I have a way of bringing out the best in women," he smiled.

Charlene looked up to see if he was putting her on. His face showed no such sign. "And how did you bring out the best in Mrs. Maefield?" she quizzed.

He showed annoyance at the direct question, struggled with it and—after a few seconds—he looked away. "Let's just say, I made her laugh. When I went by to repair something at the manse, she always welcomed me with a smile. I think she liked my clowning around and neither of us took the other too serious . . . things like that, you know, nothing personal, just general friendliness."

Charlene looked up to see a smirk so thick she could have cut it with a knife. Was he being honest, or playing her for a fool? Was he just showing false pride? Like ask me and I'll tell you a dirty secret? She thought to pursue, but then decided to go on to her next question and see if he would pick up again.

"I heard she's a very judicious dresser, likes to wear dark women's business suits, even when they're not called for. She sweeps her hair back very straight, sometimes braids it, but always pins it on top of her head and never a hair out of place. Can you confirm that?"

"Oh, yes, Mrs. Maefield wouldn't have people see her any other way, for sure! You had to look hard to find flesh showing below her neck," he laughed. You probably know, she went to law school in New York and so no one saw much of her in the last four years. But when she did show here, she dressed in black and always formal. Among our farmer squaws, she was haughty. But I know better. If you see under the wraps, as I do . . . what you see . . . is . . . " Charlene waited. She watched his face settle into another proud grin. Finally, he broke the silence. "Sexy! Mrs. Maefield, she's sexy . . . I see a sexy lady! I mean, with you, sex is out in the open, but with some women, well . . . "

He appeared to wait for approval of what he had just said. But Charlene was in her own thoughts. Everett had latched onto something that had toyed with her mind earlier . . . Madge's remarks, which had also looked behind the woman's public role. And Charlene had to agree. Based on the picture she had seen of Rhonda Maefield, her dress seemed unnatural, too much like a costume—overdone. But why?

Charlene closed her notebook. After several minutes listening to Everett's negative comments on religion and politics, as well as pestering her for a date, she excused herself and exited the diner. She hoped he wouldn't follow her.

*　　*　　*

Jerry Flynn had enjoyed the company of his mother and stepfather. In four days, they had transformed the bare floors and walls of the old Victorian manse into backdrops for a showcase of antique furnishings, paintings, draperies, and carpets. He was glad they had come and now he was glad they had left.

Proudly, he inspected the downstairs rooms with his guest, Charlene Cunningham.

She had parked on the street and walked up Cathedral Drive to the house. She had said she needed the exercise, but Jerry wondered if discretion had guided her decision. Whatever, he was glad she had done it.

He thought how striking she looked in her white shorts and ocean blue blouse. He told her she looked cool and comfortable for such a hot, humid evening. He saw her as cute, youthful and alluring.

He led her into the kitchen where he had already set their places at the breakfast nook and had set out a platter of cold sliced turkey, ham, cheeses, and rolls.

"Hope you don't mind deli delights."

"Not if the rolls are fresh," Charlene gleefully commented as she slid across the bench to the table setting in the corner.

"Couldn't be fresher. I picked them up a half hour ago at Petracelli's Delicatessen."

Out of the refrigerator, he took potato salad, lettuce, sliced tomatoes and a variety of condiments. He arranged them neatly on the table. He added a bowl of cutup fruit and beside it the remains of a chocolate layer cake. Again, he opened the refrigerator door.

"What would you like to drink? Milk, apple juice, Coke? Or, look at this! How about a glass of wine? Red? White? My stepfather's left a choice of—"

"White!" Charlene said.

Jerry took out a bottle of Liebframilch. He uncorked it and poured for each of them.

She liked the way he pampered her. He was considerate and she enjoyed his attention. His interest and intelligence appealed to her. True, she was accustomed to men showing her courtesy. She never tired of complements on her appearance. She knew, however, that onlookers could easily misunderstand this and that sometimes—when digging for information—she unintentionally signaled more than prepared to yield. She had had her share of sexual close calls, even a few which bordered on attempted rape. Fortunately, she had repulsed them all and took satisfaction in the belief that all her affairs were consensual.

Jerry could be such a man. He was handsome and pleasant to listen to, sincere, single. She enjoyed his humor and relaxed manner. She thought he looked very "Joe-college" in his red-plaid Bermuda shorts and close-fitting white golf shirt. He had none of the mannerisms and sacrosanct qualities she associated with ministers and priests, though she could admit to very little social contact with such men and had never met one for a date.

He held her attention with funny stories about his family and growing up in Philadelphia.

His tales about student days in a Catholic school and the harsh disciplines of "Sister Grace"—the school's principal—were reminiscent of her own childhood experience. Nor was there anything dull when he related how he had become a Presbyterian during his army years or his adventures as a summer intern at an urban church in Los Angeles.

He poured more wine for them and made a toast to her success as a writer. She wanted to tell him that this was a deception. She felt she could trust him. Yet, her professional side, especially as it related to the Maefield case, could scare him off. Her sandwich was delicious. She ate much more chocolate cake than she should have, but she had a sweet tooth, most of all, for anything with chocolate in it.

Their conversation turned on her. He wanted to know about her family, how she liked her job, where exactly she had lived in Philadelphia? Did they know any of the same people? How about high school friends? Talk was easy with him. She told him how her grandmother had raised her and how while still in college she had "dumbly" married. "A big mistake!" It had ended with an annulment after three months. Jerry wanted her to tell him the details, but she hesitated, maybe another time. As comfortable as she felt with him, she was not ready to open her past. With some effort, she reminded herself why she had accepted his invitation to visit.

"I think we better take that tour before it gets dark and while I can still stand up," she joked, finishing the last of the wine in her glass.

"Yah, let's start where we left off. We can make a complete circle."

"Sound's good to me," she said with enthusiasm.

Together they cleared the table and put things away. Jerry excused himself to run upstairs. Left alone, Charlene strolled into the living room and lit up a cigarette. She had yet an unopened pack in her shoulder bag, but planning to leave this behind, she removed the two remaining cigarettes from their wrapping, then, reached them up her blouse with a match-pack, securing them in the cleft of her bra. She zipped her shoulder bag closed and put it under a large, fluffy pillow. When Jerry came into the living room, she showed him where she had hidden it.

"Yah, that's a good idea," he said. "Too many people think they can walk in and out of here whenever they please. Until I change that, it's better to be safe than sorry."

"Would you like a cigarette?" she asked as she flecked her half-drawn butt on an ashtray. "Maybe later," he replied.

He did not tell her he had gone cold turkey two weeks ago.

*   *   *

Yesterday, Jerry had gotten a ring of church keys from Walter Tompkins. In handing them over, Walter had warned Jerry not to say anything to Everett. *Leave it to me to tell the custodian about the transfer.* He also handed Jerry a key to the manse's front door, saying he had cut it in his machine shop and not even Everett knew he had taken the liberty of changing that lock shortly after Maefield's murder. Jerry could rest assured that he had the only key to the front door. *Just put the slide bolts on the back and side door,* Walter advised.

All this seemed peculiar to Jerry, but he had already had one confrontation with Everett and he didn't want another. Let Walter handle it his way, he told himself. Soon enough, he would have to deal with them.

He put these concerns behind him as he escorted Charlene out the front door, locking it after them. They walked around to the cloister. He meant to pass up Shepherd House, but Charlene insisted on seeing it again; she wanted Jerry to show her exactly where Doctor Maefield had fallen. He led her through the gate in the cloister wall, down the garden steps to the entrance and through the unlocked Shepherd Door. A bluish-gold radiance shown through Shepherd Window and through the stained glass shields of the apostles, thus, providing a mysterious merge of light and shadows. Quiet as an owl searching for prey, Charlene freely inspected every corner and wall of the regal chamber. She didn't say that she thought the room cold and ostentatious, but in her heart, she felt it.

"Has any furniture been moved or replaced?" she asked.

"No. I believe everything is the same as five months ago. I have all these books from Doctor Maefield's collection to unpack," he said, looking forlornly at the stacks of boxes set along the shelved walls. "It'll be a laborious job. I looked through some of these boxes. I know I'll never need, never read, and never even know most of these books exist."

"Then why will you put them up?"

"That's a good question; probably because they'll look good."

"Do you think Doctor Maefield did that?"

"No! From what I've heard, he kept every book as a treasure of knowledge. He was as prolific a reader as he was a writer, an amazing intellect. I'm sure he could've told you about every volume. You'll have to come back when I get them sorted and shelved."

They made their way to the gray-stone fireplace.

Jerry pointed. "Doctor Maefield was found face up there, his head at the fireplace."

Charlene sat on the hearth with her arms wrapped around her knees. She imagined herself in Maefield's place, how the assailant had come at him and the fury of the attack. How violent, she thought, recalling Wheeler's description. Jerry respected her concentration. After a short while, he reached his hand down and pulled her to her feet.

Just as he had last Wednesday, he led her to the cathedral through the step passageway, entering the nave from the vestibule. As with Shepherd House, the sun streamed through stained glass, only here, it was much brighter. In its path, every speck of suspended dust was illuminated and the colors in the windows seemed to dance in the glowing brilliance of the sun.

"Strange how these dust particles float invisible at all other times," Jerry commented. "But in the light of the streaming sun, it's like looking at a billion stars floating in space."

They walked hand in hand down the long center aisle to the cathedral crossing. Jerry explained how Presbyterians served Holy Communion from the table instead of the altar and how Catholics were moving the altar out from the wall, effectively turning it into a table. "It's good we finally agree on something permanent," he chuckled. She had no idea what he was talking about and told him so. "It looks like a church, that's all I know," she added with a childlike shrug.

Jerry led her to below the pulpit on their left and—in the old style—high above the pews. They accessed it using a set of stairs laid up the side and spiraling in back. They stared down at the empty rows of dark-mahogany pews. The pale odor of furniture polish and musty, stagnant emptiness enveloped them. She took his hand firmly in hers.

"What did you preach about today?"

"I preached about love, the kind of love the Greeks called *agape*, love that makes one person sacrifice his or her life for another. Another way to explain this: Christ loved us the way a mother loves her sick child. The Mother would take the child's place if she could. On the cross, Christ took all our places."

He warmed her with his sincerity. Perhaps she had not expected him to respond in the crisp words of his faith, for she had almost forgotten that beneath his informality and easy manner, he was like a priest. Reflectively, she reached her index finger in front of his lips. She held it there, felt his breath. She did not want to cut him off, but neither did she wish to lose that other person. He seemed to understand and perhaps too he welcomed her silencing his sermonizing. He smiled and wrapped his fingers around her finger, softly kissing it.

"Thank you," she said. "Tell me more, but another time."

Jerry led the way to the sacristy off the south transept and behind the choir pews. A door opened into a stair landing connecting the cathedral and the annex. She recalled that this was where she had left him last Wednesday morning.

Up to now, they had found all doors unlocked, just as Wheeler had promised. But the door into the annex held firm. Jerry reached for a ring of keys Walter Tompkins had given him. It took him five tries to unlock the annex. He opened a few Sunday school classroom doors. There was not much to see, but Charlene had said she wanted the grand tour. They looked into the gym. Jerry found the light switches and lit the room to a glowing brilliance. There was a basketball on the floor. He ran to it. Picking it up, he dribbled to the far basket for a lay-up. The ball swished through the net and Charlene applauded his athletic antics. She kicked off her fashionable, though cumbersome, open toe shoes and ran barefoot after him. He threw her a bounce pass. She heaved the ball at the basket, but it fell several feet short. Jerry retrieved the ball and passed it back to her. She tried again, missed. She laughed and tried again. This time the ball bounced off the rim. Jerry caught it and turned it into a hook shot. Once more, she applauded his success. He threw her the ball. Charlene got up close. She aimed carefully. This time the ball zeroed in on the hoop and tumbled through the net. Jerry grabbed her at the waist and held her up, cheering as he did so.

"Not bad, not bad at all," he shouted.

Charlene laughed and then booed him as he missed a shot. She made out like a pro on the attack. He threw her a pass. She received it and turned toward the basket; she went for the shot. The ball hit the backboard and bounced on the rim before going through the net. Again, Jerry lifted her high. As her feet hit the floor, she broke into a cheer.

"Two! Four! Six! Eight! Who do we appreciate?" she roared, raising her hand in the cheerleader way. "Jerry! Jerry! Jerry!"

she shouted, each time jumping high. She was out of breath, as was he. They were like kids in high school again. It was fun. She had not played like this since college.

Retrieving her shoes, Charlene took Jerry's hand as he escorted her across the floor. He showed her the adjoining kitchen. It was equipped as if to serve a modern restaurant. Jerry explained that the church often hosted banquets and wedding receptions and—as the largest banquet hall in town—many groups rented the hall for special dinners and programs. "We don't allow liquor served, so that keeps things to a minimum." He explained how the church sponsored Boy and Girl Scout troops. And in the fall, the gym became headquarters for the county interdenominational basketball league. He commented that First Presbyterian had a championship teams in junior and adult.

"I think that's why they hired me," he laughed.

"I'm impressed," Charlene replied sarcastically.

He made a playful gesture, as if now a prizefighter, and pretended a jab to her chin. She stuck him in the ribs. He feigned injury and she poked him again. From the kitchen, they stepped out into the main hallway.

"Come September, this place will be hopping with activity. That's when church programs get under way. We do a lot with young people, so this place will be noisy almost every night. I'm glad I have the summer to prepare and learn my way around. My goal is to start a summer program for teens. The excuse that they are all working on daddy's farm isn't true anymore. And, even if some are, they still need a place for recreation. Except for the local drive-in movie or the bowling alley there's no place for teens to hang out in this town."

They paused in the hallway. "There's an underground passage through the basement. I've never been that way. Want to go? I believe I have the keys."

He tossed the ring of keys above his head and caught it behind his back.

"Lead the way!" she said.

*   *   *

Madge heated pot-roast from today's family dinner. Ordinarily, on Sunday evening they would have eaten a light meal, but as a favor to Michael, she had prepared the leftover pot-roast, his favorite. She waited an extra hour for him. When he didn't show, she and her boys went ahead and ate.

After supper, Madge gave Chip permission to stay out and play until dusk. This privilege came with the understanding that the older boy keep tabs on his little brother and they would play this side of the dirt road that separated the Todd property from that of Jorge Garcia. Garcia and several permanent farm worker families lived on lots leased to them by her father. The dirt road also serviced several packing barns and equipment garages, including one next to their home, before it wound through the fields to dormitories and cottages housing temporary workers.

The boys played tag with a half dozen other farm kids. As Madge listened to their chatter through the opened kitchen window, she washed the dinner dishes, then the pots and pans. She threw away what remained of the roast.

She never knew when to expect Michael anymore. He had called Friday night to explain how he planned to stay on after the growers' meeting and attend to other business on the Eastern Shore. He would see her Sunday but he had not said when on Sunday. Certainly, she thought, by now he would be home. And while she hated her suspicions about his whereabouts, deep down and personal, she welcomed his absence. She could not easily get over his sexual battering last Tuesday night. She remained sore from where he had forced himself on her and, though they had parted Wednesday morning on good terms, she cringed at the idea of having sex with him like that again. How many times could she look the other way after such episodes? Not many she promised herself. But what to do? On that question, she admitted her indecisiveness.

There was, however, no indecisiveness about Madge as an executive at T&T Produce.

With Michael in Delaware and her father out of town last Thursday morning, she considered herself in charge of operations. New workers, brought in specifically to rush-pick the cherished strawberry crop, had walked out of the fields during a heavy thunderstorm. The weather forecast called for more of the same all day. The workers wanted an extra three cents a quart to pick in wet, muddy conditions and a penny more on a quart after meeting their quota.

With less than a ten-day window to harvest hand-picked strawberries, rain or shine, there was never a day to spare. Jorge's way to solve the problem was to find the ringleader and "kick the shit out of him." He would force the remaining strikers into the fields by threatening to fire and blacklist any man or woman who refused. Marked workers would have difficulty finding eastern farm employment. Illegal aliens among them would find it next to impossible. If the pickers stayed on strike, Jorge would replace them with a fresh crew, pay the new team a penny more, only raise the quota to a hundred and seven quarts.

Madge, however, quickly negotiated a two-cent rain-day price increase without changing the quota. No one would get beat up, no one fired and no fruit would rot on the vine while Jorge looked elsewhere for a new crew. She believed—because of her fairness— she would get more strawberries picked for her money. On the rainy fields last Thursday, Jorge had thrown up his hands in protest. *"Why put me in charge and not listen to me?"* he had shouted as he walked off. Madge would not back down to satisfy his ego. And more, she had outright told Garcia, no rough stuff. Even when her father telephoned and begged her to explain to the workers that she had made a "miscalculation" and apologize to Jorge, she stoutly refused.

Seeing Jorge's grandkids now playing with her kids, Madge recalled she had not seen the field-boss since their confrontation last Thursday morning.

"That man's not happy unless he has some little guy to thrash," she said as she climbed up on a chair seat to reach an antique china tureen off a top shelf to wash it. With the heavy, fragile dish safe in her hands, she turned around to see Michael standing in the doorframe. He had come in so quiet, his sudden presence startled her. She almost dropped the tureen. His deadpan face, eyes empty of any warmth, signaled his anger. His words spilled out of his mouth in a nervous, accusatory manner.

"You know the men are calling me the gringo-apron farmer?"

"Hi!" Madge cheerily replied, smiling in her usual manner, trying to soften his approach before dealing direct with his distressful question. "I didn't hear you come in. You're too late for pot-roast; how about a cheese omelet?" His unresponsive face baited her for a direct reply. She complied. "Okay, why would the men," she asked in a soft, cozy tone, "call you a gringo-apron farmer?"

"Because they don't have respect for a man who allows his wife to do his business for him," he answered.

Madge turned away, bent to lower the china piece onto the counter and then stepped off the chair. In her whole motion, Michael remained idle, staring. She could feel his rage. She recalled last Tuesday night. That same tinge of fear and helplessness returned. She had no place to run. He blocked her only avenue of exit. She started to explain how she had saved the company thousands of dollars and saved workers from broken bones, when he screamed at her.

"You stupid woman, you may have cost us our field boss and I won't begin to tell you what the hell will happen the next goddamn time it sprinkles around here. You idiot! Who gave you authority to interfere? The whole shit farm may go down the tubes because of your dumb-ass decision!"

She tried pushing past him, but he stayed fast.

"Get out of the doorway!" she demanded. "I won't listen to you when you talk like this," she said as she tried again.

"Well, you better listen, goddamn you," he scolded as he seized her by her shoulders. "You stay out of company policy, you hear?" His hands shook her as if a rag doll. "I don't want to see or hear of you talking to field hands ever again!" he shouted so close she could feel his spit spray her face!" Suddenly, he let her go. Thrown back, off balance, she lost her footing. Her knees buckled, her rump hit the floor and the back of her head smashed against the kitchen cabinet. Flat out, she didn't move.

A deadening silence followed. When she remained mute, he became frightened and knelt next to her. He felt her forehead. She opened her eyes. He reached for her hand and felt relief when she gave it to him and let him help her into a kitchen chair, where she put her head into her hands. For the first time she could recall, he apologized for his behavior. Visibly shaking, he dropped into an opposite chair and rested his head in his hands. Madge looked up but said nothing as she got up to get some ice, bundled it into a towel and applied the cold compress to the sore spot on her head. She returned to her chair.

Oddly, she felt sorrier for him than for herself. Alcohol and rage, whatever the symptoms, he was suffering more than she was. She dropped the ice pack on the kitchen counter. Standing behind him, she lowered her arms around his neck.

"We need help, Michael, both of us."

He pressed her wrist to his mouth, kissed it and calmly nodded his head in agreement. After a few seconds, she kissed him lightly on the cheek, knelt on the floor next to him, resting her head in his lap. He ran his hand through her hair, reached for the ice pack and held it over the sore spot on her head. She began to cry. He helped her into her chair but could not look at her. Embarrassed by his own tears, he walked away. She waited until she heard the porch door slam. She went upstairs to turn down the boys' beds and minutes later, she heard his truck. She watched from the front window as he drove their long driveway slowly to the highway. She could only imagine his destination. But she had already resolved to face what had happened tonight as either a new beginning or a tragic end.

CHAPTER 6

SLEEPLESS NIGHT

Sunday Evening, June 10

Jerry Flynn opened the door to the annex stairwell and flipped on the light switch. Hand in hand, he and Charlene descended stairs to a landing where one door led to the parking lot, Charlene's route of exit last Wednesday. To the right another steel fire door had to be unlocked. They swung it open to a five-foot-wide, seven-foot-high passageway lit by fluorescent bulbs on the ceiling and extending, it seemed, to infinity. Besides acting as an indirect corridor between four church buildings, the underground tunnel served as a conduit of pipes for water, steam and for electric lines.

On a gradual descent a hundred yards or more from where they began, the tunnel turned sharply to descend at a lesser distance to a blank wall. Here, on their right, Jerry pulled open a no-lock steel door and looked into the dimly lit vastness of the stone-encased foundation Everett had shown him from another vantage point last Wednesday. A sour smell and a dusty, damp climate greeted them. Cautiously, they moved under dangling low-wattage light bulbs towards where Jerry estimated the stairway to the manse should be. Out of the dark, a loud roar broke into the silence.

"What's that?" Charlene shouted above the irritating noise.

"Furnace . . . probably got a call for hot water!" he yelled. He pointed to other units farther away. "Imagine the blast when they all come on?" he smiled.

Just as quickly, the harsh sound shut off.

"Let's not wait for it to come on again," Charlene said, tugging at Jerry's sleeve.

I wish I had brought a flashlight. The ceiling of this area is six feet below ground. The furnaces supply heat to all the buildings," he instructed as he gestured at the thick-padded steam pipes crossing the walls and ceilings.

"I'm really impressed," Charlene grimaced sarcastically. "Let's get out of here."

"I think this is the way."

Charlene held his hand as he led her amid the maze of walls that divided the grimy basement. He apologized for his lost sense of direction. Just then, the furnace sound revved up again. They were back to where they had begun. Jerry pulled Charlene in another direction. This time under the light of a single bulb, they came upon a locked steel door behind a facing wall. As Jerry sought the right key from his key ring, he apologized for showing her this "foul smelling, filthy place."

She rested her elbows on his shoulders as he knelt in front of the door.

"Yes, well, it has been a while since I dated a guy who showed me his coal bins."

He was about to suggest they go back the way they came when he turned the lock. He found the light switch inside the doorframe. A few overhead florescent tubes came on, but most flickered or remained a dull contrast to their potential. Remembering Everett's instructions from last Wednesday, he flipped the switch again and watched as the flickering stopped and the room filled with bright light.

"We're in the storage room beneath the manse," he said.

"Why all the bed parts and mattresses?" she asked as she moved amid the clutter.

"Civil Defense stuff. This place is actually a verifiable bomb shelter. The government began storing most of this junk here the day after a German U-boat sunk a freighter off Atlantic City. Uncle Sam never asked for anything back. In fact, they keep adding upgraded beds. I suppose with Khrushchev rattling sabers . . . Well, you get the picture."

"Yah, it's beautiful! . . . It looks like your church got a real bargain," she smirked.

Charlene skirted stacks of bed frames, mattresses and box springs, as well as other junk, piled to the ceiling. She drifted on her own to the far wall. In a playful mood, she thought she would circle behind a column of stacked mattresses, where they stood out a few feet from the wall, go around behind Jerry and scare him. But six feet forward, several mattresses stood as a blind ally and blocked her way. As she turned to retrace her steps, she saw a steel door indented inside the wall. Jerry crowded behind her.

"Got you!" he said, and pulled her close.

But Charlene's mood had changed. She shook him off and—concentrating on the mattresses in front—she demonstrated how they easily rolled along the floor.

"Look," she said, pointing to her foot, "they're on a raised platform with wheels underneath. When I push down on this metal lever . . . " With one hand, she pulled the heavy bundle toward her. "These bed pieces were supposed to guard this door. Now . . . where does this door go to?" she asked, trying to turn the knob and pushing in without success.

"I don't know. Do you think we should knock first?" he chuckled. "Maybe it's the 'Holy of Holies,'" he teased, referring to the most sacred place in the Jerusalem temple at the time of Jesus. Charlene ignored his attempt at humor, pounded on the metal surface. "It could be a closet or a closed exit," Jerry suggested in a now serious tone.

"Maybe, but someone went to a lot of trouble to hide it. If these mattresses had been rolled to the end, where I think they were supposed to be, I never would have seen this door."

Jerry fiddled with his keys, trying one and then another. He attempted almost every key on the ring before one glided into the cylinder and turned, releasing the bolt and letting the doorknob revolve in his hand. He pushed in on the door and felt for a light switch next to the frame. Finding it, he flipped on a dim lamp in the ceiling. He propped the steel door open with a doorstop mounted on the door.

"It looks like a closet all right, but there's nothing stored in here. Wait a minute," he said, stepping farther into the confined area, "What do you make of these doors in here?"

"How about King Tutankhamen's Tomb?" Charlene chided. When Jerry looked at her perplexed, she shrugged. "Well it's as good an explanation as your Holy of Holies!"

He tried the door in front of him. "Locked!" The other doorknob, however, turned in his hand. He pushed in. He found a light switch on the wall, but no light came on. With only the dull ceiling lamp behind them, it was difficult to see anything.

"The bulb must be burned out," Charlene said.

Still holding the doorknob, Jerry noticed that the inside knob wouldn't turn. "Careful, don't let the door shut. It requires a key to get out and it may not be this one."

He saw a chair nearby and braced it against the open door.

"It's furnished. Will you look at this?" Charlene said.

They could make out a bed as wide as it was long against the back wall.

"It looks like somebody's bedroom," Jerry said.

A light came on. Charlene had found a lamp on a bedside table providing a soft midnight glow. They saw then that the bed was made-up with pink satin sheets and matching large ruffled pillows. She flipped a wall switch near the head of the bed. Powerful spotlights blazed from above, their light directed on the bed as if a stage.

"Look!"

Charlene pointed to an oval gold-framed mirror hanging from the ceiling and reflecting the sleeping area. Jerry did a back dive across the bed and stared up at his laid-back reflection. He laughed at the view and made several exaggerated gestures.

"What about these sheets, Charlene? An ice rink couldn't be slicker!"

He was about to sit up when something in the mirror drew his attention.

"Is that a camera lens?" he asked with unbelief, pointing to a disk inside a tiny aperture carved out of the center of the mirror.

As Charlene came into view close by, he wobbled to a standing position on the bed, but had to bend his knees to keep his head from hitting the mirror. He examined the half-dollar-sized opening.

"I'll be damned if it isn't!"

Jerry stepped to the high brass headboard and steadied himself to gander above the mirror frame. "Hey, Charlene . . . a motion picture camera is anchored to the ceiling. It's wired so it can be operated from somewhere else."

Springing off the bed, Jerry tried looking through the mirror built into the wall facing the bed. He shielded his eyes an inch away from the mirror glass.

"This glass has a double purpose," he said. "If you get close to it . . . Turn out the flood lights, Charlene." The overhead lamps went dark. "I can barely see through but there's a room on the other side and maybe another camera."

Charlene did not respond. On her knees, she was opening drawers in a dresser.

Jerry moved to a similar mirror next to the bed and saw that it too had opposing sides. He crossed the room to switch on the flood lamps again. He opened a closet door in the opposite corner to find several tripods, flood lamp reflectors and other camera equipment, including a Bell and Howell 8 movie projector.

"Hey, Charlene, have a gander at this," he called.

She got up to stare into the closet and pulled a box off a shelf.

"Chemicals for developing film," she said. "And here's the equipment to do it," she continued, holding up a black plastic canister used for negative processing. "Wow, your church sure has nice audio-visual equipment," she giggled nervously, putting the box back.

"I don't believe the church knows anything about this. This is a photographer's studio!" Jerry replied, his voice grave and serious.

Charlene returned to sit cross-legged on the floor in front of the dresser. "And what about this?" she said, her voice burning with excitement as she stared into a drawer filled with colorful women's underwear. "Nice taste," she said, holding up a pair of red panties so sheer Jerry could see her fingers through the material. "Oh my!" she cooed and proceeded to empty the contents of the drawer onto the bed. Corsets, bras, slips, stockings, garter belts flew. She opened another drawer. She giggled as she eyeballed a long cylinder, shaped to look like a castrated, circumcised penis. "Wow!" she exclaimed, pointing it toward Jerry. "This thing could put you guys out of business," she howled, banging the sex toy against the opened drawer, a scurrilous grin on her face, her voice trailing to a nervous giggle.

"Yah, disgusting, isn't it? What is the world coming to?" Jerry laughed.

Charlene laughed louder, more amused by the object than he was and far less bashful about it. He watched attentively as she held it while rifling through a second drawer, then, seeing something else, threw the thing into the pile on the bed. She made a face as she brought out a pair of handcuffs and a long piece of nylon rope, an assortment of masks and strips of torn bed sheets. "Show and tell!" she exclaimed and made a dramatic presentation before flipping each object behind her and landing them on the bed. "Naughty, naughty," she chided merrily.

Jerry laughed and went back to examining photographic equipment stored in the closet.

Charlene pulled out a side drawer and looked in to see a stack of girlie magazines. Beneath them, she took out a set of instructional sex books, one magazine size and full of pictures and illustrations. Beneath this, she spied a pair of women's white cotton underpants. She held them to the light. She had many like them herself, an ordinary brief with a snug fit, popular among teens and young women. She wondered why they were with the sex manuals instead of the lingerie. She thought she could see telltale dried residue on the backside. She felt ashamed to do it, but a detective should never waiver in her duty, she said to herself in justification for lifting the panty crotch close to her nose. She detected a perfume scent. "It's sweet . . . familiar, but I can't place it," she said quietly. She would get them examined in a police lab. With Jerry's back to her, she shoved the panties into her shorts and flattened them there. How else could she explain taking them without revealing she was a private detective? Now she took more time with the books she had taken out of the drawer, stopping now and then to stare at the pictures. "Oh, my God!" Charlene beamed, "this is wild!"

"I think we better leave well enough alone," Jerry called from the closet, holding up a reel of eight-millimeter motion picture film to examine its frames.

"For sure, we're where we're not supposed to be," Charlene replied. She got to her feet and began returning various items to the bureau drawers.

"Yah, that's obvious. I'll question Everett. He must know about this room."

"It's probably his dirty little secret. Better be careful."

Charlene dropped the last of the lingerie into its drawer.

"Let's go! Turn out the lights!"

Jerry moved the chair away and the door sprung shut. In the tiny hallway, he tried once more opening the other door.

"Some setup," he mumbled.

He inserted the key that had opened the steel door. The knob turned.

"Yes, here, Charlene! For once, a key that fits two door locks," he said cheerfully as the door swung in.

They made their way into space only a little wider than the three-foot-wide door. Jerry reached up and pulled the string for a ceiling lamp. Before them stood a Sankyo 8Z Power Zoom motion picture camera fixed on a tripod and aimed into the see-through mirror glass. A Cannon 35 mm single lens reflex camera stood on a tripod next to it. Connected by electric wires, the cameras could operate simultaneously. There was no film in either camera.

"This Cannon is almost like mine, only it's fitted with a close-up lens attachment," he said. "Turn on the light in the bedroom, Charlene," he motioned as he peered through the viewfinder, "and remember to block the door." He turned out the light above him.

Charlene re-entered the studio-bedroom. She switched on the floods. Jerry peered through the viewfinder as Charlene threw herself playfully across the bed. She propped up the pillows and rolled over to sit cross-legged facing him. She made a scary face, then a sexy one.

"Smile for the camera," Jerry shouted through the glass partition and used a lever to zoom the telephoto lens, bringing Charlene's body features as close as his hand, then far away. He switched to a wide-angle view, where he could see the entire width of the room. She leaned back, mimicked a model striking several poses. She got off the bed and stood in front of the mirror, curtsied and walked forward to squash her nose and lips against the glass. She stepped back, played as if she were going to remove her tank top, stepped to the wall, raised the shirt a scant below her breasts, laughed, and just then reached behind to flick off the wall switch. The room changed into darkness.

"Hey, not fair! That's cheating," he shouted and laughed all at once.

He heard the door slam and looked around to see her at his side.

"What a view. You can catch the whole show from here."

"Yes, but why the need for anonymity?" she asked. "I mean, wouldn't a photographer get his best shots up close, inside the room itself?"

"Maybe! However, with these lenses he's as close here as there. The zoom lens on this camera can operate electronically and the operator may have a way to focus from inside the studio. Considering all these wires, it's obvious he uses several cameras behind these see-through mirrors. It's bad and it has to stop!" he said. "I think we better move out of here, Charlene. Let's not press our luck and get caught messing with this stuff."

She appeared less eager to run.

"But, it's your church, Jerry. You're in charge here. Maybe we should wait and see who shows up?"

"No. I don't want to face someone like that. It could make matters worse. And how do we know when someone will show up? It could be days. Let's go! Turn out the light in there!"

"Whatever you say," she sighed slowly and disappointed.

As they locked up behind them, Jerry wondered why he had the key. The possibilities of who might be responsible for the room made him nervous. He took Charlene's hand and led the way through the storage room.

"We've uncovered someone's secret," she said as Jerry maneuvered her through the maze of furniture stored in the room.

"I think it's called a pornography studio," Jerry corrected, his voice echoing a word used by law enforcement for the type of photography taking place here. "Blue movies, stag films, girlie pictures, smut, celluloid sex," he asserted. Anger had escaped his mouth as he used all the superlatives he knew to describe the purpose. "What's it doing here?"

"There were boxes of Trojans in one of the drawers," she said matter-of-factly.

He showed shocked amusement. "Why that's hard to believe," he said indignantly. But then he turned dead serious. "The idea that something like this could take place in the basement of our church is really sick! It's bizarre. And that makes it satanic! Criminal! Charlene, if word got out about this, it could destroy everything good we stand for."

He pulled up short to look at her and hold her at arms length.

"You won't say anything, will you, Charlene? At least not until I find out who's responsible?" he pleaded. "If news of this studio ever reaches the ears of the press, it could be disastrous. Can you imagine the headlines? 'Dirty-picture studio discovered in church basement.' Nothing could be more scandalous. Unbelievable!"

"Hey, you forget, I am the press." She stared blankly into his face. "Jerry, I don't want to hurt the reputation of your church, but that's not what we should worry about," she said as he tugged at her hand. She pulled away, ran her hand around him and stopped him, held him close. "Jerry! Let's think about this! Suppose what we found in that room has something to do with Reverend Maefield's murder. We could be in danger right now."

She took his arm as he urged her on. He opened the door into the old coal room; he flipped the storage-room-light switch off. The door walloped loudly behind them. He wondered why only one of the eight light bulbs in the coal room he had counted earlier remained lit. The lighted bulb seemed a mile away. As they set off in that direction, they saw dangling open sockets and their feet crunched on fine broken glass. Charlene clung to him tighter than before. Her hands were sweating and shaking. Just then, a furnace came on with a resounding burst of energy. Jerry shook his head, no, tugged at her hand and halted.

"What am I doing? We're going the wrong way," he shouted above the furnace noise. "The stairs to the manse are on the other side of that wall." He pointed toward a crack of light to their right. "Over there is the door to Maefield's liquor closet and the laundry room."

They reversed themselves. They found the door unlocked and the room lit. Relieved to get out of the dark coal area, they ran through the two small rooms and bounded up the lighted stairs. On the landing, Jerry pressed the thumb latch of the manse door. The solid oak door held firm. He hit it full force with his shoulder. It was like driving into a stone wall.

"This can't be. I unlocked the dead-bolt on the other side before we left the manse." He pounded on the door, as if someone there could open it. But he was also angry and frustrated by his failure. "Maybe I locked it thinking I was opening it. I don't know! I'm sorry, Charlene!"

"Now what?"

"We'll have to return to the annex. It's the only way I know out of here."

They scurried down the stairs and once more entered the coal basement. In the darkness, they made some wrong turns before the single ceiling light came wholly into view. They started in that direction just as the single dull bulb went out. The entire basement turned into a cave. They could not see their hands in front of their faces. With no light at all, they froze in their tracks. The furnace roared. Charlene let out a frightened scream. Jerry put his arm around her waist.

"Let's keep moving," he shouted above the abysmal noise. "The exit is dead in front of us," he yelled into her ear and tugged hard on her hand.

The furnace noise stopped. A loud, smashing noise—the sound of wood hitting steel—shattered the sudden silence. A whipping noise followed, something fanning the air. Jerry acted quickly and collapsed, pulling Charlene with him to the floor. Someone was swinging at their heads. They stretched out on their stomachs, Jerry's arm over Charlene's shoulders.

As the sound receded, he said in a tone below a whisper, his mouth touching her ear, "Someone's behind us."

She shook her head in understanding.

"Quiet as a lamb."

They lay still, heard another crack, wood hitting concrete, probably the foundation.

"Crawl like a snake," Jerry prodded.

They propelled their bodies over the gritty floor, inching their way until they could feel the wall and squirmed right until feeling the metal surface of the door. Jerry pushed. Fire regulations forbade a lock on this door that swung into the underground passage. But the door did not give. Either a person or something heavy rested against it from the other side. Jerry inched up on his knees. Every time he forced the door to open a crack, it opposed him.

"Put your hands against the door and shove," he whispered, holding Charlene in front of him. Together they strained to compel the door in a few inches. Jerry pushed with all his strength, this time moving what was behind it. He felt through the opening into more darkness. "It's blocked by a mattress! I can feel it."

A loud clang against the wall far to their left shattered the quiet dark. Charlene, on her hands and knees, bolted as Jerry pushed. Quickly, she squeezed her slim frame into the narrow opening and wiggled all the way through. On the other side, she pushed the heavy casing to the side. Jerry crawled through the wider opening. They let the door close silent behind them. With their hands, they counted two heavy mattresses crushed against the door. Charlene held Jerry's shirttail, as he bent down.

"Let's move these back!" he whispered and together— working blind—they got a grip on the mattresses and slid them one at a time against the door.

Probing sightless along the wall of the corridor, they walked slow motion, unsure of what other danger lay in their path. Behind them, they heard a rumble. Their pursuer was pushing against the door as they had. They made the mistake of hurrying. Suddenly, Jerry stumbled over a fence of metal chairs used as a barricade across the narrow tunnel. The noise of the chairs hitting the concrete floor as he fell echoed back and forth in the long corridor. Charlene, still clinging, fell with him. Her right knee scraped over something sharp. She let out a muffled cry.

"You okay?" he said. He found her armpits and stood her up with him. She trembled and took a deep breath. He held her steady.

"I skinned my knee," she said in a quiet voice. "Yah, I can feel a little blood. I've always been afraid of falling over metal church chairs in the dark."

Jerry loved her humor under adversity. "That makes two of us."

They kept their arms linked.

"As long as I can feel you, I'll be all right," she whispered. "He's in here with us. He's following us. I'm sure of it."

"Move behind me," Jerry murmured quietly and felt around on the floor to collapse a chair. "I'm going to throw a chair in front of us."

He underhanded the chair into the darkness from which they had come. The chair bounced in a wave of sparks along the floor, and skidded in a deafening crash several feet away. He grabbed another metal chair and threw it with more force than before. It too scraped and sparked as it glanced off the ceiling, shattering a florescent lamp, hitting the wall and falling in a line of sparks, before it bounced along the floor.

"Put your hand in my back pocket and lead me," he directed. Taking a third chair, he held it up and waved it in front of them as they fell back like molasses moving on a winter day until they collided against the steel door at the end of the hall. Jerry palmed the doorknob and knew he had to unlock it.

Suddenly a match came into flame. Charlene held it out toward the door.

"Where'd you get that?"

"From my bra, if you must know. I stuck matches and two cigarettes in there before leaving the manse."

"Hold it close to the doorknob."

"I could burn my bra, if you like," she suggested. She was jesting but she would do it.

"No, I don't need a bonfire."

She hit him lightly on the shoulder. "Hey, don't you wish!"

She sat with her back against the wall, lit another match and brought the flame close. It licked at her finger. She did it again. Jerry inserted one key after another.

"Here, I have it. Yes! Yes!" he said with restrained pleasure.

The doorknob turned. They scurried into the dimly lit hall and stairwell. Seeing the door to the annex padlocked, they fled up the stairs, where Jerry fumbled for yet another key.

"It doesn't make sense that these doors all require separate keys," he protested.

"Of course it does. Your custodian has the only master key."

Jerry opened the door into the cathedral. They raced up the aisle and outside.

"What time is the next tour, Reverend?"

"You're a laugh a minute, Miss Cunningham."

They avoided the cloister and approached the manse using

Cathedral Drive. Jerry took Walter's key out of his wallet. His heart missed a beat when he saw the front door wide open.

Jerry slammed and bolted it, then ran to the back of the house. Charlene went immediately to the living room to retrieve her shoulder bag. Everything seemed as she had left it. Quickly, she pulled the women's briefs from inside her shorts and stuck them in the bottom of her bag. Harnessing the bag on her shoulder, she carried it with her into the kitchen, where she found Jerry at the door in the hallway that led to the basement. There they saw that the lock-catch was in the unlocked position. Jerry pointed to where dry soil littered the floor.

"Charlene, he let himself in through the front door. He stood here. See the dirt from his shoes. He must have barricaded the passageway while we were inside his studio, then he ran ahead of us and locked us out of the manse."

"Yes, and followed us down the stairs into the coal room," she offered, anxiety etched in her voice, "unscrewed a fuse somewhere, disconnecting the electric power, and stalked us through the tunnel. He's probably down there now."

"Or, he could have doubled back to hide in here! We may not be out of danger."

On that note, Jerry reached into a closet and pulled out a police nightstick.

"The one thing I have of my father's," he said with pride and waved the heavy stick in front of him.

With Charlene next to him, they began a close-knit search of the house. On the ground floor, they went about switching lights on and off. They looked into every room, closet, the sun porch, the maid's quarters, back stairwell and the two bathrooms. Upstairs they checked the attic and each of the bedrooms. They looked under all the beds. In the bathrooms, they peered into the shower stalls and in the master bath.

In Jerry's bedroom, Charlene suppressed her amusement as she surveyed the tidiness of his bachelor quarters: the made-up bed, the neat way pants, jackets and shoes adorned the closet, how his ties hung in color-coordinated order on the tie rack, nothing out of place. Even the bathroom towels were fresh, fluffy and straight. Had she not experienced his well-prepared service at the supper table, she may have passed this off as his mother's doing before she left this afternoon. But, no, Jerry liked things in order. Her amusement came in thinking about him in her apartment right now. Jerry was as neat as she was sloppy. The comparison helped her deal with their incredible experience. Now she had to avoid a mischievous temptation to mess everything up. She looked around to see him deep in thought and peering out the opened window into the last shaded light of the evening. Humidity mixed with perspiration from physical activity showed. Jerry's shirt looked like it had mopped a dirty, wet floor. She decided this was a good time to freshen up and stole into the bathroom, where she turned on the coldwater faucet at the sink. Cupping her hands, she splashed water over her head, dousing her hair and face, not caring that water cascaded onto her shoulders and down her front. She drenched a bath towel and used it to wipe her face, then her scraped knee. She lifted her tank top and extracted the two cigarettes she had hid there. She giggled at their mangled look and threw them in the wastebasket. She smoothed down her top and draped the dripping towel around her neck while she retrieved her lipstick from her bag and applied a fresh coat. Then she got out a fresh pack of *Pall Mall* and her Zippo lighter. Leaving her bag on a short stool, she returned to the bedroom to see Jerry still moodily staring out the window.

As her frame of mind had mellowed, his had become somber. She perceived he was conflicted over what to do about their discovery. Maybe, too, he regretted her presence. Standing at his side, she asked, "Do you want to call the police? I'll leave if you would rather I not be here. You don't have to mention I was with you." A welcome breeze through the open window churned the air, taking the edge off the heat and humidity.

He turned to look at her—her blond hair soaked and drawn into tight ringlets, her eye shadow dissolved, her filthy shirt drenched and pressed more provocative than before over her breasts, her blackened white shorts and her wounded knee. But good-looks like hers do not give way to adverse conditions. Nothing could reverse the desire he felt for her.

She opened the cigarette pack and let the cellophane wrapping drop on the floor. He bent to pick it up. She put her foot over it. He grinned at her and took the pack from her hand, tapped it until a cigarette emerged. He fished it out and put the filter tip between her lips, lit it with her lighter. She dragged lightly, and held it by using her thumb and first finger as if holding a firecracker. This amused him because she reminded him of high school—how girls held their cigarettes as they gathered to smoke by a fire exit, always ready to flip the butt—as they often had to do—on a moment's notice because their sentry yelled, *"Teacher on the hall!"*

"None for you?" she asked.

"I'll share yours!"

"What if I don't want to share?"

Her eyes never left his as she put the cigarette to her lips and drew more deeply than before. The smoke floated between them.

"I'll take it from your breath."

"Oh?"

"Too bad you didn't have this lighter tucked away," he said, smiling as he flicked it.

"Yah, well, you can't carry hardware down there."

"Yes, but how many people would have thought to bring matches and offer to burn their underwear?"

"You're bad, Jerry!"

He gave her a guilty look and turned away to place the cigarette pack and lighter on the window sill. All at once, he struggled to pull his shirt over his head, the fabric sticking to his sweating body, resisting his strength. She tugged on the short collar with her free hand.

She spoke softly. "Someone was after us. He may have meant to kill us."

"I don't believe we were in danger, Charlene," he replied, his voice muffled by the shirt covering his head. "Whoever chased us wanted to frighten us and I admit he scared me. But had he wanted to kill us he would have succeeded. And, anyway, we're safe here," he continued as the last of the shirt slipped away. He looked for a place to hang it. She snatched it out of his hands and threw it across the room. She blocked him from retrieving it.

"Hey, it won't dry bunched up on the floor."

She was in front of him, close, took the end of her towel from around her neck and dabbed at the sweat on his face and chest.

"Let it be," she said, her smile rapidly evacuating her face, her eyes tearing.

He reached forward and took her hand.

"You're shaking. You're still frightened."

"In the dark, I was terrified. For a moment there, I thought I was going to die."

"And now?"

"I don't know. It's different. I don't want to be in the dark like that ever again. I don't want to be alone tonight. I really don't want to leave. But like you, I'm also conflicted. I think we should report to the police what we discovered, the sooner the better."

He took her cigarette from her fingers and put it to his lips. He drew modestly.

"I know you're right, but I have to work this out in my own way," he said. "If it was Everett Wheeler, I want to give him the benefit of the doubt. Let him come clean. Let him know I'm not his enemy. We got off to a bad start last Wednesday. If I show trust now, give him a way to explain himself, I may help him overcome whatever problem he has. If I can avoid scandal, Charlene, I should try."

"I don't agree, but it's your call." She took back the cigarette, but did not drag on it. He reached into a dresser drawer and took out a glass ashtray. She flicked the ash and drew deeply.

"How do we know that room wasn't left by Reverend Maefield?" he whispered. "Possibly, Everett knows nothing about it. We have no proof that he set it up. Maybe Walter Tompkins pursued us. He's the one who gave me the church keys and assured me I had the only other key to the front door of the manse, yet, surely, he had kept a copy. The church has nine employees and over fifteen hundred members. How can I say that any one of them didn't set up that room?"

"I think you know better, Jerry." Her tone showed her irritation, "But what difference does it make what either one of us believes? The truth has to come out! This is a police matter! Let them determine who's responsible for that studio. Let them investigate if there's a connection between that studio and the murder. Invite them to have a look."

"Give me time, Charlene."

She took a little drag on the cigarette and passed it into his lips. This time, he tasted her lipstick.

A mesmerizing smile spread over her face. "So, tell me, what would you have done if you had found someone, say, Everett, hiding in the shower stall, all dolled up in a red negligee?"

He remembered her playful mood as she sat on the bed and he focused the camera lens up close on her seductive form.

"I would have hit him in the balls with my nightstick, that's what," he said, mimicking her smile.

"Which nightstick?" she asked, relishing his surprise at her quick though earthy wit.

"Now, who's bad?" he asked.

"I am bad," she said in a near whisper and trained her eyes on him in a steady stare.

He took a deep drag on the cigarette and exhaled, enveloping her in smoke.

She did not blink. She took the dwindled butt from his fingers to her own mouth, inhaled and blew it back. They were very close.

He reached with the towel end to wipe perspiration from her brow and touched a little tear that had managed to escape down her left cheek.

"I'll take care of it tomorrow. I promise."

He removed the cigarette from her fingers. He put his mouth on hers. Her lips were soft as he imagined they would be and she opened them. But only briefly.

She stepped back a little and he wondered if maybe he had misread her invitation. She took the cigarette end from his fingers and crushed it out in the ashtray. Turning, she pulled the wet towel away from her neck, dropped it behind her, took hold of her tank top at the waist and raised it without effort over her head. Her pink bra, which daintily covered the crowning points of her high positioned breasts, came into view. She pulled him into her arms, hugging and kissing him in a way that left no question of what she wanted.

He unhooked her bra and pushed the straps off her shoulders. She let his hands remove it and roam her body at will. He had a light touch and an eager mouth, and she treasured how he used his hands and lips to explore her in concert with their rising excitement. They stopped and stared at each other.

"I'd like to stay with you tonight," he said in a hushed and affirming voice.

They cuddled and kissed several minutes before he moved her to the bed. She bent to pull back the cover. When she turned to face him, she was pleasantly surprised that he had wasted no time to appear naked in her presence. In the lovemaking that followed, there was no hesitation, no exchange of words and no modesty until exhausted and spent they rested on their sides, his body curled around hers, his arms holding her secure. An hour passed before they left the bedroom and showered together. Upon their return, she helped him change the bed linens for their cool, clean bodies. They slept fleetingly, for neither one could wait to arouse the other to new heights of passion. Only the chill air before dawn let them know they soon had to separate.

He ran a hot bath and rubbed her back as she soaked in its fragrant soapy mixture. When she worried about what she would wear to her motel, he produced one of his long-sleeve white shirts. Secretly, the picture of how Madge had worn such a shirt entered his mind. But Charlene left off her shorts, and let the lengthy shirt tails hang loose below her nakedness. They went to the kitchen where he fixed breakfast and then, in the quiet idleness of the breaking daylight, her dirty laundry in a paper bag, he walked her to her car.

"Where are you off to today?" he asked her.

They had not spoken very much. At first, she thought he was asking as a way to make conversation. Then she saw his eyes and she knew the question went deeper.

"I have some interviews scheduled, one with a police homicide detective. After that, I'm planning to question random people around town. I have to go to Philadelphia tomorrow to check in with my editor. I need time to write-up what I've learned so far. I'll call you tonight."

She unlocked the MG Midget's door and slid into the driver's seat. He got in beside her and they embraced one more time.

"And you, what are your plans?

"My first order of business is to call a locksmith and have all the locks in the manse changed. After that, I'll hang around Shepherd House. I'll talk to Everett about the basement room. If he doesn't cooperate, I'll call the police. I have to do some visiting this afternoon. There are people in the hospital I have to see. I'll be busy."

She looked away. She could not face him, but she had to ask him.

"What would happen if people learned about me staying over last night? You could lose your job, right? They could ask you to leave the ministry. Isn't that so?"

He placed his finger to her lips and she held it there as he had done to her the preceding night.

"You think I'm preaching to you?" she asked as she fed off it. "I will worry about you."

A long tear moved down her cheek. He tasted it and kissed it away. She hesitated and then decided to change the subject.

"You will tell me when you learn anything about the basement room?"

He nodded and pulled away. With some effort, he got out of the low car seat. He rolled down the window. He slammed the door firmly and almost kneeled on the ground to stick his head through.

"Hey, what have you done here?" he said, touching a band of wire holding down the convertible top. This isn't going to hold; it's already loose," he said, reaching for it. Removing her temporary repair, he forced the lever to latch the car roof.

She smiled. It takes a man, she thought. She rolled up the window and—without daring to look at him again—waved. She pulled away from the curb.

He watched her make a U-turn and disappear beyond the Revolutionary War monument.

How could he explain what had happened between them? He worried that he had fallen victim once again to his banal instincts, but wanted to believe his reasons had gone deeper than physical attraction. He wanted her for more than that. Still, she hadn't replaced his thoughts of someone else, someone he couldn't have, wouldn't dare approach and about whom he shouldn't even be thinking. Confused and feeling guiltier than any time he could remember after having made passionate love, he returned to the manse. For Jerry Flynn, there was no tonic more helpful to the forgiveness of sins than devotion to the work of the Lord.

CHAPTER 7

TEMPERATURE RISING

Monday Morning, June 11

Michael Todd ordered a breakfast of ham and scrambled eggs at Tommy's Place. He did it with a trace of regret, knowing Madge had wanted to wait on him. He should be home with her dispensing accolades and apologies.

*   *   *

After his showdown with Madge last night, Michael had driven off to meet his father-in-law and Jorge Garcia to tell Garcia the company could not renege on the deal Madge had made with the workers and to promise that Madge would never intrude again. With Walter's assurances, Garcia consented to return to work.

That done, not wanting to face Madge just now with news of what he had agreed to, Michael dropped in at the bowling alley, where he joined long-term buddies in three games. With the bowling-alley bar closed on Sunday, except for a few slugs from a hidden whiskey bottle of one of his friends, he left fairly sober and returned home about midnight.

He figured on finding Madge already asleep, but he wasn't prepared to find the bedroom door locked. He couldn't blame her, but he thought this unusual. Madge always slept with the door slightly ajar in case the children called out for her. He guessed she had waited until she heard him before getting up to lock it. He started for the downstairs guest room. Just then, he heard the key turn and, as the door opened, he saw Madge clad in nothing more than a short pajama bottom. She said nothing as she hurried back to bed and pulled the sheet snug to her chin. Michael kept his silence as well. He showered and got into bed next to her. He wanted to make love to her. He would do it slow and easy, the way she liked it. But he feared she would not respond and he hated himself for his past failures, even on her terms, to please her. And last Tuesday night, what he remembered of it, he would just as soon forget. How anxious he felt now, knowing she was awake and all but naked but with her back to him. He needed only a little encouragement. He knew that much of their sexual problems had to do with her fear of pregnancy. Chip and Dudley had been difficult births. Both times, she had almost lost her life. But she had begun taking birth control pills and for several months, he had thought their sex life had improved, that she had even consented to his "manly ways." So, why not now; let him make up for this evening. Then he heard her snoring. He guessed she had taken a sleeping pill. She had given him up completely.

At most, he slept in short spurts until dawn. He shaved and dressed. He saw her awake as he came through the bedroom from the bath. She invited him back to bed, opened her arms to him, but he ignored her. She said to wait and she would fix him breakfast. They needed to talk. But he made up an excuse that he had an early appointment and left her looking at him with big tearful eyes.

To himself, he had already admitted Madge had made the right decision about the field-worker troubles last Thursday. He had spent hours at the Dover, Delaware growers' conference listening to organization speakers recommend Madge's hands-on approach to labor management. Perhaps she had acted prematurely, Thursday. Even so, he should have backed her. Instead, he had bowed to the brute instincts of his father-in-law and their field boss. He didn't know how to tell Walter times were changing. New attitudes, laws, farm-labor boards were calling for changes in the way owners do business. Now matters were worse. He had made peace behind Madge's back. He had locked himself into future turmoil. New challenges were sure to arise over issues of workers' pay and safety. And last night he and Walter had given Jorge permission to settle matters with fists, clubs, knives, and—if necessary—guns. Why did he have such a hard time siding with his wife? Why should his pride overpower doing what was right by her? Madge was everything he was not.

*   *   *

Tommy's Place was more crowded than usual for this early in the morning, so service suffered. Millie filled his cup a second time. Michael tried to concentrate on the sports section of the paper. As he reviewed major league standings, Everett Wheeler stormed into the diner in his usual bombastic manner—shaking hands and slapping backs, patting ladies' butts, making senseless jokes about the food, Millie's bust and complaining about foreigners using up free parking space on Main Street. Some patrons ignored him, others gave begrudging hilarity and more than a few joined in with his clownish banter. Michael hoped Everett wouldn't see him.

Everett finally plopped his generous exterior over a stool at the counter and teasingly looked at his watch to time the seconds before a waitress shoved a cup of coffee in front of him. A minute later, Tommy came out of the kitchen and the two men shot off their big mouths for the umpteenth time over the loss of the Philadelphia A's to Kansas City, calling it "another communist plot" and how it wouldn't have happened if old Connie Mack still ran the show. "Stupid!" Michael said under his breath. But he had to listen on as their childish gab switched to comparison of beers and then to complaints at having to pay twenty-nine cents for a gallon of gasoline. As Millie passed to deliver her next order, Everett's eyes followed her to Michael's booth.

The two men hadn't spoken a word to each other in five years and Michael had no reason to believe their disaffection would change today, but before he shoveled one fork full of ham into his mouth, Everett was at his side. The big man stretched his long, muscular arm over Michael's shoulder as if they were bosom buddies.

"Michael, how you do 'en?" Everett roared, at the same time reached to help himself to a piece of toast off Michael's plate.

In the conversation that followed, Michael's countenance changed from bland annoyance to red anger to ghostly pain. He never finished his breakfast. He left the diner wishing he had not come here this morning.

*　　*　　*

The Tompkinsville Police Department occupied the basement and two floors on the north side of City Hall. The area included a five-cell lockup, dispatcher's room, and too little space for administration, uniform patrol and detective divisions. Homicide shared offices with other plainclothes units along a hallway that reached the length of the building. If there was any advantage in being Chief of Homicide, the chief had the very last room on the hall and he didn't have to share it with anyone else. If he wanted to pass time deep in thought, that was his business. Having just browsed through a stack of case reports from his four days off, Detective John Burroughs had much on his mind. But the desk sergeant interrupted, when he called on the telephone intercom to tell him his ten thirty appointment had arrived.

"I don't mind keeping her here," he continued. "She's a good-look'n dame."

"No, send her down, Barney, and keep your fly zipped up," he chided.

A minute later, Charlene tapped on the doorframe of Burroughs's open office.

He had to agree with his desk sergeant—"*she's a good-look'n dame.*"

Burroughs stood as Charlene came into the room. He motioned her to the solid, heavy, wood armchair in front of his desk. In spite of the dense humidity, she looked fresh in a knee length flower-print summer dress that left an open neckline amid brief sleeves on her trim shoulders. Even this tough, reserved, always-faithful-to-his-wife cop sniffed for her perfume and hoped his hair was neat and his tie on straight.

"If that fan is too much on your back, I'll turn it down, Miss," he said.

"No, it's perfect, feels great," Charlene replied as she reached across the desk to shake his hand before sitting in the designated chair.

Burroughs had the Maefield file in front of him and once Charlene settled, he too sat, then he flipped open the folder's cover to a thick stack of loose pages. Charlene got her black leather-bound notebook out of her shoulder bag and turned to the side to best use the arm of the chair for support.

"You don't mind if I take notes, do you, Detective? Usually I write them up after an interview, but if it's all right?"

He told her he had no problem with note taking and Charlene rapidly turned the pages. She had spent the morning at the motel bringing them up to date. She had a habit of decorating the margins with personal observations, drawings, and today a lipstick kiss where she had written brief, cryptic annotations about her tour of the Presbyterian manse. She hoped Detective Burroughs had not seen her mark. She had to put last night out of her mind and went quickly to a blank page, where, after scribbling the date and time, she wrote, ***Detective Burroughs, Homicide, TPD.***

After giving assurance that she would not use his name in her article, she asked for details about the murder. He did his best to describe the scene, though, out of consideration for his female guest, he left out the gore. He needn't have. She showed she was well informed and surprised him with her knowledge of forensic procedures. Burroughs now recognized Charlene Cunningham was using him to confirm what she already knew. Then she asked, "Do you suspect anyone in the congregation?"

With that question, Burroughs saw through her youth and beauty to a serious and skilled interviewer. She had neatly taken off the gloves and demonstrated she expected him to do the same.

"No one is beyond suspicion!"

"What about family members, friends from the minister's past?"

"That's under investigation. Until the murder is solved, we won't rule out anyone."

"Yes, but it was such a vicious slaying. Not everyone is capable of this."

"I suppose not; however, in the heat of an argument, with anger, drugs, alcohol, more people are capable of mayhem than we want to believe. Our death-row prisons are filled with killers who, in ordinary circumstances, would be incapable of hurting their victims, much less murdering them."

"Tell me about Mrs. Maefield. What kind of woman is she?"

Burroughs emitted a slight smile. The question took him by surprise, but, then, if you are writing about this crime, he had to admit the wife-widow angle would be necessary.

"She's ice cold, Miss Cunningham. Is it Miss? Or, do you use that new address, Ms.?

"Miss is fine," she said, showing no annoyance, though she really hated that a woman, until only recently, could not have her marital status left anonymous. But Charlene knew many men thought of "Ms." as a snotty title and she could care less about such things when she sensed she might be close to getting something extra out of him. "What do you mean ice cold, Detective?"

He leaned back in his desk chair, put his hands behind his neck and looked up at the ceiling. He did not know whether he should answer. He had already said too much off the record. But she was leading him and she leaned closer to hear. Burroughs waited a few seconds before bending a little forward, laying his hands flat out on the desk.

"Oh, I'm sure Mrs. Maefield was upset, but to me, in all conversations—I think I had four little chats with her and one very long one—she never showed . . . I don't know . . . I can't say no grief, because there was sadness, but she just seemed to take her husband's death stoically, as though hardened to things like this. I understand the Nazis killed her parents. Something like that must harden your emotions. It's as if nothing else can shock you. In any event, I never found anything in her relationship with her husband that would make me suspect her of his murder. Nor could I find information to suggest that she had conspired with another person to murder her husband."

"The report given me by my editor related that the first officer to arrive on the scene described Mrs. Maefield (Charlene slid a loose page from her notebook and read from it) *all dressed up in a charcoal gray, woman's business suit.*' The officer noted the *dark jacket buttoned over a white blouse, the matching long black skirt'* that she wore *'manly brown boots . . . that her black hair was neatly combed, pulled back and set in a bun at the crown of her head, not a hair out of place. Black horn-rim glasses framed her dark eyes. She was in makeup of rose red lipstick that stood out on her pale face and (when she removed her glasses for a moment) I noticed her accented eyebrows and dark eye shadow. She smelled of strong perfume, but pleasant to inhale.'"*

"Yah, well, I teach my officers to be observant," Burroughs said, smiling.

"Don't you think this overdone for five thirty in the morning, especially for someone who said she was in bed asleep less than half an hour before reporting the discovery of her husband's blood-soaked body?"

"True! But who are we to say how a woman should dress for discovering a murder? Mrs. Maefield's explanation was that the alarm clock awoke her at four fifty. Reverend Maefield had not come to bed, but this had not upset her. She said he often read all night in his study, sometimes fell asleep there in his chair. On such occasions, she came by to get him up. She had an appointment in New York that day at the offices of the legal firm where she planned to work. She's now an attorney, you know. She had taken her bar exams only a few days before her husband's death. Because of the bad weather, she planned on catching the eleven o'clock train from Camden. She and her husband often went to Tommy's Place, an all-night diner down the street from here, for breakfast, and she thought they could cut a path through the snow that morning. So she dressed for work, hoping she could catch the first bus to Camden whenever it left. She put on her hiking boots and headed for Shepherd House by way of the cloister."

Burroughs read from his papers. *I became frightened when I saw the door into Shepherd House ajar. I pushed and walked in. I called out my husband's name. I continued farther into the room. His reading lamp was on. I saw his body on the floor in front of the fireplace. Terrible wounds showed through his clothes and blood was all over him and around him. I knew he was dead. Fearing I could accidentally destroy evidence, I was careful not to touch anything and returned to the manse to call police.*

Burroughs looked up from his reading. "The call clocked in at five eighteen. The dispatcher recalled how she spoke in a calm, well-mannered voice. She gave her name, address and information that she had just discovered her husband, Reverend Maefield, dead in his church study. She said he was murdered. She said she would wait at the front door of the church residence and hung up. At five twenty-five, the officer on patrol—whose report you somehow got a copy of—was in her foyer and other officers were fanning out around the buildings. They had to get the custodian, who had begun shoveling the walk, to unlock the door to the scene of the crime." Burroughs closed the folder and pushed it to the side. "Now does that explain her mode of dress, Miss Cunningham?"

"Yes and no. The timeframe bothers me. I ask how long it takes a careful woman to do the toilet thing—wash, comb, raise her hair and fix it neatly in a bun, apply makeup and dress in the way your police officer described her. That's a lot of activity for twenty-eight minutes, and she still has time to walk to and from Shepherd House in treacherous weather conditions."

Charlene continued without pause. "I have a photograph here," she said and pushed a five-by-seven, black-and-white print of Mrs. Maefield across the desk. "This is not a sloppy woman, Detective. She's not the type to sleep in her clothes or leave her hair up. She showers and towels dry before putting on fresh underwear, makeup, jewelry and a women's business suit for a day at the office. She may take pains to make herself homely; however, she takes time to do it right."

Burroughs studied the picture. If he saw some new light shed on Rhonda Maefield, he kept it to himself. But Charlene did not expect him to comment on the time sequence, nor did she press him for it. Instead, she asked him a speculative question, one she had planned before meeting him.

"Let me sidetrack a moment. As a man, what do you think? Church members have told me that Mrs. Maefield dresses dowdy even for lounging around the house, just as you see her in that photograph. The church secretary, Miss Blatty stated that Rhonda Maefield [she read from her notes], *cultivated a reserved and matronly appearance,* which I take to mean, what you see may not be natural, that she created a public image as a cover for another image. It was like a role she played, even at events where such theatrics were out of place. For example, as you can see in the photograph—Miss Blatty loaned it to me—she is at the beach on a hot summer day for a church picnic. She looks ridiculous. Another church employee commented that Mrs. Maefield was 'sexy. *If you take the time to look below the wraps',*" Charlene read from her notes, *"'what you see is sexy.'* Do you agree, Detective Burroughs? As a man, now, does Mrs. Maefield strike you as sexy? Can you see under the wraps and come to that conclusion?"

Burroughs stared at the photo for a few seconds. Again, he leaned back in his chair, put his hands behind his head and looked up at the ceiling, thought deeply about her question. He balanced the chair on its back legs an inch from the wall for a few seconds before coming forward to rest his hands once more on the top of his desk. He stared again for several seconds at the photo.

"No, I can't say that, Miss Cunningham. As a man, with normal needs, if you know what I mean, I don't think of sex when I see Mrs. Maefield, if that's what you're asking. But, who's to say?" he questioned and at the same time thumped his finger on the picture. "We all have our preferences. What's attractive in a woman to one man, another man may not see. But sexy? God, no!" he laughed. "Rhonda Maefield doesn't turn me on." He pushed the photo toward her. Charlene wrote it down. She looked up from her notebook to catch the detective's eyes glued to her chest; a pleasant, receding smile fading on his bulldog face. Charlene smiled broadly, reading his mind. "In any event, let's assume, Miss Cunningham, that this," he reached across the desk and slapped the photo as he said it, "is a disguise, that underneath the veneer, Rhonda Maefield has an appealing face and a figure a man would die for. What has that to do with this case?"

"Maybe nothing, Detective, probably it has no significance whatsoever! Then again, if true, I have to ask why she is hiding. And when she gets away from playing minister's wife, what shows? And what does she do with it?" Burroughs looked doubtful as he listened. He waited politely for her to finish. "Is this a woman who lives in another world, a world where there are different rules and pleasures others only fantasize?" she asked.

"An interesting question. I suppose you think Mrs. Maefield may hide a secret life as a Jezebel and a murderess, but I believe you're barking up the wrong tree, Miss."

Burroughs removed his thick glasses and wiped them with a white handkerchief he had taken from his pants pocket. Without his magnifying-like glasses on, Charlene saw the dark pockets of his eyes and the deep groove indented over the bridge of his nose from his years of wearing the heavy lenses. Yet, without glasses, he looked younger, even handsome. Deep in his own thoughts, Burroughs put his glasses on and again looked like the kind grandfather he was. The change in appearance was remarkable and Charlene wanted to comment on it. But she knew it was too personal. Burroughs might not appreciate her using him as an example of how to study the face of Mrs. Maefield.

"It may make good press," Burroughs went on, "however, I advise you to find another angle for your magazine. In my opinion, you waste your time connecting this minister's death with his wife. We have figured Mrs. Maefield's net wealth, without her insurance claim, and before her husband's death, at over two million dollars. So, I don't see insurance money, overwhelming as the amount is, as a motive." He paused to see if that would get a reaction from her. Charlene kept her eyes glued to her page, pen in hand, waiting for his next remark. "And while the Maefields may have had a platonic relationship, and mind you I have no idea how they did sexually, nor do I care," Burroughs said softly, "we know of no marital conflict, no domestic violence, or extra-marital affairs by either one of them. For your information, I had the lady under surveillance twenty-four hours a day for a total of ninety-four days February through May. I took my own turn at it. What a bore! I will tell you we did observe Mrs. Maefield dressed more fashionably in the city, but nothing out of the ordinary, nothing—how do you say it?—risqué. We have checked her bank records, friends, immigration, education and people she works with and have not found a whisper of scandal. Before moving into her Riverside apartment, she stayed with a married couple at their Park Avenue apartment. They're both attorneys in the big leagues of corporate law. Nothing untidy there, no red lights! Now she has a job in a big-bucks law firm. Our records show that even as a minister's wife, she lived more like a princess. In that sense, she likes luxuries. She buys expensive jewelry, clothes, furs and furniture. She travels by taxi and limo, first class on train or plane. She pays high rent and has her laundry picked up and delivered. She can afford it."

Burroughs turned silent while Charlene caught up on her note taking, his little smile increasing.

In the back of her mind, she realized he had given her privileged information. Was he just being nice? Or, was he sucking her in? Perhaps establishing trust, on the outside chance, she might dig up something his police work had thus far failed to do. She realized Burroughs was no slouch. He had perfected his craft well and she fully understood he had not missed a beat on her since she had walked into the room.

"If I may go back to your observation," he began again as she rested her writing hand on her knee. "I'm curious, Miss Cunningham. You're questioning how much time Mrs. Maefield needed between rising and reporting the crime. That interests me. As a woman, what's your estimate?"

"Well, as I've already indicated, I think it took her longer. She may have miscalculated how much time it does take her. Many women would be surprised by their time getting ready to go out. Let's say, she jumped up immediately at four fifty and without pause, that is, not taking time to shower, her clothes laid out the night before, she had only to work on her face and hair. Twenty unhurried minutes could have done it for a practiced woman, but you should ask someone who fixes her hair the way you see it in this photograph how long it takes. In icy conditions, I estimate Mrs. Maefield taking seven minutes each way to walk from the manse to Shepherd House. At a leisurely pace in tennis shoes, on a spring morning, it took me six each way. And let's add in a few minutes for accessing her coat and lacing boots before going out the door. How long did she linger in Shepherd House? Four minutes? Is that reasonable time to assess and adjust to the shock of finding such a gory scene? I believe forty-one minutes to do it all is conservative. So, I believe she was up and dressed earlier than four fifty. Don't ask me why."

"An interesting idea, however, I need to know, why? And frankly, our personal appraisal of Mrs. Maefield's does not give us reason to doubt her. If not for the weather, and the style of life as we know it, I could consider a closer look at the time frame. But there is nothing to raise my interest," Burroughs said, his frustration showing in his face. "And really, Miss Cunningham, a defense attorney would have no problem defending Mrs. Maefield on this. So what if she misread her clock? Maybe it was ten to four instead of five," he smiled critically.

He hated to do it, because he enjoyed her visit, but he had no more time. He explained that he would be in court for the next two days giving testimony in another murder case and he had to prepare for his appearance. He rose to signal that. Charlene understood. She stuck the photograph, note pad and pen into her shoulder bag. She stood.

"Thank you! I really appreciate your time. But one more question? I understand Reverend Maefield had a visitor the afternoon before his death. Any clue as to who this was?"

Burroughs had to admit this lady was a pro. She had inside information from somewhere. He hesitated to answer, yet, who knows how good she might be in helping him? One thing he had learned in his police work—take whatever help you can get.

"What brand of lipstick do you wear, Miss Cunningham?"

"You know his visitor was a woman?" Her surprise was obvious.

"You find me a woman who uses pink *Royal Lipstick by DuBarry* and who chain smokes Chesterfields and I'll buy you a carton of each."

He escorted her down the hall. It amused him how many officers suddenly had business in the hall.

"By the way," Burroughs asked, as they reached the lobby and he was about to say his final goodbye, "who was that church employee who described Mrs. Maefield as a 'sexy lady?'"

Charlene would have been disappointed had he not asked. "Mr. Wheeler, the church custodian."

"I see . . . and when did you speak to Mr. Wheeler?"

"Sunday afternoon! I interviewed him at Tommy's Place." She could see the wheels turning in his head, but his voice remained cool and he made no comment. "If you learn anything more, Detective Burroughs, will you call me? Here's my card. I check in at that number frequently for any new messages."

"Sure," he said, as he took the card. "And please do the same for me." He pushed the heavy, glass entrance door open, keeping an eye on her as she passed. She had a natural, confident walk, shoulders back, trained as a model, he thought. "Now you're what I call 'sexy,'" he murmured, as she made her way beyond his focus. Still, he did not take his eyes from her as she crossed Main Street. *And I don't believe you're a freelance writer. More than likely, you work for a law firm that's snooping before it approves that insurance claim.* "So, Everett Wheeler thinks Rhonda Maefield is a sexy lady," he mused. As that image set in, amusement left his face. His gut signaled him to think as a cop again. The effect was as a dagger delivered to his stomach.

"Tread lightly, pretty girl," he said and returned to his office.

*   *   *

Everett Wheeler had gone from Tommy's Place to The Hitching Post Tavern, twenty miles east of Tompkinsville. The rustic beer joint was his favorite watering hole and one of the few in the county that opened mid-morning. At the bar, he ordered a pitcher of beer and a bottle of "Southern Comfort" blended whisky. He paid the tab and took the setup to a table in the dark recesses of the log-built tavern. He downed a shot glass of whisky before hurriedly following it with a tall glass of beer.

Drinking steadily, he lamented the position he was now in.

*   *   *

Everett could not believe his bad luck. For four years, he had kept his church basement studio secret. The new minister arrives and discovers it within the week.

In hindsight, he should have dismantled the room last January.

In the late morning hours following Maefield's murder, he had followed two uniformed police officers as they checked all the church buildings. His heart sank to his stomach when they entered the basement storage area and started nosing behind the junk scattered there. He tried to steer them away from the mattresses he had stacked close to the west wall, but one cop ignored him and tried to pull away those that were jammed between the wall and the flat stack. If the "bull" had stopped to figure out what held them in place, he would have found the secret room. Everett knew, however, the mattresses wouldn't budge without releasing the foot brake rigged underneath. After a few tries, the cop gave up and walked away.

A half hour later, they brought a blood-sniffing dog into the storage room. Everett sweated a second time when the hound put her front paws up on the bundled mattresses, but her handler pulled her away. Satisfied that the killer was not hiding in the storage room, and that there were no bloody tracks anywhere on the floor, the cops moved on to other areas in the sprawling basement. Everett correctly doubted they would have another look. Therefore, he had decided to keep things as they were.

Now this. The "preacher" and his "vixen tramp" had seen the hidden room. "Damn!" he exclaimed. "She couldn't wait to get out of Tommy's yesterday. Hot to trot little bitch!" he cursed in his beer.

Everett admitted to himself that he was to blame. They would never have seen the studio door had he exercised his usual caution. He had left himself vulnerable when he used his studio late Saturday night to do a photo-shoot of a young hooker he had met on the Atlantic City boardwalk. But she must have been high on something, because she suddenly turned pale and complained she needed fresh air. Before he took her serious, she went out like a light. When he finally got her awake, worried she might die there, he hurried her out of the building. In his haste, he neglected to roll back the mattresses.

But none of that mattered to him now. For him, the burning question was where did Flynn get a key? He considered this as critical, because the answer could explain other unanswered questions since Maefield's death. "Yah, perhaps, it would have been premature to kill those two without knowing all the facts," he muttered with indifference to anyone close enough to hear. "First, I have to know how they got in there."

He returned to the bar for a second pitcher of beer. He figured he had all day to hide out and plan his moves. The "boiler makers" helped him gather courage and he loved the collective taste of whisky and beer.

*   *   *

As Charlene Cunningham moved down the concrete steps of
City Hall and crossed Main Street, her deception bothered her.
She conceded she had not fooled Detective Burroughs. And now
she felt guilty about deceiving Jerry Flynn. She should tell him
her true purpose. She started strolling through the cool, heavily
shaded city park. With a mild breeze whispering between
branches of the tall American elm trees, the fragrance of spring
stirred her. She heard the cathedral clock as it bonged the
eleventh hour and headed in that direction. Pigeons ruled the
twisting walkways and she had to circle around their assemblies
as they fed off bits of bread spread by bench sitters, most of
them elderly folks, who appeared annoyed when their winged
friends scattered as she approached. Charlene's plan was to
exit on Church Street, cross to the church grounds and hike
over the hill to Shepherd House, where she would surprise
Jerry.

Halfway through Tompkins Park, she thought back to her
meeting with Everett Wheeler yesterday afternoon. She felt
especially guilty that she had avoided telling Jerry about it. She
knew Jerry would not reform this man. "God, what a far out idea,"
she mumbled. "Wheeler is a sexual predator, a nut case." In
retrospect, she believed him responsible for the hidden room
and everything in it, then too for the terror inflicted on them
while they fled. "Why would he have tried to trap us there, if not
to kill us?" she asked herself.

She rehearsed in her mind how she would tell Jerry about
her real job and her real reasons for visiting Tompkinsville.
Together they would call Detective Burroughs and describe what
they had seen in the hidden and locked basement room last
night. She felt she could trust the policeman and that he would
know what to do. Only her promise to Jerry had kept her from
already telling Burroughs about the room. She had withheld
information, which, as a private detective, could hurt her
credibility. Burroughs needed a reason to focus his murder

investigation on Everett and information about the studio would have been enough for a search warrant.

But Charlene could not help how she felt about Jerry. He had charmed her with his polite, gentle and kind manner. He had satisfied her with his lovemaking in a way she had seldom experienced it. Beneath his raw passion, she had encountered a warm sensitivity to her needs and had felt comfortable in his intimacy. She considered their time together as much more than mere physical attraction. Obviously, she had not been his first. Indeed, he was as practiced as she was. Still, it was different. He had cradled her, bathed her and fed her. She wanted, needed, had to have more of his affection. She refused to think of this as love. But what did she know about love? Maybe she was falling for Jerry Flynn.

Was she ready, however, to be totally up front? She worried that she might not have time this morning to explain it all, that he would misunderstand and think bad things about her. Could she divulge her whole interview with Everett Wheeler?

There were other negatives. Her meeting with Madge Todd scratched the sore surface of her mind. That interview, too, she had kept from Jerry. She was sure Madge knew more about Rhonda Maefield than she had let on. What was Madge hiding? And while Charlene did not disclose it to Detective Burroughs, Madge, more than Everett, had confirmed Rhonda as a woman in disguise. And what about Madge visiting the manse the afternoon before the murder? No doubt, Burroughs had found an ashtray full of cigarette butts. Was Madge Todd, Reverend Maefield's unidentified Sunday-afternoon visitor? So far as she knew, Madge neither smoked nor wore modish pink lipstick. But there was familiarity in her perfume. And what about those panties she had taken from the drawer in the studio? The perfume odor she couldn't place? It was as though someone had dropped them there and forgotten about them. The idea that they could have belonged to Madge Todd struck her. Could she have modeled for Everett Wheeler? On that note, her mood turned reactive and suspicious. "I shouldn't consider it," she mulled. "I'm overreacting because of her interest in Jerry. That's silly, unprofessional."

Suddenly, Charlene felt foolish. Maybe surprising Jerry wasn't such a good idea. It's too soon and we both have other things to do.

Twenty feet from Church Street, Charlene reversed herself, and strolled in the direction of her parked car. She had left it on the street in a two-hour metered space. As she left the cool shade of Tompkins Park, she felt the intensity of what forecasters were calling an unusual long heat wave for this early in June. The temperature had soared to ninety degrees. With the humidity, the clammy air was oppressive. By the time she reached her MG, she had turned irritable and uncomfortable. Going immediately to the driver's side, she flung her shoulder bag through the opened window, where it struck the opposite car door. Inside, the car was like sitting in a furnace. She thought to collapse the roof so she could get the wind, but again hesitated, fearing she would have difficulty securing it when she needed to. She turned the ignition, and pulled away from the curb. Just as she did, the passenger-side door flung open. She braked, reached across the seat, grabbed the door handle and pulled shut. Impatient now, she gunned the motor and hurried into noonday traffic.

*　　*　　*

Charlene looked forward to relaxing in air-conditioned comfort at The Green Onion Inn. Instead, she entered the Sahara Desert. An economy-minded maid had turned off the cold air unit. She looked to see what she had to do and set the knob at high cool. It would take twenty minutes to do any good. She had no plans to wait.

Stripping naked, she moved into the bathroom. She turned on the tub cold-water faucet, latched it for the showerhead, and stood outside letting the icy spray moisten and cool her body. She was about to step under when the telephone rang. Maybe she should ignore it, but fearful she might miss Jerry, she returned to the bedroom. She picked up the telephone on the third ring. She answered with a friendly hello and waited for a voice. Silence greeted her.

"Hello!" she said a second time. "What room are you calling?"

After a long pause, she hung up and returned to the bathroom, where she got into the tub shower. The force of cold water had just begun to pass over her when the telephone rang. She bounded from the tub. Grabbing a towel, she collected it around her shoulders and, dripping water across the carpet, she picked up, this time on the sixth ring.

"Yes, who is this, please?"

No one answered. She waited a few seconds before clicking the receiver dead. She heard a ready-for-dial buzz. She dialed the motel switchboard to ask for an explanation. The switchboard operator said a gentleman's voice had asked for her room. The same voice had called several times earlier. The operator had no explanation for why the caller did not identify himself.

Sitting on the edge of the bed, her address book open and motel notepaper propped up on a thick telephone directory, she had the motel operator dial her office, which also served as an answering service with a phony name. There were two messages. One was from a man named Jack Burns, a research analyst who had the information she had asked for. Jack was a pro at finding out almost anything about a person's medical history, finances and other confidential information she could use to size up a personality. His services did not come cheap. In a million dollar insurance claim, however, Charlene could afford to buy Jack Burns' time.

The second message was from a woman named Lilly Palmer. She had given no clue as to what she wanted. Charlene wrote out the number Palmer had left her secretary. She recognized it as a Tompkinsville exchange. She gave the operator the number for Mrs. Palmer.

As she waited for someone to pick up, she thought about going to the car for her notebook, but decided it was too much trouble to get dressed and suffer in the hot sun while she looked beneath her car seat. She found more motel stationary in the bed-stand. She would copy any new information into her notebook first chance tonight.

With no answer at the Palmer number, she asked for long-distance and dialed the telephone number of Jack Burns.

*　　*　　*

Everett Wheeler liked it when a woman sounded frightened of a silent phone. When he tried this tactic on Charlene a third time, he never expected she would shut him out by either taking the phone off the hook or monopolizing the line for this long. He had tried every twenty minutes for the last hour and gotten a busy signal. "How can anyone talk this long?" he asked as he slammed the phone. "Who on earth could she gab to for this long?" On his last attempt, he argued and cursed the motel switchboard operator for not interrupting and putting him through. She hung up on him. Loudly protesting, he stumbled to his chair at the table and slouched, then, looked up bleary eyed at a Moose head mounted on the tavern wall, and raised his glass as if to a living soul. "May the best man win!" he sniggered and chug-a-lugged his glass full of beer in a matter of seconds. Turning the glass upside-down, he placed it ever so gently on the table. Saluting the deer head, he said, "I win!" He filled his shot-glass with whisky and gulped it down in a flash, then slapped it soundly on the table. For a few seconds, he sat still and silent.

It was time to try again. Using the table for support, he got to his feet, emptied his pockets of all his change and, determining he had enough for one more telephone call, he staggered in that direction.

"Little bitch," he announced, "I'm going to whip your pretty tail."

CHAPTER 8

THE BURDEN OF SECRETS

Monday Afternoon, June 11

Michael Todd made his way east to New Jersey's shore. His destination was Stone Harbor, twenty-five miles south of Atlantic City, where Sarah Draper and her husband owned a remote beach bungalow. The cottage had electricity, but that was about its only modern amenity. There was neither a telephone line nor a road to its door. Michael had visited the rudimentary summer place many times. And while pleasure had prompted previous visits, this afternoon he had murder on his mind.

* * *

Michael had met Sarah Draper last July when she had offered her assistance as he and Madge worked with a group of children, including Sarah's stepson and their son, Chip, in a 4-H tomato-growing project. With five boys and seven girls, ages eight through ten, to manage every Wednesday afternoon, he and Madge accepted Sarah's offer to use her extra-wide two-car garage as a place to build a display booth for the county fair where the children would show off their project. Her palatial home on the north side of town was a perfect setting, made especially so by Sarah's open invitation to enjoy her in-ground swimming pool, a nice reward for the children after completing their afternoon projects. And Sarah, always welcoming with open arms and a counter full of cold soda, potato chips and other snack food, seemed the perfect hostess. Certainly, she appeared a far cry from her reputation as a moody, crass, insulting woman—those descriptions having come to public knowledge from people who had done business with her as owner and manager of a popular Atlantic City catering hall. Moreover, rumor had it that Sarah was a "gold digger," in that Mr. Draper, a New York banker, was her third husband after two Reno divorces from other wealthy men. Which part of Sarah Madge reacted to could be a matter of debate; however, after their third Wednesday afternoon, Madge commented to Michael on Sarah's loose midriff that revealed (in Madge's words) her "pink blossoms." Madge had said this, not to be catty, or even because she thought the children needed protection from glimpsing a woman's bare breasts. No, she had meant the remark as a way to get a laugh, or at least a knowing wink out of Michael. Instead, he gruffly responded that he hadn't noticed and added, "Madge, why do you have to be such a prude?"

Michael had noticed. If honest, he should have admitted focusing on Sarah's "blossoms" every time she leaned forward. Moreover, Michael had enjoyed Sarah's openness, her deep-throated laughter and her flashy, playful ways. Madge had never considered this nor had she perceived that Sarah had set her sights on Michael. So, when Sarah asked for help moving the finished 4-H display from her garage to the county fairgrounds, Madge volunteered Michael's truck and labor.

* * *

"Madge shouldn't have done that," Michael raged as he stepped on the gas to overtake a slow moving dump truck. "But then, damn it, maybe she did know what Sarah Draper was all about!" he shouted as if transporting a deaf passenger. Racing an oncoming car, he moved into his lane with only seconds to spare. The near miss had no effect on him. He speeded on, insensitive to the danger his impatience posed

*   *   *

Charlene Cunningham doodled on a motel notepad while waiting for Jack Burns to answer. She heard the tenth ring and was about to hang up. "Jack Burns here!"

"Wow! I was just about to slam you out of my life," Charlene scolded.

"Charlene, it's my pleasure, sweetheart."

Jack was a "sweetheart" person. He used the name for all the young women in the office and sometimes for the older ones. She guessed Jack was in his late fifties. She had met him in person only once and had found him a fatherly, caring type of man, sentimental and unpretentious. She liked talking to him and she knew he could help, not only with information about Daniel and Rhoda Maefield, but with new names as well.

"What have you got?"

"It's all in front of me. Here's what you want to know, sweetheart, about Rhonda Maefield," he began.

For thirty minutes, Jack Kelly laid out facts about Rhonda's parents. Among them, he recited the gory details of how the pastor had died in Berlin at Plotzensee Prison, a place of torture and use of a guillotine for Germans and other foreign nationals convicted of espionage. Rhonda's mother, a Jew by birth, according to Jack's investigation, went from Ravensbruk Prison to Auschwitz-Birkenau, where she died in the gas chamber just days before allied armies liberated the death camp.

"I don't have any information on how Rhonda managed to survive in Germany after her mother's arrest or how she got out of the country. That material is highly classified and, without Mrs. Maefield's cooperation, I can't crack it. All the record shows is that in January of 1937, age seventeen, Rhonda showed up in Switzerland and from there she immigrated to the United States, where she lived with a German family in Milwaukee, cousins of her father. Already proficient in English, she graduated from high school in 1938. A brilliant girl, she accepted an all-expenses-paid scholarship to Barnard, the women's liberal arts college at Columbia, in Manhattan. In 1942, she graduated. By then, she had married a Columbia history professor, twenty years older than her, who wore a second hat as pastor of a non-denominational church in Harlem. As you know, sweetheart, his name was Daniel Maefield. They were married in Scarsdale, New York, in a civil ceremony. You'd think, seeing as how he was a minister, they would have had a church wedding. But that's what the marriage record shows. The date was December 21, 1939. For the next fifteen years, they lived in the Harlem neighborhood in a church-owned apartment. He did a lot of traveling, lecturing, writing books. She spent her time registered as a full-time student. She completed a doctoral degree program in corporation law and labor relations. For a few years, she taught at NYU. I should pause here to say both Mr. and Mrs. Maefield were independently wealthy. In 1955, she took title to her father and mother's estates, worth over two million then, the collectable amount that had survived the war. And Daniel Maefield, who had also inherited from his parents, was worth one and a half million at the time of his murder. He bought the half-million insurance policy with double indemnity for accidental death from Lloyds of London shortly after marriage and named Rhonda soul beneficiary. Because of their age difference, it was a wise investment. Anyway, in 1954, the couple left Manhattan for Tompkinsville and Maefield's assumption of the pastorate at First Presbyterian Church. After four years, Rhonda went back to Columbia as a full-time student at the law school. It may interest you to know that while at Columbia Law, instead of living at her husband's campus apartment, which she could have had free, she set herself up in midtown Manhattan. At Columbia, she registered as a commuter, no New York City address. It seems she was deliberate about keeping her apartment a secret."

"How do you know this?"

"Telephone records. Calls from the Maefield number in Tompkinsville to an unlisted number in mid Manhattan. Also, Rhonda was careless a week ago and an envelope of old canceled checks found its way into the outside trash container. There's a lot there and it'll take time to sort them out, but one check that caught my eye was written to a Manhattan real estate firm."

Charlene asked for the street and number of the apartment.

"Don't have that, sweetheart. Ma Bell won't talk and neither will the real estate broker. But I'll get it. Give me a few days on that.

"After her husband's death, Rhonda stayed with Charles and Loretta Collins at their apartment on Park Avenue, north of Fifty-Second Street, very expensive."

By now, Charlene's ear was flat and aching. Jack began to go over ground about Daniel Maefield she already knew. She needed a rest.

"I hate to rush you, Jack, but can you tell me if you learned anything peculiar or surprising about Mrs. Maefield?"

"Yah, I was just coming to that, sweetheart. During her college years and after marriage, she frequented a little backdoor club in the village that opened on Friday and Saturday night named 'Paul's'. You had to pay a joiner's fee and then a cover charge to get in. Real private and cozy. Patrons sat on pillows around low tables sipping herbal tea laced with a narcotic while watching a live copulation on a sunken stage. Sometimes they viewed girl with girl and boy with boy, if you know what I mean. Of course, to stay above the law, they billed this stuff as 'art in motion'. How about that? These places were the rage in San Francisco, but according to an underground sex newspaper from the period, there were a half dozen such clubs in Manhattan. My information is that if you visited one, you visited them all."

"How do you know Rhonda was a member at Paul's?"

"The cops made a surprise raid and picked her up in the sweep. I came across her name and twenty-six others in a story printed in the *New York Daily News*. The headline read, *University Students Nabbed in Drug, Sex Raid*. As far as I can tell, they never charged her with anything. No record of her in any police files. No fingerprints or mug shot. They probably released her and the others before the sun was up. The cops shut the place down for a few months and that was what the raid was all about anyway."

"What's the date on the raid, Jack?"

"February 14, 1944! That's all I had time to dig up on the lady. Other than visiting Paul's, she appears a model of morality and virtue, sweetheart. Anything else I can do for you?"

"Yes, go deeper, Jack. Look into Rhonda's social life in the last five years. I want you to check on the lawyer couple, Charles and Loretta Collins. You said Rhonda stayed with them for two months. I'm interested in knowing about the Collins's friends. Above all, get me the address of Rhonda's midtown apartment."

"I'll go there, sweetheart. Anything else?"

"Yes, take down this name: Everett Wheeler. He served in the U.S. Army occupation forces in Japan from September to November of 1945. Why did the army dump Wheeler early?" She gave Jack Kelly Wheeler's date of birth, home address and auto tag number.

"You got it, sweetheart. You call me Thursday."

"Thanks, Jack. Keep up the good work!" She hung up.

Charlene stuffed her telephone notes into her overnight bag. She wanted to punch herself for not bringing her notebook into the room. She had so much to add. But it would have to wait.

The room had cooled to the point of freezing and once more Charlene fought with the dials on the AC unit to control both the noise and the blast of air. She thought about calling Jerry again, but decided to make it the last thing she did before leaving the room.

Last night's lost sleep had finally caught up with her. She needed shuteye. She took the phone off the cradle, set her little travel alarm clock for five thirty and got under the covers. Within five minutes, she was fast asleep.

*   *   *

Michael Todd recollected his ten-month affair with Sarah Draper.

On an August afternoon ten months ago, the weather was much like today—hot, hazy and humid. Sarah, fresh from a swim in her pool, met him in her driveway attired in a T-shirt that fell freely to the short rise of her swimsuit bottom. He did not miss the outline of her wet bikini top where the T-shirt clung to it. With her long blond hair dripping, and her trim, dark-tanned legs glistening, she looked limber and inviting.

Very athletic and with lots of energy, Sarah shared equally in lifting the heavy display-booth equipment into the cargo bed of Michael's truck. When they finished, she suggested they cool off in the pool and offered to lend him one of her husband's bathing suits.

Michael declined, but Sarah would not accept his refusal as final. The least he could do was join her in a cold beer. Besides, if he didn't mind, she continued, she needed his assistance moving another piece of furniture. She explained that her husband was away on business this week and she wanted to surprise him on his return with an antique bureau she had purchased for their bedroom. Having taken delivery, she now decided to put it against another wall.

Michael followed Sarah into the house and sat at her kitchen table where she uncapped six beers. Before he finished his first, she was on her second. All the while, the witty, wisecracking lady gabbed and chain-smoked. Indeed, she amused Michael by how she lit one cigarette from the mini butt of the dying one. After his second beer, and Sarah into her fourth, Michael said he had to get back to his office. But Sarah had not forgotten his promise to help her move the bureau. She showed him into the bedroom and pointed to a tall, bulky bureau that was unbelievably heavy. Together they pushed, pulled and wiggled the old piece across twenty feet of carpet to its new location. Perspiration poured off their bodies. As Michael rested, with his hands clutching the top of the bureau, he turned his head to see Sarah lift and discard her T-shirt, revealing her model figure in her yellow bikini swimsuit. In her hand, she held a bottle of Johnson's baby oil.

He watched as she poured it into her palms and rubbed it on her arms and upper torso.

"It guards against dry skin," she explained and looked up to stare at him while he watched. "Come over here, Michael," she invited. "I need you to rub where I can't reach."

He approached with caution.

"Don't be bashful, Michael. It'll do you good," she said laughing.

Sarah handed him the bottle of oil. In the next motion, she dropped her top from her breasts. He started to look away. She caught his arm. "Oh, come on, Michael. Don't act like you never saw them before!" She turned her back to him. "Please!"

He poured oil into his hands and brushed it on her shoulders, then down her back, but when she reared into him, he moved his hands onto her breasts. She ground her rump against him, purring as if a kitten. After several seconds, she did an about-face to surround him with her arms and engage his lips.

But she was in a hurry and quickly wrestled him on to the bed, where her haste both surprised and elated him. In all his years of marriage, Michael could not recall Madge timing an orgasm with his ejaculation. Nor would Sarah allow him to reject her because he had finished. In the hour following, she had him do things with her, which he had only thought of as the stuff of dirty books. Then, naked, they jumped into the swimming pool and cavorted into the late afternoon.

Michael had never cheated before, that is, if he didn't count sessions with prostitutes. And although at first he regretted what had happened, Sarah's fast and aggressive performance lulled him to meet her the very next day. Two days later, they met at her summer beach house. And, a week later, they spent the afternoon at a motel on the outskirts of Camden. In the months that followed, they met steadily, sometimes twice a week, in cloak-and-dagger style at various places. Sarah saw each date as a game prompting bizarre sex practices. She made up the rules and Michael followed them.

In the beginning, neither of them wanted their relationship

to interfere with their respective marriages. Yet, early on, they exchanged intimate gifts and hand-written notes. A day hardly passed when they did not use secret means to talk over the telephone. All the while, Michael worried about getting caught, fearing scandal and embarrassment if his family learned of his affair. Also worrisome was what a divorce would mean to his presidency of T&T Produce. After all, his position depended on Madge's percent of ownership. If Madge and her father joined forces against him, they would control the company. When he told Sarah this, she laughed in derision and replied that it didn't matter to her anymore. She had just told her husband she wanted a divorce. "Maybe this time I'll go to Mexico," she gloated, "and you can come with me. Then you can sell your farm interests and work for me," she roared with laughter, but he knew she meant what she had said.

This news horrified Michael, but not enough to curb his appetite for her sexual readiness. Even when her comical wit turned to belligerent ridicule, he continued to see her. Not until March, when Sarah's sharp tongue and jealous manner reached new heights of ugliness, did he make a concerted effort to stop seeing her. By then Sarah's mood swings and chronic complaining turned hostile. Violent arguments broke out between them, but to his dismay, their sexual play continued. Then, in early April— away on business—Michael did not see Sarah for two weeks. In that time, he realized he could live without what he had come to refer to as "Sarah-sex." When they met a week later, they argued and parted without even taking off their clothes. Michael genuinely hoped their affair was over.

He breathed a special sigh of relief two weeks later, when a letter from Sarah arrived informing him she had a new lover, and—in an effort to dig her dagger deep—she mocked him by writing: ***What made sex durable with you was the knowledge that I had real men waiting to fuck me good.*** Sarah was a big fan of the F-word.

Michael had no regrets as he tore the letter in tiny pieces and stuffed it in the trashcan. He was beyond jealousy. He genuinely believed he would never see his "lady friend" again. When June rolled around without further communication, he believed she was finally out of his life. He should have known better.

This morning at Tommy's Place, Everett Wheeler let loose that he knew all about his affair with Sarah Draper. Michael tried to explain that it was over. He begged Everett to keep quiet. But Wheeler simply grinned and extracted his pound of flesh. He was in a bargaining mood, he said. If Michael spread the word about "the new preacher bedding down a scarlet woman at the manse last night," he would keep quiet about him and Sarah. Otherwise, over or not, Everett threatened, "Everyone in Tompkinsville will know about Mr. Todd and Mrs. Draper."

Michael left Tommy's for his office believing matters could not get worse. Then the postman walked in with a Special Delivery envelope addressed in Sarah's handwriting and return address. His hands shook as he read the enclosed letter and viewed photos she had described as samples of what she would make public if he did not renew his relationship with her. His stomach churned as he recalled the night in her recreation room when she had photographed them as they cavorted in costumes and masks in front of a camera on a timer. She must have set up a hidden camera also to have taken him unmasked. The second photo, more shocking than the first, she must have managed at a motel. He couldn't believe his eyes. If he didn't get those photos away from Sarah, she would blackmail him into oblivion.

*　　*　　*

Michael parked his car next to Sarah's Mercedes near an abandoned boat dock that once serviced the bayside channel. This part of Stone Harbor was a bird sanctuary. From the boat-dock to the next inlet, except for the Draper house, built and grandfathered long before this area became restricted, there were no houses. Vacationers wouldn't be on these beaches for another two weeks, when schools closed. So, today, only Sarah's car occupied the sandy parking area. Still, to look less conspicuous to beachcombers, Michael changed out of his business clothes into a swimsuit. A baseball cap and dark sunglasses completed his wardrobe. He took a loaded Smith & Wesson .357 Magnum revolver out of the glove compartment, wrapped it in a towel and held it at his side.

As Michael left his car and began walking the mile of beach toward the Draper house, he didn't know whether he would kill Sarah or make love to her. He hated to admit it, but right now, he missed her sensual body and wild sex. "What's one more fling in the scheme of things?" he asked himself, resolved to do whatever necessary to learn how she had arranged for the photos and to secure any additional pictures that could embarrass him.

*   *   *

Occasionally, Everett Wheeler had ranted in his drunkenness, but most of the day he kept quiet and the bartender ignored him. By early afternoon, he had fallen asleep, conked out cold, his head on the table. That didn't look good and, with more patrons arriving, the bartender decided to get Wheeler out of the way.

It took the bartender and two patrons to carry Everett to his truck. With great effort, the three men lifted his dead weight into the driver's side of the bench seat. They gave him a final shove, so that his head fell on the passenger side. In spite of the mid-afternoon sun cooking the cab, they closed the door and left him there to bake.

*   *   *

Sarah and Sam Draper's beach house stood less than a hundred feet from where waves galloped at high tide before dying and falling inward to the eternal depths from which they had arisen. A beautiful location, but doomed by the eroding ocean, perhaps it would take only one more winter storm to wash the house off its pillars and put the front yard under high tide.

Michael approached the house from the ocean side. He felt a chill in the afternoon wind as it blew in a powerful gust and as ice-cold seawater passed above his ankles. A hundred feet off, he could see Sarah sitting on the gray-board porch, reclining in an Adirondack lawn chair, her long, golden hair trapped behind her head, her shapely body accented in a blue one-piece bathing suit. He shouted her name, even knowing she would not hear him above the ponderous surf. He wondered, however, why she made no effort to greet him. Surely, by now she must see him. Closing within fifty feet, he thought she might be asleep. Shielding his eyes from the blowing sand, he ran toward the porch, yelling and waving. But mounting the first porch step, he saw her vacant eyes staring and knew she was dead.

She bled from her left breast. Blood flowed inside her swimsuit and out the leg opening, coating the painted white chair on which her thighs rested, dripping into a puddle on the scattered sand and bleached boards of the porch. A second wound showed as a red stain surrounding a tiny tear in her crotch. Sarah had taken two bullets aimed with a message.

Michael backed off the step. The wounds were fresh. The murderer may be about. He regarded himself an open target. There was no protection and no place to hide. He retreated toward the surf, felt its icy surge ram him and move above his knees. He paused, changed his mind. Slow and cautious, he returned to the porch. This time he touched Sarah's neck below the ear and felt her warmth and stillness. She had not been this way for long. His heart pounded as a kettledrum as he passed through the opened door, his Magnum drawn and ready to fire.

He faced a ransacked living room—furniture turned over, drawers emptied on the floor, clothes flung everywhere. Magazines, wall pictures, books lay mangled and strewn. In the kitchen, the refrigerator door hung open. Food and garbage were scattered on the countertop and floor, the table upended. Only the outside roar of the surf disturbed the silence.

In quiet fashion, he made his way down the short hall. He

looked fleetingly inside two bedrooms and saw nothing disturbed. He reached the rear bedroom, the one he and Sarah had always used. The door was open.

Turning with caution into the doorframe, he saw the murderer. A man, dressed only in bathing trunks, had stretched out on his back on the facing bed. Because of pillows propping up his torso and head, his eyes stared straight at him. For a moment, Michael thought he might be intruding on someone's rest. But before that idea became reality, Michael saw blood on the pillows behind the man's head and his hands clutching a long barrel .22-caliber automatic pistol, the barrel still in his mouth.

Stunned, yet relieved, Michael took a deep breath and relaxed his revolver to his side. He stepped into the room. As his eyes searched the dead man, he saw a thick envelope tucked in the waistband of his swim trunks. He hesitated only a second before drawing it out. Holding his gun under his arm, he opened the flap and quickly browsed the contents. He saw more than what he had come for.

*   *   *

Charlene awoke on the first beep of her travel alarm. The clock hands pointed to five thirty. She sat up quickly and hammered the beeping alarm to submission. She peeled away the covers and galloped into the bathroom. This time, she took a long, hot, soapy shower. She toweled dry. In the bedroom, she showed annoyance for bringing so few changes of clothes, especially underwear. There was no time to wash anything. She decided it was too hot anyway for a bra and stockings and stuffed the ones she had taken off into her overnight bag. She pulled on her last pair of fresh panties and then the same thin cotton dress she had worn this morning. She made up her face—just a little eye shadow and a touch of lipstick. She left her hair as it was. She went around the room looking for any personal things she may have missed. At six o'clock, she had the motel operator telephone the manse. She let it ring ten times. Disappointed,

Charlene hung up and vacated the motel room. She checked out and headed north on the New Jersey Turnpike.

Her mood was one of melancholy, for she had hoped she would get Jerry to meet her. They could rendezvous somewhere for the night and go their separate ways tomorrow morning. Where was he? Miss Blatty had sounded so sure he would be at home waiting for her to call at six. Missing him grieved her so much she stopped at the next turnpike rest area. A long distance telephone call, she got the operator to dial it.

She had learned to keep a roll of quarters in her purse. It did not matter to her that *Ma Bell* profited twice off her. She dropped her last four quarters into the slot for the eighty-cent charge. She made a mental note to replenish her quarters. Jerry answered on the second ring.

"Oh, I'm so glad I got you. Where have you been?" She did not wait for his answer. "Listen, I'm at a rest stop north of exit four on the New Jersey Turnpike. Can you meet me here?

"Charlene, I would love to, but I can't. I've got a meeting at eight and then I have to visit again at the hospital. Early this morning, a tractor turned over injuring one of our church members. He was hurt real bad. They are operating on him now. I have to go by and pray with the family. His wife plans to stay the night. What time will you get back?"

"I'm due in New York early tomorrow morning, Jerry. I'll look for an overnight this side of the George Washington Bridge. That's too far for you to drive. I'll call you around eleven."

The operator interrupted, "That will be twenty cents for the next minute, please."

"I'm hanging up, Jerry. I'm out of change. I'll call . . . "

The telephone went dead.

*　　*　　*

Michael Todd sat at his desk in the management building of T&T Produce drinking Vodka and orange juice. The office staff had all gone home two hours ago, but his secretary had left him a pile of papers to read and sign. It was hard to concentrate. It would not be easy to erase from his memory the image of Sarah and Sam, her husband. Michael knew that as the identity of the dead man. There would be an extensive police investigation to confirm what had actually happened, but he was sure he had seen the aftermath of a murder-suicide.

He hadn't waited around to answer questions. He had left the Stone Harbor beach house for someone else to discover and to report the carnage. Although the scene had shocked him, and he had returned to his office fifteen minutes ago in a state of nervous tension, he felt no remorse. Indeed, he felt eternally grateful to Sam Draper for doing the nasty deed. He thanked his lucky stars he had not met another soul during his walk to and from the Draper house. And he had put behind him the thought that had he arrived ten minutes earlier he could have become Sam Draper's first kill. He counted himself doubly lucky to have snatched the envelope.

He finished his drink and poured another. He leaned back in his office chair and revisited the last three hours, the time it had taken him to get back to his T&T office.

*   *   *

Michael drove the coast road from Stone Harbor north to Atlantic City. Still in his bathing suit, he found a place to park on Atlantic Avenue at the south end of the boardwalk. There was almost no one around when he began strolling along the beach. He picked out a place close to the surf, but far away from scattered bathers. Sitting on his towel, he emptied the thick envelope containing prints and negatives. He set the negative bundle aside to examine the stack of glossy pictures. Many were no surprise.

He remembered well the evening in Sarah's recreation room when she set a camera in front of an exercise mat. Their faces covered with dog and cat masks, Sarah had him pretend he was a Saint Barnard, while she acted out the part of a female cat. But she had also managed a hidden camera to catch his face without the mask. "How nasty!" he cried out. "How she schemed!" He slipped two of the more risqué photos back into the envelope. He browsed through the rest of the snapshots. He counted fifty in all. None had anything to do with him. They showed numerous male subjects with Sarah, though it would be hard to know her because she was always in disguise or her face cleverly blacked out. As with the pictures she had taken of him, these too set a spurious tone, some boarding on bondage. The degree of her promiscuity surprised him. According to dates stamped on the back of prints, some photos dated back five years and a few showed she had played games with other men while she kept company with him. He looked hard, but could not recognize any faces. Meticulous, he compared negatives with prints and satisfied himself that at least he had negatives of all the pictures where he was the subject.

Michael could only imagine what this collection of photos had meant to Sam Draper, especially, if up to now, Sam had lived unsuspecting of his wife's extra-marital affairs and sexual interests. He pictured Sam surprising Sarah at the beach house and confronting her with these pictures. An argument broke out. Michael could perceive Sarah's sarcasm and humiliation of her husband, then, Sam raging through the house perhaps in search of more photos, while Sarah went out on the porch to sit placidly as her husband's vehemence took its course. But Sam, crazy with revulsion, steams outside and, before she has time to react, he shoots her. He is not, however, so completely out of his mind that he doesn't kill her with a sense of purpose, and aims carefully into her breast and groin. Nor is his message completed. He goes into the bedroom where he shoots himself, but leaves the pictures stuck in his waistband, a way to explain his violence. "That's what I believe happened," Michael said, a glum smile creasing his lips.

He set the pack of photos aside in the sand and looked inside their envelope for a smaller envelope. He slid it out and opened to a single picture, no negative with it, but matching what Sarah had sent him in the morning mail. This was what he had specifically come to get. Unlike the other photos, another person had taken this candid shot with a telephoto lens, perhaps from a motel closet or through a peephole. There was no question as to the identity of the subject. And the sex act was so perverted, Michael shuttered at the thought of its use for blackmail. God forbid, he worried. He had still to find others in this set and their negatives. "Everett Wheeler!" he shouted through clenched teeth. "I'll kill 'm!"

Amid the sound of the roaring surf, he used his hands to dig a shallow hole in the sand. He had brought a can of cigarette lighter fluid with him and squirted from this onto the pile of pictures he had arranged. With his lighter, he lit them, creating a mini inferno. He fed the fire the rest of his photos and then the negatives. He stared long and hard at the single photo left, but decided to put this into the envelope with the other two he had decided to keep. The flames disappeared. After picking up his towel, he used his foot to scatter the blackened sand and to cover ashes of burnt celluloid. He strolled to his car, where he changed into his business suit. He put the envelope in the glove compartment next to his revolver. An hour later, he was in his office calming himself with his Vodka and orange juice.

CHAPTER 9

EXPOSURES

Monday Evening, June 11

Everett awoke with a throbbing headache and his body in a sweat. He had no idea how he had gotten to the stifling confines of his truck cab and quickly rolled down the side windows. He looked at his wristwatch. It was six minutes to seven. Angry that so much time had passed, he peeled out of the parking field at the Hitching Post Tavern and headed for home.

* * *

As Michael Todd began putting away his papers and locking his desk, the telephone rang.

"Hi, Michael!" Madge said happily, but then in a provocative tone, "I expected you home by now. Do you want me to save supper?"

"No! I've got a meeting with the Boy Scout Council at eight. I thought you knew. I already grabbed a bite," he lied.

"Oh, maybe you'll meet Reverend Flynn there. I know he's invited. Do you know he's an Eagle Scout? Isn't that wonderful? I know you'll like him."

Madge's enthusiasm for the new minister set Michael back. He had meant to pass on to her the good news about a business deal she had single-handedly brokered. He needed to congratulate her for all her hard work. The truth was, the business could not afford to lose her, and regardless of his personal feelings, he relied on her at work. But her remark about Flynn annoyed him. He reacted to her excitement.

"Well, don't get too cuddly about him, Madge! The word's out that your hot-shot new pastor kept company overnight at the manse with a knock-out, blond hussy. She was seen leaving early this morning."

He had aggravated her. "It's nothing short of wicked gossip," she said testily.

"You mean you've already heard it?" he asked in a derisive tone.

"No, Michael! Some of us have better things to do with our time than to sit around listening to mindless snoops. But I'm curious! Who was your source of this newsworthy story?"

"None other than your own cousin, the eminent Everett Wheeler!"

Michael heard her grunt, knew he had gotten her goat with that information. In a haunting way, he enjoyed Madge's irritation.

"And when, may I ask, did you and Everett become such fast friends?" her voice bitter with emotion.

"Hey, Madge, don't get upset at me. I'm only the messenger. I'm just passing on a character evaluation so you can warn the ladies before getting too . . . a . . . cordial around the bachelor preacher. But then I guess I don't have to worry about you on that score, now do I?" he said with cutting ridicule in his voice.

"Michael, stop it! You know you can't believe what Everett says . . . And, what am I supposed to understand from that last remark?" she asked defensively, her hurt obvious in her voice.

"Madge, forget it!" he responded, unprepared for her challenge. "I thought this was something we could have a good laugh over. But obviously—"

She interrupted. "And where were you all afternoon today? You disappeared from the office without a trace."

"I had business out of town. No big deal!" he offered.

"Well, it is a big deal when people have no explanation and depend on you. Anyway, in case you forgot, tomorrow we start harvesting lettuce from the south fields. And Dad said to remind you that two refrigerator trucks are due in for loading around seven tomorrow morning."

Anything else, BOSS?" he squealed. "Can I go to the bathroom now?"

"Goodbye, Michael," her tone final. "Try to get home early tonight."

He heard the click and the dead silence following.

"She really took that news about Reverend Flynn to heart," he said to no one. "You'd think I'd tattled on her best friend. Why should she care?"

Michael gulped down the remainder of his drink. He sat motionless for several minutes. He stared ahead, his eyes tearing. Using a key on his car key chain, he unlocked the file drawer of his desk. He searched for only a few seconds. He ejected a folder. He looked into it, slipped out the Special Delivery envelope with Sarah's letter and photos. From his inside jacket pocket, he took the photos he had kept from Sam Draper's collection. Laying them all in front of him, he frowned at their gross images. Certain that Everett Wheeler was somehow responsible, he knew he had to do the man's bidding. But then a grin, more sinister than amused, crowded his face. "Who knows, I may have to thank the bastard just before I blow his brains out," he said contemptuously. Then, after a long sigh, he slipped all the photos and letter into the folder and placed it at the far end of the drawer before locking it there. Five minutes later, he was racing to his Boy Scout Council meeting at First Church.

*   *   *

Madge opened a can of dog food and spooned its contents into the bowl on the floor by the refrigerator. They had gotten their mature Welsh Corgi six months ago, but were not happy with its aggressive nature. Madge had complained to Michael that the dog didn't like children or strangers and she worried that the short legged, foxlike sheep dog would bite somebody. On the other hand, "Casper" was a good watchdog and she had to admit he acted friendly toward her.

"Probably because I'm the only one who feeds and grooms you," she said as she petted the little monster. She had taught the dog to wait patiently a yard from the bowl until she gave permission to advance.

"Okay, Casper," she said, "come get it!"

On 'get', the animal dropped his snout into the food.

"If only we could behave so well," she whispered.

She stepped onto the front porch and let the screen door slam behind her.

She relished the prospect of burning energy amid her rose bushes and dozens of other flowerbeds. She had worked at it late this afternoon, but the heat and humidity had driven her indoors. Now, with an hour until dark left, it was not as hot. She would devote what was left of daylight to her garden. From where she worked, she could also keep a watchful eye on the children as they played on the swing set and Jungle-Jim equipment Michael had assembled last summer. How much peace and happiness there is, yet, so much pain and ugliness, she remonstrated as she picked up her hand spade.

A gentle evening breeze blew across the open field. To take full advantage of it, she unbuttoned her shirt and let its halves hang open to her bare bosom. On her knees, she dug furiously into the soil. She turned out weeds and grass and shook the erring plants violently in her hands before tossing them into a nearby barrel for composting. Standing, she used her pitchfork to prepare a new patch for planting.

She thought again about the incongruity of Michael doing favors for Everett.

*   *   *

More than once as a child, Everett had put his hands on her breasts and other places. It had always appeared playful, but she had learned there was never anything innocent about her cousin's affectionate manner. She remembered when Everett had walked into her bedroom while she was getting ready for her sixteenth birthday party. He had caught her without a stitch of clothes on. Mortified by his intrusiveness, she had screamed at the top of her lungs. Instead of leaving, he had tried calming her by putting his arms around her. She had screamed again and then repeatedly until he put one hand over her mouth and another on her breast. As she struggled to get away, her mother charged into the room. Without hesitation, she pounced on her erring nephew, slapping him soundly across the face and pushing him out of the room. Her mom called him a dirty pervert and, as much as he had protested that it was all a misunderstanding, she continued beating on him and shouting hatreds until down the stairs and out of the house.

After that, Madge recalled, Everett was no longer welcome to walk into the Tompkins house without knocking. *"You wait for permission,"* Dad had scolded the only son of his only sister. In a house where strangers, including field hands, had free access, this was like a death sentence. The injunction has continued to this day.

So, there was no love for Everett in the Walter Tompkins household. And Michael, who had heard more about Everett's conduct than Madge, loathed him. Even at family gatherings, Michael avoided shaking his hand. Everett's feelings about her husband were just as bad. The two had not spoken a word to each other in the last five years. "So, why now?" Madge asked herself. "What has Everett got on my husband to make him his messenger-boy? Everett, that dirty-minded man! How hypocritical! The irony of him, of all people, spying on the minister's private guests." Yet, there was more about the news upsetting her. The thought that Charlene Cunningham had spent the night with Jerry Flynn upset her. And it wasn't just because such

news would slander the church. Jealousy, envy—whichever—
she felt it.

*   *   *

Less than thirty feet from where Madge tended her garden,
hidden eyes watched her every move. They belonged to Roberto
Ramous, who, minutes before she came to the garden, had stolen
into the packing barn a stone's throw from the Todd house.

The circumstances leading to this voyeurism began last
Thursday morning when the little Mexican in the cowboy hat
guided Ramous and twenty other workers out of the muddy
strawberry fields. As they huddled under a canvas shelter in the
pouring rain, Jorge erupted in anger. He marched into the midst
of the idle workers with a baseball bat in his hands demanding to
know who started the trouble. Manuel and several men Roberto
did not recognize held short shovels and pitchforks and, ignoring
the rain, they stood menacingly outside the circle. Any second,
Ramous expected a blow to his shins and another to his back.
He had wanted none of this. Yet, here he was among workers
whose politics he despised.

Jorge threatened, said they had three minutes to return to
work, began counting the seconds by staring at his wristwatch.
Suddenly this pretty owner lady drove up on a tractor. She turned
off the engine and dismounted. She didn't care that it was raining
hard. Dressed in men's overalls and a long plaid shirt—just as
she is now—soaked to the skin by the morning downpour, she
showed no discomfort as she broke into the circle of sixteen men
and four women.

She greeted them in friendly Spanish and never broke away
from the language as she asked how much they wanted to go
back to work. The little man stepped forward, politely removed
his cowboy hat and held it to his chest. In perfect English, he
apologized for the work stoppage and told her the workers should
be paid three cents more a quart for the rain day and two cents

more on strawberries this picking season. And the quota was not to change. The little guy called attention to unsafe working conditions, told the lady that workers demanded corrections and outlined ways to improve their welfare. She listened without comment. Then, answering again in Spanish, she asked if the representative would agree for today to two cents and one-cent increase for picking during normal weather. She promised to negotiate later about other matters. She could not offer more without consulting her partners.

There was a pause as the short Mexican calculated the offer in his head. He turned to a tall, very dark Mexican next to him and asked his opinion.

"Quick, I haven't all day," she said, switching to English, no longer sweet and patient as when she had entered the scene. "It's this or you leave our fields. I will call the local police and have you evicted if you don't go peaceful."

"We agree!" the little man snapped. "The quota, however, must not be raised."

She turned to Jorge Garcia: "It's okay! The quota remains at a hundred." Then turning to the little man, she commanded, "You go back to work immediately!"

The protesting workers cheered. Garcia walked off madder than hell. Some of those watching thought he had quit and berated him as he threw his baseball bat across the soggy field. The strike had ended. The pretty woman in pants got on her tractor and drove off.

After supper that night, Manuel summoned Ramous into a shed that served as an office.

"We know you're a wanted man, Antonio," he began, using Ramous' alias. Manuel held an overripe peach on the table and sliced it in half with his razor sharp knife. "We understand you cut up a Filipino scab in Florida last month and this after he caught you fucking his wife. That's your business. We don't give a shit. But his scab brothers want you bad, never mind the sheriff. You know why I tell you this?" Manuel smiled as he expertly carved the pit out of the fruit and poked a juicy section into his

mouth. He turned the knife tip toward Roberto's larynx and let
the soft fruit slide down his throat before speaking again. "If you
want to stay on your feet, you tell me what you know about the
little shit in the tall white hat and anyone who works for him?"

Ramous told Manuel what he knew, how the Mexican talked
to everyone in their bunkhouse about his organization for workers.
Ramous wanted nothing to do with his plans and told him so, but
he feared the man might set his bullies on him. "He looks like a
pushover, but he got muscle backing him," Ramous stammered.
"One man had a camera under his jacket this morning, waiting
to take pictures." Ramous identified the tall, black Mexican and
another man who acted as the little man's lieutenants. "They
here to organize a union."

"Ain't no union," Manuel replied. "A few big shots looking
to test the waters, seeking opportunity to shame the owners,"
Manuel told him. "But we not so stupid. We take care of
troublemakers after dark," he said, using Ramous' shirt to clean
his knife. "What else you know?" Ramous needed no further
inducement to inform Manuel that the organizer planned on
sneaking away tonight. "He boasts his friends waiting outside."

"Antonio," Manuel said decisively, plunging his knife into
the wooden table top, "how you like to fuck that gringo lady you
see in men's pants this morning? She likes Latino prick. I know
from experience," he gleamed confidently. "Man, she really
gobbles it up. Why else you think she give in? But don't you say
I told you. We want her put in her place. Grab her quick. Enjoy,
man! You put it up her ass! We'll set you up so you can watch for
best time. When done, come here; we send you north before
dawn breaks."

Ramous smiled wildly and shook his head in agreement.

When he returned to the workers' dorm that night, he saw
that the Mexican in the cowboy hat had left. Next day Roberto
heard they found his dead body along a county road, the victim
of a hit and run driver. But Roberto knew different. Nor did he
see the two men who had aided the union man. Scuttlebutt had it
Immigration picked them up and the men were awaiting

deportation. They were lucky if that was all that had happened to them.

Late this afternoon, as Ramous came in from the field, Manuel headed him off. "Tonight Jorge gets his revenge for how the lady humiliated him in front of the workers." Manuel escorted him to the dirt road behind her house and pointed to the packing barn. "Sneak in there and wait 'till dark when she gone to bed thinking about your prick."

"What about her man?" Ramous asked.

"He's no worry. If he comes home at all, it'll be after you there," he laughed. "He's got his own pussy to finish. Listen, you gag and tie her. Make sure she don't die. Understand? You finish, I meet you at the bunkhouse and get you out of here."

*   *   *

Roberto Ramous watched Madge closely from the shadows behind the lone window. He saw her beauty more now than in the rain last Thursday; he hungered for her breasts and mouth. He thought about all the things he would do to her before he did her the way Manuel wanted.

He watched as she stood to turn the soil with a pitchfork, her opened shirt fluttering in the evening breeze. For several seconds she looked toward the barn. Roberto worried she might have seen him at the window, but he could not take his eyes off her. She looked away, turned over more soil and got on her knees to smooth the area with her hands. He watched then as she straightened up and buttoned her shirt part way before tucking the tails into her pants. She gathered her tools, and with some awkwardness, carried and dragged them in his direction.

"It's almost dark and there's no escape," he murmured as she drew near.

He had found an oily rag to stuff in her mouth and an old piece of rope to tie her hands. He took off his grimy T-shirt. In his first action, he would use his shirt to blind her while he pushed the rag in her mouth. He moved behind the barn door. He sprung his knife as he listened to the sound of the door slide to the side on its rusty rails. He waited out of sight. She must be three feet from the opening. Maybe he should go out and drag her in. He heard her yell, "Chip, get your things and bring Dudley! It's time for baths and bed!" She threw the steel pitchfork into the opening. Using her foot, she pushed in her box full of hand tools. In quick succession, she slid the barn door forward in place.

"Fuck it!" Ramous said quietly, gritting his teeth.

He returned to the window to watch her take her little boy's hand. The older boy, a box of toys in his arms, followed behind. They disappeared around the house. Roberto settled into a chair to wait until later.

*　　*　　*

Everett Wheeler sat on the floor in his bedroom next to a metal army footlocker. He dialed the combination on the heavy padlock and opened the lid. Visibly annoyed and cursing, he transferred dozens of brown legal-size envelopes into an empty cardboard liquor box. He opened several to browse through pictures of women posing in various stages of undress or nude. He smiled contentedly as he reinserted each photo and packed their envelope into the liquor box. He then took two shoeboxes out of the locker. Filled with unsorted slides, he held a few up to the light to look at, then, dropped them back. Finished with the shoeboxes, he squeezed them into the now full liquor box. From the floor of the footlocker, he brought up a dozen tins of processed eight-millimeter movie film. These he placed in a large gym bag at his side.

*　　*　　*

A number of women Everett Wheeler photographed in his hidden studio were referrals from women who had already posed for him. "A few gets many," he boasted. But he was always on the prowl for new talent. He "discovered" them at bars, strip joints, cabarets or all-night diners up and down the New Jersey coast, or in the urban centers of Philadelphia, Camden, Trenton, and New York. A significant number were prostitutes. But he had also enticed those whose character was not so obvious—college girls, housewives, waitresses, schoolteachers, dancers.

His subjects posed for many reasons: an orientation toward exhibitionism, the thrill and excitement of sexual attention, a desire to please. For some women, acting out in front of his camera was a way to get even with a philandering boyfriend or husband. Others simply derided the limitations society had placed on them. Here they could do as they pleased. One thing his women all had in common: They did it for the money. Everett paid well for their services and women came away believing he had treated them fairly.

He exercised care in drawing the minimum age for any model at eighteen. Not using local talent was his other hard and fast rule. When in doubt, he asked for proof of age and residence before describing his kind of photography. For added security, he blindfolded his models before and after taking them to the church and into his studio, and did all this work long after dark.

Once he had his model in his studio, he told her he wanted to protect her anonymity and "be respectful of your privacy." He therefore offered the option of wearing a mask. He then told her that in order to enhance the drama of this "photo opportunity," he would cover his own face as the Masked Marvel, Bat Man or some other comic book character. He explained this as his way to keep the scene light and fanciful and to help his model strike a fictional mood. In truth, he had done it only to protect himself.

An electronic genius, Everett had hidden cameras wired to a console disguised as a way to adjust his lighting inside the studio. He did not divulge that behind the mirrors, before which his models primped and undressed, both motion and still cameras were operating. Nor did she know that when Everett set down his hand-held camera, the hidden camera eyes were all over her.

Pictures taken with these lenses were among his more profitable shots.

Everett sold most of his studio stills and motion pictures to a dealer in a New York bookstore just off Times Square, a growing haven for the sale of bare breast movies and girly magazines. The dealer arranged for processing and editing, then, he distributed a finished product, much of this he sold from under his own counter. In addition to this outlet, Everett maintained a darkroom in his home. Here, his wife, Marie, processed his legitimate wedding pictures, as well as what he regarded as "cheesecake." Here, too, Marie developed and printed film left off by amateur photographers, people like Sarah Draper who took "dirty pictures" at home for her own amusement and wouldn't trust to commercial film processors. Then, there were pictures Everett didn't want Marie to see. These he processed personally in his hidden church studio. Much of this he sold to trusted friends or kept for his own pleasure.

He could not avoid risks in his trade. Anyone who operated a porn studio in New Jersey was subject to arrest and jail. At the least, a conviction would bring stiff fines, not to mention public notice and continuing police harassment. The law was especially harsh on photographers who employed underage eighteen year olds. Conviction could mean long prison terms. He wanted no trouble with the law nor did he want public exposure, and for almost ten years now, he had succeeded in keeping his unsavory side of photography (literally) an underground business.

His persona as a wedding photographer protected him. But personal wealth had made his sideline into pornography affordable. After inheriting more than two-thousand acres of farmland from his deceased parents, he sold the family farm to developers. Smart investments had made him "filthy rich." All other income was for fun and games.

All that changed yesterday. First, the threats of Margo Rasmeyer to expose him. She had stormed into Tommy's Place while he sat there with Charlene, madder than hell because he hadn't called her for a second photo shoot. Then Flynn and

Cunningham's discovery of his studio. While he had destroyed evidence of the studio's existence, if that detective in homicide half way believed them and then heard from Rasmeyer, he'd start investigating. Everett planned to fix that. It did not bother him that the solution included blackmail and murder. He had used brutal tactics before to cover his tracks, and to stay one step ahead of the law.

*   *   *

Wheeler opened a brown envelope and took out photos of Margo Rasmeyer. He saw her as white trash, a wild one, who grew up among thieves and braggarts on a poor family farm just outside of Tompkinsville. Her pretty face and stunning figure had helped him overlook his rule against using locals. If she talked to the cops, they would come after him for sure. He put Margo's packet of pictures into the liquor box. He planned on calling her for a date to shoot more pictures. Only she could keep her clothes on, he smiled, because he wouldn't be shooting her with a camera.

Another studio matter concerned him and he leafed through the tight-packed envelopes. He had labeled and dated each one with the subject's initials and date of the photo shoot. He looked for two envelopes in particular. One he found right away. It held a smaller envelope with three black-and-white, wallet-size pictures. He checked them out, made a whistling sound and, absent the envelope, he pushed the photos into the breast pocket of his shirt. He had hidden larger prints of the entire series elsewhere. He searched the box again, but couldn't find the second envelope of photos. They were four years old. Perhaps he had them in his other hiding place.

By now, the sun had dipped below the horizon and dusk had fallen upon the room where he sat. He reached up and lit a lamp on a nearby table. To be sure he hadn't missed the sought-after pictures, once more, he started thumbing through envelopes in the liquor box. He was unaware of his wife, Marie, standing in the darkened area by the doorway.

Marie had grown old before her time. Her eyes sat deep in the pockets of her face and her once auburn hair, so silky and fine, hung straggly and gray. She was a fraction of the beauty that had once set every eye to follow her. How long she had stood there watching him, he could not know. Now she announced her presence.

"Is this what you're looking for, Everett? I wouldn't want you to forget this filthy snapshot," she said with intentional sarcasm.

She reached a five-by-seven, black-and-white photo toward him. It caught the light and he recognized the nude figures. The picture was from the missing set. He grunted disapproval and cursed at her. How had she gotten into his footlocker? He leaped to his feet to grab the picture out of her hand, but she sailed it across the room before he could grasp it. He stepped back and bent to pick it off the floor.

"Don't come back, Everett. Don't ever return here again!" she shouted.

He dove for her, slammed her to the floor. He pinned her down. She had no physical strength and offered no fight.

"Eat it," he yelled tearing the picture into tiny pieces and forcing them into her mouth. She gagged. "Where are the rest of these photographs?" he yelled. She spit fragments out of her mouth and struggled with words.

"Safe! And that's not all. I included a confession of all the times I lied for you. If anything happens to me, the right people will know all about your raunchy, stinking life."

He sunk his fingers into her throat and applied pressure. She began to choke. She struggled for air. He relaxed his hands.

She screamed, "Finish it! Kill me! Go ahead, that way it'll be over."

Wearily he got off her frail and shaking body.

"So, this is it?" he asked as he rose to his feet. "This is what you've been scheming?"

"I'm divorcing you, Everett," he heard, her words rasping, out of breath. "I've got enough to send you away for a long, long time and I'll use it if I have to."

He scooped up the liquor box, grabbed the handles of his gym bag and went to his pickup truck. He raced out of the driveway.

"Another score to settle!" he said to himself. "We'll see!"

Wheeler set his sights on the extended straight-a-way out of Tompkinsville and the fastest route to Manhattan. He floored the gas pedal. The headlights caught the green fields of new plantings. A stream of water pelted the windshield, sprayed by farm watering engines that drove themselves, a precaution against June's heat wave, now in its sixth blistering night.

*   *   *

U.S. Highway 46 accessed the George Washington Bridge as a heavily congested, construction riddled, four-lane thoroughfare lined by used car lots, aging diners, gas stations and motels. With darkness already a reality, Charlene pulled into a Howard Johnson's and used her company endorsed Diners' Club credit card to pay for two nights. Of course, she hoped she could finish her investigation in one day and get back to Tompkinsville late tomorrow, but the wisdom of experience informed her it would take longer. As she entered the room, she sighed with relief that it was pleasantly cool. She paused only long enough to use the toilet, wash her face and hands and thrash her curls with a comb. Without further notice, she left for the adjoining restaurant.

This was always a nervous time for Charlene. Such motel locations were the abode of traveling salesmen. There were a few families and some couples, but mostly she saw single men seated forlornly among scattered tables. A lone woman, a young woman, attractive and unescorted, was an oddity. All eyes seemed to go to her as she followed the lady with the menu to a table and took her seat. She had learned never to make eye contact with other patrons and to busy herself at almost nothing while she waited for her order to arrive. Having not eaten since Jerry's poached eggs and toast very early this morning, she was famished. She ordered a large glass of cold milk—still her favorite beverage—a plate of batter-fried clams, French-fries and a chef's salad. She ate it all and took dessert as well.

Her meal finished, Charlene returned to her room. She secured the door not only with the locks provided, but also by applying an extra trick that she had learned. Out of her bag, she produced a hard rubber doorstop, the kind used to hold a door open. Charlene wedged it into the air space between the bottom of the door and the saddle. Once in place, it would take a tank to break into the room. She was secure against motel personnel with keys or others for whom no locks were ever a barrier to entry.

For all her bravado as a woman, underneath, Charlene remained a frightened little girl. She liked the glamour of travel and meeting new people, however, when night came she felt the loneliness and danger as only a single woman could. After two years at it, she had grown tired of the singles' lifestyle and the excitement had begun to fade. Constantly on the road, enduring friendships were out of the question. In Jerry's arms last night, for the first time in a long while, she had felt secure, wanted and, well, maybe she was taking it too far, but she believed he had really loved her.

She wanted to call him at that moment. There was so much to tell him. Yet, just as she had decided not to inform him of her true purpose this morning, she knew she couldn't do it now. It would have to wait. Whatever the fallout, she had to finish her investigation. She would not blow her cover, even to Jerry.

She switched on the television. She seldom watched it, but turned it on when she was afraid of silence. She lit up a Pall Mall and inhaled deeply. She smoked maybe four cigarettes a day, usually while she was nervous about something or when alone. She thought about getting out her notebook and catching up on today's interviews. She needed to record the data Jack Burns had given her. But once more, she had left the spiral-paged notes in her car. "I'll be darned if I'm going out there for that now," she bitched as she knelt at the side of the tub. She watched it fill with hot water, tugged her slim-fitting dress up and over her head, rolled it into a bundle, and stuffed it into her overnight bag that sat on the floor next to her. She pawed through the bag to collect her used underwear and then peeled off her panties, all of which she floated in the bathtub. With a cake of Ivory soap in hand, she proceeded to wash her bras and panties as well as the satin blouse she had worn last Wednesday at her meeting with Jerry. She thought again about the panties she had absconded from the studio. She had stuffed them into her bag; she meant to get them to a police lab. Why had she thought they were so important? That perfume smell! She dried her hands and clawed through her bag, finding the cotton garment on the bottom.

She held the crotch to her nose, this time for much longer than last night. "It's lavender; I'm sure!" she said. The same pertinent thought of yesterday hit her again. "Madge Todd! No way! Lavender is so common. It could come from anyone." She returned the panties to her bag. Deep in thought, she went back to soaping and rinsing her under garments. Ringing them out, she hung them to dry over the shower-curtain rod. She stepped into the tub and sunk into the hot, soapy water. She submerged to her chin, closed her eyes and felt her body bake. Again, she thought of last night and the early morning hot-tub bath, of Jerry scrubbing her back. It had ended with him getting in with her and a grand climax. Could she get that comfortable with him again?

She cut her reverie short when she heard the television announce the eleven o'clock news. She left the tub, drying herself with several towels. She climbed into bed, dialed Jerry's home number. She appreciated Howard Johnson's updated telephone system, which let her dial her own outside numbers without going through a motel switchboard. She waited while his telephone rang seven times. She was about to hang up to try again later when he answered.

"Hello! This is Jerry Flynn!

"It's me, Charlene!"

"Where are you?"

"At a Howard Johnson in Fort Lee, about a mile from the George Washington Bridge."

"I missed you all day."

She was glad he had said it first. She would have, though, maybe not yet.

"I'll try to get back tomorrow evening, but no promises."

"Why are you there?"

"I have to meet with some New York editors. My article is near completion and needs their appraisal. I'll explain it all when I see you. How did you spend your day?"

"Mostly, thinking about you."

"That's so sweet to say."

"It'll be tomorrow before I get the manse locks changed," his mind quick to advance to less pleasant matters. "I'm not telling anyone until it's done. And guess what?"

"Let me!" She rushed to give him an answer. "You went into the basement and found the hidden room no longer hidden, no mattresses blocking your way. The door was open and the room was as clean as a whistle: no see-through mirrors, no pink satin sheets, no bureau full of kinky toys and tantalizing underwear, no—"

"Yes, all that was gone, even the inside walls and the carpet. I couldn't believe the changes. There wasn't a hint of a studio. Only the bare bed and a couple of chairs remained there; nothing to suggest more than a casual nap during a lunch break."

"My guess is your 'Mr. Cleaning Man' emptied his play room before the sun was up."

"Well, Everett didn't show for work today. I called his home and his wife said she didn't know where he was. I don't know what to make of it, Charlene. I hesitate to report how we found it to the police, especially now that I have nothing to show them. What can come of it?"

"Jerry, your predecessor was murdered in that building. Don't you think at the least that someone went to great lengths to hide their skin business? I know you don't agree, but our lives were in danger last night. He tried to kill us. Let the police decide how important that all is."

"Yea, but I can't accuse someone. If our stalker was Everett then he knows I know. He will deny it, and—"

"He'll try to blackmail you? Is that what you were going to say?"

"Possibly. But I'm more concerned about the church's reputation . . . "

She hated to hear him say this. Does he now regret sleeping with her last night? He was as crippled by fear as she and together they had sought to answer, perhaps deny, their anxiety through unrestrained passion. She hoped he didn't blame her for his procrastination. The longer he put off reporting what they found, the less meaning it would have. He disappointed her, but she would not show that over the phone. And how could she justify her own trickery? No, she could have insisted he call the police last night. She could have walked out on him. All blame was not his.

"Jerry, I think you're right. Let's keep this under our hats until I get back. Please! I'll explain. By the way, does the name Lillian Palmer mean anything to you?"

"Yes, just a minute."

She heard him put down the telephone. She could hear him shuffling papers. He came back on.

"Lillian Palmer is a church member, lives at thirty-seven Benson Place, Tompkinsville. She's a widow. Her husband's name was Luke. He died five years back. If I saw her in church last Sunday, I do not recall her face. Why? What do you know about Mrs. Palmer?

"Nothing. She may have one of my business cards with a Philadelphia answering service number printed on it. I've given several to people I don't know. She left a message for me to call. Maybe she wants to see her name in print. Anyway, if you run into her before I get in touch, please don't say anything. I'll try calling her tomorrow. Speaking of tomorrow, what are your plans?"

"I'll be in my study until noon. After lunch, I plan to visit a few of our elderly shut-ins, then I'll make a late-afternoon visit to

a minister friend in the next town. He's officially in charge here
until my ordination and installation service next Sunday. I hope
you'll be there."

"Well, thank you for inviting me. You're sure?"

"You know I am."

"Okay, what else is on your calendar for tomorrow?"

"That farmer who was in the tractor accident took a turn for
the worst. I'll have to get back to the hospital, but I already told
you about that. I've got to finish writing Sunday's sermon and
prepare the liturgy selections. Tomorrow evening, I have an
appointment with a couple planning to get married here in
September—"

She interrupted him. "Jerry, just say you'll have time for me."

"You'll be in my thoughts all day."

"But I want to be in your arms . . . " When he did not answer
right away, she said with a pout, "Jerry, goodnight! If I don't get
back tomorrow, I'll call you about this time."

She hated to hang up. She wanted to fall asleep with him
loving her.

"Good night, Charlene. I . . . "

"Yes?"

"I'll drop everything."

"I know you will. What were you going to say?"

He paused. "I'd rather tell you face to face, lips to lips."

"I can't wait that long."

She was teasing him. She did not mean to. She felt what he
wanted to say. But, yes, it was better to say it in person, especially
the first time. She waited a second and whispered, "Good night,
Jerry," and then added . . . She could go this far . . . "Love!"
She hung up.

*　　*　　*

Madge had seen her sons off to bed in the usual manner—
an hour of TV, baths, Dudley tucked in for the night, helping
Chip with his homework before he too snuggled soundly until

dawn. She then faced her most dreaded time, her hours alone when she could not chase away her past.

Her body showered and lightly scented with Lavender perfume, she wanted to be awake when Michael came up the steps. That way she could cooperate in his aggressive style of making love and perhaps guide him toward a completion more satisfying to them both. The birth control pills she took religiously did relieve the anxiety she had once felt about pregnancy. So far, she had had no known side affects. If only Michael would take his time. He had always been this way, she recalled—fast, unimaginative, destructive. But sometimes she could hold him off and even accelerate her own readiness. She did not accept Michael's explanation that it was a "man thing," the words he used to explain his quickness. For, she had been with another man, a man who had shown affection, patience and gentleness, and who had provided as much pleasure for her as for himself. Had she not had that experience, she would not know any better and therefore could believe Michael that sex with a man, any man, had to be painful and ordinary. Moreover, she was almost convinced at this stage in her life that love and sex were unrelated, that neither one depended on the other for its fulfillment.

She loved Michael. She had always loved him. Born on the same day within minutes of each other (their mothers had shared the same hospital room), they appeared knitted together for life. She could not recall a birthday cake when they weren't as one blowing out the candles. They had gone off to kindergarten holding hands, to high school kissing cousins. Michael was more like a son to her father than to his own father, a much older man.

Maybe that was part of the problem, Madge conceded, as she shed her bathrobe and got under the sheets—her body as naked as the day she and Michael were born, as naked as they were in the baby pictures their parents had taken as they slept side by side in the same crib. Dad loved Michael as the son he never had. And, Madge believed she loved Michael as a sister loved her brother, a love not meant for life naked in the same bed. Ironically, for all that, they had had two beautiful sons, and for them Madge had made up her mind to live faithful, and, if not "obey," at least endure. Yes, how much she loved her sons. She loved Chip and Dudley so much she would die for them. Or, she would kill herself if ever taken away from her. How powerful love is, she pondered, how broad its range. And to think that neither son had been conceived in any romantic way.

She recalled how she and Michael had gone off to Cornell together as virgins. It was probably too much to believe they would continue that way until graduation and marriage. Michael had already taken liberty with her body.

On their seventeenth birthday, he had fondled her and kissed her in ways she considered dirty. When he tried to put his hand between her legs, she slapped his face hard and ran from his car. She walked all the way home from where they had parked and refused to talk to him for a week. She wished she had stuck to that separation longer. She thought how much better for them both had they split then and possibly found their way back to each other later in life, maybe not as husband and wife, rather as true friends, which was all she had ever wanted from him. But a week later, she forgave him; though, to her dismay, she had still to fight his hands from wandering to her forbidden places.

She remembered how she had hoped Cornell would not accept him. Michael didn't have the high school grades Ivy League schools required, and he had failed his first entrance exam. But then he got accepted. She thought that maybe a generous gift and a word from a Trustee member of his family may have done the trick. It had all come about so unbelievably. She, however, acted happy for him, something she would live to regret. For on campus, she saw him making a fool of himself in the way he hung on her and showed such jealousy if he saw her so much as speak to another boy. He accused her of flirting. He said she shouldn't smile so much. He accused her of being too friendly. Twice she broke up with him over such complaints, but both times, she felt compelled to forgive and try to forget.

In the summer between their first and second years, she won acceptance as one of twelve college students out of a thousand applicants to work in Ethiopia, all expenses paid for by a government grant to teach American truck farming methods.

It was bound to happen, she supposed. Before the summer ended, she had become intimate with another student, a senior from UCLA. Love with Harry had been all that she had ever wanted. But like her, he had a "sweetheart" back home. He intended to break up with her and Madge had resolved to do the same with Michael. In her daydreams, she saw herself in Harry's wine vineyards as they rode off double saddled on a sleek horse into the sunset. Then she received his letter. It came two weeks after beginning the new term at Cornell. He was "dreadfully sorry," he had written. He regretted that he had presumed too much with her. He could not break off his engagement and would marry his girlfriend a month from now. He hoped that Madge too could see her way to similar happiness. The letter angered her as nothing in her life ever had. That same night, without so much as a "squeak," for her hymen had already ruptured, she felt cold as she allowed Michael to enter her. He came so quick, so simple, so irreverent, so unlike Harry, she reflected. She had thought it her safe time, but no such luck. She was then pregnant with Chip and she and Michael had no choice but marriage.

The hardest part was telling her parents. Always the perfect, well-behaved, trusted child, she viewed her pregnancy outside of wedlock as the one time in her life she had failed them. And although she and Michael married at First Church in an elaborate and proud ceremony, beneath the vale she felt ashamed that their baby would be born three months behind a virgin's count. As a woman, as a mother, she had hated what people were thinking. Michael had wanted her to quit college. She refused, however, to give up her education and, though not easy, she had graduated with her class from Cornell.

*   *   *

Madge snuggled under the bed sheets. Her mind had dwelled too long on ancient history and on what could have been, she told herself. And now recent indiscretions and conflicts with Michael upset her. Her doctor had prescribed a sleeping pill as a way to deal with nights when worries prevented needed sleep. But she hated the state the drug left her the next day. She reached up and turned off the bedside lamp, at once thankful for the deep darkness hiding her. It annoyed her that Michael was so late getting home tonight. She worried about him drinking and driving. She would make love to him, if he would let her, even knowing he had just left the bed of another woman. At the least, she would wait out the night until he was safe in bed beside her.

*　　*　　*

Prison life had taught Roberto Ramous how to wait. Having nothing to do with his time did not bother him. He simply dozed, smoked, ate Hershey chocolate bars and stared into the darkness, his daydreaming carrying him through the long, idle hours. Tonight, his imagination was especially active.

He waited ten minutes after the upstairs light went out. He figured by now the lady was in bed, maybe asleep. He stuffed the oily rag and rope into his pants pockets. He would have her gagged, tied and blindfolded before she could do him any harm. He wanted to please her, but he must take care of himself, too. He had no inclination to go easy. Speed was of essence.

He circled the house looking for an open window. He saw one on the porch with a screen, but thought he would try the door first. People around here were very trusting. Last winter he had burglarized a farmhouse with an unlocked front door.

Sure enough, the door opened freely. Without making a sound, he stepped into the dark house. That was when he heard a dog's low growl. Manuel had not alerted him to this. Before he could back out, the Corgi, without barking, lurched, biting into Roberto's down-turned hand. He felt the teeth of the beast clamp and hold around his knuckles. He screamed in fright as the dog snarled and held on. He kicked blindly, connecting with the dog's groin. The dog released his hand, letting out a loud, squealing yelp. A terrible whine followed as the Corgi ran toward more solid darkness in another room.

A light came on upstairs. Holding his bleeding wound with his other hand, Roberto ran on to the porch, the door slamming behind him. In that same moment, bright headlights swept down the driveway. A car was racing toward him. Doubly afraid, he ran off the porch and around to the back of the house. He stayed in the shadows and outside the rim of nightlights flooding the backyard. He never looked behind him. He would boast to Manuel how he fucked the lady and how she bit his hand. Whether Manuel learned the truth didn't matter. All Roberto cared about now was getting out of town before dawn.

CHAPTER 10

DISCOVERIES

Tuesday Morning, June 12

Charlene Cunningham took a wake-up call at five-fifteen.

From the shower rod, she grabbed off her pink underwear. She raised the panties to her waist. She attached her bra backwards and turned it to fit her breasts into its cups, then slid her arms through the straps. She groaned in annoyance that the brazier was still damp and cold. She smiled broadly at her temporary discomfort, a matter of correctness she had to endure. All other hand-washed undergarments she stuffed into her overnight bag. From a closet hanger, she withdrew a pair of gray denim ranch slacks she had hung out last night and quickly stepped into them and belted them around her waist. She had bought the trousers at Kaufmann's Department Store in Pittsburgh during a recent trip. They had a loose, male fit and their lightweight material did not need ironing, perfect for her planned activity. Her arms glided into her sleeveless satin blouse, which she buttoned to the top. She put on a pair of athletic socks and canvas shoes. She left off earrings and other jewelry. She combed her curls up and bunched them on the top of her head. It took several bobby pins, but she hoped she could keep her hair pinned above her ears.

Last night, at a gift shop in the turnpike restaurant, she had bought a New York Yankees baseball cap and a matching Yankees windbreaker. She put on the jacket. It would feel good in the chill morning air. With care, she fitted the baseball cap on her head and tucked the last few curls under the brim. She decided to leave her overnight bag in the room, her dirty laundry was as safe here as in her car. Her shoulder bag, which doubled as a purse, was another matter. Containing her wallet, business cards, makeup, sunglasses and a multiple assortment of other things, she could not imagine being without it. She secured the bag over her shoulder and beneath her arm.

Before leaving the motel, she stopped at the desk. She handed the clerk her room key saying she would be back later in the day. She did not want to carry it. She asked for twenty quarters for a five-dollar bill. That was more change than the clerk could spare. He handed her eight quarters and three one-dollar bills. She asked for directions to Columbia University.

It was six o'clock when she stopped at a tollbooth on the George Washington Bridge and got back two quarters from the dollar bill she handed the collector. She found her exit lane on to the Henry Hudson Parkway going south. Traffic was already building. Had she waited another hour, she would be into the thick of morning rush hour. Following the motel clerk's suggestion, she exited at 125th Street and drove south on Broadway. It would be impossible to find a long-term place to park on the street. She was at West 108th Street before she saw a sign directing her into a twenty-four-hour parking garage between Amsterdam Avenue and Broadway. Shoving her wallet, change, and a few personal items into various pockets of her trousers and windbreaker, she abandoned her car to the parking attendant. He gave her a numbered receipt and raced her little sports car into the bowels of the dark, oil-scented building. She slipped the receipt into her pants pocket and walked west to Riverside Drive. She turned north on the east side of the avenue and watched building numbers along the way.

She found Rhonda Maefield's address. She crossed the roadway at the crosswalk. Fronting a broad sidewalk was a ten-foot-wide green space to the curb and behind it was a park bench with a clear view of the entrance to Rhonda's apartment building. She sat down. "I can't do better than this," she exclaimed looking up at the ten-story apartment building across from her. A quarter mile to her left was Grant's Tomb. Behind her, down to the river and south, stretched the woodland Riverside Park, the parkway and the tracks of the New York Central Railroad. Diagonal to her was the Interchurch Center and next to it, Riverside Protestant Cathedral. She noticed how close in appearance it was to First Church in Tompkinsville.

Now six thirty, the light of dawn was replacing the morning darkness. Already she felt the June heat. The forecast was for more mean temperature and humidity. Buildings across the way and the park trees shielded her from the sunrise. She put on her sunglasses anyway. She was glad for the cooling breeze sweeping in off the river. She began to think her male disguise unnecessary. She had done it as a way to discourage attention. But in this heat, she had almost resigned herself to go back to a more womanlike appearance.

It surprised her that so many people were up and out using the park to walk dogs, jog, ride bicycles or to stroll. Many pedestrians headed for work in the office towers and factories crowding the island metropolis. A scattering of college-looking men and women were out enjoying some free time before the start of summer semester. Now and then, joggers stopped and briefly joined her on the bench. After catching their breath, they were off again.

An hour and fifteen minutes passed. If Mrs. Maefield was the creature of habit everyone had said, she should have embarked for her morning stroll by now. Charlene hoped she hadn't missed her or that she had decided not to walk this morning. She had her plan, which was to see how she looked when not wearing that black business suit. She would then stop her, identify herself as a freelance writer and ask for a few minutes of her time. Perhaps they could find a coffee shop and have breakfast, or set a date to meet tomorrow. Once again, she looked up to the eighth floor windows of the granite apartment structure across Riverside Drive.

In that moment, Rhonda Maefield bounded out of the entrance. A brisk walker, she darted left ten steps before abruptly changing direction, deciding to walk on the park side of Riverside Drive. Running to the corner, she continued into the crosswalk against the light, dodging a fast-moving cab.

A few more seconds of inattention and Charlene may have missed her. The blare of the taxi horn brought Charlene's eyes to focus on her. At first, she wasn't sure. There were no black horn-rimmed glasses. This woman wore a light, frilly, colorful summer dress hemmed above her knees. She looked like a model out of Vogue. Adorned as she was, she exhibited a youthful appearance. But as the woman drew closer, her height and the way her black hair was upswept and tied in a braided bun, confirmed what Charlene had seen in pictures. Trim and more graceful than Charlene had guessed, her gallant face—austere, almost hard, some might say, sad—gave her away. Over her sheer nylon stockings, she had put on soft running shoes that seemed out of place and a concession no doubt to the time of day and the recreation she sought. Charlene could not help notice how the thin material of the dress set off every curve of her shapely body. She also sighted on her makeup and how expert its application.

Rhonda continued toward her and hopped the curb. She was ten feet away when she stopped to take sunglasses out of a narrow, fashionable shoulder purse. She put them on and took a step toward where Charlene sat. Charlene worried she would complain about her staring up at her window. But then Rhonda turned, ignoring her, took long strides in front of the park bench, charged south on the broad promenade of Riverside Drive.

Suddenly Charlene heard, "Watch out!"

Rhonda froze, startled by a speeding bicyclist. The elderly male shouted an obscenity as he passed, angered by having to slow and steer around her. It was a revealing moment for Charlene, because she saw Rhonda growl with equal annoyance. More significant about the moment, a gust of wind swept her dress flush with her body. Charlene noted with female coyness that Rhonda's hips were trim and unencumbered by a girdle. Her breasts were large and loose under her dress. She wasn't wearing a slip and no bra. That did not level with the modest, drab ways described by almost everyone who had spoken to Charlene about Rhonda.

She waited until Rhonda walked a hundred feet south of her. Only then did she rise from the park bench to follow. The woman was fast, almost on a run, shoulders back in a quick pace, dodging rapidly left or right to avoid oncoming pedestrians. Charlene had to move with precision to keep her in sight. She started to regret that she hadn't introduced herself by now.

At West 106th Street, Charlene noticed a male stroller, who had drawn up alongside Rhonda and appeared to attempt to slow her down. Several times, the man reached for her hand, but Rhonda drew away, moved to the far side of the promenade and avoided eye contact, though the man kept on talking to her. He wore a broad-brim, strawlike hat, baggy casual shirt and trousers. He had a large build and walked in a cumbersome manner, leaning forward in a droopy way as he struggled to keep up with her more athletic movement.

Charlene started running, intent now to get a look at the man's face. She needed to gain on them, but it wasn't easy. Rhonda quickened her pace. More people had crowded the sidewalk and Charlene feared the couple could easily melt into the throng. All of a sudden, Rhonda bolted left into Riverside Drive, evading cabs and a city bus, jaywalking across lanes of south and north traffic. Unprepared, with less grace, the man followed, horns honking wildly. Charlene had no choice but to run the same dangerous course. They hurried east on West 104th Street. The light was with them as they crossed West End Avenue and Charlene got to within fifty feet. But at Broadway, once again, Rhonda broke into heavy motor traffic and against the light. Defying death, she crossed the broad avenue and the island-dividing lanes. The man followed behind.

This time, Charlene had no stomach for the near suicidal sprint and stayed in place, waiting with the curbed crowd for the walk sign. She watched as the couple turned north on the sidewalk of Broadway. If Rhonda was trying to get away from her male pursuer, she had not succeeded. He managed to rein her in and stop her flight by grabbing her arm and braking. She turned and let her arms fly against him, shaking him off.

The city was fully awake and on the run. The sun had peeked above east-side tenement houses lining Broadway, so that nothing blocked its rays in a cloudless sky. Charlene could feel the heat through the soles of her shoes as she ran on these burning sidewalks. She unzipped her wind breaker and peeled it off. On the run, she tied its sleeves around her waist.

At 108th Street and Broadway, she moved within twenty-five feet. She watched as this time the man stepped in front of Rhonda, turning and blocking her, holding her firmly, stopping her movement. He didn't care that he was creating a traffic jam of pedestrians on the busy pavement. Straining to get her first look at the man's face, Charlene collided with a woman pushing a baby in a stroller. She fell forward, losing her balance, struggling to stay on her feet, leaping around to avoid another collision. As she skirted to the curbside and came parallel with the stalled couple, she saw the face of the man restraining Rhonda.

"My God," she said as she passed, speaking to no one except herself, "Everett Wheeler!"

He had blocked his long red hair under his hat, but some strands flopped over his ears. Unmistakable were his piercing dark eyes, his chubby, round face, ruby complexion, his stumped nose, and his voice, gruff and disdainful, as he shouted cautions to the woman he now held at arms length and then hugged in a bear hold. It mattered not that they were on Broadway with hundreds of people pushing and shoving their way around them.

"Of course he thought she was *sexy*," Charlene proclaimed, "he knew her in bed!"

She moved quickly behind them and across the sidewalk to a shadowy doorway, where she could watch without them seeing her. Her stalking would be over if Everett spotted her. Winded and sweating profusely from the hurried walk, reluctantly, she pulled on her Yankees windbreaker and adjusted her baseball cap as low to her eyes as she could manage. She wished she could hear what they were saying. They appeared to argue. Showing irritation, Rhonda broke away. Again, she did not wait for the light to change and raced north across 109th Street, narrowly missed by a black limousine. Everett had not expected Rhonda's quickness. Undeterred, he caught up with her as she stepped above the curb. Again, he seized her arm and held on tight, slowing her down, halting her movement. He held both her hands in his while he scolded and insisted on something.

Charlene waited in place. She watched as they entered a small corner café opposite them. She spotted a sidewalk telephone booth a little north on the same block. She headed in that direction.

*　　*　　*

At 8:30, Jerry Flynn entered Shepherd House.

He did not get much sleep last night. After an hour of tossing and turning, he clicked on the table lamp at his bedside and began reading H. Richard Niebuhr's, *The Meaning of Revelation*. He thought this canon of theological truth should surely put him to sleep, but he was wrong. The printed pages energized him with descriptions and absorbing definitions of the chaos surrounding the human situation, yet always affirming the existence of an approachable and personal God.

Jerry had taken the book at random from his study. It was one of Maefield's books. He had recognized the title as assigned reading in seminary and was ashamed to admit, but at the time, he had opted instead to read it from another student's notes. H. Richard Niebuhr was the younger brother of a more famous theologian, Reinhold Niebuhr. Richard, teaching at Yale, had become one of Maefield's close friends. On the inside cover, Niebuhr had written, *"To Daniel—December 12, 1940, God's servant to the Word: You honor me with your friendship and humble me with your wisdom. Helmut"*

Jerry realized Doctor Maefield had stood with the giants of this theological age. Not since the Reformation had so many outstanding thinkers raised their voices: Niebuhr, Tillich, Barth, Bonhoeffer, Bultmann, Bailey, Otto, Cullmann and Maefield. In baseball terms, they were heavy hitters, superstars. With these theologians, words were never cheap. While they disagreed on much about God, all had contributed meaningful, scholarly interpretations of how God had acted in history and particularly in the first half of the warring twentieth century. Among these doctors of theology, Maefield was unique because, while they lectured in the great halls of theological learning, he bellowed sermons and prayers week after week in his own pastorate. For this, he had carried the respect and praise of them all.

As Jerry looked around his study, the half-unpacked boxes of Maefield's books greeted him. He hated this untidiness and felt guilty that he had not finished the task of organizing them all on his shelves; nevertheless, they were not first on his list today. Unopened mail sat piled high on top of his desk. Miss Blatty had collected and stacked it there for the last five months. Most of it he classified as number one junk. There was mail from denominational headquarters, most of which he classified as class number one sacred junk. Yet, he had to go through it. He had to inform himself on what was happening, where mission money was going, who was who in the several groupings of Presbyterians. There was also education material, which he gently set to the side. He would need to acquaint himself with First Church's Sunday school curriculum, its youth programs, bible study groups, women's and men's organizations. He had to get it together so he could be a useful resource person to every teacher. As he looked over the mess, he conceded that it was good he had read Niebuhr early this morning, because it might be a long time before he had an opportunity to read him again.

Nor did the profession of ministry allow much time for one's personal life. Jerry had to admit that Charlene's simple request— *"Just say you'll have time for me!"* frightened him. He was beginning to understand the practical reasons why priests and nuns were unmarried. Sex aside, how can you have time for family in this profession? You don't have time for yourself. Jesus' words to his disciples about putting him ahead of parents, brothers, wives struck true in a way Jerry had never realized and he wondered, really worried, if he had the stamina for it?

Even deciding on ministerial priorities was a challenge. Why couldn't he be like Doctor Maefield and say: "*I don't do shit!*" Jerry had heard mild-mannered Maefield had said exactly that. Yes, he now understood why Maefield showed little interest in church polity, education materials, or program development— all this "shit" on his desk. The good reverend drew the line as the thinker, the theologian, the preacher and lecturer, visitor of the sick, friend of the dying. Church policies, politics, or money-raising schemes defrauded him. He left funding matters and building management to others. If he knew how to change a light bulb, he had never let on. Jerry doubted Maefield ever saw the church basement, except to snag a bottle of his prized wine. If asked where the furnaces were, he would have given you a blank stare. So, why should Jerry be surprised that Everett Wheeler, if it was Everett (Jerry remained unsure), could operate with impunity there? Maefield certainly had not called Wheeler to account for his time, his work or his tools. And Jerry guessed no one on the Board of Trustees had either. Just then, the telephone rang. He picked up to hear Charlene in a high state of excitement.

* * *

On the corner of Broadway and 109th Street, Charlene had wrapped herself inside a graffiti-decorated, urine-smelling phone booth. She hated putting the phone next to her ear, but had no choice if she was going to hear anything from it.

"Jerry! I'm low on change, so I can't talk long," she asserted without introduction. "It's important you call Detective Burroughs. And, listen closely! This is going to blow your mind . . . "

Distracted, Charlene paused. A scraggy-looking woman was banging on the accordion door. She rudely pushed in, shouted that she had to use the phone. "I'll be finished in a minute!" Charlene shouted back. "Wait your turn!"

But the woman had no patience. She reached her bony hand through the opening and swatted the phone cradle, disconnecting the call. Charlene swatted her hand with the phone and crushed the door closed.

"Jerry!" she screamed into the mouthpiece. "Are you there?" The phone was dead. "Are you with me? Jerry!" she cried with urgency, clicking the cradle, dumbfounded by the interruption. A phone ready sound buzzed in her ear. "Damn it!"

She turned her back to the door. Keeping an eye on the café, she dug into her pants pocket for her quarters and came out with too few to complete the call. She dialed O and asked for long distance. She repeated the number and gave instructions to reverse charges.

It took forever to connect again.

Jerry picked up. The operator asked if he would accept a collect call from New York City from Charlene Cunningham.

"Yes! Put her on!"

"Jerry!"

"Yes, go on, what do you want me to do? Who's Detective Burroughs? What's going to blow my mind?"

Charlene had forgotten Jerry knew very little about the murder investigation.

"Burroughs is in charge of homicide and chief investigator in Reverend Maefield's death. You can reach him at Tompkinsville police headquarters."

"What do you want me to tell him?"

As she spoke, a shriek of police, fire and ambulance sirens overrode her words. In the closed telephone booth, the sound was deafening.

"Charlene, I can't hear you. The connection is bad . . ."

Nor could she hear him. She gave up and waited. Thirty seconds of ear-popping siren noise followed. As the string of emergency vehicles passed by, Wheeler and Maefield came out of the café on a run.

"I have to go! I'll call you later!" She hung up.

*   *   *

Where was she? Jerry could not imagine. He worried Charlene might be in danger, but he could not decide how. He looked up the number of the Tompkinsville Police. Without any idea what he was going to tell him, he dialed and asked for Detective Burroughs.

A police department operator informed him Detective Burroughs was in court today. She took Jerry's name and number and told him Burroughs would return his call first chance he got.

Jerry welcomed the message like a reprieve. He had time to think about what he needed to say. He hoped by this afternoon Charlene would call again with some answers.

His phone rang again.

He picked up to discover Miss Blatty was on duty now and that was her job. He thought he recognized the caller's voice, so he stayed on the line. It was Mrs. Hollister. Early this morning, her husband had died of his injuries, she sobbed. Could Pastor Flynn meet her at the funeral home at ten?

Jerry cut in and excused Miss Blatty. He expressed his sympathy and tried calming the distraught widow with words of assurance. He took down what information he needed and said he would see her in an hour. He no sooner returned the phone to its cradle than its ringing began one more time.

He wanted to answer, for he perceived Charlene was calling. But he trusted Miss Blatty. She would signal him if the call was for him. He waited. Nothing. The light on the intercom remained on, indicating the caller was still on the line. He hesitated. It started flashing. Hastily he picked up.

"Reverend Flynn," Jerry said. So much for his plan never to use that title for himself, he mused.

"Yes, Reverend," Miss Blatty replied, "I have Mrs. Todd on hold . . . Madge Todd, Walter Tompkins's married daughter. She is very upset. I think you better talk to her."

"Of course, Miss Blatty."

The telephone clicked to his line and Miss Blatty hung up.

"This is Jerry, Madge. What can I do for you?"

Her voice was weak and troubled.

"Reverend, I have personal problems," she managed. "Can I come in to see you?"

"Well sure! But if it's more convenient, I can come there."

"No, I'm at my office this morning."

"Okay, I sense your urgency. How about this afternoon at three?"

"Could it be earlier, Pastor? Chip gets off the school bus about then and I like to be home."

Jerry would have to cancel his afternoon calls. "Let's make it one o'clock."

"Thank you!"

"Are you going to be all right? Can you talk to your mom?"

She sounded in control again. "No, please I can't say anything to Mom, Dad, or anybody. I'll be fine."

Jerry realized he had blundered with the suggestion. If it was something her parents could help with, she would have called them, not him.

"Whatever you say, Madge. I'll see you at one."

He heard her disconnect.

"What a day." He dialed the interoffice number that would signal Miss Blatty. "Miss Blatty, you'll have to reschedule those calls I have for early this afternoon. Block me out for Mrs. Todd from one to two."

*   *   *

Rhonda and Everett were on a straight line toward Charlene.

She turned her back on them, faced the glaring, angry eyes of the street woman, who was again hammering on the booth. Ignoring her, she watched as the couple breezed by. They carried take-out orders of coffee and hard rolls, and slowed to eat and drink as they walked.

As Charlene rushed out of the booth, the cranky woman cursed at her and took a swing. Charlene blocked the assault with her arm, grabbed the woman's coat sleeves and pushed her into the phone booth. The woman screamed an obscenity, but Charlene collapsed the door against her and darted off in pursuit of her marks. She ran along Broadway, crossed with the light at 110th Street. Midway up the block, Everett and Rhonda slowed to a snails pace, so that Charlene narrowed her distance to fifty feet. At West 111th Street, they crossed, then turned the corner and strolled east. A narrow sidewalk with few people walking in either direction, Charlene feared Everett might look back and catch a glimpse of her, so she broadened the distance between them.

Ahead loomed the massive front of St. John the Divine Episcopal Cathedral; one of the three largest cathedrals in the world. Charlene reached the corner of Amsterdam Avenue in time to see Rhonda and Everett climb the steps and enter the open south portico. She crossed the avenue and made her way through the same doors.

The sudden change from bright sunlight to a cool, dark interior distressed her. She removed her sunglasses, but still had to wait several seconds for her eyes to adjust to the semi-low light of the cathedral nave. She zipped up her windbreaker and pulled down her cap.

She stood at the rear of the south aisle until spotting her prey. They sat among scattered worshippers twelve rows from the open area and on the south side of the center aisle. No worship service was in progress. Instead, this was a time for quiet, personal meditation. Many attendees had come to isolate themselves in prayer, but the cathedral was also a popular tourist stop and a refuge for homeless men. Street people were welcome to sit quietly. No one would bother them. Tourists roamed the aisles like awed pilgrims. Many stopped to read dedications in the chapels that lined the sidewall. Others chatted in low tones as they made their way toward the Choir and the Altar set in mystical light beyond the lower chancel.

There were no permanent pews or kneeling benches. Wooden benchlike chairs, locked together across the width of the nave and separated by even aisles, stood in a hundred orderly rows. In anticipation of a service that would draw a full house this evening, a staff of custodians worked from the back setting additional sitting. They worked quietly. But in this great expanse of open space, every slap and clap of a wooden chair resounded as an eerie flight of thunder.

Rhonda had taken a silk scarf from her shoulder bag and tied it like a babushka over her head. She leaned low over the empty bench in front of her. Wheeler showed no prayer stance. He had, however, removed his hat. Charlene snickered to herself, thinking of Jerry's comment that he looked like a monk with his hair stringing down from the pink bald spot that circled the crown of his head. He slouched next to Rhonda, his arms protruding like wings across the backs of chairs at his sides. His lips moved as his head turned to Rhonda's right ear.

Charlene decided to get as close as she could. She squeezed around the legs of a fat man, who slept and snored contentedly. She eased herself into a chair four empty places to the right and two behind the couple and leaned forward. She lowered the brim of her cap to her eyebrows. She prayed Everett would not look behind him.

"Let's go to your place. I swear it'll be all right," she overheard.

"Go away!" she heard Rhonda whisper, "Please, go away! I've told you. There's nothing more to discuss. We agreed not to meet. You broke your promise. You are an idiot!"

For five minutes neither one said anything. Charlene looked up to see Rhonda leaning her chin on the back of the forward bench. Everett stared at the ceiling. Without warning, he stood up. Charlene dropped her head, lowered herself farther. She heard Everett kick something, probably the bench leg in front of Rhonda and on which her head rested.

"Goddamn whore!" Charlene overheard, and it was almost not a whisper.

Slowly she raised her eyes and peeked to see Everett holding

Rhonda at the nape of her neck. He jerked her dress collar. She resisted. He turned, noticing other people, including Charlene as she dropped her head. She could feel his eyes bearing down on her. She remained motionless, head bowed, whispering the Hail Mary, which she had memorized as a child.

"Come on!" she heard. This time, he must have kicked her leg, for Rhonda gasped.

Charlene raised her head to see him shove Rhonda toward the aisle. His hand on her hip, he drove her like a cow up the aisle toward the doors. When he stopped to look behind, Charlene dropped her head swiftly. If he focuses on her it would be harder to follow. He'd remember the praying figure wearing a Yankees jacket and cap. She hoped he hadn't noticed her. Maybe she should give up the chase. She had discovered something no one else knew. She had information to put the police on their trail, reason enough for her law firm to delay payment of the insurance claim. But she couldn't quit. Her curiosity remained unsatisfied and she felt compelled to pursue the couple a while longer.

After a few minutes, she made her way past the sleeping fat man. Cautious and slow, she exited the sanctuary into the vestibule. She went to the open south portico and peered around the corner. She did not see them. She put on her sunglasses and hesitantly moved down the steps. Looking left and right along Amsterdam Avenue, she reached the sidewalk. Could they have taken a walk on the church grounds to the rear? The cathedral gardens, rectory, choir school and other buildings were that way. She walked south on Amsterdam Avenue and paused at the head of West 111th Street. She could not understand how she could lose them, unless . . . unless they had remained in the cathedral. Perhaps they went to the rest rooms. She walked farther south on Amsterdam Avenue, almost to Cathedral Parkway. She hoped to find a phone booth. She would telephone Jerry. She remembered then that she had no more quarters, not even a dime, Foolishly, she had left her unspent coins in that phone booth on Broadway.

*   *   *

The person leaning over the pew behind them had aroused Everett's interest. The baseball cap hid the face. Yet, Everett perceived he was there to eavesdrop. That was when he decided to leave. He wanted to see if the man would follow. Rhonda had to go with him. He gave her a quick kick below her knee to waken her to his urgency. He had tired of playing nice guy. There would be no more cajoling her. She complied and he continued to shove her up the aisle. He looked to the side to see that the 'man' he had seen behind them was, as he had believed, a woman. Not wearing earrings hadn't fooled him. He could see blond curls reaching out of the back of her hat. The most incriminating sign was that a Christian praying man would remove his hat in church. Of course, it peeved him that so many people these days showed no respect for God's house. "Slobs," he called them. But no, this was a woman in disguise as a man.

He held Rhonda's arm tightly. In a rush, before exiting, he pulled her into a sheltered corner as the person wearing the baseball cap came out looking for someone. He watched as the cap came up briefly and sunglasses came on. Blond hair spilled below her cap. Everett knew for sure he was looking at a woman. As she made her way down the steps, her shoulders wide and her backside straight and tight, he recognized her as Charlene Cunningham. He told himself then and there, he needed to shut her down. He watched her head slowly toward Cathedral Parkway and then about face, moving back to the cathedral.

He pulled on Rhonda's arm, forcing her outside and across the street to the west side of Amsterdam Avenue. Leading her to the corner at West 111th Street, he hailed a cab. Charlene stood less than ten feet away. Playing dumb, he shouted his destination through the open cab window.

"Rockaway Hotel on West 44th Street!"

"I know it, bud," the cabby shot back. "I'm not deaf."

"No!" Rhonda yelled. "I won't have you controlling me!"

He tightened his grip on her arm. She hit him weakly with

her bag. People close by stared, their display of friction getting attention. Out of the corner of his eye, he saw Charlene sneaking close. He repeated his destination order. Again, he squeezed Rhonda's arm, aware that he inflicted more pain. Tears masked her eyes. He pushed her into the back seat of the taxi.

"Move it!" he shouted.

* * *

Charlene was less than a hundred feet from the cathedral stairs when she saw Everett and Rhonda exit the south portico, then cross Amsterdam Avenue. She watched as Everett hailed a cab. Regaining confidence, she moved within hearing distance as Everett shouted at the hack driver. She caught the next taxi behind them. She asked the driver to follow at a safe distance.

"That's illegal," the cabby snarled, turning half way to look at his passenger.

She handed him a twenty-dollar bill. "Don't lose him," she snipped.

Without another word, the driver's eyes never left the cab in front.

On West 44th Street, Charlene watched as the couple entered the Rockaway Hotel.

* * *

At the hotel entrance, Everett took Rhonda's arm and pulled her with him. She stood alone in the filthy lobby as Everett spoke to the caged hotel clerk. They talked as if they were old friends. Everett paid and got a room key.

She wondered why he had brought her here. Other times, she had met him at the rented apartment in this same neighborhood. Since coming on to her early this morning, that's where he asked her to go with him. Then, in the cathedral, he wanted to see her Morningside Heights apartment. Now this. The

Rockaway was a surprise, a change in his plans and she wondered if she should be concerned about her safety. Everett was unpredictable. He could be brutal.

She offered no resistance as he escorted her into the scarred and smelly elevator. The scent of urine and marijuana doused by a disinfectant reached her nostrils. He said nothing as he motioned her out on the third floor and unlocked the door to room three-twelve.

They entered a threadbare room. A yellow, torn, stained bedspread covered the bed. Matching drapes, off center and one side half-fallen from the rod, decorated the room's corner windows. Everett moved to pull Rhonda onto the bed, but she evaded him and dropped into a worn-and-ratted-by-cigarette-burns upholstered lounge chair.

"Don't play games with me, Rhonda. You want me bad. I know you."

When she continued to ignore him, he went to her where she sat and reached for the top of her dress. She looked up, her face stern, but also resigned.

"Please, don't! I'll unzip it for you."

$$* \quad * \quad *$$

Charlene staked out the front entrance of the Rockaway from inside the arcade of a bargain appliance and camera store on the corner of 8th Avenue and West 44th Street. No matter this was only mid-morning and she had disguised herself as a man, she had to defend herself against women and men who propositioned her. One woman asked if she had small change, an open invitation to take a quick feel. The area was famous for this kind of activity. Adult bookstores also selling girlie magazines, movie theaters showing sex films masquerading as art, seedy-looking hotels, cheap electronic stores and souvenir shops seemed to set a trend for more of the same. The Port Authority Bus Terminal, an oasis for the homeless, loiterers, pimps and runaway teens was a few blocks south.

*   *   *

Rhonda removed her sunglasses and laid them on a side table.

All morning, she had kept Everett at bay, even when she knew it was pointless.

Her last pretense dissolved, she stood up and unzipped her dress, grasped the hem, and pulled the fine garment above her head.

Everett focused on her firm, naked breasts, which angled with her body as she leaned over to fold the dress neatly and lay it out on the bottom edge of the bed. She pushed off her canvas walking shoes. He watched with contentment as she settled into the lounge chair to detach her nylons from her garter belt and roll each one off her long, trim legs. He kept his distance until she unfastened her hair and pulled the braided strand over her shoulders to nest between her breasts.

Rhonda knew she could beguile him. Since the first time she had undressed for him, she had enjoyed his interest, the power her body held. She slid down in the filthy chair cushion so that only her head and back held a place, her legs straight as they reclined to the floor. She opened her arms to him. He was right; she wanted him. She wanted his pleasure.

He dropped his pants and shorts, then bent toward her and pulled off her panties. Taking hold of her feet, he dragged her on to the floor, flat out on her back, to engage her. He did not hurry, but waited as she moved to his rhythm and provided uninhibited affection, raising him to arousal and ultimately bringing them both to a noisy climax. For several minutes they stayed locked in each other's embrace, then parted to lie side by side. Still out of breath, he picked her up and she hugged his body before he dumped her on to the bed. She lounged there. She was looking for more, longer, enhanced lovemaking, the kind up to five months ago they had so expertly practiced. It could go on for hours. But she saw he was in no mood, indeed that he was irritable and depressed.

He went into the bathroom and did not emerge until ten minutes later. By then she had dressed and returned to the chair.

"What now?" she asked.

"I don't know, Rhonda. I really don't know. You're the lawyer. Why don't you tell me! That woman in the cathedral? She is either a newspaper reporter or a private detective. I think she's a lady dick! Whoever she is, she's looking for dirt. She tailed us here and she is now waiting at the corner. I have to take care of her."

"Everett, it's time we face our secret. If I believe what you just told me, we're already news."

She stood up and went to where he sat on the bed. She put her arms around him and pulled his head against her chest. It was a tender moment. He accepted her for a few seconds before he broke away.

"You only see the half of it, Rhonda. They'll accuse us of conspiracy in murder. Don't you see that?"

"It can't be helped. I don't believe we have a choice any longer. We'll fight it. We're innocent," she said with conviction and bowed her head again, not daring to watch him for fear of what she was about to say. "I'm planning to hire a criminal law attorney Everett and then, with him at my side, go to the police. I'd like you with me. I can't continue like this. If the authorities don't know about us already, soon enough, they will learn that you and I were seeing each other and that we were together within the time of Daniel's murder."

"They don't know and they won't unless you tell them!" he scolded. "Give me time to scare off the woman following us. Think of the insurance money. And if not that, then think about going to prison and giving up your lifestyle—all these new fancy clothes and your luxury apartment, your first class travel and wild entertainment. You better think serious about how to deal with a snooping female dick."

"The insurance company will pay me eventually. I'm innocent. I don't believe there is evidence for the police even to charge me. I'll hire the best legal defense available. I don't care what it costs. I don't care that it exposes my past and my present. I'm not hiding who I am anymore!"

"Don't talk ridiculous! What the cops don't have, they'll make up. Remember, I was out of the room during their estimated time of death. Who's to say you didn't sneak into Shepherd House. The opportunity was as much yours as mine. Besides, they won't believe either of us. If they learn we were jerking around that night, we can't even alibi for each other. They'll fix it so that we conspired to mutilate your old man. They'll develop motive and construct evidence to put me in the chair and lock you up for thirty years. And your smart-ass lawyer will tell you he won because he saved your ass from frying with mine. Can't you see how culpable the two of us look? It'll be a rush to judgment. The press alone will crucify us." She leaned forward and stared at the floor. He had more to say and he didn't want her to miss a word. He turned her face in both his wide hands. "Listen to me, god-damn you! Get all ideas of going to the cops out of your sick mind." He released her with a swat on her forehead. Before she could recover from the blow, he took a glossy two-by-three picture out of his breast shirt pocket. "Look at this!"

Rhonda stared at the picture: "You filthy man. Damn you! I thought I was cruel, but you are the devil himself. How did you take this? You were away that afternoon!"

"Don't jump to conclusions, Rhonda!" he shouted back. "I wasn't there! I didn't take this picture. But I did come into possession of the film and I did do its processing. What you see is a sample." Rhonda continued to stare at the photo, her face swollen in anger. "Don't worry," he assured her, snatching the photo out of her hand. "They're well hidden, another thing you can thank me for. Imagine what the cops will do if they see the whole affair, start to finish, sixty-four frames in all? So, be warned. Any hint about us and dirty pictures of you with your little lover friend here will find their way on to the desk of a police sergeant."

"I cannot believe you could do this to me or to your own cousin," she said, her eyes filling with tears.

"You can't believe! Hey, what do you think I said when I saw who you were with this time?" he laughed. "Not in a million years would I have believed."

"Please, Everett, grant me this. I don't care about other pictures you have of me, or what you do with them, but I beg you to dispose of this and any like it. I don't ask it to save myself from scandal, but for Madge. I promised her . . . You must do me this favor!"

"Fuck you!" he screamed, his face lit with anger. "I don't 'must' do anything!" On his feet, he reached for her hair and pulled her up to him, breathing in her face. "Now, you tell me what you did with the key I gave you to the studio? Where is it?"

"I threw it away. Why would I need it ever again?" she screamed, kicking him in the shins, backing away, throwing a wooden table chair between them.

"Before the murder, where did you keep it?" he roared, throwing the chair out of his way and grabbing her by the shoulders.

"In a pocket of my purse. No one could know what door it unlocked."

"You're sure of that?" he asked, releasing her with a flurry and turning his back.

"Yes! But why do you ask? Why do you question me on such a silly thing?

"Believe me, Rhonda!" he said facing her again, his voice more even, deliberate. "This picture came from film and a camera I found on your husband's desk hours after his murder."

"You lie!"

"No Rhonda, not about this. I believe our Reverend Maefield had a key to my studio on his ring of church keys. I believe he clicked away sixty-four nifty photos of you lady fucking little Sweetpea. Why, I don't know? Maybe to blackmail you, extort a little extra cash from your piggy bank. Maybe this was how he got off. How the hell do I know?"

"No! Impossible! Daniel had no money needs. He didn't need my money to support himself. We would always be friends. Divorced, separated, whatever I decided, he would accept it.

And sex did not entertain him. He studied sex in culture for its educational and religious values. He wrote books explaining and describing how it influenced religion, nothing more!"

"Bull shit! Rhonda! The crap about money I could possibly believe. But, sex? That is absolute fabrication! He fooled us both. And surprisingly, you more than me!"

"Daniel didn't own a camera. A brilliant man, who had no patience for gadgets, as he called them. How do you account for that?"

"Now, there you have a point, Rhonda," Everett laughed. "This picture and all the rest appear beyond the capability of an amateur. And I do agree—your husband was a klutz. I'm surprised he knew how to tie his goddamn shoes. Even so, the camera on his desk was a brand new Canonflex RM, among the most advanced you can buy. It's only been available in retail stores since last November. My best camera is not as efficient. Best of all, you don't have to think to take pictures with that thing. With a little practice, a moron can figure it out. And your husband was no moron! But, okay, suppose he didn't ogle at you and your lover through the lens? Who then? We better hope it was Daniel, because if it was someone who is still alive, we're dead in the water. Imagine what they know about us, about you. What other photos have they? For how long have they known their way in and out of my studio like it was the corner candy store? Now tell me about the key! You're sure Daniel wasn't searching your pocketbook for a little extra cash to drop in the hand of some beggar-creep and happened to come across it? He made a copy and followed you in there one night?

"Don't talk foolish, Everett! You make up such stories. My husband would never go in my purse. But what does it matter?" she said with sarcasm. "Why do you worry about that key now? You promised me in January you would destroy your studio, return the room to the way it was before you took it over for your smut photography. Now, don't tell me you didn't do that?"

"Well, I didn't, Rhonda! And today that's part of our problem. Last Sunday, your husband's jerky replacement and his overnight whore, the little piece of trash spying on this place from the street corner," he pointed, "somehow had a key and got in there."

"*Dummkopf!*" she screamed. "You deserve what you get!"

"Forget my mistakes," he sneered, throwing the photo at her, "that ain't my ass facing the camera in front of cousin fruit cup! Anyway, the studio is no more. I dismantled it last Sunday night. It's all gone. Flynn and Cunningham missed their chance to inform on me. Before they were out of their love sack yesterday morning, I hauled off or burned all traces of my picture business. So, listen big, Rhonda!" He bent to her where she sat on the bed. "If you utter one word about us in that room the night of the murder," he asserted, his finger touching her nose, "or our fucking ways for the last four years, every pervert in this city is going to whack off watching you and Madge. And that includes horny cops! Don't doubt they won't jump to the conclusion that you murdered your old man to keep him silent about your girl-faggot love interests." He pulled away his hand and towered over her. She had to look high to see him.

"You believe that? You believe I killed him?"

He went to where the picture had settled on the floor, picked it up and brought it to her. He held it once more in front of her eyes.

"No, but the whiz kids at the county prosecutor's office will."

He tried to get her to take the photo, but she refused. She looked away. Everett's supposition had stopped her cold. His treachery frightened her. When he sat down next to her, she looked at him with scorn. Nor had he silenced her.

"You said you found the camera on his desk?" she stormed. "When did you find it? The police sealed Shepherd House . . . " She stopped. The expression on her face changed from solemnity to terror, as she remembered the crash of the gate, the movement she associated with shadows of blowing cedar trees. "You were there, Everett! You saw me approaching Shepherd House that morning. You let me discover his body. Were you there for the murder? Did you catch him behind the mirror in your studio and lose your temper?" He did not look at her, but stared at the floor.

"You followed him to his office and killed him. Is that what happened?"

He said nothing as he arose from the bed and moved away, crossed the room to the window and peered out at the street below. He broke into the intervening silence. "I've got 'a go."

He helped her to her feet and brought her into his arms. He kissed her long and with passion. "Let's not argue," he whispered. "I promise to keep you and Madge a secret," he said as he slid the picture into his shirt pocket, "but you must protect me, Rhonda. I'm depending on you."

She said nothing as she fed off him. Once more, her passion for sex took over her reasoning and her emotions. He pushed her back.

"Later! Give me a few more days, that's all I ask. Come on, I'll flag you a cab."

*   *   *

Charlene moved behind a corner newsstand. Ten minutes passed before she saw Everett and Rhonda exit the Rockaway Hotel, their arms linked as they walked the short distance toward her new position on 8th Avenue. Everett signaled a taxicab. He opened the cab door and Rhonda climbed in. They waved at each other as the taxi drove off. Charlene's eyes followed Everett as he made his way west across 8th Avenue toward 9th Avenue. In her gut, she wanted to stick with her original hunt, but Rhonda was out of the picture. She could catch up to her later and so she took her chances following Everett. She would shadow him long enough to learn his next destination. Then she promised, she would contact Detective Burroughs.

At 9th Avenue Everett walked south to 42nd Street and then west again. All the while, he took his time, stopping often to browse in adult bookstores and once, he loitered at a movie theater as if planning to buy a ticket. But then he moved on. She followed at a safe distance, careful to stay out of sight by keeping to the other side of the street, dodging into storefronts, or pretending window-shopping. At 8th[h] Avenue, he walked north to 47th Street and re-crossed 8th Avenue, continuing east toward Broadway.

47th Street was another one way with narrow sidewalks. Cars and trucks parked bumper to bumper and sometimes double-parked along both curbs. Brownstone apartment houses, many with gated basement entrances under a stoop, fronted sidewalk almost empty of people. A third of the way to Broadway, she realized Everett had disappeared. She had a bad feeling, slowed her pace and soon stopped to look behind her. She wasn't ready to panic, but she thought she should play safe and cross the street, or turn back to 8th Avenue.

Suddenly, a hand seized her right arm. Everett had come on to her in a matter of seconds. Forcing her forward, he locked her arm around his waist and clamped his left hand against her hip. She jerked left to loosen his hold and felt a needlelike stab in her upper left thigh. She had a sensation that blood was running down her leg. "Keep moving, say nothing," he whispered harshly into her ear. "I can slice your artery and you'll bleed to death before anyone pays you mind. Act like you are enjoying me, you little bitch!"

Her training told her to scream, punch, run. But there was no one close to hear. Already, she felt a stinging pain in her upper thigh. He was strong, and he held her secure in his powerful clutches. They walked only six steps, when he guided her into an outside stairwell and down to the landing. He pushed her face against a windowless door. He brought his fully extended knife blade under her chin. She felt its point play on her soft flesh. She saw her own blood on his fingers. She did not move a muscle as he crushed his body against her. With his free hand, he fumbled with a key, unlocked the door and pushed in. Using his knee against her rump, he bolted her forward. She fell headlong to the floor. Her cap and sunglasses flew and her forehead hit the leg of a kitchen table. The door slammed behind them. She bled above her eyebrow.

He took a moment to collapse his knife and wedge it into his pants pocket. Roughly, he pulled her up from under her shoulders, then shoved her face first against a wall and turned her around. He drove the back of his hand into the pit of her stomach and let her collapse to the floor, where she clawed her body into a fetal position and strove to catch her breath. He reached down and took her feet to straighten her flat on her back. She opened her eyes to the face of a snarling pig, who said nothing as he dropped her feet, grabbed the lapels of her windbreaker and lifted her up only to throw her against the kitchen counter. She grabbed at things, anything to use as a weapon, but all fell out of her hands. A toaster and some dishes crashed to the floor and she followed them. She feared he was in for the kill. Stunned, she played possum, not daring to move. He cursed her and kicked her in her ribs, then tramped on her stomach. He took her by her feet and dragged her across the floor, the back of her head bouncing across a threshold as he moved her into an adjoining room. She was near unconscious when he lifted and threw her onto the bed.

He crawled on top of her. Out of the bed table drawer, he took two sets of police-issue handcuffs. Pulling up on each arm, he locked her wrists to the steel piping that made up the headboard. He got off her to spread her legs and tie her ankles to the bedposts with clothesline. Standing at her side, he stuck a men's handkerchief into her bleeding mouth and covered it with medical tape. She worried that she could drown in her own blood, for she could taste it seeping around the gag.

He slapped her face, gripped her chin, forcing her to stare at him. His face dripped with sweat and his eyes had narrowed inside their shallow pockets. He breathed hard. She could smell his sour breath. His mouth opened to clenched teeth and a cruel grin, the same she saw that night in Tommy's when he argued with the young redhead. She looked away as he emptied all her pockets, resting each found item on her chest until dropping them all into his jacket pocket.

"I'm leaving you for a little while, girl! I have an errand to run. When I return we'll have a friendly chat," he said as he stood staring at her. She tried focusing on other things in the room. "Yes, this is my other hideaway. Like it? No camera, though. Disappointed?" he half laughed and dropped his huge hand on her breast. Tense and cold, helpless and shivering, she thought only that she was going to die here. "You didn't think I could leave without a look at these gourmet tits you're so proud of, now did you?" He leaned over and unzipped her windbreaker. Her body tensed. Tears glassed her eyes and she closed them tight. Her chest heaved as he pulled open her blouse, popping the buttons. He stripped down the right cup of her bra.

"Nice, very nice. Haughty! I'd say, smooth, solid, a grapefruit variety!" he said as he pawed. "Worth a lot on the girlie shelf. Too bad I may have to cut this cute tit off," he sighed as he fingered her nipple. "I hope Preacher Jerry got a good suck, 'cause it was his last."

He patted her other breast above where the pink fabric secured it.

"But this feels just as good," he purred. "Maybe I'll keep this one intact for the coroner."

He left her that way. After several minutes, she heard the outside door slam. She shuddered. For a moment, she thought she was already dead and only pretending life.

CHAPTER 11

IDLE INSIGHTS

Tuesday Afternoon, June 6

Traffic moved at a snail's pace in lunchtime Manhattan. Rhonda Maefield could do no more than sit back and observe patience as the taxicab crawled toward her Morningside Heights apartment. But that was not the state of her mind, as all along the way, she fretted about the state of her life.

*　　*　　*

Her early years with Daniel had known little conflict and what there was had mostly occurred over the issue of money. They had very different views of its meaning and use. For Daniel money was a means to buying necessities. He did not require luxury items or new clothes. He preferred to travel as cheap as possible, drive a used car, live in "squalid" church housing (which was how Rhonda had described the manse provided by their Harlem church) and eat only enough food to ward off abject hunger. Moreover, Daniel appeared impervious to how much things cost, or, when he found out, he usually shouted—much to Rhonda's embarrassment—*"Highway bloody robbery!"*

But charity was another story. Daniel supported missionaries and the church's benevolence budget with generous contributions.

In Rhonda's mind, he gave extravagant gifts to the March of Dimes, UNICEF, Red Cross and other charitable organizations he considered reputable. His out-of-pocket cash to beggars was legendary. If a man or woman came to the church with money problems, he was quick to open his wallet to help stave off professed starvation and to pay their rent or utilities. He could never pass a supplicant without dropping something into his or her box.

To Rhonda such people were panhandlers, lazy, drunks and thieves. She constantly scolded Daniel for getting conned out of his last dollar.

Rhonda believed money was the route to happiness. She liked to live in grand style, travel first class. She gloried in service at expensive restaurants and resorts. Even her dreary clothes came from high-priced stores. And the apparel she purchased to grace her body for those discriminating times came from the finest dress salons. She surrounded herself with costly furniture, jewelry and artwork. She never thought about how much these items cost or how far she dipped into her personal savings to pay for them.

So, when the opportunity for her husband to take over as minister of First Church at Tompkinsville presented itself, she begged him to accept the call. His salary would quadruple (to her a matter of pride, not need), the housing was exquisite, the gothiclike cathedral as beautiful as any in Europe; the importance of ministering in a more-than-a-thousand-member church, she believed, fitted his renowned reputation.

As it turned out, the move was a mismatch, if ever there was one. Intellectually and theologically, church and minister were as different as sugar and salt. They differed on politics, interpretation of the bible and most of all on social responsibility. But Daniel was faithful and caring in his pastoral duties. He ignored criticism and attended to pastoral needs with decorum and dedication, a nature that infuriated Rhonda. She likened the church elders, who often plotted behind his back, to the ancient Pharisees, who—with few exceptions—had opposed

Jesus and had actively sought his crucifixion. She had worse words for the trustees, who managed the church's buildings, and made policy respecting the church's millions in endowments. To Rhonda they were the equivalent of "Nazi fascist pigs."

But Daniel seldom complained. "His meekness drove me crazy."

She believed his lifestyle and passive attitude reflected his identification with Indian teachers. In India, his father had translated much of the bible into a half-dozen Indian dialects. To do this, he went off to live within their community for many months, even for a year at a time. Neither the poverty nor the absence of luxury discouraged his research. Indeed, he became so engrossed in his work he had difficulty adjusting to the lifestyle of his wife, who lived in royal elegance as an English lady—crinkled dresses, afternoon teas and servants to answer every need.

As young as six years old, against his mother's wishes, Daniel's father took him with him into the Indian world. But his father's sudden death, when Daniel was fifteen, separated him from that environment. With Daniel in hand, his mother returned to London, where, six months later, she died after a short illness. Everett would not return to India for ten years and then only as a scholar and a traveler. But he had remained essentially a product of meager Indian living standards and of a nonviolent philosophy to achieve political ends. He studied *Satyagraha*, Gandhi's principle of nonviolent behavior. He spoke of Gandhi as his friend and had met the popular leader in his simple, yet utilitarian home. In 1955, he encouraged a young, black, civil rights leader named Martin King to visit Gandhi. From that experience, King more clearly defined his own understanding of the power of nonviolent politics.

For Rhonda, however, Passivism in the face of evil showed weakness.

She believed with many Germans—who fought Hitler in the beginning—"*You don't kill a snake by stepping on its tale. You chop off its head.*"

When she first met Daniel, he agreed with that view. He once considered men like Neville Chamberlain weasels and as lambs led to the slaughter. Daniel changed. Like many liberal thinkers, after the war in Europe, and the surrender of Japan, Daniel turned from hawk to dove. He once compared his transformation to that of Julius Oppenheimer, who had as much to do with creating the atom bomb as anyone, but then adamantly opposed further development. Daniel agreed that the human death toll and total destruction powered by one atom bomb made future war indefensible, regardless of the evil it deterred. So, he participated in demonstrations against nuclear bomb testing. He joined peace groups and supported them with his writing and his money. Never mind that a third of Europe now lived in slavery under communism, Rhonda argued back. But Daniel had become more like a deaf man, never hearing her anger or recognizing how much she and her family had suffered. "How dishonorable he was," she sulked, "his pious indifference made me sick."

*   *   *

Rhonda made her way into the luxuriant lobby of her tenement where floor to ceiling mirrors reflected her tarnished view—hair down and disheveled, dress uneven and wrinkled, makeup smeared. She wished to hide, but she could not avoid the security man who greeted her by name and with a smile. A credit to his training, he hid his true thoughts behind his helpful manner. Standing silent, he engaged the elevator and rode Rhonda to her floor.

Once inside her apartment, she stripped off every item of clothing and deposited them all in the hamper. A hot, soapy shower followed and then, in her nakedness, with a stop at the mini bar in her living room to fix a strong gin-and-tonic, she moved into the extra bedroom, which she used as her office. Sitting at her writing table, out of the drawer she took a pen and a box of fine stationary, her name and address emboldened on paper and envelopes.

Dearest Madge, I cry for you every night, she penned.

The letter was brief, but filled with emotions she found rare to express. Finished, she addressed an envelope and affixed more than the needed postage. She wedged open her apartment door to the hall. Seeing no one, she dashed the few seconds it took her to drop her letter into the mail shoot. Returning to her apartment, she fixed herself another Collins and went to the bedroom where, on her bed, she propped up her body with pillows.

Her letter to Madge had not lessened her anxiety. If only she could suppress her worries, drive the darkness into her subconscious. But it was no use. While tasting her drink, she recalled how after four years at First Church, she and Everett Wheeler had become lovers. He had seen through her masquerade as the good and faithful wife, had broken into her defenses and made her his "slut." But then she was to blame for that. It would never have happened had she not followed him into the basement apartment, which was then not a studio but a half-hidden room where he snuck away for an afternoon nap. Had Everett Wheeler lived in Nazi Germany, he would have served as one of Himmler's henchmen, the perfect sadist for the Gestapo mentality and the kind of man she had learned to hate and fear. By the date of her seventeenth birthday, many "Everett's" had invaded her life. And strangely, they still pleasured her, brought her body nothing less than relief, indeed, freedom. But then, so did lovers like Madge. If only Madge was not so conflicted. She recalled that afternoon. After years of friendship, they had come to intimacy; how pure and unreserved their first time like that had been. How much she wished she had that to do over again. Given time, Madge could forgive her. But Everett's pictures proved they had run out of time. She owed it to Madge to get Everett to destroy them, or else—she quivered at the thought, and drank from her tall glass until the ice lay bare. Her hands shook as she set it on the table at the side of her bed. She eased back on to the pillows and soon lost herself in alcohol-induced sleep.

*   *   *

Madge Todd sat across from Jerry in a wingback chair by the fireplace. Her cheek-length ravenlike hair set off her striking facial features, though, in her sodden eyes, he saw she had been crying. A white summery dress, politely drawn an inch or so above her knees, rose tightly to stretch across her chest, where sparse sleeves secured it on her bare shoulders. She exalted female beauty by every standard of measurement. Pleasant speaking and sincere, intelligent and personable, she made conversation easy and Jerry imagined how pleasant life could be with such a woman as a wife.

As she conveyed the details of her and Michael's confrontation last Sunday night, tears filled her eyes and she took a tissue to them. Before she finished explaining things, she excused herself to use the restroom behind her chair.

What was he supposed to do or say? He had had little training in pastoral counseling. Although this was one of the most called-upon roles in the pastorate, seminary had offered him only one course in dealing with marital conflict and virtually nothing in understanding the dynamics of marriage role expectations.

All he could remember was a bland lecture on professional ethics. "*Now boys, for lady visitors in distress, always sit behind your desk, place folded hands on top like this,*" the professor had demonstrated, "*and keep your eyes focused on your ring finger. Remember the Apostle Paul's injunction that a wife must obey her husband. Close with prayer.*"

Well, he had already broken those rules. He wasn't sitting behind his desk, he didn't have a wedding ring on his ring finger to look at and he considered that "*obey your husband*" counsel as hogwash. Nor was he planning to close with prayer unless she asked him to do so. Even more, he couldn't understand how a husband could act so stupid as to let such a beautiful, appealing, smart wife become his enemy. But he knew he must suppress his emotions. He had to deal with what university studies had shown—that married women predominated as those most likely to come to their minister with a problem and male infidelity was most often at the root of that problem. Jerry wanted to ask her if she suspected Michael of being unfaithful. But thinking he would appear forward, especially this early in hearing her, he would not ask. Besides this, he had absolutely no idea how to treat her once he broached the subject. When she returned from the restroom, he sought a way out.

"Madge, do you think that Michael and I could get together?"

"You mean for counseling?"

"No, I 'm not suggesting anything that formal, just a chat. If you two are going to stay together, you will have to work on your problems together. I have no training as a marriage counselor, nor have I the time it requires. Besides, I'm sure your disagreement goes deeper than how you two manage the farm. I have to tell you that I suspect there are personal matters here you can't talk about, nor should you talk about them to me. But a special concern of mine is for Michael to trust me. The best I can do is get you both to a family therapist who can help you identify personal differences and can suggest ways to cope with them. I realize Michael won't consider a referral without meeting me. Perhaps if we could sit down over a couple of beers, it might break the ice."

Madge brightened at the suggestion. Michael played on the church basketball team, which she knew interested Jerry. He was also active in the Boy Scout troop that met at the church. She asked if Jerry had met Michael at Boy Scout Council Meeting last night, and showed disappointment when he replied he had sent his regrets. Due to an emergency call at the hospital, he had to miss his first meeting.

"Perhaps you'll meet at next month's meeting," she suggested. Madge doubted Jerry would see Michael at church until Christmas.

"Well, why don't I just trot into his office tomorrow, introduce myself, and say: 'Let's go out for lunch?' There's no need to be shy. I'll be up front with him if he wants advice. It may take more than one meeting before I'd even broach the idea of marriage counseling."

She liked Jerry's practical approach. He didn't get clinical with her and ask a lot of uncomfortable questions as Reverend

Maefield had. He would not try to solve her problems by handing her a book to read, or give her advice on how to please her man. She did not, however, know how to tell Jerry that Michael was already prejudiced against him. She dabbed her eyes with her handkerchief. "I don't know if he'll ever go for that. He's not one to admit he has a problem. What if he won't go to counseling?"

"Then you have to go alone. You have to seek help for yourself, not for him. But Michael might surprise you. You told me how he reacted when he saw you hurt. That's a good sign. It shows sensitivity. It's a beginning. He does love you, even if it doesn't always show."

"I don't know. I just don't know what his feelings are. I'm not sure of mine."

"Tell me more, Madge. Tell me what you perceive as Michael's problem."

She took a deep breath. Did she dare? She opted to keep herself out of it.

"Michael may have a big problem with alcohol. It seems to have gotten worse in the last few months. I've seen him out of control because of his drinking more times than I like to admit. Last night, he came home so intoxicated I don't know how he drove from wherever he began. I awoke to find him stretched out on his stomach on the living room floor. I couldn't wake him, and left him there. I'm thankful he recovered before the children were up. After seeing him like that, and the Sunday-night incident, I made up my mind to come in to see you. I am at my wits end."

"Are you afraid to live at home?"

"No. As I said, I don't believe Michael meant to push me."

"What about your father; do you think Michael would listen to him?"

"My father?" she said, raising her voice in despair.

Jerry knew he had asked the wrong question.

"My father's views are worse than Michael's. Sure, he'll listen to him! He's been listening to my father all his life. Dad will tell you that a woman's place is in the home. I think he's softened to some degree of late, but, no, Daddy would never see me as an equal. My father, O God, no! He does homage to the ground Michael walks on and when he finds out I may file for a divorce, he'll be furious with me."

"Sorry, I had no idea."

"Well, you'll learn soon enough! I'm sorry. I love my father dearly, but I would never expect him to agree with me as a business woman or to support me in my disagreement with my husband."

"What about your mother?"

Madge smiled, but then her eyes turned glassy in another move to tears.

"My mother subjugated herself to my father many years ago. That's what they both think I should do. I can't. Life is too short. I'm not a pet dog and I refuse to have someone treat me like one."

Matters were more complicated than Jerry had originally perceived. He now saw Madge's anger and depression. For the first time, he considered she might be a candidate for a nervous breakdown. She had no one to turn to and things looked hopeless. He wished he had someone he could refer her to immediately, but it takes time to find the right people. Thus far, he had not begun consulting counseling agencies or private-practice marriage therapists.

"Madge, alcoholism is a cover for deeper matters. I believe you know that. We're not going there today."

He watched her nod her head in agreement.

"Okay . . . well . . . let's see how it goes tonight. Don't talk business. Find agreeable things. Try to protect your children from hearing you argue. For their sake, you and Michael have to do whatever is reasonable to avoid divorce."

Madge reached into her purse for fresh tissues, blew her nose. She looked at Jerry with sincerity and sadness. "My children are all that keep me from leaving," she cried.

He rose with her. They both knew the session was over.

"Thank you for listening. I know I disrupted your afternoon."

She walked past him and he kept his hands behind his

back.

"I have to get home before the children. Chip will be getting off the school bus in a half hour and Mom drops Dudley by about the same time."

Jerry walked Madge to Shepherd Door. She started out, then paused and came back in. Jerry waited for her to speak. She took her car keys out of her purse and nervously fiddled with them. She hesitated, looked down at her shoes, then directly into his eyes. She turned away and took a deep breath, met his eyes once more, but she did not smile.

"I have to warn you. Be very careful what you do or say around Everett Wheeler! This is between you and me. He knows everything that goes on around here and he can't be trusted. If that were all, it wouldn't be so bad. The church should fire him and—if possible—excommunicate him for all the terrible things, known and unknown, he has done. He's no good as a cousin, worse as a friend and—believe me—you don't want him as your enemy. Anyway, this is a friendly warning about keeping female company at the manse."

Jerry frowned. That Madge was the one telling him this shocked him as much as hearing it at all. How quickly their roles had reversed. She knows about Charlene. He could feel his face redden and he knew his surprise was all too obvious. He wanted to deny anything happened, instead, he said, "Thank you! I appreciate your advice."

She lowered her eyes as if ashamed she had said anything. She knew it was none of her business. His embarrassment had touched her. She looked up to see his pain. In an instant, his eyes had lost their confidence. She took a step toward him and took his hand.

"I'm sorry, but I believed you'd be better off knowing this now than later. You can be on your guard," she said; then, she lightly kissed him on the cheek and left him with his thoughts.

*   *   *

As afternoon hours ticked away, Charlene Cunningham fought against panic and despair. To succumb to either mental state could kill her. As best she could, she stayed motionless and quiet, conserving what little physical energy she had left.

Thanks for little things. Intended or not, Everett had allowed enough slack in the ropes to permit her to pull up to a partial sitting position. By nudging the pillow behind her, she supported her shoulders and head. But the metal cuffs around her wrists hurt every time she flinched and her arms grew weak and weary in their upraised positions. Soon her skin showed raw, so she found it more comfortable to skid into the footboard and rest flat on her back.

She counted it in her favor that the blood from the cut over her right eyebrow had coagulated. Maybe, it was not as deep as she had originally feared. And while it was difficult to swallow, she believed she no longer bled inside her mouth and maybe she hadn't lost her tooth.

Now and then, she felt nauseous, but she knew her life would be over if she gave in to that feeling. She considered how black and blue she must look where Everett had punched her; she hurt plenty when she took deep breaths, and she could hardly see out of her left eye. In spite of these difficulties, she appraised her situation, estimating the apartment consisted of two main rooms and a bath. The outer room was a kitchen that also served as a sitting room. She remembered its linoleum floor and the aluminum table leg against which her head had smashed. The bathroom faced the hallway through which Everett had dragged her and a closet may be on the opposite side. Her bedroom prison was neat and nicely furnished. A ceiling fan directly over her head circulated air and kept the temperature bearable. Dark imitation wood paneling covered the walls. From what she could see of the floor, which she could see in a mirror attached to the back of the door, it appeared covered by a deep pile green carpet. A small window, close to the ceiling with curtains and a drawn shade, emitted a little daylight. Everett had left a bright lamp lit on the bed stand. A tall bureau against the opposite wall and a huge reading chair with a floor lamp next to it in the north corner completed the ensemble. Her body stretched out on top of a white comforter, her head cushioned by a soft pillow.

By now, Charlene figured Everett had gone through everything personal in her car.

He had taken her wallet, thus, her driver's license, private detective ID and employment card. He had her appointment and address book with telephone numbers of every person she knew in the world. He had the address of the law firm for whom she worked, a picture of her deceased grandmother, and the address, phone number and even the key of her Philadelphia apartment. He had the parking-garage receipt, thus her MG.

A new fear suddenly flashed in her mind as she thought about him reading her notebook with all her interview notes and other information. It occurred to her that when she looked earlier this morning, she had not seen it. "Could I have lost it? God, I hope so." All her entries through Monday morning, as well as her observations, conclusions, and questions filled its pages. And most incriminating of all, next to Everett's name, she recalled, she had doodled a hangman's noose. "Dumb!"

Ironically, if Everett believed she had communicated vital information to Officer Burroughs this morning that could work in her favor. His fear of an imminent police investigation might save her life and make him think twice before hurting her anymore than he already had. How to persuade Everett that she would be more beneficial alive than dead occupied her thinking.

*   *   *

Frank Scarpelli ministered to the Presbyterian Church in the next town, and had pastoral oversight at First Church during the interim months. Jerry knew Frank as friend and mentor. With these titles on his mind, and to drop off a copy of his ordination service for Sunday, Jerry pulled into the gravel parking lot of St. Andrew's Presbyterian Church.

A Presbyterian minister for more than ten years, Reverend Scarpelli had served in his present church all of that time. His responsibility for the cathedral church was due to Maefield's death, an appointment he accepted as in addition to his regular pastorate. Besides some administrative duties, Frank Scarpelli was on call for pastoral services, which—in a membership the size of First—meant a lot of extra time. Working an eighty-hour week was usual for pastors like Scarpelli. Their skills and dedication were what kept the church going.

Like Jerry, Scarpelli had graduated from Princeton Seminary, and grown up in the Catholic Church. But Frank's experience was more like that of Jerry's stepfather. An ordained priest for eight years, Scarpelli had served the Newark Diocese as pastor at two churches. Frank, too, had fallen in love with a woman and married. It wasn't his affair that had so upset Mother Church (that could be forgiven), but his decision to marry her. Fortunately, for the Presbyterian Church, that woman was a Presbyterian.

Walking through the little fellowship hall outside Frank's office, Jerry had to exercise caution not to trip over boxes of used clothes, canned goods and an assortment of children's toys. People were dropping off these goods all week, Frank had explained yesterday, and on Friday, church deacons would begin their quarterly distribution.

Jerry stopped to look in at Scarpelli through his open door and saw the man at a table at the side of his desk busily typing. His wide desktop looked as though a dump truck had backed into the office and unloaded over it. Jerry beheld stacks of typewritten papers on top of prayer books, bibles and catalogues. He recognized volumes of Calvin's Institutes and New Testament commentaries by William Barclay. There were coffee cups, a paper plate with a half-eaten sandwich and candy-bar wrappers. Off to the side of the room was an A. B. Dick manual mimeograph machine. Fresh ink oozed from its drum, injured copies of worship folders were scattered about the table and overflowing the wastebasket. Jerry knew Scarpelli's church could not afford a full time secretary and he guessed what there was of one was a volunteer.

He recognized that Frank Scarpelli at St. Andrews Presbyterian Church—overworked, understaffed, underpaid and working out of a rambling, deteriorating building—was more typical of the Presbyterian Church than what he represented at First. In one way, Jerry envied this genre of pastor; in another, he did not think he had the guts for it.

Behind Frank, Jerry saw bookshelves stacked with books, magazines, notebooks, file folders, and Scarpelli's state-of-the-art stereo system, his one luxury in this world. Scarpelli loved classical music, opera and—as if in rebellion to all that—Elvis Presley. But Bach's Oboe Concerto in D Minor played softly in the background today.

Politely, softly, not wanting to startle him, Jerry rapped on the door. The big man looked up, his dark eyes flashing, his face a solid grin. His hands went to his combed, straight back, generous carpet of shinning black hair.

"Hey, Jerry!" Frank shouted.

His six-feet-four, 280 pounds of muscle and flab came out of his chair like Mt. Vesuvius erupting. He hurried around his desk. Frank had that classic Italian exuberance and he reached for Jerry like a bear to cuddle her young, pulling Jerry to his chest, pounding him hard on the back of his shoulders.

"Here, here, sit down, my handsome friend."

Frank grabbed up what was in the one visitor's chair and threw it—where else?—on top of his desk.

"Gee, Frank, who's buried here?" Jerry laughed as he sat and toyed with papers in front of him. "You got an old mob boss under this?" Jerry lifted up a stack of debris, pretending to search for an un-named suspect.

Frank Scarpelli laughed all the way to his desk chair, where he plopped down heavily, out of breath from his little exertion.

"You kill me, Jerry!"

"How's Angel and the kids?"

"Great, absolutely wonderful! Marriage, Jerry, bambinos, ha—it's the life. You know, I can't think of myself as any other way. Angel loves every piece of this," he said, patting his stomach. "What about

you? You ready to settle down, get married? I got two widows here
and a divorced lady. Jerry, the divorcee, she's beautiful. Great legs
and a heart of gold. Her ex-husband's an alcoholic, a mean one.
The asshole beat her up once too often. She finally got up the courage
to quit. We had her and her two kids hiding out with us for three
weeks. Gorgeous girl. Let me set you up."

"Tell me about the widows, Frank?" Jerry said jokingly.

"Wooeee! One's a little old for you, though, maybe you need
a mature lady. The other, frankly, she's not ready, a bitter girl.
Her husband's been dead for three years and she still cries herself
to sleep every night. Killed in a tragic accident. Thirty-eight years
old. He was driving home from work late at night, the car broke
down, he pulled over on the shoulder, opened the car door, put
both feet on the pavement, and 'wham!' An on coming car carried
him away. Killed instantly. It's tough, Jerry, you can't do much
else with the survivors except cry with them."

Jerry looked down into his hands. He knew the script.

"I have my first funeral Friday. The man's tractor flipped
over on him while he was heading out to the fields to plow. They're
still trying to piece it all together. A combination of wet grass and
worn tires caused it to slip. The rear wheel slid too far over a
drainage ditch. The family believes it was his time, predestined.
That's real Calvinist thinking, isn't it?"

"Sure, I suppose it helps if you can believe that crap. It isn't
your fault or the victim's. Let God take the blame. Technology
has nothing to do with death. According to that belief, God writes
up our deaths before our births. Deep stuff, Jerry. And sometimes
I have to agree. You think your life belongs to you, but it doesn't.
I don't know! Paul, Augustine, the Catholic Fathers, Luther,
Calvin . . . they all mirror that belief, don't they? Man has nothing
to say about his own destiny. In all due respect to the fathers of
our faith, they were more fatalistic than we like to believe. It's all
written ahead of time."

Jerry shook his head. "I 'm not sure I agree. I don't think of
myself as God's puppet. I believe God creates us with freedom
and we suffer the consequences of that. We are free to drive

potentially dangerous machines. Their very imperfection puts us at risk."

"Right on, Jerry! But be prepared to defend yourself, especially there at First Church. Your predecessor, Daniel, he was—I think—the greatest free thinker ever in our church. He argued with the big boys that man is not predisposed to heaven or hell, but he is capable of deciding whether to do good or evil on any given day of his life. Depending on what he decides, he may suffer or enjoy the consequences or the pleasures of his choices. Daniel Maefield honestly believed our responsibility as Christians is to change the social order into the Kingdom of God, to move there by good deeds. If Daniel Maefield didn't get into heaven for what he said or wrote, he made it for what he did or tried to do. I never knew a more Christlike man, Jerry. Yet members of his congregation called him a walking devil."

Frank leaned back in his chair, loosened his tie and unbuttoned his collar. He looked to the side and out the open window, as if waiting for a gust of cool wind off the sultry fields. When the climate remained unresponsive to his silent wish, he turned back to Jerry, his eyes sharp and unsmiling.

"You know Daniel died of a broken heart! Yes, I understand the knife cut into his heart and let the blood out, but spiritually, he had already begun to die. And it had nothing to do with his critics. He loved arguing with them. But, something terrible lived in that man's mind, Jerry, something dark and sinister. He struggled with the devil as sure as Jesus did in the wilderness."

"You were friends!"

"We were friends—poker and good wine, jokes and long discussions. Sometimes we got into personal things, as priests do. We met almost every Monday morning at Tommy's Place for free sausage and eggs. Daniel genuinely relished his breakfast. Every other meal he could stuff into a thimble. That was about all he ate. But breakfast for him was the banquet of life. That last Monday morning, a week before his death, he hardly took a bite of his meal. He was deeply saddened, melancholy. He talked about Rhonda's unhappiness. He said he was a failure as her husband. He warned me they would separate and divorce before the end of this year. He told me the decision was Rhonda's and he wouldn't be able to save her, his exact words, *from fire worse than hell.* For a man who didn't believe in hell as most people envision it, his words were uncommon. But, sometimes I couldn't decide whether Daniel was speaking figuratively or just being melodramatic. That morning, however, I took him serious. Whatever he had discovered was somehow linked to Rhonda and it had depressed him beyond his faith."

"I've heard mixed things about Rhonda," Jerry interjected. "Most people in the church say they didn't know her. People describe her as aloof and unfriendly. I take it she wasn't around very much in the last four years. Word has it she and Daniel already lived separate lives."

"Yah, I believe that was true. Still, she was all he had and he would die for her. Whatever wrong she had done, Daniel forgave her. He loved her very much. I don't want you to misunderstand me, Jerry. I don't want to give you a false impression of Rhonda, but the way Daniel spoke about her that morning, it was as if he loved her in the same way the prophet Hosea loved his whoring wife, Gomar."

Scarpelli paused for a moment, dropped his eyes to his desk. Jerry thought about the room he and Charlene had discovered. Maybe that was the connection. Jerry poised to say something about it to Scarpelli, started to, but too late. Frank had turned away again. He hadn't seen Jerry leaning forward, desperate to make his own confession.

"You got a tough job, Jerry. If you aren't careful you'll be torn apart." Again, he faced Jerry. "First Church is an aesthetically beautiful church, great bunch of folks to work with and such an opportunity to serve our Lord. Yet, I wouldn't trade my rinky-dink building—with its leaking roof and broken down organ, a furnace that waits to shut down on the coldest day in February—" he laughed loudly, "for your cathedral and all its wealth."

"Why do you think they called me to serve them, Frank?"

"Because you got balls! Because you're young and they believe . . . the energy of youth will set fire to their souls. You're likable. Because in appearance, experience and the way you present ideas, you are the total opposite of Daniel Maefield. I think they believe you will help them forgive themselves. In spite of what they say now, Jerry, many of those people hated Daniel so much they treated him as already dead. They paid no attention to his example. Then, when death happened and because of its violence, they cried like Judas and Peter did for their betrayal of Christ. There's a lot of guilt in that church, Jerry. Anger, pity, shame, they're all included."

"And what if I disappoint them, Frank, when they find that I don't live up to their expectations? That I am also very human, have balls, as you say. What then?"

"Tell them, Jerry! Make clear from the start who you are. Don't let them hold you to a standard that defies normality. You're a sinner like everyone else."

"Well, I guess I've already shown that," he whispered and dropped his eyes.

If Scarpelli heard, he ignored it. "Jerry, you'll do fine. But don't stay too long. Anyone who comes to First Church is there for the short haul. That's the way I see it. Presbytery should have insisted on that anyway, a one—or two-year assignment, someone to come in to clean up the mess, and it's not all about Daniel Maefield's murder. That's what the Catholics would have done and on that score, they're right; enforce the parochial disciplines. But the powerful people at First Church would have nothing to do with an in intermediary minister. Those tyrants went along with your nomination because they believe they can mold you to their views and if you fail, they can turn around and say, 'Told you so!' You, son, are their bait. If I were you, I would turn the tables and purge the old fools. They want to go worship somewhere else, give them your blessing and the toe of your foot. Tell them to go take a shit, the one they've been holding off on for so long. They'll feel better."

"You mean people like Walter Tompkins?"

"He's exactly who I mean. But he's not alone. In fact, Walter is one of the more progressive minds. Stand up to him. That means getting younger people involved in governing the church. See if you can't get the congregation to vote some women on to session. Personally, I would eliminate the Board of Trustees as a separate entity from session. The constitution of the church doesn't require us to have a separate financial board. Put the finances and management of the church building where they belong, under the authority of the session."

"Frank, I feel like David against Goliath and I don't know if I can find the smooth stones to do the job."

"You'll find 'm, Jerry, God will help you."

He had to ask Frank one more question. "Did you have any dealings with the custodian at First Church?"

"Did I? Wheeler's mind is always in the gutter. He has a nasty view of sex and a racist view of anyone who he doesn't like. If you get on his wrong side he'll find an ugly name for you."

"Yes, I've learned that first hand."

"Unfortunately, the trustees will keep him on. He's got them eating out of his hand. He does a good job maintaining the church, I suppose. I never heard anyone complain about that. He's dependable and efficient. That counts more to them than moral character. But I'll tell you, I wouldn't want my daughter or my wife left alone with him."

"Yes, I've heard rumors, accusations, but no charges . . . "

"It may surprise you, but Maefield was as much to blame for keeping him employed as anyone. It's hard to understand. I can't decide whether he did it out of kindness or fear. But this is for sure, Jerry—Wheeler has to go and you're going to make it happen."

Jerry hated to leave. Frank Scarpelli was a pastor he could talk to and he needed to talk more. But it was late now and they both had obligations. He handed Frank a copy of his ordination service and waited quietly as he read it through. Frank would deliver a brief message.

"This is good, Jerry," Frank said approvingly. "It looks like you got it all here."

Scarpelli came around his desk and wrapped Jerry in his

long arms. Then, as the good priest he still was, he grasped Jerry's shoulders. "God shall bless you as he did David and give you courage while you fight Goliath."

Jerry returned to his office to find four messages left there by Miss Blatty.

Detectives Burroughs: call him at home, first chance. DO4-8760

Lillie Palmer says it is urgent, says to call her. She insists she has to speak to you tonight. DO4-9825

Pennington Funeral Home: Mr. Pennington called to confirm that the Hollister family decided on 10:00 A.M. funeral service, Friday, at the cathedral. Visiting will be Wednesday and Thursday, 2-4 & 7-9, at the funeral home. Please call to confirm: DO4-7772.

Everett Wheeler called. Said he would call back. Told him about the Hollister funeral plans. He said I should get Roger Jones, assistant custodian, to handle it. He was taking vacation time.

*   *   *

Charlene heard the sound of the outside door. Seconds later, Everett stood in the bedroom entrance staring at her. A sly smile creased his face. He approached the bed and continued surveying her body, contented she remained helpless and afraid.

"I'm going to remove the gag. You scream and I'll change my mind. Understand?"

Charlene nodded her head. He tore the adhesive tape from her skin. Excruciating pain swept across her face as the tape pulled at her cheeks and burned her lips. She suppressed her need to yell. He yanked the handkerchief from her mouth. She breathed deeply. He opened the blood-stained linen cloth and used it to pat her mouth, which bled again. He unlocked her right wrist from the handcuff. "Hold the handkerchief," he ordered.

"Would you dampen it?" she groaned over swollen lips and a parched tongue. "Please!"

She took a deep breath as he left the room. Self-conscious, she pulled the cup of her brassiere in place and tried buttoning her blouse, hoping against hope he would leave it be. When he returned, he held a soaking dishrag and a can of Coca-Cola. She took the rag and cautiously dabbed her lips and the cut above her eye. She put the rag down and accepted the cola and a straw. The can was ice cold. She sipped through the straw. Nothing ever tasted better.

He sat on the bed beside her. "Now then, why were you following me?"

"I wasn't following you, not at first. I set out following Mrs. Maefield."

He looked surprised. She drew again through the straw. The cold sweetness of the cola lent her new strength.

"I'm an investigator for a law firm that represents the company holding Doctor Maefield's life insurance policy. I came to Tompkinsville to do last minute checking before the company pays Mrs. Maefield a million dollars. As with you last Sunday, I wanted to interview Mrs. Maefield today without her knowing my employer. I was about to catch up with her on her morning walk when I recognized you walking with her. You were a total surprise. I never suspected you had a personal relationship with her."

"Yah! And what conclusion did you and your preacher-man come to about the basement bedroom?"

"We didn't! In fact, until you mentioned it now, we had no evidence to connect you to it. We assumed that since you are the custodian of the church you could explain it. We thought what we found in the room was strange, but I've seen stranger things. And Jerry Flynn wanted to talk with you before deciding whether to inform the police."

"What'd you tell the cop Burroughs?"

Charlene knew this could be a life or death question. If Everett had read her notebook, she was dead meat, if only her appointment book, she might buy time. She took the chance that he had not read her notebook.

"Do you mean at his office yesterday? Or, what he learned this morning?"

"Go ahead . . . You tell me!"

Charlene drew from the straw.

"Well, yesterday, at the police station, I never mentioned you or the hidden room."

"Yah and what about this morning? You talked to Detective Burroughs?

"No, I tried calling him," Charlene lied, "I was told he would be in court all day."

She had taken a stab in the dark, a guess based on a passing remark by Burroughs yesterday regarding his schedule today. Everett could check it out. He would know if she was lying. She hoped he would believe what she would say next.

"So I called Jerry Flynn and asked him to inform Burroughs that I saw you and Mrs. Maefield together this morning and you looked like you were having a lovers' quarrel. I called him while you two were in the coffee shop."

"You're lying!"

She stuck to her story. "No! And, if I disappear you'll be the first one the police will want to interview. Don't make matters worse for yourself, Everett. I can help you."

She took a long sip on the straw, sucked the cool, sweet liquid into her mouth. She hoped her show of confidence would impress him. But it had the opposite effect. After staring for a few seconds, his eyes narrowed and his cunning grin turned into a cold scowl.

Everett wrenched the coke can from Charlene's hand and poured the remainder of its contents over her. Any hope he might be gentle and caring to her faded. When the last drops dribbled down her neck and over her chest, he squashed the metal can in his iron fist and threw it across the room.

"And how can a slut-dick help me?" he replied, wiping his sticky hand on her slacks.

Again, he used the handcuff to lock her wrist to the headboard. Beads of perspiration appeared on his forehead. He showed her the same sharp knife he had driven into her thigh earlier. He unnerved her by using it to cut the shoulder straps on her brassiere. He nudged the fabric beneath her breasts and touched the knifepoint to her throat. Her whole body tensed as he used his free hand to grope her breasts and taunt her nipples between his fingers.

"So, you were saying," he said, his fiddling continuing, his voice reflecting his heightened excitement: "How you going to help me?"

She forced herself to stay calm. She had to suppress the fright she felt.

"You told me you hoped the police would find Reverend Maefield's murderer and you wanted to see his killer fry. You said you liked him as a pastor and that he had been a decent man who didn't deserve to die like he did . . . " She paused as Everett laid the knife between her breasts, its point toward her chin. She broke out in sweat as he slowly slid his hand along her stomach and under the waistband of her slacks.

"Go on," Everett said. "I'm listening." He moved his hand over her panties feeling for her opening through the material. "Continue!"

Charlene shuddered and let her breath out slowly: "I believe you. I believe you only look guilty. Your affair with Rhonda and your photo studio are coincidental to Reverend Maefield's murder, but you're afraid they make you suspect for the minister's murder. But think about it, Everett. If you harm me, no one will believe you. Your innocence won't matter and you'll have what you do to me to answer for as well."

He withdrew his hand. She took a deep breath. He appeared to relax some.

"Maybe! Open your mouth . . . Wide!"

He picked up the dishrag, freshly stained by her blood,

pushed it into her mouth, heard her gag on it and showed amusement at her distress. Using the same medical tape as before, he pressed it to her face. A piece of the rag hung over her chin.

"I'm going to keep you here until I'm sure."

He lifted the knife that lay between her breasts, collapsed the blade into its sheaf. Standing, he put the knife into his pants pocket. He closed the bedroom door behind him as he exited to the adjoining room. Charlene could hear his muffled voice as he made several telephone calls. He stayed in the kitchen a few more minutes before she heard him go out. She settled back to await his next visit. She relaxed some. She had made a point. She was still alive, thankful. She worried, however, that she had now put Jerry in greater danger. With that new thought resting on her mind, she began to cry. She wished Jerry were here to free her and gently wipe away her blood and tears. Then she noticed that the tape over her mouth was not as tight as before. Her perspiration and the coke mixture he had dribbled over her had weakened its adhesive power. She used her tongue and had some success spitting out the washcloth. She breathed heavily through her nose and continued to blow the rag out of her mouth. At last, she sucked air through her teeth. She closed her eyes and prayed. She recited as she had this morning in the church, only now with sincerity, "Hail Mary, full of grace . . . " She played with her fingers, as if little Rosary beads were passing between them. The words of Jerry's Sunday sermon came to her mind. *Christ loved us the same way a mother loves her child.* She knew it was true. Her mother had died giving her birth. What greater love is there? She had never thought of that until now. She sobbed for the mother who had died loving her so much.

*   *   *

Everett Wheeler headed west into the fuming mouth of the Lincoln Tunnel. He could not have chosen a worse time of day to return to Tompkinsville. Because of construction and homebound commuters, traffic moved like turtles on a rutted path. If he could turn around, he would do it. He had left too much unfinished business in Manhattan.

His first priority would be to kill Charlene Cunningham. It pleased him to think about her warm, soft body and the pleasure he could derive while squeezing the last breath out of her lungs. He could drop her body in a Jersey swamp before continuing to Tompkinsville later tonight.

Only her insistence that earlier this morning she had communicated incriminating information to Detective Burroughs by way of Jerry Flynn prevented him from killing her this afternoon. He must find out if she lied to him. She had told the truth about Burroughs spending today in court. That much he had looked into. The dispatcher had told him: "*Detective Burroughs is in court today. Please leave me your name and number so he may . . .* "

But what did it matter? So what if Flynn got through to the detective and told him about Charlene seeing him and Rhonda together? What did that prove? He had only to say he had gone to the city to offer the widow assistance moving heavy boxes out of storage into her new apartment, a good deed First Church would want him to extend to its grieving widow. It was true. Rhonda kept lots of her junk in a downtown warehouse. Before going there to move it in his truck, they went for a walk and stopped in at St. John's Cathedral to say prayers for her dear departed husband. He would say he hadn't seen Cunningham since last Sunday afternoon at Tommy's and he had no idea how she disappeared. And no body, no crime! His explanation was that simple. So, it didn't make sense keeping her alive. She knew too much about him. He didn't believe she could add anything to his defense if tried for Maefield's murder.

Rhonda represented another threat. Under interrogation, she could spill everything they had thus far covered up about the hours just before her husband's murder. He wanted to believe he dominated her, that she would obey him, however, he conceded she could also play him for a patsy. After today, he counted on her fear of him and especially his threat to expose Madge. She seemed genuinely upset by the picture he showed her, and by his knowing about her affair with Madge.

Nor was he confident he had left the contents of his footlocker in good hands. His 42nd Street dealer was under a lot of police scrutiny. If the cops raided the man's bookstore, his treasured pictures and films would become some lawman's pickings. He thought he should have taken the three thousand dollars the dealer offered him for the lot. They were worth much more, but if he had to flee the country, he would lose everything in the box anyway.

That too was unfinished business. He had paid plenty for false passports and other documents. His 'fence' wanted additional information and money. If all his efforts to hide his guilt failed, he planned on fleeing to Argentina. He would jump bail if necessary, assuming a lawyer could get him out while awaiting trial. Rhonda had said the South American country was the place to hide. She had boasted about German friends in Buenos Aires. If he fled, he wanted her with him. He needed her friends and especially her language skills. So, it was important to stay on her good side, satisfy her with sex and promises of a golden future.

*   *   *

Taillights abruptly brightened. Everett applied his brake to avoid colliding with the car in front of him. A chain reaction of near misses, tires screeching, flooded the semidark Lincoln Tunnel. Everyone came to a hurtling stop. When traffic moved again, it took twenty minutes to climb the last half mile out of the smoky tube and into the light of evening. There he saw the reason for the traffic delay. In the eastbound lane, blocking all access to the tunnel from New Jersey, he saw an overturned fuel tanker and autos upended or smashed against it. What a mess. It would take hours to clear and get things moving again. He decided to go on to Tompkinsville.

He had plenty to do at home and maybe on balance, he

thought, it was better to get that out of his way tonight. He had to deal with his wife, Marie, Jerry Flynn, and Margo Rasmeyer. If he could free himself from their incrimination, he would solve his problems and would not have to think about fleeing the country.

"That bitch, Marie!" he screamed. Maybe he had lost his touch. "I thought I had her scared shit, afraid to spit without my permission." He rolled down the window to toss out his cigarette butt. "Yet, last night she sassed me like a seasoned whore," he snarled.

Marie had gotten into his footlocker. However she had managed it, she got hold of the envelope containing four-year-old photographs of him having sex with Rhonda. Those pictures alone would make him a principal suspect in Maefield's murder. One way or another, he planned to get them back.

He remembered taking his Rhonda pictures a few days after transforming the basement room into a first rate photographer's studio. She was a way to check out his new camera equipment and to test his wiring. Everything had worked perfectly. Even Rhonda didn't know that behind the mirrors, cameras were clicking. He never showed her the pictures. Since he did not intend to use them commercially, neither of them had worn disguises. And he hadn't blanked out faces when he printed the film. "How stupid I was!" he roared to himself. The enlarged five-by-seven black-and-white prints were sharp and explicit. There was no doubting his identity or, considering all the pictures laid out in sequence, hers.

He concentrated on his other big concern. "How do I involve Preacher Flynn in the pending death of 'Goldie-locks'?" He had laid the groundwork by using Michael Todd to spread the word about the new preacher entertaining the sexy blond overnight at the manse last Sunday. He considered it a stroke of luck to find Michael in Tommy's yesterday morning. "And ain't I a genius to use Michael for spreading the story?" Everyone believed Michael, the Eagle Scout, the All American Boy, a member of the school board and successful businessman. "Why there's talk of Michael running for Congress in the next election," Everett said through lips puffing a near-spent cigarette.

A couple of days from now, Everett imagined he would start circulating the pictures he had taken of Jerry and Charlene from Tompkins Park as they stood in the upstairs manse window Sunday at dusk. His long-range lens had caught them embracing. "It'll be easy for the cops to concoct a lovers' quarrel scenario. After a desperate search, they'll find Charlene's beat-up, raped and strangled body in a locked, deserted room of the church basement. Three days later, the cops will find the missing minister dead of a self-inflicted gunshot wound under an ocean pier. "Yes, that's a better plan than having her body rot in a Jersey swamp," he laughed.

Everett applied his brake with force, then hit the gas peddle, steering into the center lane, car horns blaring as he swept ahead a few spaces. "Damn construction! Will they ever finish fucking with this shit-ass road?" he shouted. He maneuvered into the moving right lane, zooming ahead a hundred feet before braking to another dead halt. He laid his head back and sulked as cars in the lane he had just left passed him. As his lane of traffic began creeping again, a convertible in the middle lane kept pace with him. He could not help a glance at the pretty woman in the front passenger seat. For a few seconds, he thought he was staring at Sarah Draper—long blond hair, come-hither-smile on a painted face, a cigarette casually puckered in her juicy red lips. The woman waved suggestively . . . *a tease just like Sarah*. In that moment, her female companion gained the lead and slipped to the outside lane, running far ahead.

Although tempted, Everett did not give chase. Instead, he smiled and mumbled his recollection of the day he had discovered Michael Todd was having sex with Sarah Draper. "I almost walked into them as they left that Camden motel . . . What a small world. I picked up so much pussy at that whore house, you'd think I was its franchise taxi service!" he bawled. "Let me think . . . That was nine months ago. I had to drop between parked cars to avoid them seeing me. What a surprise! I had never thought of

Michael as less than straight and narrow, same as Cousin Madge. Wow! Hot damn! They both let me down!" he chuckled.

Traffic started moving in slow motion. Everett saw an opening and sped into the center lane. Soon, everyone was moving at normal speed. But, two miles north of New Brunswick Exit 9, traffic came to a dead stop. Everett leaned out the window to talk to a trucker with a police band radio and learned that a mile farther a major accident blocked all south lanes. Police estimated an hour to get things started again. He lit a fresh cigarette and settled back to wait. He closed his eyes.

*   *   *

Since the day of Maefield's murder, Everett periodically sifted through his memory for clear answers to what happened. "I downed so much booze that cold Sunday. Maybe I did kill him. I really don't know," he lamented.

He recalled how he woke up naked on the bed in his studio, the lit flood lamps blinding him. He rubbed his temple in an effort to calm his pounding headache. Images of weird sex with Rhonda were the first to parade into his consciousness. He looked at his watch: 4:15. It was then that he saw dry blood staining his hands and caking his forearms. He looked closely to see if he had cut himself, but saw no wounds. He worried if the blood belonged to Rhonda. Suddenly, he began to sweat and he wondered if he was hallucinating as images of Shepherd House blazed through his head—the sad eyes of the shepherd Jesus staring down from the leaded stained-glass window, blood splattered on the glassed-in bookshelves beside the fireplace, the bright glow of the lamp lighting a grotesquely bloodied body. He shook his head no and used a pillow to wipe perspiration off his face. His head pounded as he struggled to sit up. He thought he would faint as he got to his feet, and he had to use the wall to support himself and to keep from falling. Groping his way, he stumbled onto his shoes and his clothes lying in a heap a few feet from the bed. He reached for them and saw blood on his shirt and down his right trouser leg. From the pants pocket, he took out his switchblade knife, its blade locked inside its handle, clean, no blood on it.

He would take no chances. He gathered the bed linen and his clothes in his arms and went into the coal room where he burned them in the incinerator. In the bath, he poured disinfectant over his weather-beaten shoes and left them there to dry. He stood under a hot shower soaping his body for what seemed an eternity. Securing the studio behind him, he went out to the storage room and dressed in fresh clothes and shoes he took from his locker.

Flashes of the mutilated body rocked him again. Why? Why was he seeing this? Were these mindsets leftovers from a nightmare? Seeking relief, he stood silent clutching the metal frame of his locker for several minutes. Longer images of the same things continued and one brightened into the bloodied face of Maefield. He pounded his fist against the locker, banging until his hand hurt and his arm muscle became sore.

He had to know. He ran underground to Shepherd House, entering from Miss Blatty's office. The smell and gore of death greeted him. On the floor in front of the fireplace hearth, he saw his nightmare. He trembled in realization that what he had seen was real. He had difficulty catching his breath. He sought fresh air and the shortest way back to his studio. He skirted the body in its pool of blood. He crossed the room to exit by Shepherd Door. As he passed Maefield's desk, on top, amid papers and books, he spotted a Canon SLR camera and next to it, a thirty-six exposure roll of black and white film. Without any idea what they might hold, but unwilling to let them fall into the hands of the police, he made off with the camera and the exposed roll.

Although not dressed for the weather, he ignored the cold and icy rain, trudging through deep snow, ascending the garden steps to the cloister just as the great bell chimed five o'clock. In the dim light, he saw Rhonda's cautious approach. Caught by the wind, the gate crashed loudly against the wall. He panicked. He feared her seeing him, and he ran into the hollow dark shadows cast by the cathedral, crouching there until Rhonda made her way down the steps to Shepherd House, knowing she would be the one to discover her husband's brutalized body. When she was out of sight, he hurried through the unlocked door of the manse and, using its basement stairs, he returned to the studio where he hid the stolen camera, film and his knife. Once more, he locked the studio and moved the mattresses across its entrance. At his locker, he put on a pair of galoshes and a coat to return to the cloister where he started shoveling snow off the steps and walkway to Shepherd House. Less than twenty minutes had passed before a cop with his gun drawn interrupted his work. At his insistence, Everett unlocked Shepherd Door and followed inside, where once more, he saw the putrid scene of death. He acted surprised, shocked and cursed the mayhem! Outside, he continued shoveling the walk, blabbering insults as useless ambulances arrived and within the next hour reporters, television network trucks, church members, townspeople, funky politicians and even the priest from St. Joseph's Catholic Church.

*   *   *

Traffic started moving. It took a blast of a horn to awaken Everett to his present time and place. He put his truck in gear and picked up speed. He lit a cigarette and went back to his thoughts.

*   *   *

He had waited a week before processing the two rolls of film. For all he knew he had pictures of the Sunday-school Christmas party or of the church basketball teams. Perhaps Maefield had found the camera in the gym and held it for someone to claim. But as he scanned the uncut negatives, fresh from his washing solution, the wild story of Rhonda's seduction of Madge Todd came into view. On the second roll, the one found inside the camera, he saw that the cameraman had come back for a second shoot, finishing the roll with eight photographs of him and Rhonda with a male prostitute. He thanked God he had stolen the camera and films off Maefield's desk. "Imagine if the cops had gotten hold of this," he sighed. He wasted no time destroying the last eight negatives. The remaining sixty-four frames he made into three-by-five and five-by-seven prints, careful to shade Rhonda's identity. While he worked, he appraised the professional nature of the photographs, and acknowledged that in order for them to turn out this sharp, the operator had known precisely how to set the camera for focus, light and motion.

"Yah, it seems impossible Reverend Maefield could have achieved such excellence with that camera," Everett said, talking to himself as he sped south on the turnpike. "You don't reach that level of efficiency without practice and I never saw Maefield as much as pick up a box-camera. He couldn't and wouldn't have hidden such talent." Nor could Everett think of anyone employed by the church or a church member who had the wherewithal and knowledge of the church basement to carry it out.

Traffic slowed again. Coming to a complete halt, Everett stuck his head out the window and spit into the mall dividing north and south traffic. He took the ashtray out of its pocket and emptied it into the breeze created by cars speeding past in the opposing lane. Cigarette butts were so crammed, he had to toy them out with his finger. Suddenly traffic began moving again. He slid the ashtray into its compartment and lit up a cigarette as he resumed normal speed.

"That was some romp, Rhonda and Sweetpea!" he laughed. "Hell, I get a hard-on every time I look at those photos. To think my little cousin fell into Rhonda's web. God, I was dying to ask Michael if he knew! But why give myself away? Ha! Ha! Still, the bastard has a right to know how his wife puts out. Hot damn, not for a man, but for a lady with style. Ha! Ha! Wow! But then I saw too the way Madge stared starry-eyed at the new preacher . . . Jesus . . . last Wednesday at the manse she looked like she wanted to eat him up. It couldn't have been more obvious if I had caught her in bed with him. Those big eyes of hers were all over him. I'll be damned but the guy attracts beautiful women the way pollen attracts bees. Madge must like it both ways. You got to wonder about that girl [he tapped his breast pocket]. Who knows?"

Everett roared with laughter and pounded his hand on the dashboard. He snaked around slower moving traffic and soon burst free at eighty-five miles per hour. He lit a fresh cigarette from the one still burning. He flicked the last remains of the old butt out the window.

* * *

Madge, Michael and their children ate an early supper at the kitchen table. Michael, in a lousy mood, showed irritation at the boys' antics and gruffly criticized Madge for not disciplining them. She made the mistake of asking him how the loading went today. Getting ready for frozen food shipments had always created turmoil at the factory. Michael responded with a frown and a blank stare. She recalled what Reverend Flynn had cautioned: *"Don't talk business."* She held her tongue.

If anyone should be angry, it should be her, especially after finding him dead drunk on the living-room floor last night.

That was such a surprise to discover him there, for she had seen no headlights before she had heard a terrible shriek and then the dog howl and yelp in agonized pain. The sounds had caused her to fly from the bed, and reach beneath it for the shotgun that was always there and ready. She had flipped on the hall light and then had heard the door slam. She had sat on the top step waiting. When she had heard the door slam again, she had warily made her way down the stairs only to see Michael passed out on the floor. A false alarm, she thought, until this morning, when she had seen spots of dry blood on the floor, found candy bar wrappers and crushed cigarette butts strewn about the packing barn, then a chair facing out the barn window.

She had to pull the dog from behind the sofa and, seeing his pain, take him to the vet. Someone had been in the barn watching their house and had entered their door. She wanted to tell Michael that a stranger had come in just before him and that the dog must have scared him off. Had the prowler tried to come up the stairs, she would have blown him away. From now on, she planned to lock doors at night. She wanted Michael to know so that he would have his key.

And just as critical, she had made several decisions regarding work. For the good of their children, and to foster family peace, she would resign her position at T&T, and put off going to graduate school. She would be a stay-at-home mother. Wasn't that what Michael wanted all along? Wasn't that what was behind his rage? They had so much to discuss.

A knock at the front door called Chip from the table. His best friend and the friend's mother had come by to pick him up. Madge joined them on the porch. The boys had completed a joint science project. Because they would demonstrate their research tomorrow morning in a school science fair, Chip planned to stay overnight with his friend. That way, they could get to school rehearsed and ready. Madge wasn't thrilled about the overnight adventure. She believed Chip wouldn't get the sleep he needed. Nevertheless, she gave her permission. Chip had already packed. He acted so grown up. After polite conversation and saying goodbye, Madge returned to the kitchen table.

By then Michael had gone into the den to read the evening newspaper. She was disappointed he showed so little interest in Chip's project and hadn't come out to join in their little "good luck" farewell. Michael had business in Vineland early tomorrow and he would miss attending the school program.

But she said nothing. Maybe after getting Dudley to bed, she thought, they could get started on their discussion. As she tucked her little guy under the sheets, Michael yelled up the stairs that he had a late appointment in Atlantic City with an out-of-state produce buyer, added that he didn't know what time he would get home and not to wait up for him, as if she did anymore. Without listening for her to respond, he left the house.

*　　*　　*

Traffic now moved well and Everett considered more delays unlikely. As he breezed south of the Pennsylvania interchange, he concentrated on ways to assure that he would never have to reveal his tormented memory of Reverend Maefield's murdered body. It was almost dark when he drove into the next rest area. He needed gas, cigarettes and food.

CHAPTER 12

LONESOME TONIGHT

Tuesday Evening, June12

Michael's impersonal way of leaving home never failed to hurt Madge's feelings. But tonight it especially upset her. She did not believe Michael had a business appointment. She watched from the upstairs bedroom window as he turned his company pickup truck onto the county road. She considered repealing her earlier decisions. Instead, she went about the task of making them reality. With a sense of urgency, she sat at the dining-room table and typed out her letter of resignation. She had a lot more to do. In front of her lay paperwork to write a report detailing the status of all her marketing accounts. Tomorrow she would submit the letter and account information to the monthly board meeting of T&T Produce Company.

*   *   *

Everett paid the toll at the turnpike exit and sped east into bean-land. At a pay phone just inside Tompkinsville, he called the cabaret where Margo Rasmeyer worked. After a few minutes, she came on the line.

"Margo! This is your photographer."

She was quick. "What do you want, Everett? I'm on duty, so make it fast."

"Slow down, beautiful. Don't be harsh. Anger hides your pretty face. I told you I'd call when I had an opening. I need you for a hot photo-shoot. How about it?"

"Are you putting me on?"

"Margo, doll, don't I wish," he laughed loudly. "Listen, I'm sorry I showed you my mean side . . . really I am. I lost sleep thinking about it. I want to make it up to you. And here's the good news. I'll pay you a hundred twenty-five to pose in a special outfit I purchased just for your lovely body; you get to keep it. How's that for a bargain? I'll pick you up at eleven."

"I don't know," she replied. Her voice had softened. "I don't get off until one."

"So, you got cramps. Or, tell your boss you have to go home early to care for your sick momma. Hey, modeling is money in your bank, beautiful! You'll find an excuse." He listened to her silence. "I'll meet you behind the cabaret at eleven!" he commanded and hung up.

*   *   *

At nine o'clock Everett turned into the long driveway of the Tompkins' homestead. Every window in the farmhouse glowed. This was something Everett never understood about his uncle— how he could be so frugal in business and his personal appearance, yet, so carefree in spending on his home and family. Walter would reprimand a farmhand for leaving a forty watt light bulb lit in a holding barn. In contrast, he would never say a word about lights left on and unused in the main house. But Walter's spending on his three daughters exceeded everything. Walter had been extravagant in his gifts of jewelry and clothes. Each daughter had a new automobile to drive before graduation from high school. When Madge married Michael Todd, Walter gave the couple money to build their own house and the land to build it on. The way he spoke about his girls, they were models of decency and purity. They could do no wrong. As Everett thought about this, he tapped the photos inside his breast pocket. "Wait till he sees these!" he exclaimed. He knocked hard on the screen door.

"It's open! All you have to do is pull it!" he heard.

It was Bob, speaking in her more-than-usual condescending voice. She gave the door a hard shove and Everett caught the handle, pulling it open to step inside the great hall that led to the body of the house.

"You're looking for Dad, I suppose? He's in his office."

Her rudeness toward him was nothing new. He saw her as beyond his charm. He'd like to take her over his knee and spank her bare little ass. That's what she needs, the nimble brat, he believed. He passed her in silence and headed to the double set of open French doors at the end of the hall. He looked in to see Walter at his huge desk, which was crowded with record books and account papers. Tompkins still kept the books for his farm, though of late, the business had grown to such a degree he left payroll and taxes to others.

"Everett, fancy seeing you this late at night," Walter said cheerily.

"And you, don't you ever get away from those books, Uncle? Why you should be out with Greta doing the Highland-Fling," Everett replied, knowing Walter and Greta had taken up Scottish dancing in the last few years and had formed an organization to keep old customs alive. Walter laughed at this.

"Oh, not tonight, lad. You need to do those dances on cooler nights, you know."

"Do you mind if I shut the doors, Uncle? I've got some private things I need you to advise me on."

Everett didn't wait for an answer. He closed the double doors and sat in a chair opposite Walter Tompkins' desk. Walter dropped his pencil and leaned back in the great swivel chair, his hands going to the back of his head, as if in surrender to his visitor.

"I'll only take a few minutes, Uncle. I'm concerned about security of the church buildings. Last Sunday evening, although there were no activities scheduled, I happened by, as I always do, to double check the buildings. Low and behold, I find lights on in the annex classrooms, gymnasium and the kitchen. I find the fire door to the basement tunnel wide open. I'm sure it was our new pastor going through the place, but I didn't know he had been given free reign yet. I was wondering if by any chance you had given him his own set of keys."

"I did! He's here now, moved in and will be ordained and installed on Sunday. I think we ought to trust him with keys to the church."

Everett could see he had put Walter on the defensive, unsure of the significance of his inquiry.

"Oh, I don't question that at all, Uncle! It's only that . . . shouldn't I, as chief custodian, know who has keys and, indeed, shouldn't I be the man to determine which keys he should have? He's not very responsible. Maybe you haven't seen that yet, Uncle, but Reverend Flynn appears to regard our holy place as his private playground."

Walter came forward. His hands went across the desk and his manner changed.

"Everett, I take it you don't get along. He's young and this is all very new to him. I think you need to be patient. We don't want any trouble this early in the call."

"I've no trouble, Uncle. I just think you, as president of the board, you should be aware that the pastor may not be as virtuous as you believe."

Walter showed his annoyance. "What are you saying, Everett?"

"I'm saying he had a lady friend overnight in the manse just last Sunday, a very pretty young woman, I might add. Now, you could say that it was just a platonic sleep over, but if you've seen her, I'm sure you'd doubt it."

"How do you know this?"

"I'm in charge of the buildings of our good church, sir. I count it my duty to notice who comes and goes there. And, if you need proof of this illicit affair, I've got photos I can show you. I caught them embracing in front of his bedroom window Sunday night and again as they walked out the front door yesterday morning. Just as soon as I get them developed, I'll give you a look, Uncle."

"That won't be necessary. I'll speak to young Flynn. In the meantime, I want you to keep quiet about this. Let's not create a problem until we're sure of the facts. I need to hear our new minister's explanation."

Everett smiled. He leaned back in his chair and kicked the desk.

"That's not satisfactory, Uncle. Are we to close our eyes to adultery in the house of God? Imagine how our community will react . . . Our last minister murdered . . . his successor using the church property to fuck little girls . . . "

"Shut your foul mouth, Everett! You're overstating what's involved here. I said I don't want to hear anymore about this until I review it with Mr. Flynn."

Tompkins was angry now. He showed it in his red face and his clenched fists. Why had he supported this man in his church position for so long, he couldn't explain? Had he carried kinship too far? He was about to lecture Everett on his own failed behavior when the man reached for the pictures.

"I hate doing this, Uncle, but you leave me no choice," Everett said as he took the photos from his shirt pocket. "You need to see something, which I've guarded and kept quiet about since first viewing them not long after the regrettable death of our former pastor. I wouldn't want these photos to get out and tarnish the reputation of your beautiful daughter, you know. And please don't ask me how I came into possession of such lowly scenes. Nor have I any idea who the other woman is. Just be grateful I've kept these in a safe place and shown them to no one."

He laid three wallet-size photographs face down on the desk.

"These are samples, Uncle. Out of respect for your sensitivity to such things, I took care about my selections here. The more graphic photos I wouldn't chance removing from their hiding place," he chuckled.

He turned them face up one at a time, savoring with delight the diminishing strength of Walter Tompkins as he recognized Madge in the embrace of an unidentifiable woman. There was no mistaking his daughter.

"You vile, depraved man! . . . What do you want?" Walter begged, shoving the photos across the desk. "You show those to another soul and I'll shoot your brains out!"

"Now, now, Uncle! Don't get angry at me. I didn't have anything to do with this," Everett said, acting casual as he slipped the photos into his breast pocket and, looking up, added, "I'm not the one whose daughter makes love to a dyke."

Walter lunged across the desk, but fell short, his swing fanning the air.

"I'll kill you! Mark my words on your parents' graves, I'll kill you!" he shouted, his finger pointing straight as an arrow at Everett's face, his cold eyes bulging from a face wild with hatred.

Everett got to his feet. Cautiously, he moved around the desk toward the French doors. "I want Jerry Flynn out of here, Walter! He's not welcome. I'm sure you'll find a way. And you're not to believe anything he tells you that infringes on my puritan reputation. He'll do that, you know, to try to save his own soul. But it ain't true. Do you understand? Flynn's to keep his mouth shut about me and be out of town by this time Friday. Also, about those pictures of him and the blonde? When I'm ready, you're going to say you asked me to take them because you had a bad feeling about the preacher from the beginning."

Drained, his heart pounding, his body weak, Walter slumped into his desk chair.

"And one other matter, now that I really have your undivided attention. Where did you get the ring of keys that you gave to Jerry Flynn?"

Walter looked up, curious about the question, reminded that this was how their conversation had begun. He had no problem telling him, but he couldn't figure out why those keys were so important?

"They were Reverend Maefield's set of church keys. They were in the man's jacket pocket at the time of his murder. The police returned them to me a few weeks ago with other church property they had held during their investigation. So far as I know, the keys were the same set I gave Daniel when he first arrived as minister."

The answer did not surprise Everett. It confirmed his presumptions. Nevertheless, it did not solve his puzzle. How had Maefield gotten hold of a key to the secret room? If he had lifted it from Rhonda's purse, how did he know what door it unlocked?

"Tell Flynn you want those keys returned, Uncle. They belong to me. I don't want him snooping around in the time left him. You get those keys to me no later than tomorrow night. That's it! You take care of those matters and I'll see to it that Sweetpea's photos remain our secret. And Walter, from now on, you and your family show me respect!"

Having said this with elation in his voice, Everett silently walked out of the house.

*   *   *

Walter dropped his head into his hands. The photos had shocked him to his core. He felt disillusioned and confused. How could Madge disgrace herself and her parents like this? he moaned. He patted his eyes with his handkerchief and wiped away the sweat that had collected on his hands and forehead. He had to protect Madge, Michael, his grandsons, friends and the T&T Produce Company from scandal. For the present, he believed he had no choice but to bend to Everett's wishes. He had to act quickly to prove his willingness to cooperate.

*   *   *

Michael Todd had told Madge the truth when he said he had a late meeting in Atlantic City with a customer.

At 9:30, he arrived at the appointed place, a cabaret a block from the boardwalk. There he met an executive for a supermarket chain building new stores in and around Philadelphia. Michael liked the place for its entertainment, modern atmosphere, low lighting, and terrace seating arrangement. The *maitre d'* ushered them to a tiny table above and away, but having an excellent view of the entertainment area. They watched and listened attentively as an attractive woman, dressed in a formal white gown, sat at the piano playing and singing a medley of popular songs. She had a strong, mature voice, a pleasant delivery, which made her a popular performer, and Michael relaxed as if under her spell.

For the first time since yesterday morning, Michael had confidence his affair with Sarah Draper would remain private. He thanked his lucky star that he had stopped seeing Sarah six weeks ago. With that thought behind him, his attention focused on a young cocktail waitress with flaming red hair. She wore a black costume that accented her enticing figure, particularly her breasts, which parted and pointed under a bodice that dramatized size and sharpness. Except for a thin strap circling behind her neck and supporting the bodice, the outfit left her freckled back exposed to her waist. From there the outfit traveled midway down her thighs, where it ruffled out and relied on black stockings to cover her graceful legs. The look was different from that of a "Bunny" in the recently opened New York's Playboy Key Club, which Michael had visited last month, but it conveyed the same playful message.

During an entertainment break, the redhead served Michael and his business customer a second beer. On this visit to their table, she surprised Michael by calling him "Mr. Todd." She then announced that her name was Margo Rasmeyer and she too lived in Tompkinsville. She explained how after graduating from high school two years ago, she had worked at T&T canning factory and had known him there as her boss. She volunteered that she had quit after less than a year. Margo then inquired about some of the people at the plant. She asked about "Mrs. Todd." Margo remembered Madge Todd as in charge of personnel and had seen her on a daily basis. Michael replied that Madge continued at her post and suggested Margo stop in to say hello.

He then flattered her by commenting on how a smelly canning factory was no place for a pretty girl like her and that her new uniform was far more appealing than those baggy white smocks and coveralls his employees have to wear. She smiled broadly at his complement and said, "That's such a nice thing to say, Mr. Todd." Twenty minutes later, Margo brought another round. The lady at the piano had just begun to sing, "*Are you lonesome tonight . . .* " As Margo set clean glasses on the table and poured bottled beer into them, she leaned over Michael in such a way that her breasts pressed against his neck and shoulders. He interpreted this as intentional and believed it represented her interest in him.

"Next time, bring me a Scotch on the rocks," he said quietly.

*   *   *

Rhonda Maefield had fallen into deep slumber and now, as in other forced sleep, she sweated in the vividness of a nightmare. This time, she heard herself scream and bolted up straight, confused and shaking. Through the open window, she saw light in neighboring apartment windows, and far off she heard car horns and a screech of brakes. She swung her legs over the bedside so that her bare feet touched the carpeted floor. For several seconds, she sat with her head low in her hands and waited for her faculties to register that she was alive. A cool breeze whipped the wispy curtains, and suddenly she felt chilled. Looking at her wristwatch, she marveled that it was nine o'clock. Rising to her feet, she steadied herself by the window. Finding the cord to the Venetian blind, she lowered it from its valance to the sill and adjusted it closed. She turned on a table lamp and saw her way into her bathroom, where she took a cold shower before applying makeup, combing her wet hair out long and fastening it behind her neck in a silver cord. She chose a necklace with a dime-size cluster of diamonds and let it hang to the division of her breasts. She fastened loose bracelets of Turquoise around one wrist and a Lady Hamilton watch around the other. She stepped into black panties and zipped up a matching stretch corset that supported her breasts without covering her nipples. She rolled up dark stockings and attached them. For outer garments, she chose a short, red, rubberlike skirt and slipped into a tight V-neck, black sweater, which clung like a second skin and left her shoulders and arms bare. Finally, she eased her feet into stylish, high, broad heel shoes and strapped them around her ankles. Filling a black leather purse with keys, a compact, lipstick and cash, she swung its long, thin strap over her shoulder. She appraised herself one more time in the mirror before exiting her apartment. She crossed Riverside Drive at the light and caught a southbound cab.

*   *   *

Within minutes of leaving Walter Tompkins' house, Everett Wheeler went to a telephone booth and dialed the number at the Presbyterian manse. Jerry answered on the first ring.

"Hey preacher, how you doing?" he asked with sarcastic amusement. "Had any snatch today?"

"What do you want, Everett? I'm in no mood for your bantering."

"Oh, my goodness," he said, his tone belittling and acid. "I can't believe preacher's got a temper!" Then he turned assertive and angry. "Now you listen to this preacher. You keep your nose out of my business and the next time you see that blond piece of ass you like to play with, you tell her she's got you in a whole lot of trouble. Hear me! Your days in this church are numbered, Mr. Preacher."

"Everett, do you know where Charlene Cunningham is?"

Everett believed Jerry had just given him the answer he was looking for. If Charlene had called Jerry this morning, had given him the information about Rhonda and him, he would not ask that question.

"You tell me, preacher? You're the one who shot it up her

ass. She stood me up today," he lied. "She made a date to meet me at the Green Onion Inn, but she checked out yesterday."

"Charlene had business in Manhattan; that's all I can tell you. I expected her back by now."

"Yah, well, when she shows up, you tell her I'm next in line for what she gave you."

Jerry wanted to tell Everett to go to hell, but instead he softened his tone of voice. "Everett, I don't know if you had anything to do with that room in the basement. I can only assume its purpose. You believe I know more, but I don't. You tell me the truth and I'll help you all I can. Let's call a peace, Everett."

"Reverend Flynn, I don't know what you're talking about. What room? In what basement?" Leaving the phone dangling on its cord, he left the phone booth. He felt relieved. He could get on with his next task.

*   *   *

Jerry Flynn had hoped to bridge the differences between him and Everett, but he now believed the man impossible to reason with and that he could not be trusted. He decided to try telephoning Lilly Palmer again. All earlier efforts had failed. Either he got a busy signal or no one answered. He dialed and listened to it ring eight times before he heard a tired voice.

"Hello! This is Mrs. Palmer. Who may I ask is calling, please?"

"Mrs. Palmer, this is Pastor Jerry Flynn. I've been trying to reach you all night. You left a message with my secretary earlier today for me to call you. I know it's late, but you said it was urgent. How can I help you?"

Her voice brightened. "Yes, Pastor. I'm sorry about any inconvenience I may have caused, but I thought you might help me locate Ms. Charlene Cunningham. I found a leather-bound notebook next to the curb on Main Street yesterday. There was no address, but *'Property of Charlene Cunningham'* and a Philadelphia phone number were written on the inside cover. I left a message at that number for her to contact me, but I haven't heard from her. The notebook appears rather important; something a reporter might have lost. Among others, I saw your name and notes about you on a few pages. So, I thought you might know—"

Jerry interrupted her. "Mrs. Palmer, can I come by and pick up that notebook right now?"

"Well, yes, of course!"

"I have your address, just give me directions."

She told him how to reach her house from the church.

*   *   *

Detective John Burroughs and his wife, Emily, were homebodies. It had always been that way. They had almost no outside interests beyond family, Sunday Mass at St. Joseph's Parish and John's job at police headquarters. In their home, Emily kept busy sewing, cooking and decorating the house with things she made after seeing them in *Better Homes and Gardens*. In his spare time, John considered himself a woodworker. His basement was a treasure house of tools for crafting everything imaginable. While their children were growing up, Emily was their seamstress and John their toymaker. Now they used their talents making things for their grandchildren.

This evening, John Burroughs worked on a redwood chest for his granddaughter, who had come into the world three weeks ago. Several times, he had stopped to smell the dark purple of cedar wood and to study its grain. But even this did not take his mind off his day in court. He hated that part of his job, but recognized the significance of his testimony. After he left the stand, the man and woman defendants in the murder of the woman's husband looked defeated and wishing they had coped a guilty plea of involuntary manslaughter. Now, both faced New Jersey's electric chair, though, Burroughs thought it more likely a comet would drop on his roof than they would die that way. Still, spending fifteen to twenty in prison was no free ticket.

And the way things were, these two would grow old there without much chance of parole. He wished he had had as much luck arresting a suspect in the Maefield case, an achievement he was no closer to today than the morning he examined the body.

He thought back to yesterday's conversation with Charlene Cunningham. She had raised new suspicion of Everett Wheeler when she told him about Everett's comment regarding Mrs. Maefield as a "*sexy lady*." When Cunningham told him that, he had silently laughed it off. But now, he let his imagination run at full power and asked himself why Everett would see the homely woman as sexy unless he knew something that other men didn't know or see. To catch a criminal, you have to think like that criminal. As he set an end piece of cedar into its grooved base, Burroughs tried to visualize Mrs. Maefield with her glasses removed, her hair down and her business suit jacket off. Turning the wood, he imagined Rhonda from behind, bending over, lying down. "No! It couldn't be! Lovers? Everett and Mrs. Maefield?" He wanted to say this was absurd, but he had been a cop long enough to believe anything and everything are possible. "My God," he said to no one, "could this case be any way close to the case in which I just testified, where an adulterous affair led to the murder of the woman's husband? Were Everett and Mrs. Maefield? . . . " He dropped the cedar wood piece he had so delicately sanded to fit. "Damn right they were! Holy shit!"

He bounded up the stairs and into the kitchen where Emily was ironing baby clothes. He kissed her gently on the cheek and told her he had to go out on a case. Emily appeared unruffled. It was almost ten thirty and she was ready for bed. She knew it was useless to ask him if it could wait until tomorrow. When John is on a case, there is no tomorrow. She helped him find his things, handed him his holstered gun and watched him from the front door as he backed his unmarked police cruiser out of the driveway.

*　　*　　*

Lillie Palmer was a gracious woman and First Church's most benevolent person. She was in her late seventies and had buried three husbands, the last one just a few years ago at age eighty-one. Her wealth was legend. She enjoyed giving money to deserving causes. She had set up endowments for such diverse causes as an inner-city family counseling clinic and a college scholarship fund for the children of migrant field workers who earn acceptance into an accredited New Jersey college. The cause for which she was most enthusiastic was her own church. *"If there is anything the church needs and you can withstand Lilly's grilling, she'll buy it,"* Jerry had heard from one of the church elders. Daniel Maefield had more than once named her a saint. She, in turn, had been his most enthusiastic supporter. She had admired his strength of purpose, his Christian compassion and his limitless love for learning. People said Lillian Palmer was the only member of First Church who could speak on his level and who truly embraced his social theology. When the Board of Trustees battled Maefield for using the church building as if it were a welfare hotel (an embellishment of the fact), Lilly was the one who stepped into the fracas and said, *"Shame! Shame on you! How low can you get? Would you deny the Lord his place in the inn as well?"*

The murder of Reverend Maefield shook her to the core. At the funeral service, she gave one of the eulogies, a passionate testimony of her faith in God and her trust in Daniel Maefield's spiritual leadership. She had quoted from the Book of Jeremiah, leaving no doubt as to her belief that the pastor had died a martyr. *"Daniel Maefield has become a victim of violence and hatred— the same that crucified our Lord. Let us respond with love as Christ taught us to love, as Daniel wished us to love."* There wasn't a dry eye in the packed church. No one would forget the funeral sermon of Lillian Palmer for her friend and patriot, Daniel Maefield.

* * *

Lillian welcomed Jerry with open arms. She would accept no

apology from him for the lateness of his visit, and—without asking—she escorted him into her kitchen where she had set the table with her fine china, a plate of cookies and finger-sandwiches.

"Something left over from afternoon tea," she explained. "My bridge club meets here every first Tuesday from one to five. No one calls on me then, you know, not even you," she said with obvious humor.

He pulled out a chair for her and held it as she sat down.

"Such a gentleman. You're mother taught you right. Listen, Jerry, maybe you'd rather have a brandy this time of night. That's fine with me."

"No this is great, Mrs. Palmer," he said as he sat opposite across the small kitchen table.

"Well, you needn't worry about that here. As Paul the Apostle said, 'a little wine is good for the stomach.' On that observation, I agree with him. Trouble is it interferes with my medicine, so I don't drink it anymore. Damn the pills!"

Jerry liked her immensely. She was all so real and honest, spry and full of down-to-earth humor.

"You are a handsome cuss! I suppose you've heard that you show a distinct resemblance to a young Cary Grant. So, I want you to know you can court me anytime."

He laughed with her. He waited as she poured tea from a beautiful hand-painted china teapot. He thought about his Aunt; she would have paid a king's ransom for an antique like this.

"Sugar?"

"Three, please."

"Cream?"

"Just a little, thank you."

"You young people have such a sweet tooth," she said as she dropped the rectangular lumps from silver prongs and poured cream from a tiny silver pitcher. She pushed the tea cup across to him. "Help yourself to the sandwiches and cookies, because what you don't eat here goes home with you."

Jerry was famished. He had missed supper. He dove into the eats, remarking on how tasty everything was.

"So, are you and Miss Cunningham dating?"

Jerry couldn't believe it. Was there anybody in this town who didn't know about him and Charlene? He looked at Lillian in an innocent, questioning way.

"Sorry, I don't mean to be personal, Jerry. It really is nobody's business. I just thought it very sweet."

She handed over the leather-bound notebook opened to pages Charlene must have written out afterwards. There he saw her lipstick kiss implanted over his name.

"Oh, yes, we're just friends," he said, an uncomfortable smile lighting his face. "I know she'll be looking for this book. She's doing research for a magazine article on the aftermath of Reverend Maefield's death. She thought I could be of help and I showed her around."

"Yes, I read that."

There was a long pause in which each one digested its intimate implication. Lillian broke the silence.

"I know all the people she's interviewed. That Wheeler fellow—they ought to string him up by his feet." She looked away for a second. "Sorry, I shouldn't be so candid. I didn't read every page of Miss Cunningham's notes, but enough to know they were very important."

Jerry finished his tea and she filled his cup a second time. He wanted to talk to her more, but it was almost eleven and he was anxious to go through the notebook himself in hopes he might find some clue to Charlene's whereabouts. After exchanging a few more pleasantries, he took his leave. At the front door, just as he stepped out on to the porch, she said, "You know ghosts inhabit our beautiful church. You will probably think this the imagination of an old woman, but I believe the ghost of Daniel Maefield also walks the sanctuary and corridors of First Church, including the manse. He's a good ghost and he'll protect you from whoever killed him."

She didn't smile or wait for a reply. "Goodnight, Pastor. See you in church Sunday."

*　　*　　*

Protocol required Detective Burroughs to call in his return to duty and to specify his purpose and destination. He considered that premature and decided it could wait until he got to a pay phone. There were too many reporters and lawyers scanning police radios these days and, like many detectives, he didn't want to broadcast what he might later have to explain or defend. Besides, he had made up his mind to have a look before announcing himself. So, he parked his car on a dirt farm road a quarter mile south of the Wheeler home.

There were no other houses in sight. Acres of flat, cultivated fields surrounded the wood-frame structure. Burroughs attached his badge to his belt where he also fastened his holstered .38 Smith and Wesson Chiefs Special. To avoid the main road, he walked through a planted field, "probably potatoes," he grumbled judging from the ground foliage. Several times, water from revolving field cannon pelted him, so that he had to stop to dry his glasses. By the time he got up close to the house, his clothes were soaked. Fortunately, he had not bothered to change out of his workbench duds. Had he dressed in his usual double-breasted blue suit, white shirt and tie, he would be upset getting them wet and muddy. Burroughs was fussy about his appearance.

As he came out of the potato field on to mowed soft turf surrounding the house, he heard a male voice shouting curses. He headed toward sound and light coming from an opened ground-floor window. The shade was up and—unusual for these parts in spring and summer—there was no screen in place. Once more, he took out his handkerchief to wipe his glasses. Without them on, nothing near or far was in focus. Back in place, he could make out the large form of Everett Wheeler in the living room less than twenty feet away. Burroughs crouched down to peer over the top of the waist-high window sill.

A woman sat on the floor leaning back on her elbows. A fallen lamp lay next to her and loose debris surrounded her. The woman wept loudly and while Burroughs' perception of detail was a little fuzzy, he presumed from the scene that she had sustained an injury. Wheeler knelt at her side facing the window, his eyes focused on the woman.

"One more time, Marie, one more time," he shouted, "I'm going to ask you. Who has those pictures?"

Burroughs could smell a burning cigarette and ascertain that the man held it in his left fingers. He tried seeing what was in his right hand, but the woman's body blocked his view. He watched as Wheeler reached the cigarette to the woman's upper thigh. She screamed uncontrollably. She started crawling away. Everett clenched his cigarette between his lips and grabbed her foot. As he did so, Burroughs saw that his right hand held a handgun. The woman turned on to her stomach and tried again to crawl loose, all the time screaming and crying. As Burroughs began to remove his weapon from its holster, he watched Everett take the cigarette from his mouth and hold it close to the woman's butt.

"This time I'm going to shove it up your ass, if you don't tell me!" he shouted.

In all his years on the force, Burroughs had never drawn. He rose to full height in the open window and pointed his Smith and Wesson.

"Police!" he shouted. "Put your hands over . . . "

He never finished his sentence.

On his knees, the lit cigarette dropped, facing the window, his gun extended in both hands, Wheeler fired his Colt .45. The bullet drove into Burroughs sternum and slapped him from the window. He hit the ground on his back. Wheeler charged into the window and aimed at the level body. He saw the badge secured next to the belt buckle. Only then did the extent of his act sink in. He squeezed the trigger twice, hitting the detective in the head and heart.

He ran out the door to the yard. Fearing another cop close by, he crouched defensively behind the fender of his pickup truck for several minutes. Hearing no one and seeing no movement, he stood up. Convinced the cop had come alone, he returned to Marie still stretched out on the floor, her face hidden in her hands and crying uncontrollably

"Now look what you made me do!" he scolded. Clutching the back of her shirt, he dragged her to the window, where he lifted her by the arms to look over the sill at the dead man. "You made me kill a cop, you bitch!" He dropped her onto the floor, bent over, slapped her face and demanded she stop crying. When she continued, he put the barrel of his gun to her ear. He shouted in her face. "Where are those pictures, Marie? I'm out of patience!"

She fell silent. Waving off his gun, she struggled to her feet. She stumbled across the room to a writing table that stood against the wall. She balanced herself there for a few seconds before pulling out a bottom drawer and extracting a tiny envelope. She waved it at him.

"Safety Deposit Box in my name, New Jersey State Bank. You can't get into it unless I'm with you. If I die, an officer of the state has to be present to open it. I'll get the pictures for you tomorrow."

She backed into a chair and slumped down. Exhausted and ruined, she whimpered in a quiet way. Everett placed the key in his pocket and went outside to attend to a burial.

He pushed his hands into work gloves and, along with a battery-operated lantern, he got a pick and shovel out of the garage. At the death scene, he picked up Burroughs' Smith and Wesson. Examining the weapon, he saw the safety was on. "Stupid cop!" he exclaimed as he slid the handgun into his side pocket. Shinning his lantern at the body, he saw that the head shot had blown through the left eye frame of the man's glasses, shredding the lens, but the frame and right eyeglass remained intact. In spite of the bloody eye, Everett recognized the dead man as John Burroughs. He recalled Burroughs as the detective in charge of the Maefield murder investigation. He took a deep breath as he recalled Burroughs interviewing him shortly after the murder and several times after that. "I think he suspected me all along," he exclaimed as he bent his knees to hoist the body over his back. He recalled how Cunningham had said she got a message to Burroughs through Flynn this morning. "I guess she told me the truth after all. Fortunate for me, old John here was a bit slow on the follow up." Everett now believed Jerry Flynn knew more than he had let on. "Another problem to solve!"

He carried Burroughs to where tall grass grew in the far end of the yard. Discarded farm machinery and rusting cars occupied the area. Behind a stack of rotting wood crates, he dug through the tough, deep-rooted grass, chopping out a shallow grave. He would hide the body here until he had time to drop it where it couldn't implicate him.

He was about to begin burial when the thought occurred that the detective's badge might be helpful and so dislodged it from his belt and put it in his pants pocket. He thought about keeping the policeman's revolver, but then threw it into the grave. "Too easy to trace!" he said, as he booted the corpse into the shallow ditch. "He shoveled dirt and sod into the grave and moved a rusting cultivator above the fresh-turned soil. As he walked to his house, he decided Cunningham was more valuable alive. He needed her to lure Flynn into the secret room, get him to leave his prints and some personal things there. That way, he could kill them and leave them in the old studio. When the stench of death got bad enough, they would be found and a great missing person's case would be solved. At that thought, he panicked.

"The car—where did Burroughs park his goddamn car? He didn't walk here from the shit-hole police station!"

He checked out the road that ran in front of his house. He tried looking through the darkness from where Burroughs had fallen. He started walking in an ever-widening circle around the house and then he heard the chatter of a police radio, a dispatcher making routine calls. He rushed to the car. The key was in the ignition. He had worried he might have to dig the body up to search for keys. He had to move the car away from his property.

Everett returned to his house to force Marie into his cover-up scheme.

She appeared comatose, pale and silent, eyes staring at nothing. He smelled a burn-ointment and saw where she had dressed her wound. A good sign, he reasoned. She was more awake and aware than letting on. He splashed her face with cold water and shook her until she acknowledged him. He marched her to his pickup truck and pushed her in. He drove to the dirt road and parked. "When I back that car out, Marie, you follow me. Stay close." He put on a fresh pair of gloves and walked down the dirt road to take his place behind the wheel. He backed out to the highway where Marie waited. As ordered, she fell in behind him. To avoid detection, he drove along dirt paths that ran on the boarders of several planted fields. He came out twenty minutes later at the parking lot of Grady's Bar and Grill, a local hangout for Mexican workers. He drove Burroughs' cruiser behind the windowless building to a dark, isolated space. He turned off the engine, lights, and rolled up the window. He checked the logbook and saw no entry since six o'clock when Burroughs had parked the cruiser in his own driveway. He left the key in the ignition, went to his truck, where he shoved Marie to the passenger side and, careful not to draw attention to himself, slowly drove away.

He felt safe. Cops like Burroughs were protective of their sources. If right, Burroughs hadn't reported his conversation with Flynn or told anyone his destination tonight. Nor did he have to worry about the cops finding the police cruiser too soon. He idealized that before dawn, an unsuspecting Mexican would stumble onto the unlocked car and take it for a joyride, then, abandon it where it would take weeks to find. No matter, a few nights from now, Burroughs's body, weighted down with concrete blocks, would sink into the ocean off a Jersey pier. He turned to Marie who leaned heavily against the opposite door.

"Marie, you listening to me? I'm taking you home. Lock yourself in and don't talk to nobody. You hear?" She appeared to have returned to her listless state, but he believed she had heard all right, knew what she was doing. "I won't hurt you anymore, Marie. Whatever you want, you got it. I won't contest a divorce.

And I'll be generous, set you up so you won't have to work a day for the rest of your life. Just keep your mouth shut." He pulled into his driveway and reached over her to open the door. "You're home, Marie. Go to bed. I'll be back tomorrow night."

He gave Marie a hefty shove. She staggered before she fell forward onto the ground. For the longest moment, she did not move. Everett thought he would have to carry her into the house. But she managed to pull herself up and, supporting her weight on the truck frame, she got to her feet. He watched her stumble into the house. "She'll drink herself silly," he cursed, "the drunken bitch!"

$$*\qquad*\qquad*$$

Charlene had slept for several hours. Now awake, she shivered. Pain gripped her body and fear raced across her mind. When she heard the sound of the outside door, she dreaded the very worst and believed she had said her last prayer. Shortly, she expected Everett Wheeler to rush into the room, and—after torturing and raping her—kill her. She hoped it could be quick. Strangely, if he granted her one wish it would be the use of the toilet. She thought that her bladder would burst, yet, up to now she had held it in. But she knew she might not even get the chance to ask.

But nothing happened.

Sounds from the outer room were gentle—water running, a chair scraping the floor, dishes rattling. Charlene wondered if someone other than Everett might be there. She pulled up as far as she could and with renewed fury, she rubbed her mouth against her shoulder. Spitting and blowing, exhausting her strength, she moved the soggy gag farther out of her mouth. She used her tongue and pushed hard. She had nothing to lose and, with all the vocal power she could muster, she scrammed. "HELP!"

The door flew open. Before her, she recognized an altogether new version of Rhonda Maefield.

$$*\qquad*\qquad*$$

Charlene and Rhonda caught a cab at the corner of 47th and Eighth Avenue and were uptown to Rhonda's apartment in less than twenty minutes.

Charlene found it hard to believe that her odyssey had begun here almost sixteen hours ago. She watched as Rhonda unlocked the outside security gate and closed it behind them, then rang for the night attendant.

"You can't get in here without a key before seven in the morning," Rhonda instructed, her tone reassuring, "when the night watchman goes off duty. The doorman and lobby staff won't take over until nine, but for those two hours, the only way into the lobby is if someone buzzes you through."

A uniformed guard appeared in front of the steel-grated glass. For several seconds he stared out skeptically at Rhonda and especially at her beat-up friend. Rhonda took a card out of her purse and held it to the glass. The security guard's face brightened and quickly he unlatched the door.

"Sorry, Mrs. Maefield. I didn't realize . . . "

"That's all right, Bill!" she said as they passed into the lobby. "Please be on alert if someone rings asking for me. I'm not in to any callers."

Bill acknowledged her request. The elevator was open and waiting. One of Bill's duties was to see residents and guests to their floor. He stepped in after them and without uttering a word, road them to the eighth floor, then watched as Rhonda, with Charlene limping behind her, unlocked her apartment door. Only when they were across the threshold, did he close the elevator doors and return to the lobby. Rhonda led Charlene through the apartment and into her bedroom.

"The main bath is in here," she said turning on lights. "You must be famished. I can scramble eggs."

"That'll be fine. I'd like to use your telephone."

Rhonda pointed to the phone next to the bed and left her alone. Charlene asked for Tompkinsville long distance and gave the number for the manse. As she waited, she thought she had never seen a more grotesque-looking bedroom. Strange! The phone rang four times.

"Hello!"

"Jerry, it's me, Charlene!"

She started to cry. She had wanted to sound cool and collected, but had lost it the moment she had heard his voice. "I'm all right, but I've been through hell. I can't explain everything now. I need you."

"Where are you? I've been on pins and needles with worry."

"Right now, you're not going to believe this, but I'm at the apartment of Mrs. Maefield. She was the one I came here to see. Whatever you do, don't tell Everett Wheeler where I am."

"He called here about two hours ago with a mouthful of garbage. I asked if he knew where you were, but he provided no clue."

"Oh, he knew where I was! Listen, it's very important you call Detective Burroughs right away. Give him Mrs. Maefield's telephone number and ask him to call me here. I don't know where to begin. It's extremely involved. Burroughs needs to know that Everett and Rhonda have been having an affair."

"What?"

"I can't repeat it, Jerry. As I said, it's very involved. Everett's a dangerous man."

"Detective Burroughs was out of his office earlier and when he called me back I was out. He left his home phone number. You want me to tell him Everett and Mrs. Maefield are lovers? . . . You're sure?"

"Yes! I'm sure! There isn't time to explain it all now. Please forgive me. I lied to you about what I do for a living. I'm not a freelance magazine writer. I'm a private detective working for a Philadelphia law firm that represents Maefield's life insurance company." She was in tears and sobbing. She held the phone away. "I'm ashamed I deceived you."

"Don't be! The important thing is you're safe!" He waited a few seconds before continuing. "Did Everett hurt you?" he asked.

She took a deep breath. "Fortunately, Mrs. Maefield rescued me. I'll tell you about it later. I'm going to stay here for the night. If I don't hear from Detective Burroughs by eight o'clock, I'll call the New York police. But I really want to talk to Detective Burroughs first." She paused. "Jerry, you have to be careful. Did you get the locks changed?"

"Yes, this morning. I have new keys to all the outside doors." He hesitated. So much, he didn't understand. He wanted answers. "Charlene, this is all very confusing. I'll leave now for Mrs. Maefield's apartment."

"Jerry, I want so much to see you, but it will have to wait until morning. I'm exhausted and I still have to talk with her. Call me at seven. We'll plan from there."

"I have Mrs. Maefield's Manhattan address and her telephone number. I can find you. It'll probably be seven before I get there."

"We're on the eighth floor. Until nine, you'll have to ring the apartment through the intercom and be buzzed up—"

"One other thing," Jerry cut in, "the reason Lilly Palmer tried to call you. She found your notebook in a gutter across from City Hall on Monday afternoon. You must have dropped it out of your car. I retrieved it from her less than an hour ago."

"Well, that's a relief and losing it may have saved my life. Keep it in a safe place. And, Jerry . . . I love you! I love you so very much!"

With the lightness of a feather landing, she returned the phone to its cradle and sat motionless as tears streamed down her cheeks.

* * *

At 11:30, Madge Todd put away her Olympia portable typewriter and prepared for bed. Fluffing the pillows behind her, she unfolded the crumpled newspaper her husband had discarded in the trashcan.

"How thoughtless!" she said as her weary eyes took in the bold headlines: **BANK PRES., WIFE DEAD**—and underneath— **Police suspect murder-suicide**. "Oh, my God," she exclaimed in almost a whisper as she read on, recognizing the names of Sam and Sarah Draper. "Why didn't Michael say anything?"

Madge glanced through the news report.

STONE HARBOR, NJ: Police theorize Sam Draper 47 shot his wife, Sarah 36 after learning of her affair with a partner in his banking firm . . . He may have come upon her suddenly as she sat on the porch of their beach bungalow . . . On a bed in one of the bedrooms, Draper lay dead, the same handgun believed used to kill his wife clutched in his hands . . . A police spokesman reported the deaths probably occurred mid-afternoon on Monday. Miss Ellen Stover, also a Stone Harbor summer resident, after having walked her dogs past the Draper cottage about 8:00 o'clock, called police, saying she had just seen the body of Sarah Draper sitting in a porch chair. Miss Stover also alerted police that she had seen Mr. Draper drop anchor for his speedboat in the channel behind her house as early as two Monday afternoon . . . Rumored to have a checkered past, Sarah Draper owned and managed Sunshine, a popular bar and catering hall in Atlantic City. The investigation is continuing . . . Funeral plans are incomplete . . .

Madge dropped the newspaper at the side of the bed and put out the light. She recalled she had not seen Sarah since last September at the county fair and had never met her husband. Her only contact since then had occurred in a phone call to invite her stepson to Chip's Halloween party. Sarah had answered that Sam's son was in prep school in Massachusetts. Madge had to bite her tongue. She couldn't understand how parents could send a nine-year-old away for four months at a time. After exchanging a few pleasantries, Sarah had ended the conversation. It was obvious the woman did not want to talk to her. Madge had to admit, she never liked her and she guessed the feeling mutual. "But I would never wish this on her," Madge heard herself say. "How terrible, unbelievable, that their lives ended in such violence. It all goes to show, you never know what kind of pain people are harboring." Thinking about her own safety, she got up to double check the downstairs locks.

Back in bed, she stretched out on her stomach. She had a wild thought. Which is worse? A rape by your husband or a stranger? At least with a stranger, if you survive, you have the possibility of criminal prosecution. Then she entertained a more frightening question. Would Michael murder me if he discovered I had had an affair? Would he kill me out of passion? Jealousy? Or, hatred? What would he do if he learned about me with Rhonda? She reached for a tissue to blot her eyes. She knew his views on homosexuality, had heard his revolting words about men or women who engaged in such sex. Did they still try people for sodomy in New Jersey? She would have no defense. In a divorce, Michael would take their children. He would deny her all she had.

She turned out the light and snuggled a pillow to her midsection. She entertained the notion of what it would be like to commit adultery with Jerry Flynn. How could she explain his appeal? Why was the minister so attractive to her? "Maybe with the right man, I could be normal," she sighed. She recalled reading that women who engage in sex with other women are more likely to find fulfillment in a heterosexual relationship than men who have had homosexual relationships. One doctor writing on the subject reported that women with lesbian experiences, as opposed to strictly heterosexual women, had enhanced libido when having sex with their male companions. She imagined Jerry in bed with her. She longed to cradle him in her arms and have him love her to completion.

She wished she could fall into natural sleep with that thought in mind. But the old doubts and hungers that had made her so vulnerable to Rhonda returned. She compared Rhonda to a seed buried in compost. It burst forth in a beauty all its own and she couldn't resist the temptation to accept its pleasuring scent.

She turned on to her back and stared at the ceiling. She hated such moments. She needed her sleep. She got out of bed and pulled out the lingerie drawer in her dresser. In the darkness, she felt beneath the silken textures and shuttered as she touched the shotgun cartridges she had unloaded from her rifle last night.

Whether Michael agreed or not, she had decided to no longer keep the shotgun loaded and under the bed. Finding the container of prescription sleep medication, she took it into the bathroom, filled a glass with water and downed a pill. The heat and humidity had gotten to her. She undid her nightgown and pulled it off. Naked, she crawled on top of the sheets. If Michael found her like this and forced her again, so much the better. Why ruin another gown? And sex with him would be over that much faster.

*   *   *

At eleven thirty, Everett telephoned the Atlantic City cabaret where Margo Rasmeyer worked. He waited five minutes before she came on the line. When she heard his voice, she became irate, said she had been outside waiting for him. He ignored her complaint, said he had to cancel their date due to unexpected business and couldn't make it back in time. He would call tomorrow with new plans. Suddenly, she wasn't on the phone. After a long pause, he heard the bartender again. "She walked off," he said. "I'm hanging up on you, buddy." Everett slammed the phone. "Bitch!" he screamed and pounded his fist on the wall. "I'll make you pay!" he yelled. A half hour later, he raced north on the turnpike.

CHAPTER 13

LOST MOMENTS

Wednesday's First Hours, June 13

Jerry Flynn telephoned Detective Burroughs at home. Now past midnight, a sleepy Mrs. Burroughs answered.

"John isn't here, Mr. Flynn. I can take your number and have him call you as soon as he comes home. There's no telling when that will be. If it's urgent, I suggest you call police headquarters. They should be able to reach him."

Jerry gave Mrs. Burroughs the manse number. "If I'm not home, he should call Charlene Cunningham." He dictated the Riverside Drive apartment telephone number and name of Rhonda Maefield. He apologized again for telephoning so late and thanked her for her help.

In truth, he was disappointed. Jerry had hoped Burroughs could accompany him to Manhattan, or advise him on what to do when he got there. He remained unsure of himself. Pieces of the puzzle were missing and what information he had didn't fit together. Charlene's news that Mrs. Maefield and Everett Wheeler were lovers sounded outlandish, unbelievable. He wondered if maybe Charlene had jumped to conclusions. It's not possible, he thought. Ridiculous!

He dialed the Tompkinsville Police Department. A dispatcher came on and asked if he wanted to speak to Burroughs's backup, who was on call. "No, that's okay. I best stick with Detective Burroughs. If you hear from him within an hour, ask him to call Jerry Flynn at home." He gave the dispatcher his number. "In any event, I'll try again later. Thank you."

Jerry went into the bathroom and two minutes later, he stood beneath the force of the showerhead.

*　　*　　*

Charlene Cunningham had not waited for Jerry's response to her profession of love. Maybe she shouldn't have said it. As a captive, her thoughts about him had given her hope and she could not recall any man who had ever occupied her mind this much. But was she fair to him? Her emotions had overcome her. Her body and mind would take weeks to recover. She walked into Rhonda's bathroom and turned on the shower. While waiting for the water to run hot, she removed her sneakers and socks, disposed of her blouse and pushed her gray denim slacks and her panties to her feet. She turned to face the mirror and saw herself. Her upper lip was swollen, an ugly half-inch gash protruded above her right eyebrow. Her left eye looked horrible. Her wrists were sore and red. There were rope burns around her ankles. Her stomach was black and blue where Everett had hit her and her breasts remained sore from his harsh fondling. On her upper left thigh, the stab wound looked rather deep and fresh blood oozed again. It probably needed stitches, but she wasn't going to any emergency room at this hour. She worried how a scar would look there when she put on a bathing suit. "Such a silly concern," she cried. Remembering she had gotten a tetanus shot a few months ago, she felt less concerned. She got under the fast spray of steaming water. She began to feel alive again.

When she pulled back the shower curtain, Rhonda stood waiting for her. She had changed out of her "street-walker-like" apparel into a long, white, silk robe. She held a large fluffy towel and a red flower-print, silk pajama robe over her arm. In her serious dark eyes, her straight black hair and her body encamped in white silk, Charlene saw the woman's beauty and sex appeal. Rhonda's transformation from the woman in her picture was close to miraculous.

Charlene sat on a short stool as Rhonda knelt on the floor and applied peroxide and a dose of Iodine to her cuts. The application was sheer torture. Then Rhonda doctored the wound on her thigh and dressed it with a gauze bandage.

"It doesn't look infected," she assured Charlene. "Keep it clean and covered."

She put a Band-Aid on the cut over her eye. Then she rubbed a strong-smelling liniment on Charlene's back and midsection. She handed over the kimono and Charlene stood up to tie it closed.

"If no ribs are fractured, that should cure you," Rhonda said.

"Thank you! I'm so indebted to you," Charlene replied.

"Don't think anything of it. After you hear me out, you may not thank me so much. Come into the kitchen. You'll feel much better after you've had some food in your stomach."

Rhonda was right. Charlene consumed everything on her plate of soft scrambled eggs, sausage, toast, then a dish of fresh-cut fruit and an extra large piece of *Black Forest Cake*, something Rhonda said she had bought yesterday at a German bakery. She chose a tall glass of cold milk over wine and she thought her taste buds couldn't get enough of it. All the while, Rhonda stared at her, but Charlene saw empty eyes and believed the woman's mind focused on some long-ago time and place.

On the kitchen table was a **Voice of Music** four-track tape recorder. Rhonda explained how two Christmases ago, the congregation had made it a gift to Daniel. She thought he never appreciated any "modern electronic" more. He had used it often to listen to recorded music and to practice his sermons. Of all Daniel's personal things, this one she had kept. As Rhonda threaded the recording tape, she spoke about how she used the machine for her own work. "Recording my thoughts now will help later when I speak to the police," she said. She pushed down on the switches to record and they watched as the reels turned. Resting the microphone in its stand in front of her, after saying the date, time, her name and address, and announcing Charlene Cunningham as her witness, Rhonda began slowly.

"You notice I have an accent. Until 1937, my home was in Germany. The Gestapo killed my parents. They arrested my father in 1934. He was tortured and executed—a judicial murder—three years later at Berlin's Plotzensee prison. The Gestapo arrested my mother, a Jewish convert to Christianity, a few months after my father's arrest. Charged with espionage, they put her in a labor camp. I don't want to imagine what it was like for her, a beautiful, intelligent woman. She died at Auschwitz in the gas chamber a few weeks before Americans freed survivors, by then no more than skin over their brittle bones. Three days before her arrest, my mother deposited me at the country home of my father's brother. I never saw her again. A month later, the day after my fourteenth birthday, plain-dressed Gestapo men came to my uncle's home and took me back to Berlin, where they enrolled me in a school for girls supposedly operated by Hitler Youth. In truth, a special branch of the SS had charge. Some girls were as young as ten, others as old as eighteen. We had one thing in common. All our parents had betrayed the government and either our parents were already executed or in prison. The stated purpose of this institution was to educate daughters of convicted traitors. That way we would grow up as worthy mothers for heroes of the Third Reich. But that was only half the purpose. My third night there, I was taken with another new girl my age to an officer's hotel room in Berlin. He raped us both until we bled. Then he called the principal of the school and said, 'Send me two more virgins while these girls get fixed up!'

"I was less than cooperative at my next outing. I cried and resisted, and the officer complained that my behavior was an embarrassment to him and his male friend. When returned to the school, for a whole week they kept me locked in a windowless room. They took away my clothes and fed me sparingly. When let out, the matron escorted me to the school principal, a woman in her late forties with a nasty temper and a firm hand. She switched me on my backside. When my flesh turned raw, she said I had one opportunity to redeem myself and to serve the citizens of our new Germany. If I failed, I would have an accident and die. In the months that followed, they treated me well. In addition to my regular school lessons, they taught me how to stand, sit and walk properly. After dark, other teachers taught me things of a sexual nature, which they said would endear me to people pledged to save my life. Confident that I would do their bidding, one Sunday afternoon, they dressed me in a pretty gown, made up my face to look older and, explaining this was a rehearsal, they took me to the house of the feared principal and her officer husband. That was my introduction to lesbian sex and other acts of a sexual nature. Every weekend thereafter, for almost two years, I met men and women of the Third Reich, most of them officers in the SS. These people played with me and other girls from the school. We might have been mechanical toys strewn on the floor of a children's room, for all they cared. Nothing was out of bounds. Mild disrespect or hesitations we paid for with harsh punishment when we returned to the school. But I never suffered these. I don't know why, I don't have any way of understanding how my sexual experience conditioned my mind the way it did, but beginning that night with the principal, I enjoyed and looked forward to my weekends of pervasive play. I suppose I had learned that by obeying commands I could survive. The more I pleased these people the better they treated me. I became a favorite. High-ranking officers of the security police fed me and dressed me, took me for week-long vacations to country villas and fine hotels. They indulged me with kindness and gave me gifts. And nothing bothered my conscience.

"I will say too that the school itself employed high standards of learning. Weekday teachers showed no awareness of what was happening to their students, or—if they did know—they chose to ignore it. Under their supervision, classes were regimented and scholarly. There was never time for play, another reason I suppose I looked forward to weekends and other breaks. Holidays became my escape from the dull, cold, repetitive methods used by the school. Yet, I excelled under their tutorage in languages, learning English as well as French. Math, classical literature, art and the Nazi view of history were also part of our curriculum. In those ways, the school provided a disciplined and diversified education and I am grateful for that.

"One day a very influential Prussian general learned what was going on beneath the school's intellectual surface. A man of honor, a grandfather and a gentleman, he became so irate he complained to Hitler. At that time, this general was in the good graces of the leader. I have learned, however, that in the end the SS executed him after his conviction with many other officers for plotting Hitler's failed assassination. But I digress! Say what you may about the Fuhrer. There is rumor enough at the time to believe he was a deviate who preyed on young women. He was known to have murdered his own niece and lover. Perhaps he wanted this general to view him differently. In any event, as I understood it then, Hitler ordered an investigation and threatened to punish anyone found guilty of sex with underage girls of the school. I don't know if anything came of it. I believe, so that I could not testify against them, officials arranged for my transportation out of the country. I was also pregnant. Issued a passport and travel papers, I journeyed by train to Basil, Switzerland, just across the boarder from Germany. An aunt on my father's side took me in and arranged for my passage to Wisconsin, where I have other relatives. Before leaving Switzerland, four months into my term, without my consent, *Herr Doktor* opened my womb to take the fetus. I would never have another pregnancy. While he was at it, he had fixed me for good. I tell you this, not for sympathy, but for your understanding in what I tell you next.

"I married Daniel Maefield with him knowing very little about my years at the girls' school. He knew the Nazis had conditioned me for inordinate sex, but we never discussed details or personalities. He knew I could not have a child."

Rhonda turned away from Charlene, as if listening to the silence, her proud face pale and sadder than before. She gripped the arm of the kitchen chair next to her, her knuckles turning white from holding it so firm. She wept as she spoke.

"The things they did to young girls . . . Considering our age and the duress, it was wrong, evil, callous and insane. But I am living proof of how abused children deny their past and protect those who compromised them. Only two years ago, a reporter from a popular German magazine asked me if there was anything to the rumor that the SS used this girls' school to breed child sex slaves. I had never heard myself described that way before, yet, it was accurate. Nevertheless, I told him the rumor was a lie and offered no encouragement in the story he wanted to write. How curious that other women who survived the school and the war have also kept their silence. And what is worse, I do not want to free my life from the slave I became. I was in psychotherapy for years, Charlene! Ultimately, the therapist dismissed me. *As long as you do not want to change, there is no cure,*' he said. But for me there is no disease to cure. 'Abnormal' is in the minds of others, not mine."

Rhonda appeared in a trance. For a long moment she sat with her head bowed, her eyes on her wine glass, her memories rising and falling from the tomb that held them.

"When I first met Daniel Maefield I was nineteen. He was a few weeks from turning forty. I was a pupil in his Renaissance History class. We were marrieed after christmas in 1939. For most of our married life, we were reasonably happy.

"This part of New York was and remains today a wonderful neighborhood for people like Daniel and me. I completed college and then a Masters' program in political science. I went on to add a doctoral in industrial relations. Daniel continued his work as minister of a small, racially diverse, but poor church in Harlem. He lectured at Columbia and at Union Seminary. Those were his most prolific years. He wrote several books on religious themes and I can't tell you how many articles he contributed to professional journals. He did editing and writing for a forty-volume Bible commentary. I took on a teaching position at New York University. We had an active social life among people in the arts and humanities. Our lives were never dull and mine uninhibited by moral conventions.

"A modest man, Daniel showed no carnal interest in sex. He treated the subject with cold detachment, writing about it as a way to understand human development and religious expression. The fact is he preferred to talk about sex, not participate in it. He was like a person who knows everything about the sport of tennis, but doesn't play it. I don't mean to imply we never had sex. In his way, I suppose we did, dispassionate and devoid of intimacy, infrequent and unimaginative. I will not pretend that one man could have satisfied me and I believe he accepted that I craved what you call 'deviant sexual behavior.' The 'unusual and twisted' excite me. Sex with a stranger compels me. Pleasure comes in pleasing a man or a woman and in receiving the same in return. While Daniel did not condone my extramarital activity, he tolerated it. He kept his views to himself and showed no interest in my absence from home, sometimes overnight, other times for longer. I was discreet and managed to keep this side of me very secret. If we saw abnormality in each other's behavior, we accepted those aspects as honest expressions and did not try to change them. I cannot recall our arguing about my conduct. I believe Daniel loved me very much and feared if he offered objection to my lifestyle, I would leave him. He was probably right.

"I had thought that our move to Tompkinsville would enhance our lives. But it had the opposite affect. For no two places could be as different as a church in Harlem and a church in the center of New Jersey's farm industry. In the beginning, I made up my mind to fit what I saw as their mold. I had the memory of my mother as a pastor's wife as an example. I did everything I could to show hospitality. Daniel and I held dinner parties and I hosted afternoon teas. I attended women's meetings and church socials. In all these events, I tried to show interest. I had always dressed to appear more Daniel's age, but at Tompkinsville, perhaps I carried this too far. Underneath, I hated the cultural boredom. And soon, I despised the boundaries I had drawn around myself.

"In private, I looked for diversions and began leaving town for weekend excursions to New York, where I have friends and where I am free to satisfy my sexual interests. Or, when we traveled in the Far East, while Daniel plodded through monsoons in India, I enjoyed exotic hotels in Bangkok and Hong Kong, which are in fact brothels for the young and daring. In Europe, while Daniel attended university lectures and met with theologian friends, acquaintances entertained me in Berlin, Hamburg and Paris. I counted these safe retreats and they should have been enough. But one day, against my own better judgment, I seduced the church custodian, Everett Wheeler, in a basement room once used as a housekeeper's apartment."

For the first time, Rhonda looked up to stare at Charlene, her blank facial expression waiting for a response. Charlene presented a doubtful smile.

"You are surprised," Rhonda observed. "But, yes, I saw Everett as an opportunity for amusement and gratification. It never would have happened if I had not wanted him. In the first few months of our amorous affair, we saw each other repeatedly, everyday if convenient and safe. I had to be cautious, because as open and liberal as Daniel was about me sexually, it would break his heart to learn I had taken my infidelity to people he knew, especially anyone in the church. That had always been the unspoken dividing line. Yet, strange as it may seem to you, Everett Wheeler satisfied me as few men have. For almost six months, I even remained loyal, saving my body just for him. We knew we played a game. Yet, preposterous and sad as it sounds, Everett is the only man with whom I have had a sustained sexual rapport. This does not mean that we were or are in a romantic relationship. We feel no jealousy over other lovers. We do not exchange gifts. Promises of deviant sex guide any affection we show each other. As time went on, and as I became absorbed in my law studies at Columbia, we saw each other less and less. I rented the apartment on 47th Street. Once or twice a month, Everett traveled to the city for business and stayed overnight with me. Now and then, I returned to Tompkinsville. When I was at home in Tompkinsville, I met Everett in the basement room. By then, my marriage had become more fiction than fact.

"A year ago, Everett took over the lease on my downtown Manhattan apartment. Traveling to New York more frequently, he needed a place of his own. We agreed that I should continue to reside there until I could find my own place. I already had plans to join the law partnership I work for now. I had it in the back of my mind that Daniel and I would work out a legal separation within this year. When I learned this apartment would become available in April, I bought the lease. I tried to discuss these changes with Daniel, but instead of agreeing, he became belligerent toward me. We argued over incidental matters. I had not, however, anticipated his depression. I came home a few days before Christmas and planned staying until after New Years' Day. If Daniel learned about Everett and me, he may have discovered our affair that week."

Rhonda looked up at Charlene, her eyes pained. Perhaps she wished she hadn't begun. Her hands trembled, especially as she filled her glass and sipped more wine.

"This would explain why Daniel was so on edge all of New Year's Day. He drank more than usual. He lost his temper and swore at me. He threw a book across the room that hit me in the head. We had exchanged roles. He had become the nag. He was far from the passive, condescending man with whom I had become familiar. I had never seen him like this. New Year's Day, I walked out on him and returned to the city. Our combat couldn't have come at a worse time, since I was scheduled to begin my bar exams ten days later. While deep in my studies, Daniel telephoned the apartment, sometimes late at night, or early in the morning. He did it two and three times a day. He was terribly depressed. He cried like a child, begged my forgiveness, wanted assurance I would not leave him. At times, he sounded suicidal. I tried to calm him by lying to him about my intentions. I needn't have bothered, because he didn't believe me. His belligerence became more abusive and he started swearing and ranting over the phone on how I didn't understand and never could. I perceived alcohol was affecting his thinking. He slurred his speech, he rambled on for an hour about nothing. Friday, the calls stopped. Sunday night, I tried reaching him at his university apartment. I thought we could meet for lunch on Monday. But he didn't respond to the message I left. Now I was into taking my exams and so I did not pursue him. After three days of silence, I became anxious. When we finally connected by phone Friday morning, he didn't want to talk and hung up on me.

"Did he say why he was angry?"

"Other than confessing his unhappiness about a separation and my plans to live here, he did not say. And, I didn't ask him. But I know he was unhappy about my private life. He wanted me to renew contact with my therapist. He offered to make the appointment and go with me. I refused. I believe this made him very angry.

"I finished my bar exams Saturday morning and caught the first afternoon train. I didn't know in what kind of mood I would find him. To my surprise, he had calmed down. He acted jovial and more like his confident self. We spent a pleasant evening together. We went to see a silly movie that night: **The Absent-Minded Professor**, starring Fred McMurry. For the first time in many months, I heard Daniel's loud laugh. I believed things were back to normal.

"As I was leaving church Sunday morning, Everett stopped me to say he had to cancel our three o'clock rendezvous. He joked about afternoon business in Atlantic City. I was disappointed, perhaps I should say sexually anxious, considering I had locked myself in my apartment with law books and papers for nearly two weeks.

"Following our usual routine when I was home, Daniel and I went out to Sunday dinner at a local restaurant. By now, news about the weather was on everyone's mind. Daniel canceled his Monday classes at Columbia. I spent the afternoon reading. I thought Daniel would join me. We had planned to read to each other in German parts from Goethe's poem, "**Faust Two**." We had often spent Sunday afternoons like that. Daniel derived much satisfaction from such readings. But he had a two o'clock caller and left for Shepherd House. He returned to the manse a little after five. By then the snowfall had turned into the forecast blizzard. News broadcasts advised everyone to stay home. We watched the news on television and ate a light supper. At eight o'clock, Daniel left again for Shepherd House. He had lots of reading to do, so he planned to stay there all night, a common habit. He asked me to come by before dawn. We would walk over to Tommy's Place for breakfast, something we often did, regardless of the weather . . . "

Rhonda had dabbed her eyes with a handkerchief while speaking. Charlene saw none of the ice-cold stoicism Detective Burroughs had described. In her presence, Rhonda was teary and fumbling, her speech slow and hesitant. Every so often, she lapsed into her native German, showed irritation when she caught herself and returned to her deliberate, succinct English.

"After Daniel's death, police conducted a systematic search at Shepherd House. They went through files of sermons and research papers. They listened to recorded tapes made on this machine. They examined marginal notes in every book on his shelves. To assure thoroughness, Detective Burroughs had each book catalogued and put into a numbered box. That way he kept tabs on what his investigators had browsed. He spent many nights in Shepherd House doing the work alone. He told me he was searching for a note, a confession. I don't know for sure. The detective believes Daniel left a clue, perhaps the name of an old enemy. It frustrated him that he could not learn who had visited Daniel that afternoon. But no record of the visit has shown up. Daniel had not entered a name or anything about the caller on his calendar. Nor had he told me.

"When permitted to take back Shepherd House, the elders didn't know what to do with the boxed books and had them toted to the manse basement for me to claim. They should have kept them in the study. I had no interest in them, so I gave them to the new minister."

"Yes," Charlene interrupted, "Jerry, a . . . Reverend Flynn, has returned them to Shepherd House. I saw them there last Sunday. They will look very nice."

Rhonda managed a polite smile. "I'm glad for that. I hated to think of those books rotting in that damp cellar."

"Do you think they could hold a clue as to why Reverend Maefield was depressed?"

"It's possible. Daniel often stuck notes inside pages of his books and wrote personal thoughts in the margins. If he read something that reminded him of someone, he would star it and write a name. And it's true—there are fanatics who saw Daniel as the devil who vilified their image of Jesus. As a social activist, he had made other enemies. He received many threatening letters over the years, most of which he laughed about before he burned them. I told this to the police and that may have prompted them to spend time searching through his work. It must have been a very boring investigation."

She paused and looked down at the table. "Maybe I don't really want to know."

Charlene heard an opportunity. "What about the keys, Mrs. Maefield, the pastor's personal set of keys to all the rooms in the church? Do you know what happened to them?"

Rhonda looked up. There was that question again, the same one Everett had asked her this morning. "Daniel had a ring with a dozen church keys that hung from a hook by the kitchen door. Now that you mention it, I looked for them when I went to Shepherd House that morning. Not seeing them in their usual place, I assumed Daniel had them with him. I relied on him to open Shepherd Door when I rang the bell. But as you may know, I found the door already opened a crack. Why do you ask?"

"Because if those were the keys Walter Tompkins passed on to Reverend Flynn, one of them unlocked the door into your hidden room. That's how we got into the studio."

For several seconds Rhonda said nothing, her eyes seeming to focus on the tape recorder reels as they revolved. "I don't know how my husband would have gotten a key to that room,"

Rhonda replied. "Both Everett and I had a key. I carried mine in a pocket of my purse. Daniel could have taken it from there." She looked up at Charlene. "I dare to think that he wouldn't do something like that. He respected my personal things. He never mentioned the room to me. I had no indication he knew it existed. But, yes, if he had his own key and saw us there, that could explain his depression . . . "

"You must have known then that Everett used the room to photograph obscenity?"

"Yes, I knew! And, no, I did not discourage him. I am not proud to say this now, but there were times I watched Everett with his models . . . A few times, I even participated, though always in disguise. On the Monday night after the murder, Everett and I met briefly at the manse. Fearing what the studio would imply in a police investigation, I thought I had persuaded him to destroy the room as a studio. I know now he did not do so. The morning after my husband's murder, we had also agreed to have no contact. If the police learned of our affair, we feared a rush to judgment. Today, Everett broke that promise as well."

Without warning, Charlene reached across the table and pressed the stop button on the tape recorder.

"Why did you do that?" Rhonda questioned with annoyance.

Charlene's face was grave. She hesitated to go on, but could not let the moment pass. She looked point blank into Rhonda's eyes. "Off the record, strictly between you and me—though it may return to haunt you later—I have to ask. Did you have a Sunday afternoon visitor January twenty-first? Did you use the hidden room to make love to . . . Madge Todd?"

Rhonda's hands came up to cover her eyes as astonishment flooded her face. How could Charlene know? If she lied about Madge, how could Charlene believe anything she told her?

"How do you know?" she asked without taking away her hands.

"A guess! But, in honesty, it is more than that . . . intuition! And a little evidence! When I met with Madge last Sunday afternoon, she turned crimson at my mention of your name. I understood that you two might have a casual relationship. I had no reason then to think of it as sexual and I didn't. I did, however, ask myself if maybe you shared a confidence, perhaps you knew something about Madge that could embarrass her, or if it might be the other way around. During my interview, Madge revealed she had seen you the afternoon before the murder when she stopped by the manse to return borrowed books belonging to Reverend Maefield."

Rhonda laid her hands out flat on the table. She avoided Charlene's eyes and bowed her head to stare at her own hands.

"But there is more," Charlene went on. "When Jerry and I searched through Everett's studio, I found women's underpants stuffed in a drawer filled with adult books and magazines. The panties were a common brand, nothing out of the ordinary. That and the fact that they were there instead of in a drawer full of costume lingerie made me believe they had a personal relationship and someone had meant to retrieve them. They were my size and style, popular among teens and young women, so I had some idea as to the weight and age of their owner. What got my attention was the strong odor of perfume they carried. I didn't associate this with Madge right away, but I had gotten a whiff of her perfume only hours earlier—a scent of Lavender, not especially unique, but distinctive! I was, however, a long way from thinking of Madge in that room with you. I thought it probable that Madge could have modeled in secret for her cousin, Everett. And maybe you had learned about it. Incredible as that connection is, this was how I saw relationships last Sunday evening. But tonight, your admission of sexual interest in women made me realize what had happened. So . . . , Madge's nervousness about you, the mention of visiting you that afternoon, the panties with their scent of Lavender, well, I decided to ask, off the record."

"You're a good detective, Charlene," Rhonda said, focusing on Charlene's battered face. Reaching across the table, she took hold of Charlene's wrist, held it gently, used her other hand to massage the red area where the handcuffs had held her. "For Madge's sake, I hope you will keep this our secret. Madge was an innocent victim. Let me assure you, she is no more a lesbian than you are," she purred in a quiet tone. Her eyes then looked plainly into Charlene's eyes. "That doesn't mean you can't respond in a positive way to another woman's sexual appeal. You may even prefer intimacy with some women compared to some men. I do, and I am not ashamed to say so."

Charlene resisted pulling away her hand. Rhonda's warmth and passion were not without sensation. A quiet moment passed before Rhonda continued.

"I took advantage of a girl starved for affection, a girl repeatedly raped and browbeaten by her husband. I showed her how she could feel when someone took the time to give her both love and pleasure. She found herself conflicted between conscience and powerful urges for gratification. Afterward, shame and guilt returned. My husband's murder six to eight hours later made our relationship even more forbidding. Madge remains tortured and confused by what she considers unforgivable, sinful behavior. She has to get over that. I have to get over her." Rhonda's eyes swelled with tears and she let go of Charlene's hand. "I did then and I do now love Madge. I am responsible if she becomes a casualty of our indiscretion. I have begged her to forgive me. Whether we meet again for love or for just friendship is her decision." Rhonda looked away dismissively. She appeared destroyed. Her eyes stared at the tabletop and again she put her palms to her cheeks, covered her eyes with her fingers. She hunched forward as she cried. "I beg you, Charlene, keep our secret! Whatever happens because of what I confess here, please don't include Madge as a suspect in my husband's murder.

Rhonda pushed the record buttons on the tape machine. "What else do you want to know?"

"Tell me about the night of the murder?"

Silence followed. Rhonda took long, deep breaths, used a linen napkin to wipe perspiration off her face. Her mind had arrived at the place of no return. She took a long sip from her wine glass. She looked as though she might not continue. The tape recorder reels revolved with an hour of unused tape on the reel.

"I was reading in bed when Everett telephoned. He said the way was clear, that Daniel was secure at Shepherd House for the duration. At first, I protested. I could tell from the way Everett spoke he was very drunk. I ranted at him for breaking our date that afternoon. But he humored me, said he had a way to make up for his absence. He instructed me to meet him at the bottom of the cellar stairs at ten o'clock. I dressed for him. Everett liked my dowager look, the only man I know who does. I met him as planned. He said he had a special treat that would excite me, but I must put on a blindfold.

"For Everett and me, sex often began by acting out a fantasy. I offered no objection. We had done this before. He led me to our secret room. There he stripped me naked. I sensed someone else in the room and asked if this was so. He told me he had a present for completing my bar exams. He took off my blindfold to show me a man on the bed, naked from the waist down. He was masked and gagged and Everett had tied his hands behind his back. Everett said he wanted to watch. He removed the man's gag but left him tied. Strange and perverted as it may sound to you, I accommodated him. The man pleaded with Everett to untie him and allow him freedom with me, but Everett refused. Only after I brought the man to achievement did Everett end the game. He blindfolded and gagged him again. Together we pulled his pants up. Everett said nothing as he ushered him out. I disappeared into the bathroom to shower and went back to the studio bed to wait for Everett's return.

"What time did Everett leave with this visitor?" Charlene interrupted.

"About ten forty-five. I'm guessing. I didn't look at my watch but I sense no more than an hour had passed since I went to the basement.

"After my shower, I turned out all but a low-level lamp at bedside. I slept until Everett awoke me. Again, I did not take note of the time. I do recall, however that Everett was drunker than before. In spite of that, we made ardent love. I sense it went on for much more than an hour, perhaps two. When I heard Everett snoring, I decided to leave and did not awaken him. I did not dress or even put on my shoes. I merely gathered my things in my arms. Before I left the studio, I recall turning on the studio lights to look at my wristwatch. It was then three fifty. I thought too that the blinding lights would awaken Everett. He had said he needed to go home before starting early on shoveling snow from the church walks. Upstairs I took a hot bath, redid my hair and face and dressed in the same outer clothes I had on earlier, added storm boots, muffler and overcoat. Just as I stepped into the cloister, the bell in the church tower began to peal five o'clock. The snowfall had turned to sleet and the walkway had become treacherous. The instant I saw the gate to Shepherd House wide open and clanging in the wind, I began to worry. I had a premonition things weren't right. When I saw Shepherd Door ajar, I feared the worst. Hesitantly, I entered the study. Besides a lamp lit on Daniel's desk, light came from a single floor lamp next to the reading chair at the far end of the room. The fireplace fire had burned down, but some logs smoldered and flared. It was enough light to see the body of my husband on the floor. He was face up, his eyes open and blood all around him. His glasses were off. The police found them smashed where they had slid under a chair. I think I stared at him for a whole minute, not wanting to believe what I was seeing . . . "

In the silence that followed, Rhonda stared blankly at the tabletop, but what she saw was the death scene as if it had appeared all over again.

"My shock was total and I had to sit in a chair at the table with my head down to keep from fainting. I didn't want to call the police from there for fear of disturbing evidence. As a lawyer, I'm conscious of such matters. I recall leaving in a hurry and pulling Shepherd Door closed behind me. I made my way to the manse, where I dialed the operator to get me the Tompkinsville police."

Rhonda laid her head on her arms, which rested on the table. Except for the whine of the tape recorder, all was quiet for several seconds. Charlene broke in.

"Mrs. Maefield, it could be crucial to your defense. Do you know who Everett brought you that night?"

Rhonda lifted her head, stared blankly into Charlene's eyes. "No!"

"Can you describe the visitor?"

"Everett had covered the man's head in a birdlike mask. I do remember some physical things. If the police ask, I will describe them. I assume Everett picked him up at a bar in Atlantic City, since that's where he had been all afternoon."

"And how was Everett when he awoke you for sex?"

"What do you mean?"

"Well, besides his alcoholic condition, was he dressed and if so . . ."

"He had removed his clothes. The only light was from the bedside lamp . . . I saw him as a shadow."

"And after you turned the bright lights on, did you see Everett then?"

"I did not take notice of him. He was snoring loudly, that is all I recall. I did not linger."

Rhonda reached for the stop button and pressed it. The room was very silent and once more, she lowered her eyes. Charlene waited for her to start recording again. Rhonda raised her eyes to meet hers.

"I know you ask: Where is my shame? How could I allow such defilement to happen in my own house? In God's house? How could I seduce Madge, a pure, innocent, young mother? How could I allow Everett, a man of despicable character, to make love to me? You want to know why I would exploit another man's weakness to entertain my and his degenerate needs. I wish I could answer you, Charlene. The truth is I can't. I have no honor when it comes to sex, no revulsion, only hunger. I am every man's fantasy and more often that of a woman. And my crime? I do these things for pleasure. I do them for myself. I do them for free."

*　　*　　*

Jerry Flynn had stayed under the shower so long his skin shriveled, not that this was unusual. As a young man, his mother had threatened to turn off the water at its source if he didn't get out. Now time and circumstances drove him out. He toweled dry and dressed in casual clothes. Believing he would not get back from New York much before noon, he wrote out several notes for Miss Blatty and left them on her desk outside Shepherd House. He worked another hour in his study before returning to his bedroom. He was anxious to get on his way, but decided to read Charlene's journal. Her handwriting was neat but crowded and she had often drawn pictures instead of words. Laying the notebook down, he wished she had shared what she had learned about Everett Wheeler after her interview at Tommy's Place. Maybe he would have called in the police Sunday night. But, no, that's wasn't fair. He knew Everett was a bully and a racist. And in retrospect, had she given him proof he was a killer, it wouldn't have changed his mind Sunday night. "All I wanted was sex with her. Short of her refusal, nothing could have kept us from making love." Still, did she have to hide that she was a private detective? And thinking back to her notes, he wondered why she hadn't mentioned to him her meeting with Madge Todd on Sunday? The dagger she had drawn next to Madge's name puzzled him. And why had she written *"beauty inside the beast"* next to words where Madge described Mrs. Maefield? There were other graphics and he smiled at her lipstick smudge in the margin by his name. He realized that Charlene's interview book was as much a portrait of her likes and dislikes as they were a record of her investigation. He hated to think what Everett would do if he saw her comments and pictures relevant to her interview with him.

Over the phone, Charlene had told him she loved him and, while he was less certain if he felt that way about her, he yearned for her closeness. He worried that Everett Wheeler had hurt her real bad and wondered where the mad man was now. But more puzzling than all, he couldn't for the life of him comprehend how Rhonda Maefield fit into all this. He looked again at the picture of Rhonda Charlene had slid between the pages of her notebook and smiled depreciatively. He did not like to

use the word "ugly" for any of God's creatures, but that was
what he saw.

* * *

After concluding business and saying goodnight to the grocery
store executive, Michael lingered at his table. He hadn't seen
Margo Rasmeyer since an hour ago and had accepted that she
had checked out early when he saw her walking toward him. His
spirits rose. A broad smile cresting her face, Margo put a Scotch
on the rocks in front of him. "On the house," she said, pulled out
a chair and sat across from him. "I'm off duty and was wondering
if you could do me a favor, Mr. Todd? Can I thumb a ride back to
Tompkinsville? My car is in the repair shop and rather than stay
the night with a girlfriend in Atlantic City, seeing as how
Wednesday is my day off, I would like to get home."

Michael readily agreed, and fifteen minutes later, they sped
west over Pleasantville Boulevard. Margo began making
conversation and volunteered that after she left the job at the
canning factory, she worked for a fashionable clothing and jewelry
store in Camden. She left out the fact that she had stolen from
the place for family, friends, and anyone else who would pay her
discount price. One evening, the store detective stopped her for
a routine security check. It was hardly routine. A search of her
person discovered more than five hundred dollars worth of
jewelry. From her locker, among other things, police confiscated
a matchbox filled with marijuana. For this and another three
thousand dollars of unaccounted merchandise, she had pleaded
guilty to a charge of first offence larceny, which let her out on
probation after half time served. Since then, she had stayed clean
and, after turning twenty-one, her probation officer had approved
her employment as a cocktail waitress. The tips were good and
she was making it on her own.

Besides fine jewelry and clothes, Margo had a weakness for
well-healed men. She dated for the pleasure of sex, and if they
cared to leave her a "gift," she didn't turn it down. While she fell

easily in and out of love, she did not do well with rejection. She had seen Everett Wheeler as her sugar daddy, too old for her tastes, but rich and exciting. She believed he owed her another opportunity behind his camera and, catching him in Tommy's Place with that blond last Sunday had ignited her anger. In the exchange that followed, he had made matters worse by telling her she was no more than one among many models he chose to entertain and she had to wait her turn. She had then made the idle threat to make an anonymous telephone call to the police and inform them how he was using a room in the basement of First Presbyterian Church. He hadn't realized she knew that, but she did. After turning her down again tonight, she might just do what she had threatened. Maybe tomorrow she would turn in the bastard, she thought. With that on her mind, she asked Michael if he knew Everett Wheeler. Michael turned his head to stare at her and it was not a pleasant look. "Unfortunately, to live in Tompkinsville is to know Everett Wheeler." He did not reveal Everett as his wife's cousin. Instead, he asked Margo how she knew him. She certainly was not going to tell him, among other things, that she had posed in the nude for him. She therefore lied that Everett had once tried to pick her up. She would rather date *Dr. Julius No*, a reference to the sinister, bad-guy character in the James Bond movie thriller showing in movie theaters. Michael commented that Margo reminded him of the movie's female titan, *Honey Ryder*, played by Ursula Andres. Margo laughed at that, but also accepted it. She liked the comparison. That this handsome man pictured her as the popular movie sex symbol bolstered her confidence. "Well," she responded, "you look like Sean Connery, Agent Double-O Seven." Michael showed a doubtful smile. "I mean it," she insisted. "I find you very handsome."

Michael smiled broadly. But he kept his face forward and drove in silence.

Margo wasn't sure what to say next. It flattered her to think that she could attract such an important and high-class guy. She did not however feel confident. Filthy rich, college man, married to a Tompkins, how could she hope to succeed with him? But then, if he chose her over his pretty wife, so much the better. She would do her best to please him and keep him coming back for more. She interrupted their silence to test his openness. She asked how Madge stayed so young and gorgeous. She mentioned how all the guys at the canning factory were "wild" about her. Michael replied he wished she would change the subject. He wasn't in a mood to discuss his wife. His manner on this showed his alienation. That was all Margo needed to hear. She slid across the seat to his side and, stretching her bare arm over his shoulders, she kissed his cheek. Instantly, his right hand traveled along her exposed thigh. She kissed his neck and trailed her tongue into his ear. Easing back, she whispered, "Is that a better subject?" He replied that he knew of a motel a few miles up the road where they could stop to discuss her question, and when she offered no objection, he floored the gas pedal.

*   *   *

It was one o'clock when Rhonda closed down the tape recorder and set it on the floor inside a kitchen closet.

"You need sleep and so do I," she said dryly to Charlene as she showed her into the guestroom. "I'll set the alarm for seven. Then we'll see about the police."

"One more question. Why did you go to Everett's apartment tonight?"

Rhonda took a deep breath. "Frankly, I was on my way to a private club on the Upper East Side to meet a female friend for a few hours of sex in a club cubicle, but decided first to stop off at the apartment to pick up Everett's handgun. He usually hides it under the kitchen sink. He paid a lot of money for a compact Colt .45, very powerful for its size, and supposedly untraceable. I really thought I would come back here and blow my brains out."

Rhonda never flinched and Charlene cringed at the thought that she had meant it.

"I don't think that would be very smart, Rhonda," she asserted. "And, the gun wasn't there, was it?"

"No! But you were!"

"So, what does that mean? That you thought to rape me or leave me there tied up for Everett?" she replied, a hurt ring in her voice.

Rhonda waved Charlene off. "I meant neither. I can't be party to murder. You must believe me. But enough of this. Come on, I'll show you where you can sleep."

She led Charlene into her office and pulled open the Simmons Hide-A-Bed. She spread sheets over the mattress and laid out a blanket and a pillow. She raised the window and Charlene immediately felt cool night air sweep the room.

"You'll be comfortable here. I don't know how well my clothes will fit you, but you're welcome to whatever I have. Do you want something to wear to bed?"

"No, I'll be fine, thank you."

Rhonda turned out the light. If she had any reason to distrust this woman, she was too tired to worry about it now. Charlene was asleep before her head hit the pillow.

* * *

Jerry went downstairs just as the great grandfather clock chimed two in the morning. He estimated it would take three to four hours to find Rhonda Maefield's Manhattan apartment. He would get there before Charlene expected him, but he could use the extra time. In any event, he was too anxious to wait any longer.

The manse was in darkness and he had to grope his way around. He was still unfamiliar with the placement of furniture. More than once, he stumbled over things. He lit a table lamp next to the living-room sofa and another on the sun porch. "Better I leave lights on." He went into the kitchen and switched on the ceiling lamp. He walked outside to the garage, which stood detached from the house at the west end of the property.

In the last few days, Jerry's troubles with starting his Crown Imperial had increased and he wanted to kick himself for not taking it in for service. He raised the garage door, got into the driver's seat and said a silent prayer of thanks as the engine roared to life. He backed out. He left the car lights on and the motor running while he went back to lower the garage doors. He thought he should ask for an electric garage-door opener. If Everett could hang one on the maintenance garage, why not here? *Oh well, I have to get my exercise one way or another.* Laughing at himself, he slid onto the car bench again. He began backing to where he could turn out of the driveway, but extra bright high beams, reflecting in his rear view mirrors, blinded him. He jammed on his brakes to avoid a collision. Putting the transmission in park, he jumped out of his car to see his way blocked by a noisy truck. The person behind the wheel kept revving the motor. Jerry started toward the driver's side of the cab, but stopped when he heard the passenger door open and someone get out. As the passenger passed in front of the headlights, Jerry recognized Walter Tompkins.

"Walter, what are you doing here this early in the morning?"

"Well, I might be asking the young preacher the same question. Seems to me you should be in bed resting for the busy day you must have before you."

As Walter said this, the engine of the truck went dead.

"No rest for the weary, as they say," Jerry replied and cautiously added, "I have kind of an emergency. I really have to get away."

Walter shined a flashlight into Jerry's car, opened the back door of the Imperial and shown the light over the floor. He slammed the door closed.

"I hear you've been keeping some early hours with the ladies, Mr. Flynn."

Jerry muffled a laugh. Walter had probably heard he had a harem at the manse and foolishly believed it.

"Walter, let's talk about this another time. I really do have someone waiting for me."

"Yes, of course you do. And who do you have waiting inside?"

A silly grin settled on Jerry's face. "No one is waiting for me in the manse, Walter. Go in and have a look, but first, move your truck. I don't want to be rude but I have to be free to leave."

"I want you to leave all right," Walter said, his voice more high pitched than usual. "And I don't want you to come back. I'm calling the elders as well as the trustees to meet with me on Thursday evening. You can be there if you like, but I'll tell you right now, they will vote to block your installation on Sunday."

"Walter, do whatever you have to do, but right now, move your truck!"

"You listen to me, young man! This church doesn't need another filthy embarrassment. Your conduct is unacceptable." Walter angrily spit out his words while his finger jabbed the air a few inches from Jerry's nose. "You know I was the one person on the search committee who voted against you. I told the others we needed a man with more maturity. You were . . . "

"Walter, move you're goddamn truck or I'll move it for you!"

Jerry brushed Walter's pointed finger aside and moved toward the cab. He saw that it was empty. Too late, he realized that the driver was behind him. Jerry was on the step to pull down the door handle when he felt a hard punch in his ribs. Strong arms gripped his legs and roughly dragged him to the ground. A powerful fist pounded his back, a foot kicked him just below his rib cage. As he climbed to his knees, another kick flew to his groin. He rolled on his side, paralyzed with pain.

"Stand him up!" he heard Walter order.

Jerry didn't have time to catch his breath before his assailant pushed him face forward against the truck fender. A knee struck his butt. He would have fallen to the ground except a heavy hand held him in place. Several glancing punches to his back and shoulders followed before a hard kick hit his leg just below his knee. As he turned to take one feeble swing at his tormentor, his arm was blocked and two hands pushed his head on to the hood. Pulling him into a chokehold, once more he faced the blinding flashlight and Tompkins's screeching voice.

"This is just a warning, Mr. Flynn!" Tompkins's lips were an inch from his ear. "You'll make a confession about your misdeeds and tell everyone that a guilty conscience won't allow you to accept ordination. You prayed all night to God and he has judged you. You'll tell the elders you need sex counseling or something. You'll find the words. You're good with words."

Jerry wheezed and held his stomach, desperate to fill his lungs with a full breath of air. Again, Walter bent close to his ear.

"That way you can resign with some dignity and, who knows, maybe our mother church will find you a little congregation far from civilized people, a place where you won't be a threat to our little children and young ladies."

Once more Jerry took a sharp jab to his midsection, but this time his protagonist let him fall on his knees. He vomited on the truck tire. He thought his insides had burst. He collapsed on his side, his lungs desperate for a painless breath of air. He turned to lie flat on his back and opened his eyes, catching a look at Jorge Garcia, Tompkins's field-boss.

"If you feel you need police protection, Mr. Flynn," he heard Walter say, "tell the coppers you were mugged in your driveway by an unknown rascal. A little fib just might save your life. You call me around suppertime tonight and let me know how you are. Show me a wee bit of humility and I'll make it worth your while."

Jorge took hold of Jerry's feet and dragged him away from the tire. He heard the two men gab quietly as they entered the truck cab. The engine roared to life. He watched as the truck backed off from his Imperial and turned on to the circular church drive. He lay in utter misery for five minutes or more, slowly rose to his feet and staggered to his own vehicle, still idling with its lights on. He thought of all the things he should do. Go in the house, apply ice packs to all the places he hurt, call the police and swear out a warrant against Tompkins and his field boss.

The more he thought about it, the more he believed that this was all connected to Everett Wheeler and included not only what he and Charlene had uncovered in the basement, but the murder of Daniel Maefield. And the scariest, hardest realization? Walter

Tompkins's involvement. But Walter and Everett underestimated him if they believed they could scare him off. As he backed his car out the driveway, he recognized they had much more to hide and to be ashamed of than he had. Let them expose his indiscretion. Let people believe what they want. He had nothing to hide. Before he drove past the Revolutionary War monument at the juncture of Main and Church streets, he had made up his mind and—as Frank Scarpelli had encouraged him—to meet his Goliath. He had only to find the right stones. And for those, he looked to the secrets Charlene had uncovered in Manhattan.

*   *   *

In spite of his gruff show of force, Walter Tompkins was not by nature a brutal man. He hated what he had just done. He knew it was wrong. His nephew, Everett Wheeler, was his real enemy. Yet, protecting his family and the integrity of his daughter outweighed Walter's more noble instincts. He hoped his ordered beating of Flynn would work, that Flynn would count his own survival, if not his reputation, as more important than a plush church job and he would take his advice to leave First Church. Walter was prepared to keep quiet about Jerry's "adultery"— that's how Walter thought of it—provided he attest to the elders that he now had second thoughts about answering a call for becoming a pastor. Jerry could say he suffered a crisis in faith. In the meantime, he would refuse ordination. The church could pay him a generous severance and that would be that. Walter believed such action would get Everett off his back for a while. Given time, he would deal with Everett. Nephew that he was, he would pay for his bad deeds.

"Take a turn at the next corner," Walter instructed Jorge Garcia. "I want to assure myself Flynn went into the manse to lick his wounds."

Garcia followed directions. He returned to the church property by entering the parking lot behind the main buildings.

As headlights passed over the pitch-black area, the two men saw a familiar pickup truck parked in front of the annex entrance.

"Isn't that Wheeler's truck?" Garcia asked.

"Right! Can't imagine why he's here at this hour. Park behind that stand of pine trees."

Garcia backed in facing the annex and cut the lights and ignition.

"You want to go in and have a look?"

"No, Everett's locked himself in there and I don't have keys. He must be in a mad hurry. Otherwise he'd have parked his truck in the maintenance garage."

"Look at the sparks flying," Garcia said looking up at the chimney housing. "Must be burning things!"

"Yah, he's up to some kind of mischief," Walter exclaimed and took his handkerchief out to wipe his brow. "Sure don't need heat tonight. Hand me those binoculars under your seat. Let's wait and see if Everett comes out alone."

"What about the padre? You want me to walk over there and check to see he's home?"

Walter looked in the direction of the manse, which stood above the parking lot, lights beaming from its kitchen windows.

"I think we can safely conclude Mr. Flynn is running scared and wherever he was venturing to at two o'clock in the morning, he canceled. No, right now, if the padre knows what's best for him, he'll be holding ice cubes on his balls."

He laughed loudly and Garcia joined him in his hilarity.

CHAPTER 14

COMPLICATING CIRCUMSTANCES

Wednesday before Dawn, June 13

Everett Wheeler lathered his body and stood under the pulsing shower in the bathroom adjoining his disbanded studio.

The church basement was his best place to destroy evidence. He couldn't count how many times he had used the old furnace to incinerate material that could prove embarrassing to him. Last Sunday night, that had included everything from lingerie to bed sheets. This morning, he had thrown in everything on him that a police lab could connect to the dead detective.

He grabbed up his Colt .45, keys, switchblade knife, Burroughs's detective badge and sample photos, and left the bathroom. Out of frustration that the best dirty picture studio in the Northeast had gone under, he banged the gun butt against the wall. "I'll make them pay," he shouted as he passed the forlorn wide bed that had once been the centerpiece of his studio. "Tomorrow night I'll strangle her with her stockings and get Mr. Preacher down here before I clobber him. Fuck 'm all!" he shouted going out the door.

He unlocked the steel wardrobe cabinet where he kept changes of clothes and personal items. When he dressed up, he did so in clothes he saw as dapper, but others saw as gaudy—a pair of green lightweight slacks, a yellow silk shirt, a dark blue tie with orange balloons printed all over it. As each piece went on, watching himself in a full-length mirror by his locker, he scrutinized how he looked. Finally, he slipped into a pair of white leather, Italian-made, shoes, and put on a sporty double-breasted sports jacket with deep pockets and tailored from a polyester fabric of red plaid with dark to light squares and stripes that sometimes drifted between red and orange-red. Because he had become self-conscious about his growing bald spot, in recent months, he covered his head in a fedora. This hat was green with a yellow band. After filling his pants pockets with essentials, he strapped the holstered Colt behind him and dropped Burroughs's detective badge and his knife into a side pocket of his jacket. Off a shelf, he took a camera equipped with a long-range lens. Opening its back, he retrieved its spent film. "A little added insurance," he murmured, recalling its use to photograph Flynn and Cunningham. He stuffed it into his jacket pocket.

Midway along the south wall of the storage area, a pair of pipes rose to exit through a hole in the plaster sub-ceiling. Against the wall stood a stack of metal chairs. Everett used one of these as a stepladder. Standing on the seat, the chair straining to support his weight, he reached up into the hole. After feeling around for several seconds, he slid out a sturdy cardboard box once used to store legal-size file folders. He got off the chair and rested the box on a short pile of nearby mattresses. He removed the box lid. He took out a six-cartridge magazine and a box of ammunition. He retrieved his Colt .45, reloaded its partially spent magazine and dropped the extra one, plus a few loose bullets, into his jacket pocket. He returned the remaining .45 bullets to the box and his handgun to its holster.

Reaching into the box again, he extracted the top envelope and took out a batch of negatives, and vest size as well as enlarged prints. Shuffling through them, he gave out a low whistle and shook his head. "Darling, Sweetpea . . . My! My! My!" he cooed, his eyes staring wildly at the top photo. "How I wish I knew for sure who took these fine photographs," he gasped as he browsed through other photos. "I hate the possibility anyone other than the late Reverend Maefield had freedom to do it. Oh, my, what an eyeful! How did he hold the camera steady? Just think what they're worth in the bookstore market," he exclaimed. He held a particularly revealing photo close to the light. "Wasn't I a good cousin not to show this one to Daddy?" After returning the prints to their envelope, he dropped in the photos he had shown Rhonda and Walter, then, laid the envelope in the file box. He got the undeveloped roll of film from his pocket. "First chance, I'll have a look at what I got," he said as he put the film in the file box. His last business here was to check a brass door key, a duplicate of the one on his key chain. He looked for tiny scratches that might indicate use. "The damn thing's clean . . . never left this box," he assured himself then put back the key. Again, mounting the chair, he shoved the slender box into place. He stepped down, walked to where three six-foot shepherds' crooks stood, stored there for use in Christmas pageants. Selecting one, he returned to the chair and stood on it again. This time he threaded the long pole through the hole to push the box as far back as he could. "That ought 'a do it," he said. "Can't be too cautious." He got off the chair, returned the crook to its storage place, then went back to fold the chair and leaned it against the wall. Locking doors behind him, he made his way out of the building.

*　　*　　*

Everett Wheeler paused in the dark parking lot to light up a cigarette. The first match failed and he struck another. This time he cupped the match in his hands as he inhaled and slowly dismissed the smoke. He flipped the match to the side.

Walter scrutinized him through binoculars, got a good look at his face, hated that the low round eyes had the likeness of a Tompkins. When Everett opened the door of his truck, the dome light came on. He stood in its illumination for a few seconds feeling in his deep pockets for his car key. It was enough light for Walter to observe Everett's garish attire and to comment to Jorge "Looks like he's off to a whore house."

Everett drove off by way of the east exit.

"Do you want me to follow, Mr. Walt?" Jorge asked.

"No, he isn't worth our time. It'll be light before we know it. We best get a few hours shuteye while we can."

"Well, I got an hour of work ahead of me, Mr. Walt. Your son-in-law will drive a load of lettuce and strawberries to the Vineland Produce Auction in the morning. I promised to have it stacked and loaded and behind his house by six. I'll get a few men up to help me."

"I guess there's no rest for the weary, Jorge. Isn't that what our preacher said? Don't bother to wake the bunkhouse. I'll give you a hand. Let's go!"

*   *   *

It was after two in the morning when Michael parked outside the office of the Starlight Motel. He had used this roadside place with Sarah, so he knew the routine. He returned to the truck proudly holding up the room key.

From the slender crevice behind the seat of his pickup truck, he fished out an unopened bottle of whiskey and tucked it under his arm. He unlocked and opened the motel door. Before closing it behind them, Margo pressed against him, causing him to drop the bottle, which wobbled around their feet on the linoleum floor. Her body molded to excite him as her lips engaged his in sensual kissing and feeling. Michael, lifting her, kicked the door shut and elbowed the light switch on. She stayed frozen to him and he had to jostle her to release her hold and drop her to her feet. She stood to the side, at first uncertain of his rough way of handling her, but then made herself comfortable on the bed.

He watched her from a corner chair as she glided her stockings off her legs. He enjoyed the private show, but dismissed her view in order to break the seal on the whisky bottle. He unscrewed the cap and tossed it into a wastebasket. He raised the bottle to his lips as if it contained soda pop, felt the liquor burn in his throat, run into his stomach and further lighten his already alcohol-shocked brain. Margo giggled at his drunken demand to show more and then at his direction, "Get down on the floor and crawl over here like a pussycat." It was a chapter from *Sara-sex* and he wondered how his new "feline" would compare.

Margo was all too willing to play a part. She sunk head first off the bed to slink across the floor, meowing as she moved up his legs to sit facing him on his lap. She knew he was aroused. She tilted and slid her crotch provocatively against him. She played at scratching his face before she took the bottle away to her own lips. Several times, they passed it between themselves. She drank with less gusto and stopped after a few swallows.

Leaving the depleted bottle in Michael's hand, Margo slithered off his lap and playfully undressed him, pulling off his shoes, pants, tie and long-sleeve shirt. All the while, he stared at her and swigged his liquor bottle, which was near empty when she took it from him to rest it on an end table. She got his full attention as she turned her cocktail dress up and over her head. He took special interest in her scant crimson panties and then the way her nipples peaked under their pasties. Enjoying his open-mouthed smile, she bent to kiss his lips. But when he tried to gather her in close, she teasingly pushed out of reach, stripped her panties down her legs and kicked them toward him. Turning her back to him, she picked her dress off the floor to hang it in the closet saying she didn't want to get her uniform soiled. He collected her into his arms, his hands holding her breasts. The action was electric. She spun around and faced him, buried her mouth in his, then helped him remove his T-shirt and get out of his shorts. Alighting on him, as a bear would hold a climbed tree, she forced him across the bed. Hurriedly, she positioned him inside her and rode him to completion. He was, however, exhausted and limp long before her passion diminished. And feeling cheated, she berated him. If he heard her, he did not show it, for the alcohol had taken over by now. Before another minute had passed, he was snoring, oblivious to her naked young body, which remained over him, her kisses trying to arouse him.

Frustrated that she could not get his attention, she slapped his cheek lightly. There was no response. Determined to awaken him, she got a cup of cold water from the bathroom. Mounting him, she poured the icy liquid over his face. He came to life with a jerk and hit the water cup, spilling it on them both. She laughed and tried to wrestle him, but he drove her off and left the bed. He found his clothes and began putting them on, demanding she do the same. He had a busy day ahead of him, he complained, and had to get home in a hurry.

*   *   *

Jerry Flynn hurt all over. Jorge's blows had not drawn blood and, mercifully, the pain had begun to dissipate. Or was he just fooling himself. He continued north on the New Jersey Turnpike.

He wished he had taken time to read a road map. He had never driven in Manhattan and had only a fuzzy idea how to reach the Riverside Drive apartment house of Mrs. Maefield. He knew the address was in the vicinity of Columbia and the uptown Protestant Interchurch Center, where the Presbyterian Church had its national headquarters. He had lunched at the Protestant Center a few months ago, along with a hundred other seminary seniors. But he had gotten to the building by train and then subway. Driving there was another story. He remembered Charlene saying she had stopped for the night in Fort Lee by the George Washington Bridge, but he deemed that it would be more direct using the Lincoln Tunnel.

To be sure, he stopped at a turnpike rest stop to get a New York City road map. He also needed to buy gas and to freshen up. After the attendant filled the Imperial at the service station, he picked up a free map and shuffled into the Howard Johnson restaurant to the men's room. Inside a toilet stall, he examined those parts of his body that had already discolored from Garcia's punches and kicks. It did not appear he had any broken ribs; at least no bones stuck through his skin. A cracked rib was a possibility. But he was breathing normal now with less pain and he understood that as a good sign. Best of all, he saw no blood when he spit into the toilet. His testicles were sore, but he had been hurt there in college basketball and knew there wasn't much he could do to stem the discomfort. He wished he had worn briefs instead of boxers for the added support they could give him. Although his bruises were tender to the touch and covered a wide area, he considered himself lucky. Or, maybe Jorge was just that expert at beating up people. Jerry made an asserted effort to stifle his pain. From a machine dispensing everything from potato chips to fingernail clippers, he got a pocket tin of aspirin.

He entered the restaurant area where he ordered orange juice, coffee and a stack of buttered toast. He studied the highway map of Manhattan Island. Exit 16 on the New Jersey Turnpike would lead him to the Lincoln Tunnel. From there it seemed an easy loop north on to the West Side Highway. He would exit at 95th Street and find his way from there. He saw nothing complicated about it. He took his time finishing his coffee and toast and downed two aspirin. When he returned to his car, it wouldn't start. The gas station had no mechanic and he could only wait and hope that after letting it rest a little longer, the engine would turn over. It had worked before. What else could he do at three thirty in the morning?

As he waited, he thought about his work and all the items of church business he had to manage as soon as he got back. Sermon writing and preparation led his list. A funeral service on Friday. He had shut-ins to visit and other calls to make, committee meetings and special events to attend It was expected that he would join Rotary, take a turn as chaplain of the volunteer fire department, work with Boy Scouts, Girl Scouts and American Legion. Someone had called to ask if he would become a member of the board of Planned Parenthood. He thought about what a terrific secretary Miss. Blatty was. Where would he be without her dedication and organization?

He had left Miss Blatty the details she needed to type the service for his ordination and installation, scheduled for four o'clock, Sunday. Besides his entire family, long-time friends, the congregation of First Church and the ordaining presbytery, he had invited local clergy and a few professors on the Princeton Seminary faculty. The ladies of the church were putting together a big reception afterwards. In his opinion, the service was unstoppable. And, anyway, the service did not belong to the local church but to the presbytery. Walter Tompkins may cause him embarrassment, but unless Jerry gave in to his threat, the service would go on as scheduled.

Almost an hour had passed since pulling into the turnpike rest stop. Jerry waited another five minutes. He turned the ignition and floored the gas peddle. The engine turned over instantly and he gave a sigh of relief. "Thank you, Jesus!" He drove out of the parking lot and headed for the Lincoln Tunnel.

*　　*　　*

Madge Todd awoke to the loud roar of a truck engine idling. She looked out the window to see a fully loaded T&T flatbed parked on the dirt road that serviced the packing barns. She supposed Jorge Garcia was behind the wheel.

"Who else would annoy me at four in the morning?" she asked, stealing a look at the clock on the dresser. Then she remembered Michael had to be at the Vineland auction market today at six and this was Jorge's way of reminding him. This too was her first clue that Jorge was back on the job after their Thursday clash. Another minute of sustained noise passed before Garcia killed the engine. She watched the barrel-chested man walk under the security flood lamps toward his house, which stood a mile up the road. "I'll bet he's drinking again."

Getting back to sleep would be a lost cause. She did not consider a second sleeping pill. She found her cotton robe and slipped into it. She left the bedroom for the kitchen to brew a pot of tea. Sometimes the change was enough to wrestle her away from whatever worried her. But to no avail, hard worries preoccupied her mind.

She stirred honey into her steaming tea. One of the few sweets she permitted herself, she used it sparingly at best on everything from bread to corn flakes. She smiled to herself when she remembered herself as a child. I must have been four, she recalled. Daddy saw me spooning a glob of golden honey on my green peas and affectionately nicknamed me Sweetpea. The name lingers today. Her eyes flooded with tears as she thought about the father who loved her and the awful disgrace he would feel if he ever learned his Sweetpea's secret.

She hoped Michael would appear any moment. Anxious to greet his arrival, she got up frequently to look out the window for his headlights. He would be delighted to hear her decision regarding work. She would have him read her letter of resignation. Maybe they could begin getting their lives on track.

She resolved to stop thinking of the minister as her knight in shining armor, here to rescue her from her perversion and unhappiness. She had to face reality. If Michael accompanied her to counseling, so much the better. She determined she would go. She could only help herself. Jerry Flynn was right about that.

She sighed deeply and her eyes narrowed as she wondered what would happen if the dark side of her life became someone else's business. Adultery with a person of the same sex was the unforgivable sin. She could have an affair with the minister. If exposed, people would ring the riot act, but few would hold it against her for the rest of her life. It was a sin but forgivable. Not so in a lesbian relationship. All those names they had for such people, she would have to endure. And she would have no hope of winning in a divorce proceeding. They would declare her unsuitable as mother of her children. No, Michael could blackmail her for life. She had to make her peace. She had to hide her guilt. She had to stay away from Rhonda, from Jerry and anyone else, male or female that tempted her. She had to live the decent, respectable life everyone believed she lived.

*   *   *

At 47th Street, Everett backed his pickup into a space. Usually he had to drive around for half an hour before finding a free spot, which could be a three—or four-block walk from his apartment. Boasting this must be his "lucky day," he lumbered into his apartment and immediately knew things were not how he had left them. The kitchen light was on and the mess he had left was not there. The door to the bedroom was wide open. He looked in on an empty bed, the cuffs still dangling from iron rails, the ropes he had used to tie Charlene's ankles, cut. He saw her pink bra bunched up on the floor next to a bloodstained towel and the bloody washrag hung on the bedpost. He checked the alcove behind the kitchen where a door led to a back alley. There was no sign of forced entry. The only person who could have freed Charlene was Rhonda.

"Whoring bitch!" he shouted at no one.

Thinking fast, he reasoned that if they had called the police, they would have arrested him before he put his foot on the bottom step. Either vanity or fear had ruled and they had decided to seek a safer place. He had a fighting chance. He left the apartment, returned to his truck, drove to 8th Avenue and turned north.

*   *   *

Michael Todd used the bathroom of the motel to pee and wash-up. Margo would have douched; however, her kit was in her car. Most guys she laid with she would have insisted on a condom, not Michael. Besides, she was kind of in her safe time and, if not, she saw Michael's seeds as trophies of conquest. She was not going to let it worry her.

She invited Michael to shower with her but he declined. She figured he didn't want his wife asking why he smelled *Ivory* clean. She wanted to tell him that a passionate woman could just as easily smell another woman on her man, but thought better of it.

She toweled herself dry and tugged her toylike panties to her hips. She stuffed her stockings into her handbag and then she slid into her cocktail dress.

While she readied herself, Michael sat watching in silence. When she finished dressing, she strutted about to his admiring eyes. He got up and wrapped his arms around her, told her how good she had been and apologized for "conking out." He kissed her so passionate, she thought he would take her to bed again. But then he folded a rolled bill into her hand. She protested, saying this made her feel cheap and unappreciated. She feared it might mean finality. He stopped her, arguing that the money was a little gift. "Use it to buy a sexy outfit for our next date." She agreed to it then and kissed him long and hot. Once again, they shared the whisky bottle, Michael gulping down the last drop. In the parking lot, he heaved the bottle into the air. It broke as it hit the pavement and glass splintered across the surface. In the truck cab, Margo snuggled to him. He put his right arm over her shoulders. He burned rubber as he released his foot on the break of the already in-gear truck. There was no traffic this early in the morning as he headed west and pressed the accelerator to the floor. He turned his head to kiss her on the mouth. The moment was quiet except for the whine of the engine and the cry of pleasure that arose from her throat. It was also dangerous due to construction crews having scraped away the road shoulder in preparation for new blacktop. A warning sign LOW SHOULDER meant nothing as they raced into the dark morning mist.

His mind numbed by alcohol and distracted by her moist lips, Michael took no evasive action as the right front wheel of the vehicle dropped off the road to ride on rough gravel. Speeding eighty-five miles an hour, the tire rapidly tore on the sharp road edge and exploded. The wheel jumped back to the pavement and bounced over a deep crevice, shocking them out of their embrace. Michael's head hit the roof hard. His cry of panic had not emptied from his mouth before the truck careened left along the concrete divider and turned sharply right, throwing Michael into the steering wheel and propelling Margo's lithe body forward.

There was nothing to slow the truck's forward motion, or to stave off Margo's rapid ascent as the vehicle came to an instant stop against the trunk of a giant pine tree. Nor was anyone near to hear the ponderous sound of steel splintering the monster tree, or to see blood flaming out of the shattering windshield as Margo's head hit the heavy glass and separated from her neck, flying twenty-five feet forward of the wreck, her freckled torso and pretty legs sliding across the crunching hood to land in a broken heap on the smoking ground. And Michael? His last breath wheezed from his lungs as his chest flattened in the crush of metal and chrome that rushed forward to entomb him.

*   *   *

At the east end of the Lincoln Tunnel, a collection of confusing road signs waited for the disoriented and uneducated motorist. Jerry had no second chance. Too late, he saw the entrance ramp for the West Side Highway North and within seconds, he found himself spewed onto 9th Avenue, going south. He didn't know what else to do, so he turned left at the next street one way east and then north on to 8th Avenue. At Columbus Circle, he merged into the north lane of Broadway and kept going. At this hour of the morning, with traffic lights working in his favor, he drove as far as 96th Street before a red light stopped him. When green, he chugged less than ten feet into the intersection. That was where the Imperial turned itself off and refused all attempts to start again.

*   *   *

At 96th Street and Broadway, Everett Wheeler passed a cab pushing a black 1957 Chrysler Crown Imperial across the intersection. The luxury car heralded his attention. He doubled back for a second look, and—sure enough—New Jersey plates. As he passed the stranded vehicle, he saw Jerry Flynn! "Well I'll be damned!" Everett delighted in punctuating each word.

He made another swing around the short block and parked in a curbside space on 96th Street. He walked to the corner and crossed to observe Flynn looking under the hood. *How convenient.* In less than a minute, he overpowered the already weakened minister and locked him in the Imperial's trunk. From his pickup truck, he got his toolbox and within five minutes, he had the engine purring.

CHAPTER 15

DRIVEN

Wednesday Morning, June 13

Madge Todd heard the mantle clock chime six times. Night was on the verge of losing to the advancing dawn, the heavy dew hanging over fertile fields to the opening rays of the sun and the wakeful dreams, longings, fantasies of the sleepless ones to the hard rules, limitations and sober morality of the day.

With reluctance, she left her vigil at the kitchen window to go to her bedroom. After making the bed, she showered, dressed and returned once more to the kitchen window. She had made an asserted effort to believe everything was all right, but a sense of dread continued. With each passing minute, she became more worried and nervous.

She wanted to get in her station wagon and search for Michael. She thought to call her mom to ask if she would come by and see to Dudley. If she didn't hear anything by seven o'clock, she would have to do that. Then she saw the state police car moving toward the house. Like on many farms in this part of the state, the Todd house stood a long way from the main road. It seemed an eternity before the car reached the pavement in front of the garage. Madge went out on the porch. The rising sun shown directly in the trooper's eyes and, even with his sunshades on, he had to shield his eyes as he walked toward her.

"Mrs. Todd?" the officer asked as he passed into the shade of the house.

"Yes, I'm Mrs. Todd."

He moved to the porch steps and she now saw he was an older man, a state police captain.

"Is your husband Michael S. Todd, ma'am?" he asked, as he stopped in front of her.

"Yes!"

"And does he drive a white T&T Company, nineteen-sixty Ford pickup truck?"

"Yes, that describes his truck."

The officer needn't have said anything more, for Madge's tears had already begun to flow.

"Mrs. Todd, I have very sad news for you. We have tentatively identified your husband as the driver in a truck of that description in a fatal accident earlier this morning. Do you have a relative close by I can call?"

There was no scream, no calling God's name, only silence, followed by burning tears. She stood motionless, gripping the porch post for a few seconds more. The policeman moved up the steps ready to catch her if she fainted. She did not wait for him.

"Excuse me," she said, "I have to check on my son."

Madge disappeared into the house, climbed the stairs to Dudley's bedroom and there, as she rocked her sleepy little boy firmly in her arms, she began to grieve.

*   *   *

Charlene Cunningham slept soundly during the hours left to her. If she had a nightmare about what had happened to her over the past twenty-four hours, she forgot it the moment the alarm clock rang. She awoke knowing exactly where she was and why, so that she immediately bounded out of the convertible sofa to stop the alarm Rhonda had set for her. It was quarter to seven and she knew a long day answering questions by police awaited her. Any minute she expected Jerry and wanted to be ready to greet him. She used the small bathroom adjoining the guest room. She felt comfort in seeing that the swelling around her eye had retreated, and while still quite sore, overall, she felt much improved from six hours ago. She wanted to shower, but decided that could wait. Rhonda had thoughtfully laid out a matching set of white underwear. Charlene put them on. The panties fit appreciably, but the bra hung humorously loose. A short blue cotton dress hung on a hook behind the door. That could wait and she settled for now on the silk kimono she had worn last night. One problem with it. She had to hold it up when she walked or trip on the hem. She thought that she would find Rhonda still asleep. She should have known better.

Rhonda looked as though yesterday had not happened—fresh, scented, makeup applied, hair combed straight down her back, dressed in a trim brown skirt, yellow print blouse. All was in balance. Tall, straight, high breasted, with her hair down and no horn-rim glasses on, once more, Charlene admired her looks.

"I have strudel and coffee?" she offered.

"O yes," Charlene replied.

"Drink your juice first!" Rhonda said insistently plunking a tall glass of grapefruit juice in front of Charlene.

Charlene tried to look pleased, but didn't do a very good job of it.

"Vitamin C; very important for your lovely skin."

Tentatively, meekly complaining that her lip hurt, Charlene made a face as she drank from the glass. She smiled as Rhonda joined her at the table.

"I'm surprised we haven't heard from Detective Burroughs," Charlene exclaimed. "Maybe I should try calling him from here. I know he'll tell me to contact NYPD about my abduction."

"You have my tape recording, Charlene. Before you do anything, allow me to call a criminal attorney I know. I want him present when the police arrive. I would like to convince Everett to surrender with me. But I don't know. He is dangerous, probably a killer. He has to be stopped; yet, I am not the one to trick him. He has to surrender willingly. It is better that way, better for both of us."

"What will happen when he doesn't find me in that apartment?"

"To be honest with you, I am surprised we haven't heard from him. By now, I would think he has discovered your escape. He'll know immediately that I freed you. How will he be? Crazier than before!"

Charlene picked at her strudel. She stirred four heaping teaspoons of sugar into her coffee, stirred it black, looked up to see Rhonda staring, a doubtful smile on her face.

"You like your coffee sweet. How do you stay so in shape with all that sugar?"

"By playing decoy to psychopathic killers."

Rhonda laughed with her, but it was short lived, interrupted by the harsh buzz of the intercom next to the wall phone. Rhonda was on her feet before the buzzing stopped.

She pressed the answer button and spoke into the mouthpiece. "Yah?"

Dead silence followed. Charlene had come to her feet and stepped forward to speak.

"Jerry? Is it you?"

"Yes! It's me," she heard. But then nothing. A few seconds passed before he spoke again. "Are you okay?" he asked in a gagging whisper.

"I'm fine. How are you?"

Suddenly, there was the sound of a scuffle. Jerry shouted, "Charlene!" and yelled, "Don't answer the door!" Again, there was silence. Suddenly, Everett's voice broke in.

"Sorry to disappoint you, Miss Cunningham! Lover-boy here is alive! I'll say that much, but it seems he's had a little accident. Can you believe his car broke down several blocks away on Broadway? And who do you suppose became his Good Samaritan?"

Charlene was already shaking and her flesh had turned pale and cold. She turned to look at Rhonda whose back was toward her.

"By the way, talking about Good Samaritans, did the good woman there tell you how much she likes to take care of me?"

Charlene said nothing. She wanted to cry, but was too frightened.

"Talk to me, little girl. You and I had a date today. Did you forget?"

"The police have been called, Mr. Wheeler!" she bellowed into the intercom.

"Liar! Don't bull-shit me," he fired back. "Now tell the fucking good woman there to buzz me in."

Charlene turned to see Rhonda had left the kitchen. She ran after her, but failed to catch up. She saw Rhonda touch the signal button at the hall door, admitting the caller to the apartment lobby. Charlene ran back to the kitchen to the wall phone. She dialed the operator and asked for police emergency. Rhonda disconnected her.

"Nein!" I can't let you."

"Yes, you must go through with it now!" Charlene screamed, pulling Rhonda's hand away.

Rhonda grabbed the phone. The two women struggled for possession.

"I can't do it! I can't allow you!"

"Stop it, Rhonda! You just told me he's a killer. Why are you protecting him now?" Charlene rasped, falling against the table, upsetting plates and cups, losing possession of the phone. "Can't you see he's going to murder us all?"

She grabbed Rhonda around the waist. Rhonda seized the wall piece and yanked it off the wall, the wires snapping. She threw the disabled mechanism across the room and shook Charlene off. Charlene could only hope the extension in the bedroom worked. In some homes, phones operated independent of each other. She ran into the living room. Her foot stepped on the hem of her robe, tripping her. She went down hard on her belly. Rhonda pounced on her and held her. She was strong. Charlene's efforts to get free got nowhere. Already weakened from Everett's abuse, she paused, concentrated on catching her breath.

"Don't move!" Rhonda commanded as heavy knocking commenced on the hallway door. Rising to her feet, Rhonda went to answer it. Charlene reached, caught her foot and pulled it toward her. Rhonda stumbled, but fell against the door, reaching to undo the chain and dead bolt, turning the knob. Immediately the door opened with the thunder of Everett rushing Jerry through, pushing him hard, so that he fell to the floor next to Charlene. Jerry's face was blood stained, his body immobilized. Charlene clutched him to her, but only for seconds. Everett Wheeler's powerful hands lifted him from the floor and threw him headlong across the dining room table.

"Rope! Get me some goddamn rope!"

Charlene saw Rhonda exit to the kitchen. While Everett's attention centered on Jerry, who wrestled in Everett's grip, she pulled herself up. Everett had his back to her. She picked up a tall ceramic vase from a table and brought it crashing on the top of his hat. The vase shattered, tiny pieces pelted her face. Stunned, Everett collapsed on top of Jerry. Charlene hit Everett, this time with a chair from the dining set. The table that had supported their combined weight buckled and they fell with it on to the floor.

"Out, let's get out!" Jerry shouted as he uncoupled from Everett's dead weight. He took Charlene's hand and pulled her through the still opened apartment door and into the hall. There was no elevator waiting.

"Over there! Use the stairs! We've got to get away."

Charlene was hardly dressed for a life-or-death escape. She hiked up the silk robe and tried to tie it high with the sash as she ran. She was barefoot and had all she could do to keep the robe closed. She offered no complaint as she hobbled along. Neither one of them were in shape to go too far. Jerry limped and his wrist was sprained. His forehead showed dry and new blood and he had to hold it with his handkerchief. They flew into the fire exit stairway.

"Did he beat you?" she wanted to know.

"Later!" He pulled her hand as they half fell and jumped down the stairs. Three floors below, they heard a heavy door above them slam shut and footsteps in fast order. They continued down the stairwell.

"Keep going," Jerry urged.

"I should have hit him harder. I held back. I didn't want to kill him," Charlene whined as she plodded along slightly behind Jerry.

They reached the first floor landing.

"He may be ahead of us if he used the elevator. One more flight to the basement."

Cautiously, they looked into a dark, gloomy, brick hallway.

"Reminds me of you know where!" Charlene heckled.

"Shish!"

They made their way through a low-lit corridor and out a back door to a filthy courtyard. Garbage cans, wooden crates and cardboard cartons littered the concrete-paved ground. Broken bottles and discarded newspapers were everywhere. They ran into a narrow alley and squeezed single file between the tall buildings. They came out on a side street, which they crossed and ran east to Claremont Avenue. A car turning into the parking garage at the Interchurch Protestant Center almost hit them. Jerry screamed at the driver to call the police, but the driver honked and waved him off, then sped into the shadowy bowels of the building. Everyone who saw them either pretended not to or hurried away as if they were from another world.

Once more Charlene stumbled on her robe. This time it tore along the seam and she took it apart above her knees. Jerry dropped the silk material in the gutter. Charlene was free to run. Her feet, however, were tender. Pebbles and tiny objects that topped the sidewalk pained her. She bled from cutting her toe on a piece of glass. Jerry led her past the back entrance to the Interchurch Protestant Center, which had a sign posted at the doors directing early entrants to the main entrance on Riverside Drive. They rounded the office building and crossed another side street. They came out on Riverside Drive and ran for the entrance to Riverside Church Protestant Cathedral.

"This way; I'm sure we'll get help here," Jerry assured Charlene.

They accessed the narrow narthex through its fast-paced

revolving door, a measure to keep the inside air cool in its air-conditioned climate. On their left were swinging doors into the nave where a prayer service was in progress. Jerry hoped Charlene had injured Everett good. Perhaps he was in no condition to follow, especially in here. They stopped to catch their breath and to look at each other.

They were a sight for sore eyes. When the sleeves of Charlene's robe fell away from her wrists, Jerry saw her bruises and raw flesh.

"How did this happen?" he asked, holding her hands out. "And your face?"

"Everett had me handcuffed to a bed in an apartment on 47th Street."

"Shish! Shish!" An usher stormed toward them. "Can't you two see people are trying to worship inside the cathedral?" he whispered and scolded at the same time.

"Sorry," Jerry replied, "but we need your help. Will you call the police for us? A man with a gun is following us."

The usher was a tall black man with a ruddy complexion and sad eyes. He looked at them in a skeptical way and Jerry could tell he did not believe him. While it was his duty to be kind, he was also committed to clear out individuals who looked like they might create a disturbance.

"Goodness gracious," the usher said in a troubled voice. He took a step back to better inspect the couple. For the first time he saw Charlene in her bare feet and adorned in the torn and tattered silk kimono. He saw the bumps and cuts that matted both their faces.

"I will call the police, but we don't want a commotion here. Take the elevator to the seventeenth floor where we have a counseling center. You wait there. I'll let the receptionist know your coming and I'll call a policeman."

Jerry and Charlene ran toward the elevator as the usher turned toward a little desk with a telephone. All at once, the doors of the cathedral burst open and hundreds of worshippers stampeded into the narthex. The prayer service had ended. People were anxious to get to jobs, meetings, daily chores. They quickly engulfed the couple in their forward movement, and pressed them to the back of the elevator. The elevator dove down one floor instead of up and emptied, its occupants rushing toward the smell of hot coffee in the downstairs fellowship hall. Jerry hit the button for the seventeenth floor. The elevator rose, but stopped at the cathedral level. The doors slid into their pockets. The large figure of Everett Wheeler blocked the opening. He smiled as he fidgeted with the gun in his jacket's right-hand pocket. He solemnly tipped his green fedora. That hat must have a steel lining, Charlene thought. How silly he looks in his gaudy jacket. He reminds me of Red Skelton in a clown suit. But then he reminded her of her own attire.

"I like your dress, lady," Everett gestured toward Charlene, a knowing grin spanning his broad, red face. "But I think I can find something more suitable for you. Please, step this way!"

In that moment, the usher came up behind Everett. "O good! I see you found them, Detective! This is the couple. We're so fortunate you came in when you did."

It was then that they saw the police badge attached to Everett's vest pocket.

"Thank you, these two are suspected of fleeing after they beat a man to death," he asserted. "You've been a big help," Wheeler continued, his grin now changed to a friendly, wholesome smile. Jerry started to explain, but to no purpose. The usher hurried off. Charlene wanted to run. When she tugged at Jerry's hand, he resisted and held her back.

"Step out of the elevator and walk ahead of me to the street exit. I have a car waiting and I believe, Mr. Flynn, you already know I hold a loaded gun in my pocket."

They did as directed, Everett immediately behind them. "Don't do anything stupid. I'll kill you in a moment if you bolt. I don't care for anything more than suicidal revenge. Believe me, you're dead if you don't cooperate."

"We're dead anyway!" Charlene whispered.

Jerry held her hand tighter than before. There were people

everywhere about the church's narthex and if Everett began shooting, there would be more dead and injured people. Charlene had not needed Rhonda to inform her he was crazy. She pulled Jerry's hand close to her side in a way that let him know she would not try to flee. Everett avoided the revolving door and pushed them through the auxiliary entrance to the outside steps.

Jerry couldn't believe it. Parked at curbside, immediately in front of them, stood his 57 Crown Imperial, the motor running. Everett yanked open its front door. How the car had gotten here was obvious when he saw a pretty, middle-aged, neatly dressed woman sitting behind the wheel. He had no idea who she was. Nor did she turn to acknowledge him.

"Flynn in the front seat!" Everett growled while taking hold of Charlene's arm.

Jerry obediently slid onto the passenger side of the front seat. Everett slammed the door. He pulled the handle down to open the back door and pushed Charlene onto the floor so that he could take the seat behind. He dug his heels into her back. He pulled the door shut.

"Move!" he ordered. "Head for the turnpike and use the exact change lane on the bridge."

They drove in silence. Wheeler kept Charlene pinned beneath his feet as the big car bounded across the George Washington Bridge. After throwing coins in the toll baskets, Everett broke the quiet.

"So, tell me, did you girls have fun last night? . . . I'll bet you did. Two beautiful, sexy women licking each other's wounds—hey?" he laughed.

There was no response. Jerry sat forward and pressed his head into his hands.

"Are you praying, Mr. Preacherman? Why, I guess we could all use a little prayer right now. Rhonda, pull into that Texaco station. Go around back! There, park next to the garbage truck."

Jerry wondered if he had heard right? Did he call her Rhonda? Could the woman driving his car be Rhonda Maefield?

She sat there cold, expressionless. All the while, she had kept her face forward and even now, she made no effort to look at Jerry.

"We're going to switch seats. Reverend, push over! You drive! Now listen closely, punk! Do not exceed the speed limit. You got it?" he emphasized by tapping the gun barrel on Jerry's shoulder. "Rhonda, you get in the back with me and sweet Miss 'Private Dick'. You bring her clothes?"

"In the bag," Rhonda said.

For the first time Jerry had heard Rhonda speak. She eased out of the car, opened the back door as Everett removed his feet from Charlene's rump and ordered her to sit up. He reached in the bag and pulled out a blue cotton dress and her canvas shoes. Rhonda pushed in next to Charlene and pulled the door closed. Jerry moved behind the wheel. He set the gear in drive and merged into traffic.

"Well, isn't this just one big, happy family?" Everett cooed. "You keep your eyes on the road, young man. No looking back here at the pretty ladies, especially while Miss Cunningham changes into a suitable Sunday dress. I don't want you getting hard here while we have business to conclude. O my," he said, as Charlene undid the robe and pulled it away from her body. "Looky, looky at this bra. Too large for your tits, ain't it?" He pulled at the elastic strap and let it snap on her shoulder. "Why, I do declare that Mrs. Maefield's boobs are two sizes larger than Miss Cunningham's, but then, I already knew that. My, my, I'll bet you never dreamed you could cross your heart in a D-cup." Everett teased, ridiculing a popular add. He laughed a belly laugh and reached forward to slap Jerry solidly on the shoulder. "Pay attention to the road, Mr Preacherman! I'll keep you abreast" he laughed, enjoying his pun, "of titillating things," he laughed some more, "back here."

Charlene ignored Everett as though beyond his humiliation. She dropped the dress over her head, eased it down her body and buttoned the bodice to her neck. She slipped her feet into her canvas shoes. Rhonda opened her purse and took out packets of pre-moistened paper tissues. She tore away the protective coverings.

"Here, this will help," Rhonda said as she handed one to Charlene and used the other to clean dried blood off the younger woman's face. Charlene spread the wet, scented, paper towel behind her neck and ears. Rhonda handed across her lipstick and a makeup pack. Reluctantly, Charlene accepted the items and, using the tiny mirror, tried to tidy up her face. If Everett had thoughts about any of this, he kept them to himself. He appeared content to keep his left arm tightly wrapped around Charlene's shoulders while he stared ahead of Jerry.

"Hey, preacher, turn up the air conditioner," he yelled. "We're cooking back here."

"Doesn't work. It's broke. Roll down your window."

"Shit! Some luxury piece of junk! Where'd you get this crate from anyway?"

"You don't like the transportation, catch a bus!"

"Oohheee! That don't sound very Christian, Preacher Flynn."

Jerry kept his feelings to himself. So far, he had had no favorable opportunity to take a stand against Everett. In his weakened and pained condition, he considered cooperation as the best course. Stay calm, he repeated to himself. Don't challenge Everett. Jerry was now convinced Everett had murdered Daniel Maefield.

*　　*　　*

Chester Walsh was the first police officer of color to accept detective grade in Tompkinsville and was now second in command of Burroughs six-man homicide division.

At eight thirty, Emily Burroughs called police headquarters to ask if her husband had come on duty. Informed by Chester Walsh that he too was waiting for John, Emily described her husband's late-night departure and confessed she was worried.

Quickly, Walsh traced the local telephone number Emily gave him to the Presbyterian manse. There was no answer. Ten minutes later, he knocked on the door of the residence. When no one responded, he drove to the parking area for Shepherd House off Cathedral Drive. Miss Blatty had just gotten in. Reluctant to open Shepherd Door to the black man, even though he showed his badge in the little window, Chester scurried around to the main entrance. There, Miss Blatty recognized him as one of the detectives who had worked on the murder case, and who she had known since his youth as a member of First Church. She apologized for her discriminate caution. Chester said he understood, yet, deep down, it always hurt.

Miss Blatty had no idea of the whereabouts of Reverend Flynn. As she looked through the many papers and notes he had left her, she saw one that explained he had an emergency call and that he would telephone the office first chance this morning. Walsh asked Miss Blatty if the name Charlene Cunningham had any meaning to her.

"O yes," she replied. "Miss Cunningham is a freelance writer. She kept an appointment with Pastor Flynn last Wednesday morning and returned here in the afternoon to interview me."

"Can you describe her, Miss Blatty?"

"A very pretty girl, I think about twenty to twenty-five years' old, short, blond curly hair and a beautiful complexion. I'd say she was five-five in her bare feet. Has wonderful posture, but I thought her not properly dressed to have met with the minister. I mean she had on a very short skirt and a . . . Well . . . " Walsh waited for her to finish. "I shouldn't say it, but I don't believe a lady ought to dress in so revealing a manner."

"Do you know this phone number in New York, Miss Blatty?" Walsh wrote it out on a pad. "Does it look familiar?"

She adjusted her glasses and stared at the number Walsh had written.

"Yes, I think I do know that number. Just a minute." She thumbed through her Rolodex. "Yes, here it is. I thought so. It's the number of the former minister's wife, Mrs. Maefield. This is her Morningside Heights, Manhattan, telephone number. It's a very fashionable apartment, I understand, up town by Columbia University."

"Can I have the address?"

Miss Blatty wrote it out on the same note pad, tore it off, and handed it to him.

"Do you mind if I call this number from here?"

"Not at all. You can use the telephone in Reverend Flynn's study."

She showed Detective Walsh into the room. He accepted her suggestion to sit in the pastor's chair behind the wide desk. He dialed long distance and gave the operator the number. He listened as it fed back a busy signal. He dialed another number, gave his name, police rank, badge number and asked the operator to check the Riverside Drive number. A minute later the operator told him the phone was out of order. "It may be disconnected." Walsh thanked her, hung up, opened his book of telephone listings and dialed New York City Police Homicide. He had only to identify himself and say he was engaged in the investigation of a missing police detective and needed their cooperation. He presented the address of Rhonda Maefield and asked if they would check it for occupancy. There was no hesitation. The detective on duty said he would connect Walsh with the Manhattan precinct for that address. In the meantime, he would order a car to the Riverside apartment building.

"How shall I advise them?" he asked Walsh.

Walsh responded without equivocation, "Proceed with caution. I don't know if there is a connection, but the woman at this address is the widow of a minister murdered here in Tompkinsville about six months ago by an unknown assailant."

The New York detective put Walsh on hold. Six minutes passed. The officer came back on the phone.

"Detective Walsh, we have four uniformed patrolmen in the apartment building. It's a high class place, lots of inside security. No one answers the door to the apartment. The super is reluctant to allow us entrance. We may have to get a court order."

"Damn, this could be critical."

"Hold on! Okay, I've got Officer Kelly. He's inside. We're

splicing into the police radio unit, so you'll have to speak-up. Here he is."

"Officer Kelly, Detective Walsh here! What can you tell me?"

"No occupants," he said over static. "The living room is a mess. There appears to have been a brawl. A disturbance-interrupted breakfast. The phone is off the wall. We're reconnecting it. There's blood on the carpet. A neighbor in an adjoining apartment heard a racket a little after seven. That was enough for the super to let us in. So far, no corpses on the premises. The entrance door to the apartment is intact, no sign of forced entry. Who are we looking for?"

The line went dead. A long pause followed before Officer Kelly came back on. "We've got the phone working. Hang up and dial us here."

Walsh went through the operator to dial the Maefield apartment. Kelly picked up.

Walsh continued without the static and faraway sound. "I suspect two white females, one white male—a minister. Don't know how he was dressed. I'm going to put the minister's secretary on and ask her to give you names and descriptions."

"What about a vehicle?"

"Yah, right!"

Walsh rested the phone on the desk. He returned to the secretary's office.

"Miss Blatty, I want you in communication with New York City Police. Give the officer your best description of Miss Cunningham, Mrs. Maefield and Reverend Flynn. Tell him their estimated ages, heights, weights, how they might be dressed, anything you feel pertinent to identifying them." She started to pick up the phone. Walsh saw her nervousness, but he knew she could describe the people in question. "One more thing. What kind of car does Pastor Flynn drive?"

"A big black car, I don't know? I think it's a Cadillac. Mr. Wheeler would know, but he's on vacation."

"Who's Mr. Wheeler?"

"He's our church custodian. What's wrong, Detective? Is Reverend Flynn in trouble?"

"Just do as I ask, Miss Blatty. I'll explain later."

She picked up the phone and began speaking just as Walter Tompkins entered the reception area outside her office. He was ashen faced, obviously troubled. He looked for Miss Blatty to attend to him, but she waved him off. Glancing into Shepherd House, he saw the black man at Flynn's desk writing on a yellow pad. Walter stepped into the room and demanded to know what was going on in here. Walsh looked up and at the same moment, Walter saw his badge.

"Sir, I'm conducting a police investigation. Are you here to see Reverend Flynn?"

Walter was speechless. He didn't know what to think? Had Jerry called the police about his getting beat up? He had actually come to apologize, to beg Jerry's forgiveness. And, he had to ask him for his help in the terrible new crisis affecting his family. He wasn't sure whether to excuse himself or answer the detective's question.

"Yes! I'm a member of the church," he stammered. "My son-in-law was killed before dawn this morning. His pickup truck ran into a tree on Route Forty, twenty-five miles east of here. I came to make funeral arrangements. I'm looking for Reverend Flynn."

"Mr. Tompkins, I didn't recognize you," Walsh said as he came around the desk.

"I'm Chester Walsh." He reached out to shake Walter's hand. "You don't remember me, sir, but you were my Scoutmaster. That was many years ago. Please, don't tell me your news is about Mike Todd?"

Walter nodded ascent and lowered his head. Now he remembered Walsh. He was the big colored kid who had made such an impression on him. Walsh was the first Negro in the county to accomplish the award of Eagle Scout. And who could forget Walsh as a Tompkinsville High School football hero? He hadn't seen Chester since his graduation, when he had presented him with one of the T&T college scholarships. Walter took his hand firmly, half relieved, and overwhelmed.

"Yes, Chester," Walter replied, "it was Michael."

Walsh's eyes dropped as they filled with sorrow. He and Michael had remained close friends since high school. The news shook him to the core. He raised his head in unbelief, searching Walter's face for news that there might still be some hope. When it didn't come, Chester wanted to cry. But he caught himself, forced his emotions into the background, concentrated on the urgent matter that had brought him here.

"I can't tell you how sorry I am, Mr. Tompkins. Michael and I . . . Please forgive me, but right now, I'm trying to locate Reverend Flynn. It seems he's disappeared and so has my boss and partner, Detective Burroughs. We're concerned there might be a connection. I hate to bother you with this, however, it's important—can you describe Flynn's car?"

"Sure! It's a black Chrysler, a 1957 Crown Imperial."

"Well, that should be easy to spot. Do you know the plate number?"

"Only that it is New Jersey registered. I can find out."

"That's all right, we'll get the numbers. Would you have any idea as to why Reverend Flynn might want to visit Mrs. Daniel Maefield of New York City early this morning?"

"No, not at all."

Miss Blatty poked her head into the room to say she had finished giving information to the New York police. The detective on the line wanted to speak to Detective Walsh. Walsh picked up the phone on the pastor's desk. Walter walked into Miss Blatty's office to see a woman in distress. She had caved into her desk chair. She looked up to see Walter and knew immediately his presence meant more distressful news.

"Walter, shall we ever be free of evil in this place?" she asked. "God help us! I fear something terrible has happened to Reverend Flynn."

Walter tilted his head. What had he done to contribute to the current problem? He hesitated to tell her more sad news. With

Madge, Michael had been a favorite in the church. Michael and Madge, "The Inseparable Two." "M&M" everyone called the couple.

"Marion," Walter said, easing himself closer to her desk, "I came to arrange for a funeral . . . Michael is dead."

He fell silent and let his own tears fall graciously. Miss Blatty stared in disbelief, unable to comprehend what he had just said, trying to understand the news and the grief of the proud and anguished man in front of her.

"Okay, I've got to go," Walsh said, rushing in from the study. "If you hear from any of those people, call police headquarters immediately. Whoever answers, give your information, and tell them to call me. Sorry about Michael, Mr. Tompkins. I'm on duty and can't help you and your family right now. Jerry Flynn was the last known citizen to try to contact Detective Burroughs. That's why I came here this morning. Everything happens at once."

Walter walked him through the study and out Shepherd Door. They climbed the steps to the cloister. Chester had parked his cruiser on Cathedral Drive. Walter looked over at the manse, hesitated, and turned to Walsh.

"Chester, this is only a suspicion, but I've got to suggest it to you." Walter paused but he knew he had to say it. "You will want to speak to my nephew, Everett Wheeler."

"The church custodian? He's on vacation, according to Miss Blatty."

"Then you know about him!"

"What should I know?" he said, all detective again.

"I believe he may be mixed up in this, whatever it is. Everett had some kind of dispute with Reverend Flynn, perhaps because of Miss Cunningham and I know Everett doesn't like our new pastor—"

Walsh stopped Tompkins. He heard his number and name loud and clear on the police radio. Someone wanted him in a hurry. "You realize Mr. Tompkins that anything you tell me I have to investigate and write into my report. I'll have to question you further about this later. Where does Mr. Wheeler live?"

Walter gave him the address and Walsh, on the run, waved goodbye.

Walter thought about driving to Everett's house. If he wasn't home, maybe Marie would know how to reach him. But then he decided he'd better get back to the house. He had a lot to do. His family needed him. He had to take charge.

As Walsh drove out the church driveway, he received word that Detective Burroughs's car was behind Grady's Bar and Grill. Walsh turned on his flashers and siren and raced east on Church Street.

*   *   *

Wheeler watched in silence as the car approached the New Brunswick Exit. Almost too late, he poked Jerry on the back of his neck.

"Get off here!" he screamed in his ear. "Exit nine! Nine!"

Jerry put his foot on the brake, turned sharply into the exit lane and caught the horn of a tractor trailer truck as he swerved in front. He accelerated ahead on the narrow ramp. Rhonda and Charlene, who had nodded off, came awake with a fright.

As they neared the tollbooth, Jerry thought about his options. On the dashboard clock, he saw the time at 9:45. This might be his opportunity to overtake Everett or signal trouble. He stopped third car in line. Rhonda handed him the toll ticket with the exact change.

"Don't do anything stupid, Reverend," Everett whispered. "Arouse suspicion and the toll man goes first, you second."

He reached out to the collector with the ticket and money. He felt the barrel of Everett's gun at his right armpit. The toll transaction completed, the crossing rail lifted. "Have a nice day," the collector said. Jerry wanted to shout they were in trouble, let the man know they were hostages. He thought about slamming the car door into the toll abutment. But he would never have a chance.

"Easy does it preacher, no heroics here!" Everett whispered harshly.

Jerry drove away from the booth. Everett ordered him on to Route 1, south. Again he cautioned against speeding and passing through red lights.

Traffic lights had positions about every quarter mile on this fast major artery between New Brunswick and Trenton, but with good timing, a driver could go a long way without having to stop for one. Nearing the Princeton exit, Everett directed Jerry to turn off Route 1, then east on to County 571. East of the little town of Holson, he directed a southerly direction on to County 537, another baron road through the rural landscape of central New Jersey. Everett knew his way and was circumventing roads likely watched by police. At Chambers Corner, he picked up U.S. 206 and directed Jerry to make a beeline through the Pine Barrens and Wharton State Forrest. The desolate, rustic setting seemed a world apart from the concrete and the confusion of the city.

*   *   *

New York City Police detective Irvine Harpolsky was the first plainclothes officer to arrive at the Maefield apartment. He immediately sealed off the floor and ordered an around the clock guard. He directed officers to check public areas of the building and interview anyone who may have heard and-or seen anything suspicious from six o'clock on. He telephoned Judge Harry Deitch to request an order to search the apartment.

While talking to Judge Deitch, a policeman interrupted to report that an usher at Riverside Church had seen a couple answering the description of Charlene Cunningham and Jerry Flynn at 7:45 this morning. The usher was about to call police when a detective showed him his badge. Saying he was looking for a drug dealer and his prostitute girlfriend, the usher told the detective where to look. The last he saw of them, the cop escorted the couple out to the street. Another person saw the couple and a large man in a colorful jacket as they got into a black Imperial. The witness said the driver was a woman, but he did not get a good look.

Harpolsky repeated the information to the judge. "Undoubtedly, the big guy is impersonating a police officer," the detective said. He urged Judge Deitch to act on his request.

"You got it," he replied. Harpolsky turned to his assistants.

"Do a quick search, then, start all over again! Take fingerprints, the usual."

"Maybe you'll want to start with this, Irv," one detective replied and showed Harpolsky the tape recorder he had found in a closet. Harpolsky set it on the kitchen table and plugged it in. He rewound the tape and started it on play. Rhonda Maefield's voice came on clear as a bell.

CHAPTER 16

SINNERS OR SAINTS?

Early Wednesday Afternoon, June13

Marie Wheeler sat glassy eyed in front of the TV as it broadcast news relating the disappearance of Detective Burroughs. The story hadn't changed since early this morning. Without waiting for the segment to end, she switched it off. Slow and halting, she made her way upstairs. In the bathroom, she turned on the hot water in the tub.

The clothes she took off were the same she had on last night and she looked at them in disbelief—the torn dress Everett had tried to rip off, the stockings with open runs. She looked closely at her burn mark. Nothing could hurt as much. She had applied a suave and the blister appeared less tender. Now she dabbed the wound with the same remedy as last night but worried it would leave a nasty scar.

She reflected once more on what happened after she had returned to the house, how she shook uncontrollably and took a tranquilizer and when that didn't help she drank "Jack Daniels" until passed out. She wished she had never woken up. Her head throbbed. She felt sick to her stomach, the burn areas on her thigh continued to throb.

She dropped her hand over the side of the tub to test the water. It was as hot and deep as she wanted it, so she turned off the faucet. She did not however get in. Instead, she opened the door to the shower stall, turned on the cold-water spray and—with the water flowing—she stepped in with her underwear on. It had become a ritual for her, something she had learned during her weeks at a rehabilitation center for alcoholics. Cold shower, hot bath, cold shower. Marie had followed the routine to regain sobriety after previous lapses into alcohol binges.

As the icy water poured over her flesh, Marie reminisced about her life with Everett.

*   *   *

She couldn't believe things had gone so wrong. She once loved him so much she gladly lied about his whereabouts, protecting his alibi for whatever crime he had committed. He could be kind and jolly, generous and affectionate. She liked his gifts and their house with all its modern features. She had once taken great satisfaction in his jealous rage if another man showed her any attention.

But pleasant things aside, most of their married life, she had lived in fear of him. He had physically beaten her several times. He had forced her to do uncommon sexual things and had threatened to make her disappear if she ever mentioned such activities to another soul. The decisive spark turning her against him occurred four years ago.

After several miscarriages, she had a healthy pregnancy. As the baby grew in her womb, Everett reacted with increasing amusement and disappointment. He accused her of having an affair and offered to arrange for an abortion. Then, in her seventh month, tests showed the fetus had died and she underwent surgery to remove it. Mentally, Marie did not recover. Depression and all-day drinking followed. Everett was unsympathetic. He scolded her for getting behind at processing his wedding pictures and other photographic work. Their relationship turned more argumentative and cold. Her drinking had become a problem and she did not want to stop.

*　　*　　*

Marie turned off the shower and removed her underwear. Waiting until now was part of her ritual of cleansing. She stepped into the heated bath water. She lathered her body and eased down, covering her frail frame in the hot water bath.

*　　*　　*

For more than a year now, Marie meant to force Everett to cooperate with her in a divorce. She believed he should compensate her for her years of work in his business, as well as for pain and suffering as his wife. Everett was worth close to a million dollars. He would, however, leave her penniless unless she held something against him, something so valuable that he would pay her to get it back. She knew he was making dirty pictures. She had done her share of processing them without protest. But to catch him in the act: that had become her objective.

She recalled the night she had gotten into his footlocker.

Everett came home drunk, but not so far gone that he couldn't work the combination padlock. Setting the lock aside, Marie watched in secret as he dropped new envelopes and movie film canisters into the large metal box. These were pictures he had processed himself or had had them done elsewhere. They were for his eyes only, though she perceived he was also selling copies to private collectors. In his inebriated condition, Everett forgot to return the lock to the hasp. She watched him leave the room for the toilet and then for the downstairs sofa, where he stretched out flat on his back while the television blared. Thus, she felt safe to do the unthinkable. He would have killed her in an instant, she believed, had he caught her rummaging through his footlocker.

She could not take the time to look at very much and ignored the reels of film resting on the bottom. She opened several envelopes, each one containing photographs and matching negatives. She saw that he had taken cheesecake photography to its ultimate limits by producing full frontal nudity. Then she came upon an envelope marked simply "*R*" and a date that went back almost four years. Here, Marie's curiosity turned to astonishment. She knew instantly she had what she needed as she viewed photos of her husband with Mrs. Maefield. They were untouched and faces were clear and unmasked. There was no mistaking Everett. Recognizing Rhonda Maefield as his woman was the biggest surprise. Had the envelope not included a few pictures of Rhonda in her black-rimmed glasses, bun hairstyle and clothes more suited for a jail warden, Marie may not have made the connection. But as the pictures showed a progression to nudity and intimacy with Everett, Rhonda looked younger and attractive. Nor did she appear shy about her raw exposure. Now Marie believed she had proof of Everett's infidelity. She wondered if it was a one-night stand or an ongoing relationship. No matter, Everett would pay plenty for the return of these untouched pictures and their negatives. She realized, too, if she wasn't careful, he would torture her to get them back. Setting aside her nervousness, Marie spun the combination lock. There was no turning back. The next day, she purchased the right to a safe deposit box at the New Jersey State Bank and placed the envelope there. "*Yes,*" the bank officer had assured her, "*you alone have access to the volt. In the event of your death, no family member can open the box without an agent of the state present to examine its contents.*"

Marie wished she had gone further. She should have met with a lawyer that day and begun divorce proceedings. There was no way to know when Everett would discover the theft. She had enough money saved to live on her own for six months, the amount of time she thought she would need to convince Everett to settle with her. He would have fumed, but he would have traded a hundred thousand dollars for those pictures, especially now, knowing that they could be used to convict him of murder.

But she had delayed. She believed that the pictures were so damning, in and of themselves, they would protect her from Everett. But much more influencing was her hesitancy to hurt

Dr. Maefield. How could she, of all people, be the one to use photographs of Rhonda's infidelity for her own selfish means? She knew herself as no saint, but neither was she a cad.

* * *

Marie shivered as she stood a second time under the icy spray of the showerhead. She endured for less than a minute. Invigorated, believing her mind and body cleaned from the poisons of alcohol, she wrapped herself in a full-body towel and went into her bedroom, where she stretched out on her bed. Staring at the ceiling, she recalled her attempt to save the minister from learning of his wife's affair.

* * *

Everett Wheeler opened a fresh pack of Pall Malls and lit one up. He did this as an annoyance to Charlene. He knew she smoked, but she wouldn't ask him for one. Repeatedly, he blew smoke in her face.

Charlene tried to ignore him. She sat with her arms folded over her breasts, her eyes staring ahead or across Rhonda at the passing scenery. Everett took off his fedora and fanned the smoke, then leaned forward to throw the cigarette butt through Rhonda's open window. Charlene saw the swollen area where she had popped him with the vase. There was a square bandage inside the circular bald spot at the back of his head. A little blood showed through and Charlene guessed it hurt plenty. His hat had probably saved him. For reasons she could not understand, Rhonda had gone over to his side. She must have aided him in recovering so he could chase them and then brought Jerry's car to the cathedral. Why had Mrs. Maefield betrayed her after saving her life yesterday? It didn't figure.

Everett broke into the silence with more directions, so that they continued south on to another rural highway, Route 54, toward Vineland. Jerry recognized some of the places they passed.

Wheeler was taking them by way of the old highway system, but skirting Tompkinsville. They proceeded another thirty miles.

"At the next intersection turn left! You hear me? . . . Okay, slow down! . . . You see that abandoned gas station on the right? Turn at the corner! We're dropping in for a little sleep over."

A hundred yards off the main highway, Everett directed Jerry to drive onto the gravel parking area of Sunrise Motel, a place that had seen better days and which now appealed to the off-road sleaze trade or truckers who drive all night. There were a few trailer rigs parked close to the road. Deep in farm country, the motel anchored a thick grove of pine with a sea of apple orchards on one side and open fields on the other. Except for the closed gas station, Jerry did not see any commercial buildings and only a few farmhouses in the far distance.

"Rhonda, you're elected. Get us a cottage in back. You know what to do."

Rhonda entered the office, which doubled as the owner's house. A few minutes passed before she came out, key in hand, and walked toward a group of cottages lined up behind the main building.

"Follow her," Everett ordered.

Jerry parked the Imperial in front of a cottage at the far end of the line. One other car stood five places away.

"Not here, dumbbell, over there! Park behind the trees!"

Jerry drove the Imperial inside a grove of pine trees, seventy-five feet from the cottage.

"All out! It's time to rest our weary bones and, who knows, Reverend," Everett yawned, "maybe get one up?" he roared, laughing so hard Jerry hoped he would break a blood vessel. Everett's amusement was short lived. "The keys?" Jerry dropped them into his hand.

They entered a cottage furnished with two full-size beds and a long countertop against the facing wall. Below the counter were clothes drawers and above it a mirror was mounted on the wall. The counter held a television set and an electric hot plate with a metal teakettle. A bath with sink, toilet and tub-shower adjoined the room.

Everett yanked the drape across the room's double windows, sheltering the place in instant darkness. He flipped on the wall switch lighting the ceiling lamp, then turned on the air-condition unit mounted below the windows. Jerry looked for a telephone, but saw none. He had noticed a phone booth next to a cold beverage machine by the office. Clearly, Everett had used this place before and, judging from Rhonda's familiarity with the surroundings, he figured she had too.

"Okay, these are the rules children. No talking unless it's to me. No one leaves this room for the can without my permission. If you need to piss or take a shit, you do it with the door open. To discourage ideas about wandering off, I'll take your clothes. Strip! Get naked! Shoes, socks, underwear, leave nothing on. Nothing! Do it! You, too, Rhonda! Get your ass naked!"

He took his gun out and waved it at them. Jerry shrugged and pulled off his shirt. "Surely he isn't serious about everything," he murmured to Charlene.

Charlene didn't answer. She knew he meant business and undid the tiny buttons that held the dress closed. She pulled it up and off and threw it at Everett's feet. Jerry saw Charlene's black and blue marks across her midsection and the large bandage on her left thigh. She discarded the loose bra and closed her arms across her breasts. She, too, paused, hoping against hope Everett would not insist on her panties as well. She then saw Jerry's bruised side and cursed Everett for his brutality. Jerry wanted to explain, but there was no opportunity.

While they stood fearful and poised, Everett stripped the beds. He threw all the bedding into the bathtub. Rhonda folded her blouse and skirt and neatly laid them on the counter top. She then pulled her slip up and over her head and gently draped it on a chair near her clothes. She unfastened her black brazier and dropped it on top. She wasn't wearing panties, only a thin garter belt and sheer black stockings. Everett returned from the bathroom.

"Hey! This ain't no two-bit strip show," he screamed. "Take off those stockings!"

In an ugly mood, he reached down and grabbed Rhonda's feet, knocking her off balance, causing her to fall on the mattress. He grabbed Charlene by the hair and yanked her across the same bed. In a second, he drew her panties down to her ankles and slapped her soundly on the butt. Jerry moved to stop him, only to receive a solid punch in the stomach. He fell to the side of the bed gasping for breath. Already sore from previous punishments, he bent low in audible pain.

"I said everything! Skinny dip!"

In agony, holding his stomach, Jerry struggled to his feet and dropped his pants and boxer shorts on the floor in front of the bed. Charlene remained on the bed and kicked the white satin briefs Rhonda had loaned her to the side. Everett ordered Rhonda to collect the discarded garments and all their shoes and pile them on top of the bedding in the bathtub. He pulled the mattress closest to the window free from the box spring and folded it against the door. He used his foot to push the empty box spring next to the window.

"All naked now? My, my, aren't we pretty! I wish I had my camera. Do you know how much this scene would be worth in Times Square? Preacher, you must drive the ladies wild."

By now, it was obvious the air conditioner did nothing more than grind and blow warm air. Everett fiddled with the control. Suddenly, he kicked the unit, cursing it and haranguing at motel management. But it was too much trouble to change to another cottage. And he didn't want anyone coming by to repair the unit. He kicked it again, shattering the control knob, killing the incessant noise. Exhausted by his tirade, he eased himself onto the spare folded mattress, his gun steady in his hand. As he talked, he waved the gun, stopping now and then to point it at one or the other of his hostages.

"Now stretch out on the bed, relax, roll over on your bellies, hands at your sides! No talking! I hear one word and you get your face dunked in the toilet. You hear?" he growled.

Jerry realized that Everett was as much fatigued as he was. If he had slept in the past forty-eight hours, it had not been for long. Whatever he planned for them, he wanted it dark when he did it. His caution and craftiness made him that much harder to overtake. Jerry needed to recover his strength. He needed sleep himself. He worried more about Charlene's physical condition than his own. She lay stretched out between him and Rhonda. Her thigh touched his, their hands clasped. Jerry tried to reassure her. He kissed her shoulder. She turned her head to look at him. They stared deeply into each other's eyes. Rhonda had turned her face to the wall and Jerry thought she may have fallen asleep. Time passed in the semidark, hot, humid room. In spite of conditions, Jerry and Charlene also drifted off.

*   *   *

In Marie's mind, Doctor Maefield was a saint.

He had counseled her when she lost her baby. He had held her hand and prayed with her when she turned to alcohol as her only solace. He had persuaded her to join Alcoholics Anonymous and drove her to a private hospital just over the boarder in New York State for ten weeks of rehabilitation. She watched him sign her in and guarantee her expenses with his own check. In the three years following, she had lived free of booze. A year ago, the pastor had come to her door late at night after she had called him because Everett had beaten her up. He had given her a black eye, fractured her wrist, and cracked four ribs. Maefield took her to the hospital and pleaded with her to file charges of assault. She had refused. So, the minister found her a place to hide until strong enough to return home. In the meantime, he parlayed an agreement with her husband, which permitted her to live at home in a kind of separate but equal living arrangement.

For such personal kindness, Marie adored the minister. She feared losing his friendship. That night when she had discovered the pictures in Everett's footlocker, she felt sorry for his wife. After all, the demeaning photos were almost four years old. Marie already knew Everett as a philanderer. He had destroyed marital relationships before. He had rigged photo shoots of unsuspecting wives, as much to assure their silence as any other reason. Marie believed Rhonda had become one of his many innocent, unsuspecting victims. She wanted to spare Reverend Maefield and Rhonda from news that could only cause heartache and shame. Thus, she needed a second line of attack, pictures showing Everett with someone else, photos illustrating his deceit and vile conduct. She resolved to find where Everett photographed his subjects and to catch him in the act.

One cold night in early January, she spied on Everett as he left an Atlantic City bar with a young Hispanic girl and got into his pickup truck. It was dark, but Marie was sure Everett blindfolded his passenger. She then followed to, of all places, the parking lot of First Church. Was Everett using the building for his illicit affairs and pornography? Marie knew Everett as callous, but to this degree, he turned her stomach. She kept a safe distance as he drove his truck into the annex garage and lowered the remote-operated doors behind him.

A week later, she hid in the annex as Everett locked up for the night. For three hours, she kept vigil from a classroom window facing the parking lot. When she saw his truck approach his workshop-garage, she ran ahead and watched through the semi darkness of the hallway as he led a blindfolded woman into the underground passage. Fearing discovery if she followed, she retreated from the scene.

The next night was Saturday. Knowing more about the church basement than Everett would have given her credit for, Marie ran through the underground passage and into the old coal rooms of the basement. She found her way into the pitch dark of the storage cellar under the manse. She had brought a flashlight, so did not bother to switch on the overhead lights. Everett was so skilled as an electrician and photo genius she feared he could have rigged a camera to shoot a picture of anyone switching on the lights. Reasonably familiar with the room, she hid behind a high stack of mattresses. It was a long wait. But just before midnight, the door opened, a few overhead fluorescent lamps switched on. Several bulbs flashed on and off, in need of adjustment or replacement. In the temperate light, she spied on Everett as he escorted a blindfolded woman in a long winter coat and scarf. She saw them disappeared behind the wall of stacked mattresses and grasped that Everett was using the abandoned housekeeper's apartment as a pictures studio. He probably believes no one would remember this damp, dingy, old bedroom, but Marie did. Thirty years ago, her aunt had lived there.

Like many Eastern Europeans who immigrated to America in the 1920s, her aunt had taken a job as a domestic servant. The job provided housing and a little income while she assimilated. Working for the minister, her aunt cooked, cleaned and baby sat. At that time, the housekeeper's apartment included a stairwell to a combination kitchen and sitting-room with a door on the backyard. During a major renovation of the manse, the trustees had the upstairs room torn down and in its place built the manse's sun porch, then a new housekeeper's apartment off the kitchen. They then abandoned the room completely by bricking in its basement entrance.

"How clever," Marie conceded as she heard the door slam behind Everett and the blindfolded woman. "One must marvel at Everett's ingenuity for concealment. He's broken through that blocked wall and fashioned a studio for himself."

Marie decided to stay put. Fifteen minutes later, she heard a door from behind her open and shut. In the flickering light, a tall, lanky man, wearing a dark suit, warily approached the wall. An uncommon beret capped his head. His back was toward her, so she missed seeing his face. In spite of that, she believed she knew him. She hoped against hope she was mistaken. Her heart beat harder as he walked hesitantly and stopped several times as if listening for sounds that would alert him to danger. After several seconds pause, he pushed the mattresses, as Everett had done, and followed the thick bundles into the opening. Marie watched as the mattress barricade rolled back in place.

An hour passed. She heard Everett before she saw him, his voice booming as the mattresses were pulled in and as he came out with the blindfolded woman holding on to his belt. They walked under a working fluorescent light and stopped. Everett held the lady's winter coat. She wore a brazier and shorts, and boots that reached halfway to her knees. The blindfold did not hide her smile. She laughed loudly and playfully kidded Everett, enjoying her masquerade. Everett rolled the mattresses once more into the narrow passage. He took the woman in tow. They exited through the door into the coal room, leaving the blinking fluorescents on. Marie moved to a position closer to the wall and waited for the next shoe to drop. Five minutes went by. She heard the mattresses rolling again and then saw the tall, thin man at the entrance of the snug corridor. Now facing the glare of a florescent lamp, Marie saw the unmistakable face of Reverend Maefield.

Sadness filled her eyes. Every suspicion conceivable ran through her mind. New questions tore into her imagination. Is the minister in cahoots with Everett? Is he too spying on Everett? Perhaps he already knows about Rhonda with my husband. But how did he get into the room without Everett seeing him? Marie watched as the minister left the storage room the way he had entered. With many questions troubling her, she left the building.

She felt doubly betrayed by what she had seen. It was degrading enough to catch her husband in blatant criminality, but to realize that the minister—who represented the highest moral values in society—was somehow culpable, struck her harder. Her feelings ran deep and she determined to learn the truth. This time, she acted immediately. She telephoned Reverend Maefield five minutes before the beginning of Sunday's eleven o'clock service and told him she had to see him that afternoon. She knew Everett would be out of town. She swore the minister to secrecy about her visit. Maefield knew she lived in constant fear of Everett and—always sympathetic to her cause—he told her to meet him at Shepherd House at two o'clock.

*   *   *

Deep in these memories, Marie did not move the first time she heard the doorbell. The second ring brought her to her feet.

Startled and frightened, she shed the towel for her robe and went to the window. She peeked through the Venetian blind to look down on a gray Ford Galaxy parked in front of the house. She did not recognize the car as belonging to anyone she knew and her first reaction was to ignore the bell. But then she heard the caller banging on the door. Hesitantly, she descended the stairs. Again, the doorbell rang. Cautiously, Marie opened the door a crack and stared at the badge and photo ID of a police detective. Dressed in slacks and a short sleeve, open at the collar, white shirt, the black man introduced himself as Detective Chester Walsh. Politely, Walsh asked if Mr. Everett Wheeler was at home.

Marie grew nervous as she told Walsh she hadn't seen her husband since early this morning when he dressed for work. She couldn't remember exactly what time he left the house, but thought it was about seven thirty.

There, she had lied for him again. The lie was instinctive. Walsh contradicted her, saying he had heard at the church that her husband was on vacation today. Marie responded, irritation in her voice, that she knew nothing about vacation. Everett left for work. That's all she knew. Walsh handed Marie his calling card and told her to ask Mr. Wheeler to call him as soon as he returned home. He thanked her for her time and slowly walked to his car. She watched him drive off.

She waited five minutes before she opened the liquor cabinet and poured a glass of whiskey. She carried glass and bottle to the dining room table and stared at them for the longest time. The memory of her afternoon visit with Reverend Maefield flooded her mind. She began sipping her liquor.

*   *   *

Jerry wandered in and out of sleep. Gently, he rubbed the sore skin on Charlene's wrist, and worried about their present situation.

He tried to figure Rhonda. From all he knew about her, she was a bright woman. He could not understand her attraction to

Wheeler. Intellectually, socially, politically, she was his exact opposite. Yet, she obeyed Everett as if a subordinate. Was she under some kind of spell or hypnotic suggestion? Jerry considered she may be on some kind of drug and based his notion on her blank stares, expressionless eyes, rigid face, a body that appeared more robot than human. She had also surprised him by her looks. She didn't appear anything like her pictures in the church photo album. If Everett hadn't called her by name, Jerry would have never guessed that the alluring woman driving his car was Rhonda Maefield.

Nor had she shown modesty about her nakedness. He could not free his mind from the memory of her as she had crossed the room and stopped to support her weight by placing her hand on his arm while she bent to pick up their clothes. Her chore completed, she had crawled onto the bed next to Charlene, and laid flat on her stomach.

Now Charlene awoke, and whispered she had to use the toilet. Jerry watched as she backed off the bed. Everett came to his feet behind her and pushed her along to the entryway dividing the bath from the rest of the room. They disappeared behind the wall. In that instant, Jerry felt Rhonda's hand massaging his bruised rib section. When he turned to face her, she was on her side staring at him.

"Don't worry," she whispered, "you'll survive this."

He rose up on one elbow to watch as Everett trailed Charlene to the bed. Timidly, she crawled on to the mattress to her former place between them.

"It was awful . . . I've never been so humiliated," she whimpered.

Tears streamed off her cheeks. Jerry took Charlene's hand and squeezed tight. All was very quiet as they toyed with each other's fingers. They closed their eyes and tried once more to sleep. Then they heard Rhonda leave the bed. Without coercion, she mounted Everett and wrapped him in her nakedness. A smile broke out on Charlene's face and Jerry snickered as Charlene's eyes rose and fell in time with the heaving noises of the couple copulating inches from their toes. When Rhonda returned to rest next to her, Charlene, with Everett snoring loudly, whispered scornfully, "How could you go so easily to him?" Rhonda replied in a raspy voice, her tone sharp and insulting. "Would you have rather he raped you and forced Jerry to fuck me? You should thank me. Now he's like a lion with a full stomach. There's less chance he'll hunger for another body." But Jerry surmised Rhonda could have just as well have spoken of her own hunger. He recalled Frank Scarpelli relating that Daniel Maefield seemed to have loved Rhonda the way the prophet Hosea, loved his whoring wife, Gomer!

*　　*　　*

Marie struggled to open a second pack of cigarettes. Her hands shaking, she tore the cellophane and half the under-wrapping away. She had a problem steadying a match to light it. She took a long drag and exhaled, then emptied her glass of the liquor that had remained. Staring blankly out the window beside her, she thought about Reverend Maefield on the last day and night of his life.

*　　*　　*

The sky was dirty gray and Marie Wheeler felt chilled to the bones by the time she reached Shepherd House. It hadn't begun snowing yet, but Marie knew the storm was close, that any minute now the clouds would burst and spew their white ash upon the dry earth. She had parked her car outside Nick's Delicatessen on the other side of Tompkins Park. After her visit with Reverend Maefield, she planned on stopping in for groceries and a six carton of beer. Nick sold beer on Sundays to established customers. He just put it in the bottom of the bag. One beer now and then couldn't hurt her, she reasoned.

She climbed the hill and came in through Shepherd Door. Cordial and polite, Maefield rushed to greet her. Taking her coat, he remarked how thin it was, "not suitable for the weather outside," he said as he hung it in a cloak closet built into the shelving along the east wall. He made her comfortable in a chair facing his desk and went back around to his chair. She lost no time lighting a cigarette. After much preliminary discussion about the weather, the church's activities and listening to the pastor's worried concerns about the state of the world in the nuclear age, she explained the purpose for her visit.

"Pastor, you need to know my husband is misusing church property. He has set aside a room in the basement below the manse as a private studio to photograph women in compromising poses and in stages of undress. Sometimes he photographs himself in disguise as he has sex with them."

Reverend Maefield showed shock at her allegation, saying, it would trouble him deeply if things like this were happening in his church. He became immediately defensive, his voice reflecting irritation as he asked why Marie would make such a "nasty accusation."

His reaction stunned her. She had expected more openness and cooperation. She decided not to answer him directly and instead told him about a basement room, how as a little girl she had visited her aunt who lived there as a housekeeper and how the church trustees had since then built a new apartment on the manse and blocked the old entrance.

Maefield interrupted. "The last I heard, Marie, Everett transformed that room into a walk-in closet. I don't even know where the door is," he said with a laugh. A smile still held his face as he threw up his hands in a gesture of innocence, "It's not my business or interest what's down there. It's so much space; I don't know how Everett finds his way. Of course, I know he stores photography gear somewhere in the basement. Is this what you are referring to?" He didn't wait for her to reply and surprised her again by going to Everett's defense by warning her about making too much of hearsay and, "While rumors about Everett's flirting and voyeurism abound, we mustn't believe all we hear. Remember, Marie," he lectured, "it is important for you to maintain the peace pact you and Everett agreed to. Accusing your husband of something as preposterous as this will not build trust."

Marie couldn't believe what she had just heard. Doctor Maefield apparently thought he could play her for a fool. She grew inwardly angry. She crushed her third cigarette into the ashtray on his desk and lit up another one. Without missing a beat, she continued.

"Doctor Maefield, late last night and into early this morning, I hid out in the storage room below the manse. I saw my husband enter and leave that closet—as you call it—with a blindfolded woman." She watched Maefield's face turn red. He leaned close into his desk and tapped the desktop with his fingers. Marie paused. She had gone this far, she would go all the way. "The woman was young, short, brunet. She giggled a lot, and . . . well . . . Why don't you describe her appearance?"

Maefield ignored the implication of her question. His discomfort with her news was more than obvious in the way he shifted in his chair. He picked up a pencil and started twirling it in his fingers. His face stern and his voice firm, he promised Marie that if Everett was using the room in an unsavory way, he would put a stop to it. "I deny knowing anything about this, Marie." Then, incredulous to her ears, he asked, "Are you drinking again?"

She took a deep breath. She would not let him distract her from the facts of last night.

"Reverend, I believe you know for certain how Everett uses that room for the purpose I have described. And, no, I've never been more sober." Instantly, Maefield's face turned pale. He looked like he would cry. His hands shook. He swiveled his chair so as not to face her. Marie's sympathy rode to the surface. Turning down her accusatory tone, she said in a hushed voice, "I'm sorry, I really am. I had hoped you could be straight with me about this. You always impressed me as that kind of man. 'Tell it like it is!' you advised. I owe you so much . . . believe me; I am not here to embarrass you. I don't want to hurt you. Please look at me, Daniel! Don't treat me like I can be ignored." Slowly, he revolved his chair to face her. "What's behind that door?" she asked. "How do you get in there? If you are not assisting Everett with his pornography, what is your purpose?"

Maefield showed exasperation by letting go of the pencil he had gripped for so long, then, loosening the clerical collar that bound his neck, he admitted he had seen inside the hidden room. He described the false walls and the see-through mirrors behind which Everett operated preset cameras electronically while he acted as photographer before his unknowing model. He related how easy it was to hide, that once Everett began shooting his pictures inside the studio, he rarely returned behind the false walls. When he did look in to adjust a lens or change out a film, Maefield described how he had only to move around to the far wall.

"I can watch with impunity as Everett poses his models," he said, his voice relaxed and confident. "When I first discovered what Everett was using the room for, I meant to close him down. He has no right to use church facilities in this criminal way. Yet, studying his sexual belligerence fascinated me. Mind you, as an intelligent human being, I see no harm in pornography. It can be a form of education as well as artistic expression. Adults should have freedom to look at anything they please. I have studied sexual expression in hundreds of cultures where sex is often a way of acting out religious rites. But my intellectual arguments aside, Marie—I will not be hypocritical—free expression has boundaries. Its presentation can be carnal and depressive. It can offend other values in human relationships. It can be exploitive. And even if I defend Everett as an artist, I can't defend his using church facilities for that purpose. So, why have I let it go on? Because, Marie, I am debased by what I see."

He stretched back in his chair and stared up toward the disciples' windows. Marie waited for his long silence to end. But his mind appeared to have ground to a stop.

"I am sorry, so sorry," he continued, as he skulked in his chair, his eyes dripping tears, strained in their focus on her. "I have let it go on!" He turned to the side. "God forgive me!" he cried, his lips quivering. "I have let it go on because behind those walls, I can see live action, Marie . . . Everett has no idea I watch."

He removed his glasses to wipe them with a handkerchief. He touched the cloth to his eyes. "Obviously, you've been spying on me, Marie! Now you know my secret, my sin, if you wish to call it that. One way or another, I suppose every human is vulnerable to powers he or she cannot drive off. Reason cannot protect us from everything. I see the evil in my ways . . . I do feel ashamed, Marie. I wish I could stop!"

"How long have you known about Everett's hidden studio?" she asked.

"Please, child, I beg you not to ask me that. Why should it matter?" When she showed no sign of softening, he went on. "Marie, forget this! I'll find a way to make Everett close his studio. He'll never know you informed on him."

It was Marie's turn to look away. She took her time crushing her cigarette in the ashtray. He had confessed to more than she had wanted to hear. She had not meant to bring him to his knees, or on her part to infer any judgment. If she had, she walked in the light of hypocrisy. How many years had she developed and printed Everett's films and those of others? Her protests and complaints had been mellow, if at all. She had processed erotic orders for the money. And if put to the test, she had had no conscience about what she did. Who was she to stand in judgment of her minister?

"What do you want from me?" he asked, reaching for her hand, holding it against the desktop as smoke continued its escape from simmering tobacco. She looked up and stared.

"I want you to help me get a divorce. You can do that by acting as a witness to his infidelity. You can also help me turn the tables on him in such a way that there will be no need to take him to court. I want to catch him in that room before he puts on a mask. I want pictures of him with at least one of his models and thus confirm his criminal photography with my own pictures. When Everett realizes I have indisputable proof of his adultery, and that he could go to jail for his pornography, he will come to terms with me for a divorce."

"That's blackmail, Marie!"

She smiled at the innocent way he had said it. She hated his retreat into an appeal for legal justice. When her smile turned into outright laughter at his absurdity, he made a vigorous protest. "There is no way I can go along with such a scheme. I cannot add more fire to my disgrace or use this church as a seat of injustice."

"You needn't let your conscience bother you, Reverend. Everett's been blackmailing people with his pictures for years. Consider this an eye for an eye, a tooth for a tooth . . . Isn't that what the Bible sees as justice?" she said in a mournful voice, her eyes now unwavering in his. "And besides, the way I see it there won't be any scandal. Hear me again. He'll destroy his studio rather than chance a raid by the vice squad. I'll be safe in hiding, so he can't hurt me. He'll never know about your helping me. It's that simple."

"I can't do that!"

"Bull shit, you can't," she said angrily. "What you're really saying is you can't give up your cheap way to jerk off! Or, are you tying to protect your whoring wife?"

They both fell silent and dropped their eyes. She had said it. Her sharp tongue had pointed her to say it. She had shown she knew more than he could imagine and her willingness to involve Rhonda, if it came to that. She had said what she had not wanted to say, its effect instantaneous. She looked up to see him slumped in his chair, stunned and defenseless.

"I'm sorry!" she said. "I didn't mean to say it that way. But, yes, in case you're wondering, Reverend, I have found pictures of your wife with my husband. They will never see the light of day, if you help me with this."

He stared ahead, unseeing, pained. She crushed the last cigarette from her pack of Chesterfield's into the ashtray. She welcomed the silence. She used the time to take a Canon 35 mm camera and two rolls of thirty-six exposure Kodak black-and-white film out of her bag.

"I figured things were about as you described them. See-through mirrors are nothing new. Everett used a similar setup years ago," she said while placing the camera in front of Maefield. "He knows tricks with cameras the CIA hasn't thought of yet. Anyway, I purchased this camera yesterday. It's simple . . . well . . . almost. I've added a few features to allow close-up photography. Reaching across the desk, she demonstrated how to focus the camera as well as other camera functions. "You adjust for light, motion of subject, focus, aim and shoot. Try it." She waited for her instructions to sink in, watched him practice. He fumbled just looking through the viewfinder. "Reverend, you must hold the camera steady."

"Marie, I can't do this!"

"Then let me! Tell me how to get into the room and I'll hide behind the wall all night if I have to."

Maefield struggled with her suggestion. Just then, the telephone rang.

If he welcomed the opportunity for diversion, he did not show it. With obvious irritation, he grabbed the phone off its cradle. He listened without comment, then explained that he was busy and could not be disturbed. A long pause followed. Marie overheard Rhonda's voice. Who else would scold him in German? While he talked, Marie loaded the camera and tried to appear uninterested in his conversation. Suddenly, he changed to German and his tone became harsh and excited. When he switched back to English, he weakly explained he had a visitor. If the caller at the manse wanted to come over and wait outside his study, she should do so. He could not say how much longer he would be. There followed another period of listening. Abruptly he hung up. He smiled at Marie.

"I apologize for the interruption, Marie. My wife reminds me I have someone waiting at the manse. Now, where were we?"

"The studio! You were going to tell me how to get in there without notice. I want to try tonight."

"No one will be there, Marie. With this bloody storm forecast, we've cancelled everything at church. Before Everett left this noon, he informed me he had alerted his staff to finish their chores and lock up tight. He's ordered them here by six tomorrow to shovel snow. I took his instructions to mean he has no plans to return tonight . . . "

"Yes, I know. He spends Sunday afternoons barhopping in Atlantic City. I rarely see him at all on Monday. But I have a feeling he'll show up here late tonight." She held her hand across the desk. "You do have a key, Reverend?"

He took out his wallet, fumbled inside a change pocket and slipped out a brass key. "Please be careful. If he catches you . . . " She didn't wait for him to finish, plucked the key from his hand and stood up. "If he loses his temper, he could kill you!"

"Don't worry. I know my husband," she said, enclosing the key and her camera in her bag. "I'll return your key after I get what I want."

"No need to. I keep a second copy on my key ring."

"Anything else I should know?"

"Yes and this is very important. If the ceiling lights are on and flickering when you enter the storage room, leave them that way. If you flip the light switch again, as it is almost instinctive to do, the restart will correct the lighting problem. If he comes in the room after you and sees the fluorescent lamps glowing normal, he knows an unsuspecting person has been there or is there then. He's very clever. I'm surprised he hasn't caught me by now. Somehow I've always managed to get in there while he's busy posing his model or before he has arrived with one."

Maefield removed his glasses and sat back to stare at the ceiling. He made no effort to get up as Marie stood and got her coat. She paused by his chair before opening Shepherd Door.

"I know what addiction is, Reverend, and how hard to break bad habits," she said sympathetically. "I'm sure there are people who can help you."

She saw his head nod ever so slightly as she let herself out.

*   *   *

It was snowing lightly as Marie climbed the garden stairs to the cloister. Proceeding to Cathedral Drive, she recognized a yellow Ford station wagon parked a hundred feet beyond the manse. She wondered why Madge Todd was visiting on a day like this. She reflected on the telephone call from Rhonda. Madge must be the person who was waiting to see Maefield.

Madge, younger by eight years, had once treated Marie like a big sister. Nor was Marie happy about Madge "kowtowing"— as Marie understood it—to Rhonda. "They get a college degree and they think they're better than the rest of us," she intrigued.

In the next moment, Marie turned off Cathedral Drive, made her way behind the manse, crossed the back lawn and skidded down the steep, wooded hill to the parking lot. From there she made her way to the ground floor entrance of the annex. It had taken fifteen minutes to complete the roundabout trip, but she felt confident she had made it this far without anyone seeing her. She had, however, one more obstacle to overcome. Everett's assistant custodian's car was in the parking lot, a sure sign that Roger Jones was on duty. Fortunately, he had left the door to the annex unlocked, so that Marie slipped quietly into the building and then along the corridor that serviced classrooms on the ground floor. Midway, she heard the familiar sound of metal chairs collapsing and getting stacked in a chair cart. A light was on in the room and Marie looked in to see Roger's back toward her. She quickly moved past the doorway; then, carefully cushioning the sound of every door she opened and closed, she advanced into the tunnel passage to the furnace and coal room where the obnoxious noise of steam heat blasting to distant registers filled the dark, dirty room. Glad to have that behind her, she opened the door into the storage room and sure enough, just as the Reverend had warned, fluorescent ceiling lights flickered. Following his advice, she let them be, and found her way through the erratic darkness. Sighting the foot brake, she released it to roll the mattresses into their slot. At the hidden door, she confidently rolled them back. Just enough light filtered over the mattress barrier to see how to ease her key into the doorknob, so that without hesitation she proceeded into a dark outer hallway. Right away, she realized she was not alone.

Women's voices, an argument, Rhonda's gruff German accent penetrated where Marie stood. She should flee this instant, she thought. Instead, she opened the door into the narrow space behind the walls, where, under brilliant lighting, behind the window-mirror, she saw a naked Rhonda backing Madge into a corner. Madge had a frightened look on her face. Marie set the f. stop on her lens, adjusted focus and began shooting. Madge tried to get around her and Rhonda stopped her with a slap to the face, then, shoved her across the wide bed. The action troubled Marie, but she would not get into the middle of a lovers' quarrel, which was how she saw the drama unfolding before her lens. In quick sequence, she shot again as Rhonda fell on top of Madge and held her down. After adjusting her camera's focus and light, she clicked up close through the tenth frame as Madge fought to free herself. She took a picture of Madge's face as if six inches away, a spit of blood trailing off her lip. Backing the lens off, Marie focused on the two women as they lay motionless. Marie focused again as Rhonda moved to the side and began massaging Madge's back and—without Madge resisting—undressing her, then fornicating over her. Marie took the moment to duck down and crawl around the corner to the see through the phony mirror at the side of the bed. She had eight pictures left on the first roll and popped up to photograph from this different view. Now, she caught Madge standing over Rhonda, enjoying her oral attention, and wrestling her to the mattress where she became the aggressor. Marie focused and clicked until she ran out the roll and had to reload. She changed film and, after taking several shots, she decided to go back to the other mirrored window. She was about to crawl around the corner when she looked ahead to see someone standing in front of the glass. With horror, she backed off. Seconds passed before she summoned courage to peek and—as she suspected—Reverend Maefield stood staring at the women wreathing on the bed. She hid from view until she heard the door slam. Rising to her feet, she stood to look through the mirrored glass and clicked away as Madge left the bed. She could hear muffled shouts, but mostly there was silence as Madge went around the room picking up her clothes, and soon disappeared into the bathroom. She then photographed Rhonda as she dressed and reclaimed her classic appearance.

Marie sat on the floor and rested her camera, her mind conflicted and pained by the incredible and wild scene she had imprinted on film. Suddenly, she heard vague voices on the other side of the wall. She peered into the studio to see Madge and Rhonda standing across from each other fully dressed. Madge looked more composed, though her face remained grim and her eyes teary. Marie took a final picture as Madge rebuffed Rhonda's attempt at a kiss. Then the lights turned off and doors slammed behind them.

Marie waited ten minutes in absolute darkness before exiting. She near panicked when the mattresses didn't move, but soon figured out how to disengage the brake. She came out slowly, carefully returning the mattress bundle to their former place. She toured through the storage room, the fluorescent bulbs continuing their irritating flicker, and opened a door leading to the manse stairs. Along the walls of the well-lit room, she saw exactly what she had prayed for—rack on rack of bottled wines and liquors.

"Maefield won't miss one" she said to justify her theft.

She removed a fifth of twelve-year Scotch and unscrewed the cap. Everyone knew the minister drank only the best. She returned to the storage room, where she climbed on top of a shoulder-high stack of mattresses and bundled her coat into a ball to use as a pillow. Hot and sweating, she unbuttoned her shirt and pulled it out of her blue jeans, then, took off her boots and stretched out on her back. Bringing the liquor bottle to her lips for her first taste in over a year, she fought off vulgar feelings seeking outlet in her body. "God, don't they arrest people for that anymore?" she said, "and Madge; of all the women I know, she's the last I would expect of that kind of thing. If ever I wanted to commit blackmail . . . " She could not complete the sentence. "Scandalous! Fucking scandalous!"

Marie had always been a loner. Everett, so extroverted, was supposed to have taken that away from her. Instead, she had wrapped herself more completely into her shell, though, if she had learned anything from all her therapy and AA meetings, it was to break away from dependence on an abusive husband. Stealing the pictures from his footlocker, coming here this afternoon, her whole desire for divorce, were ways to liberty. She sucked from her whiskey bottle like an infant with a nipple and thought again about the scene she had witnessed, how her record of it could give her the easy life forever. She muttered and not too quietly, "All that hatred Everett has for the Tompkins. What he wouldn't pay for a show like I just saw and to know his own mistress had led the assault."

Marie knew the liquor would float her into unconsciousness. Once begun, she couldn't stop. She recalled a speaker at AA confessing, *"Twelve year scotch is especially good after the wagon. Nothing runs as smooth."* "I agree," she cooed and gulped a long swallow. She didn't stop until she emptied the bottle. Soon she fell as close to comatose as a person can without inviting death.

What awoke her were loud voices. Again, she couldn't miss Rhonda's accent. Were they coming back, she wondered, Madge and Rhonda? She looked at her wristwatch. It was ten minutes to ten. She had been out like a light for five hours. In the light of the blinking fluorescents, she peeped over the side of her perch at Rhonda, blindfolded like one of his regulars, Everett leading her. "Hell, he's drunker than I am," she exclaimed in a low woozy voice, as Everett swayed and almost fell, then slid the mattress section in. He did not push them back. Marie slipped into her boots and hung her camera by its strap over her shoulder. Her legs waddled as she climbed down and moved across the floor. This time she would have her own pictures, she thought. She got out her key and ever so carefully, she made her way into the enclosed little hall.

Perhaps she was too drunk to consider the danger, the rage that would be committed against her if Everett caught her. She listened against the door to the studio, heard laugher and excited voices. She opened the door into the tight space behind the false walls and mirrors, the glass looking out on another scene of debauchery. Her camera focused on a masked man naked from the waist down, his hands bound behind his back as he lay on the bed and as Everett and Rhonda engaged him in sexual acts. Eight pictures, that was all. The roll of film ran out. She wished she had another, but it was enough. She had more than what she needed. This time she didn't care that Rhonda would serve her purposes.

She raced from the secret room to the parking-lot exit, thinking she would go up over the hill, the same way she had come in. She would go through Tompkins City Park to Nick's where she had parked her car. But that plan changed abruptly.

Opening the door to the parking lot, the storm exploded in her face. A great snowdrift lay across the path. She didn't even have her coat. She had left it on top of the mattress stack. She had no choice but to stay. She ran up the annex stairs, through the hallway to where the secretary's office joined Shepherd House. There were no lights on in the hall. She looked out a window on to the parking lot below. She heard the garage doors before the truck appeared from underneath. Everett, the crazy fool, was backing out of the garage, off to somewhere, plowing through the snow as if driving a bulldozer. She watched him as he swayed and ripped his way out of the parking field and was gone. She began to tremble, the first time she had done so since her binge began. She felt a gentle hand rest on her shoulder.

"Marie, are you all right?" she heard and recognized the pastor's voice. She turned and looked into his face. She didn't know what to say. She wanted to ask how he could not know. He had looked through that window as she had. How could he love Rhonda? She said nothing, but began to sob. He put his arm over her shoulder and led her through the office into his study.

"You don't have to say anything, Marie. I knew you were there this afternoon. I could feel your presence," he said as he sat in a comfortable chair by the warm fire and bade her to take the seat across from him. Suddenly self-conscious of her open blouse, she buttoned it to her neck. He acted as though he hadn't noticed, but she was sure he had.

"Madge Todd was a surprise," he sighed. "I feel badly for her. Yet, I should have suspected it. Rhonda has few friends who are not also lovers. When I saw Madge just before she left the manse this afternoon, she appeared nervous. I reacted stupidly and I believe she suspected me of having seen them. As for Rhonda, all these years I have ignored her ways." He leaned back in his chair. He put his feet on the ottoman. "Rhonda is mentally incorrigible, you know. It goes back to when she was a teenager in Nazi Germany. She thinks I am ignorant of those years and to some degree, I am. The Nazis stole her life when they conditioned her, made her crazy for sex, a nymphomaniac. Yes! You have to call it something and that is as good a description of Rhonda as any I know. She can no more control her compulsion for sex than you for a drink of whiskey."

Marie stared at the floor. She had to listen. She wanted to argue against the comparison, but didn't know how. He paused to watch her face, seeking some sign of understanding. When she showed none, he went on. "As you saw, Rhonda is bisexual. Only with women, she controls the situation and with men, she lays down like a slave for her master."

"So, you were back there, behind the side mirror when Rhonda came in with Everett . . . and that other man?"

"Yes," he nodded. "While you clicked your pictures in front, I was at the other glass. I wouldn't have cared if you had discovered me. I don't understand my mental state anymore." He moved out of his chair briefly to ease a new log on to the fire. Sparks and glowing embers spit onto the hearth. He sat back in his chair and rocked as he stared at her. "Maybe I'm sicker than Rhonda," he said wistfully and just as quickly dropped the subject. "Your coat, Marie? Where did you leave it? Do you remember?"

"I left it downstairs . . . I think on top of a pile of mattresses. I had fallen asleep."

There was a long silence. He lit his pipe and, after puffing several times, he turned to his sherry and sipped slowly.

"It gets very chilly in parts of India. My father had his coat stolen one night, and the next morning, we saw it on the back of a tall beggar boy. It was obviously too nice a coat for this lad, although, in fact, it was a cheap garment by the English standard. I said to my father, 'There is your coat! Will you ask for it?' Father stood behind me and placed his hands on my shoulders. I was a child of eight at the time and felt instantly cold as he took my warm coat off of me. He walked to the beggar, whose little wife or sister—I don't know what their relationship was—stood next to him. My father draped my little coat over her shoulders. 'There,' my father said, 'the son of Christ makes this gift to you,' and he pointed at me, my lips chattering in the cold. As we walked away, I asked my father why he had given away my coat. He said, 'Because you believed the coat belonged to you. In the presence of misery, son, nothing belongs to us.' Marie, I will find your coat and give it to someone in need. In the meantime, take my coat. You are cold and in misery; you need my coat more than I do."

Abruptly, Maefield rose to his feet and went to the bookshelf closet, where he took his coat off a hanger and walked back to drop it across Marie's lap. After smoking another cigarette, and as he puffed on his pipe, she told him she had to get home.

"I worry Everett might start searching for me."

"Well, what do I know?" he responded. "You can't tell about that man. I didn't expect him here tonight, now did I? How bad a judge of character I am and a worse judge of a guilty man's intentions. But no, Marie. He'll drop off his passenger and then he'll return to the studio. He and Rhonda will stay together until morning. I shall go down shortly for another look."

He appeared unruffled by the thought, but struck his pipe aggressively against the hearth, shaking out the dead ashes before fitting the pipe stem into his breast pocket.

"Well, I want to go," she said, standing. "Thank you for your kindness. I'm sorry for what you have had to learn. I know it hurts."

He sighed deeply. "I will have to resign, Marie. I've already written my letter, described everything. I'll call the police in the morning. It's all over. I said my wife needs help? Me too!"

"I have to go."

"How will you get home? Your car is snowbound by now. If you parked on the street, the snowplows have certainly buried it."

"I'll walk. It'll do me good. It's less than four miles. Everett will pull my car out when I tell him I had to abandon it after going into town for beer," she laughed. "Will you do me one favor, Reverend Maefield? Can I leave my camera and film here?"

"And what do you want me to do with them?"

"Throw the film into the fire, if you wish. I leave it to you."

"The fire is a good idea, Marie! I will stand with you against Everett. You don't need pictures. We can't let what we learned today destroy Madge Todd, or reduce our own character, low as they may have reached."

As she passed to exit through Shepherd Door, she slid the camera strap off her shoulder and laid it and the roll of exposed film on his desk. She bundled Maefield's heavy coat around her against the wind.

Without his coat, she would have frozen to death that night. It took her almost three hours to walk four miles, most of it over unplowed roads. At home, she collapsed in exhaustion.

Like everyone else in Tompkinsville, Marie awoke that morning to the news of Reverend Maefield's murder. Her shock and grief were limitless. She shivered in fear that Everett was somehow involved in the killing, and her heart skipped a beat when, a week later, she saw Everett with the new camera she had left on Maefield's desk. She hoped Reverend Maefield had burned the film before Everett found it, but inwardly she believed otherwise. Three weeks later, she found her light coat hanging in the church's clothes-for-the-needy room. That afternoon, she learned police were looking for Reverend Maefield's winter coat, described as heavy black-dyed wool and well worn.

Petrified that Everett or a search by the police would find the coat, she took it from where it had hung in a hall closet and burned it in the backyard fireplace.

*   *   *

Marie lowered her head into her hands and sobbed, her glass drained and her bottle empty.

CHAPTER 17

A DEATH IN THE FAMILY

Late Wednesday Afternoon, June 13

News of Michael Todd's death had spread quickly across the land bursting with new life from its spring planting. By noon, a constant flow of visitors had begun arriving at the home and farm of Walter Tompkins, for it was here that Madge Todd cuddled in the warm embrace of her mother. Madge knew, however, that others depended on her for solace. For their sake, she had to show strength. Thus, she left her mother's side, wiped her eyes dry and announced it was time for her to inform Chip and Dudley about their father's death.

The Grimms volunteered to get Chip from school.

When the nine-year-old saw them, in his heart he knew something was amiss. Indeed, he had thought it strange when the school principal had told him his mother would not make it to the science fair. So when his aunt and uncle arrived, saying only that his mother would explain things to him, he knew something awful had happened.

Early this morning, a neighbor had taken Dudley to play at their house. Bob went to retrieve him.

*   *   *

Madge waited for the boys in the backyard of their home, where

Michael had built a play area fifty feet from the old packing barn. Swings, a long slide, monkey bars and a tree hut made this a fun place. Close by, Michael had built a picnic table and a large brick fireplace. He had wanted to put in a swimming pool, but Madge had objected by voicing concern about the children's safety. Maybe in another year, they had agreed. She thought about her worry about the safety of their children. And yet, life is a risk at every age. She wished she had let Michael go ahead with the pool project.

In faith, Madge believed God had a place for life after death. This belief consoled her, and she assured her sons that death meant passing from one home to another, from a visible life on earth to an invisible, spiritual one in heaven. She had no use for those who preached about purgatory or sinners sentenced to hell. She did not believe God caused the death of Michael, only that now in the course of his death, Michael could take his place with other saved sinners. If she had learned anything from Reverend Maefield, it was that pain, suffering and death are part of life. God built them into creation. No matter how good or bad a person lives, he or she could not avoid suffering, no more than Jesus did when he died on the cross. We have to accept heartache and death, Madge believed, not as the consequence of sin, but because of our freedom as creatures of God.

She could not explain this faith to a four—or a nine-year-old. She could hardly explain it to herself. But, as she folded her arms around each child and kissed his tears, she knew she had both given and received the peace of Christ. She admired how resilient and accepting her children were. She answered their questions with as much honesty as she dared and—after saying a prayer with them—she let them return to their play. They would need more time to come to terms with it all, just as she would. Surprisingly, she returned to the home of her parents more at peace with herself than she had felt in years.

*   *   *

By early afternoon, more information about the accident

began to surface. Rumors were flying. Walter tried to dispel them by explaining how Michael had simply tried to do a good deed by giving the young lady a ride home from her place of work in Atlantic City. Walter refused to believe anything more than that was possible and he bristled with anger every time anyone suggested otherwise.

Only telling her children of their father's death was more difficult for Madge than when Michael's father and mother came by. Madge had always treasured their love and she knew how deep the tragedy wounded them. Jessie Todd, Michael's father, like her father, had worked hard all his life. As with so many of the older truck farmers in the county, his hands were tough as leather, his face cracked and browned by too many suns, his body stooped and tottering from lifting heavy wooden crates and burdensome farm machinery. Michael, their only child, born when they were past child-rearing age, was seen as a special gift from God. They had often said, "Only old Abraham and Rachel of Bible fame were more blessed than they were."

Just as the elderly couple took seats on the porch, the county coroner telephoned and asked for a member of the family to come by to identify Michael's body. After that, there would be an autopsy. Jessie said it was his duty to go. Walter said he would drive. Jessie left his wife, Wilma, at the house and, with Walter steadying his arm, he got into Walter's shining white Cadillac. Heart wrenching and touching, the gallant old friends clung to each other in a common grief. When they returned an hour later, neither one could control his emotions. Walter fell into Greta's arms. He had seen the twisted and mutilated body of his son-in-law and he would have to remember it that way for the rest of his life. Jessie looked like a ghost and neither did he make any effort to hold back his tears.

In the lingering silence of their arrival, Walter overheard Madge asking when Reverend Flynn would be calling. She fully expected his pastoral visit by now and did not understand his absence. She wanted to plan the funeral and begin the long march to reclaiming her own life. Walter decided he better tell her

Reverend Flynn was out of town and no one knew when he would be back. He didn't say anything more, except that he had telephoned Reverend Scarpelli and he would be by presently. At that awkward moment, Detective Chester Walsh drove up the long driveway. Michael and Madge could trace their friendship with Chester back to high school. Madge had acted as Chester's campaign manager when he ran for Senior Class President. His victory ushered in a big change in the way classmates related to Negroes then and Chester considered Madge and Michael's support as making a big difference in his own attitude. There wasn't any contact between them during their college years and beyond. But one night four years ago, Michael had come home after men's basketball practice at First Church and behind him stood Chester Walsh. He was the best surprise Madge had had in years. She really adored him. The three of them talked for three hours. Chester told them he had just joined the Tompkinsville Police Department to work in the detective division. A difficult task lay ahead. He would be the first Negro hired in that division and had won the appointment over more experienced white officers. Nevertheless, good at what he did, decorated for bravery, he had an excellent record in the Jersey City PD. Confident that the majority of officers understood and would accept him, he went to work in the homicide division. That night he also related that he and his wife of two years were expecting their first child in another month. As it turned out, Dudley and Chester's boy were born within hours of each other and Madge had made it her mission that they should be friends and grow up together.

Madge ran to greet Chester and hugged him as she would a brother. That's when he broke down. His partner missing and presumed dead and now Michael. Chester could hold his emotions for only so long. How was he ever going to get back to being the policeman who had also come here to inquire about Everett Wheeler?

Arm in arm, Chester and Madge walked the rest of the way to the house. She introduced Chester as Michael's and her friend. She took him inside where a great spread of food occupied the dining-room table. Chester filled his plate while Madge brought him a tall glass of ice tea. She found him a TV tray and sat opposite him. She picked at a piece of pie and drank coffee as Chester enjoyed his samplings of hot and cold dishes.

"Tell me, don't spare me. I want to know, Chester."

"In time, Madge! Not now. The fact is I don't know anything. I've been on another case. My partner is missing and that's all I've had on my mind. In fact, your dad broke the news to me about Michael. I met your dad at the church early this morning. Oh, these turnip greens are good! Who do I have to thank for this?"

Madge ignored his attempt to distract her.

"What's going on, Chester? Why were you at the church? I overheard someone say that Reverend Flynn has disappeared. Is there a connection?

He reached over and took her hand, felt it tremble.

"Madge, believe me, I don't know!"

"Who was the woman with Michael? Chester, I know he had a female with him and that she was also killed."

"Listen, girl, you're telling me something I haven't heard. Believe me, when I learn more, I'll let you know."

She realized it was useless and unfair to continue probing.

"Are you ready for dessert? Apple pie, pudding?"

"Madge," he said, looking directly into her flushed eyes, "I need to talk to your dad about Everett Wheeler."

"So that's it! He has something to do with Jerry's absence, hasn't he? Was Michael working for Everett, delivering one of his hussies?"

"Madge, please! I've no information that would connect Michael's accident with Everett Wheeler."

Just then, Chester looked up to see Walter standing behind his daughter. Walter rested his hands on her shoulders. His eyes were riveted on the police detective.

"Sweetpea!"

It was his very affectionate name for Madge.

"Will you excuse Detective Walsh? He and I have a personal matter to discuss."

She started to protest and Walter became firm. "Sweetpea! I don't want you to hear this."

More neighbors and church folk had arrived, all of them carrying plates of food or soft drinks, offerings expressing grief and willingness to do anything for the family. There was no more space on the table and the kitchen refrigerator was full. As her mother greeted the newcomers, Bob busily accepted their casserole dishes and platters, carried them out to a waiting car in which to shuttle food to the Todd house or the company freezers for safe preservation.

Madge saw her mother signal her. She had people to greet. Plaintively, she stood up, cuddled in her father's gentle arms and then reluctantly moved away. It concerned her deeply that her father could not discuss his business with Chester Walsh in her presence. As she moved off, she said her farewell.

"Thank you for coming, Chester. And please call me when you know anything new."

Walter pushed the chair closer to the little table at which Chester ate and sat down.

Walter had begun to grieve his own sins a few hours before he learned of Michael's death. After helping Jorge load up the produce truck, Jorge dropped him off at the house. Walter knew sleep would be impossible, so he planted himself in a porch rocker. From there he waited for dawn and recounted the mistakes he had made in the last several hours as well as many more over the course of raising his children. Mostly, he felt ashamed of himself, and more so, he hated how he had reacted to Everett's pictures. While thinking how to make amends, he heard the phone ring. Greta picked up to hear Madge sobbing and her anguished words.

Things could not get worse, but they had. After leaving Greta with Madge, Walter tried calling Jerry Flynn at the manse, but there was no answer. He drove to Shepherd House only to find Walsh there and to learn that the minister was missing. He would bet his life that Everett was involved. But most of all, he considered what a mess he had made of things.

Now he told Walsh why he should be on the lookout for Everett Wheeler.

*   *   *

At the Sunrise Motel, Everett slept soundly on his makeshift bed until six o'clock. He awoke with a start and shouted his hostages into wakefulness. He instructed that each one had five minutes to visit the "head" and dress. All the while, he stood by the open bathroom door waving his gun and watching every move.

"Rhonda, go get us some food! There's a supermarket a mile south of here." Everett handed her the car keys.

During Rhonda's absence, Jerry and Charlene sat idly on the edge of the bed as Everett lounged across from them seated on the counter. He fiddled with his *Colt .45*, chain smoked and lamented the evils of racial integration. When Jerry tried challenging him, he responded by pointing his gun at him. Jerry stopped in mid sentence. Charlene asked if they could watch television. Everett offered no objection as long as they held the sound to a minimum.

They tuned into a Philadelphia station broadcasting national and regional news.

"Tompkinsville police are puzzled by the disappearance early today of one of their own. Detective John Burroughs, a twenty-six-year member of the force and Chief of Homicide, was last seen Tuesday night . . . " The TV screen switched from a police portrait photograph of the detective to a distraught Mrs. Burroughs outside her home. " . . . when he left his Tompkinsville residence." The television commentator reported Burroughs was last seen backing out of his driveway at ten thirty last night on police business in his unmarked police cruiser. "Later this morning, the Ford Galaxy was discovered behind Grady's Bar on Highway Twelve . . . " Newsreel showed Grady's and the police car under scrutiny by police.

Charlene and Jerry stared in disbelief. They were afraid to

look at each other, but each one felt the other's hand turn cold. Everett reached across and turned the television off.

"We don't need to know more about a dumb cop. Probably got dropped by one of Grady's drunken spics."

Jerry and Charlene sat in stone silence. Everett amused himself by polishing his gun again and every now and then taking aim, first at Jerry, then at Charlene. He smiled each time, and made shooting noises in the same way a child would do with a toy gun.

A knock on the door brought him to his feet. He opened to Rhonda. Out of paper bags, she drew the makings for sandwiches, cold beer, a bottle of apple juice and potato chips. She included a bottle opener, which Everett quickly grabbed to lap off a cap from a beer bottle. She laid out the food on the counter. They took turns making sandwiches. All the while, Everett complained about Rhonda's choice of cold cuts.

"Never send a Kraut to get food. All Krauts know is sausage and pumpernickel. It don't matter if it's breakfast, lunch or supper . . . sausage and pumpernickel."

Jerry noted Everett wasn't complaining about the beer. He sucked two bottles of cold brew into his gullet before Rhonda handed him a sandwich. Charlene and Jerry shared a beer between them.

"Reverend, did you thank the Lord for our bounty?" Everett asked with his mouth full and his hand raising his third beer. Jerry ignored him. "Well, preacher, ain't that what you're supposed to do? What the hell do we pay you for?"

"Pray yourself, Everett," he finally muttered.

Everett looked around. "Bless you, Father!" he offered and threw the empty bottle toward the wastebasket, missing. The bottle bounced across the floor.

Using a paper cup from the bathroom, Rhonda drank a small portion of apple juice.

"Now look at Rhonda here drink'n the sweets of the apple. She don't like American beer, you know! Thinks it's too watery. Ain't that right, Rhonda?" She ignored him, turned her back so she would not have to look at him. He made a sour face and then an obscene gesture.

When Jerry started to pick up the trash that lay about the room, Everett laughed at him and called him *Miss Jerry*. "I wonder about you, Miss Jerry?" he said. "How'd Miss Jerry do in bed, Charlene? Did 'she' fire a burst in you? Or, all over you? What you need Miss 'Pee-Dick' is a real man," he yelled and stood up to demonstrate, moving his hips back and forth.

They frowned at Everett's amusement but said nothing. Suddenly he grabbed Rhonda, who sat on the bed close to him, in a killer headlock and pulled her up as he rose to his feet. With his right hand, he tore open her blouse and pulled down her brassiere.

"Come here, Miss Jerry!" he shouted. "Put your mouth on that sucker and know what it's like to milk a real whore."

Blood had rushed to Everett's head, his face red and sweaty. Rhonda tried to pull away. Jerry feared he would snap her neck and shouted to stop. Everett finally relented and loosened his grip. Rhonda angrily slapped him hard across the face. A second time she hit him in the stomach with her fist and fled to the bathroom. He laughed, unfazed by her response. Charlene started to follow Rhonda, but Everett blocked her, spun her around and locked her in a bear hold, his hands clawing at her breasts.

"You dirty perverted slob!" she screamed as she kicked his shins and wrestled free. Jerry took a step forward and swung. The blow struck Everett's shoulder, but before Jerry could throw another punch, Everett pushed Charlene into him. The two fell backwards on to the bed. As they tried to recover, Everett was on to them, smashing his knee into Jerry's chest and wrapping his hand around Charlene's throat. Instantly, he had his gun out of his jacket pocket and pressed to Jerry's temple.

"Now or later?" he screamed, his mouth so close Charlene felt his phlegm spray her face. Jerry, frozen in fright, feared the gun would discharge. His chest ached as the heavy man applied more pressure. Charlene felt her breath slipping away. Her eyes filled with tears. Everett tightened his grip on her larynx. Coughing and retching, she started turning blue.

Rhonda was there now patting Everett's shoulder, begging him to stop. Her comforting may have saved their lives as slowly he relaxed his grip and released his hold on Charlene's throat, got off of Jerry and stood at full height above them, the muzzle of the gun still pointed at Jerry's head. He turned the gun on Charlene. Rhonda continued to appease him. His voice cracking with anger, he said to Charlene, "Don't think you're not going to get yours before this night is over." Charlene struggled to sit up. Her hands and knees shook to the degree that she couldn't have held anything or walked any distance. This time Everett raised his jacket and slid his weapon into his holster. As he did so, oddly, the most ludicrous observation entered Charlene's mind. As Jerry held her close, he heard her whisper, "Not once has he taken off that sick jacket; animal!"

"All right, enough of this. We're leaving. Let's get the hell out of here."

CHAPTER 18

FLIGHT TO MIDNIGHT

Wednesday Evening, June 13

Once more Jerry drove the Imperial, but now Everett lodged himself between Rhonda and Charlene, his gun, as before, resting on Jerry's right shoulder. His menacing mood, as evidenced at the motel, continued in the way he badgered Jerry with directions that took them onto rough-graveled or all dirt roads.

In the distance, lightning strikes signaled an approaching thunderstorm. In less than an hour, it would be dark.

*   *   *

Marie Wheeler watched from the window as two police cars and the unmarked cruiser she had seen earlier arrived. They had driven up with only their flashing lights in the early dusk alerting her to their presence. One policeman held a dog on a leash. She heard the dog bark excitedly and watched as the men in blue followed the hound around the house.

Marie moved to the kitchen table and waited. She poured another glass of whisky and lit a cigarette. She heard a knock on the back door and got up to admit Detective Chester Walsh and three uniformed officers. Without saying a word, Walsh held out his badge and showed her a search warrant. She became unnerved when she saw the policemen had their guns drawn and rushed to different locations in the house. More police vehicles arrived and two additional plainclothes detectives entered the house. Police were everywhere—attic, bedrooms and the business area in back. She could hear noises below in the crawlspace. One officer searched the kitchen, opening drawers and cabinets. Another asked for a key to the darkroom. She handed it to him without protest. Chester Walsh came in to ask her for the combination to the upstairs footlocker. After she showed ignorance, she heard an electric saw cutting the lock.

She looked out the living room window to see a fire engine had driven across the lawn to the far corner, its engine noisily generating electricity to floodlight the area as police personnel cleared away old farm equipment. Marie knew it was all over. She went back to the kitchen table and waited for Detective Walsh to ask her cooperation.

*   *   *

Everett knew the back roads and farm paths of southern New Jersey in the same way a fish knows every hollow in its small pond. He directed Jerry over trails that appeared to go nowhere, but suddenly emerged from forested areas, crossed county roads and resumed on the boarders of open fields. Tractor paths ran under power lines and alongside orchards and grape arbors. In spite of the solitary darkness, Everett knew where to halt, turn and weave. For the last fifteen minutes, Jerry had followed Everett's orders to drive slowly with only his parking lights on. Charlene now sat up front between them. In the back seat, Rhonda appeared in a trance, seeing and hearing nothing. Charlene believed she had taken a narcotic of some kind. All the while, Everett leaned, watched, searching the darkness for landmarks. It was ten minutes to ten on the dashboard clock when he shouted at Jerry to stop in front of a small utility shed and to turn on the headlights.

Drops of water pelted the windshield and Jerry wondered if they were getting residue from the spray of rolling watering cannon. He realized, however, as flashes of lightning ignited the sky and thunder followed in rapid succession, rain was falling. The storm, threatening since leaving the motel, had caught up with them.

Everett reached to turn off the ignition, then, he took the keys and put them in his pocket. He motioned Jerry out of the car and directed him to walk in the beam of the headlights. He followed close behind. Standing in front of the utility shack, Everett aimed his Colt .45 at the padlock and fired one shot. The lock shattered. The smell of spent gunpowder amid the pungent odor of steaming fields filled the air. Everett pulled open the rickety door and took out a full five-gallon metal container of gasoline.

"Fill it up!" he told Jerry.

Jerry lifted the heavy can and carried it to the car. The Imperial had run on empty for the last half hour. Everett was no fool. Indeed, Jerry estimated his intelligence off the charts. Add to this his cunning and resourcefulness, and you had a dangerous mind. Whatever he planned for them, Jerry figured Everett would leave no trace of his own culpability.

As Jerry poured gasoline into the tank of his car, he saw Everett take a telephone from the shack. Farmers often had such an arrangement for emergencies and telephone lines crisscrossed the fields. A telephone pole stood just ten feet from the shed. Jerry surmised they couldn't be too far from highways and houses. They may even be close to Tompkinsville. He scanned the horizon for the church bell tower, which stayed lit from dusk to dawn. He reasoned the high trees to the north were hiding it. He listened for the ten o'clock toll, but did not hear it. After emptying the can of its last drop of fuel, he walked to where Everett sat in the open doorway of the shack, the phone poised at his ear. He tried to overhear, but Everett mostly listened.

"That's far enough," he shouted as Jerry approached. He covered the mouthpiece with his hand. "Drop the can on the ground. Turn the car lights off."

Jerry walked back to the car, reached in and pushed the

throttlelike switch. The sight of the shack and Everett's figure blended into the darkness surrounding it. Everett came up behind him and pointed the gun over his shoulder into the Imperial.

"Okay, Miss Fancy-panties, slide your little ass across the seat and get out. Stand here with boy-wonder."

Charlene complied. She took Jerry's hand. She feared worse things about to happen. Lightning flashes lit the fields, louder thunder cracked the air and rain fell steady. Wheeler shoved them to the rear of the car and touched along the trunk lid until he found the opening for the key. The lid sprung up and an interior light lit the compartment.

"Okay, preacher, into the trunk. And you get in there with him," he yelled slapping Charlene on the rear. "Keep your mouths shut. Any screams and I'll shoot through the back seat. Got it?"

They had no room to move. Jerry had felt cramped when Everett had put him here early this morning. He crouched into a near fetal position and Charlene folded into him.

"Maybe I'll kill you both now," Everett said.

He stood over them waving the gun, his face illuminated by the trunk light, and aimed. Jerry waited, his body tense, his mind resigned. Presently, Everett slammed the trunk lid, locking it. Jerry considered he might just as well have shot them. He worried about having enough air.

The car began moving at a fast pace over the bumpy field road. The back of Charlene's head rested against Jerry's chest. Again, he realized how brave she was. She's every bit as frightened as I am, he thought, but she isn't going to let on. If they died like this right here, it would be all right. He loved her very much. He folded his arm across her stomach and whispered into her ear, "Whatever happens I love you." She nodded and relaxed in his arms.

A little while later, they felt the car lurch over a high curb and abruptly they rode on smooth pavement, picking up speed. They went on like this for maybe twenty minutes. There were several turns and stops before they came to a complete standstill and the engine went dead. The air in the trunk had turned weak and stifling. Charlene coughed quietly and Jerry knew the signs; they were exhausting their supply of air. They heard car doors open and shut, then silence. It seemed an eternity. Charlene began straining for breath. Jerry tried to give her room, but his back was wedged against the frame. He managed to turn on his back and Charlene nudged her body around to face him. He thought it was over for them when the trunk lid disengaged and fresh air rushed in. So did strong arms lifting Charlene out and the lid slammed closed, banging Jerry's head as it fell.

Everett held his hand tightly over Charlene's mouth and his arm around her waist as he dragged her inside the church annex. She had no energy to resist and in minutes, he half carried her into the narrow underground passageway. Her head spun and she felt nauseous. She started to struggle. Everett pushed her hard against the wall. He held one hand to her throat and used his other hand to press the gun muzzle to her left breast. After holding her like that for several seconds, he yelled she was dead if she didn't cooperate, and pulled her around in front of him, her arm up behind her back, then, steered her like that all the way into the room she and Jerry had discovered four nights ago. She hardly recognized it until she saw the large bed—now stripped of its fancy sheets—and a few other furniture pieces. In the little light left on, seated motionless in a corner chair, she saw Rhonda.

Everett lifted Charlene off her feet and threw her heavily onto the wide bed.

"It's time," he shouted, staring down at her, a piece of Nylon rope gripped in his hands. "Rhonda gets you first. I promised her first licks. Right, Rhonda?" he sneered.

He pulled Charlene's wrists close to the headboard and wrapped the rope around them. She opened her eyes just in time to see the blow coming. As he bent over her, Rhonda had taken a batting stance with a length of two-by-four. She swung down on his back. Charlene saw his stunned face. He turned to see and ducked as she swung again, by inches missing his head.

"Why? You said I could have her after you! What are you doing, you crazy bitch?"

"No more!" Rhonda yelled. "You won't hurt anyone else," she stammered and again she swung the two by four, this time brushing his shoulder as he staggered to stay standing. Charlene rolled in Rhonda's direction to the floor. Scrambling beneath Rhonda's feet, she heard the gun go off. One shot! Rhonda legs buckled instantaneously, her upper torso dropped on to the mattress, the two by four dropping with her. Charlene crawled away from the kneeling body. She got to her feet to see Everett standing statuesque, his gun smoking, his face ruby red, his eyes flushed and showing surprise.

"No! No! No!" he screeched, the full meaning of what he had done taking over his emotions. And, in the next second, he stooped over Rhonda and began shaking her. "Get up, Rhonda! Don't die! Don't! I didn't mean . . . O Christ! . . . "

He rolled Rhonda on to her back. She bled from her chest. A dark stain grew broader and redder on her shirt and the pool of blood spread beneath her. Everett dropped his face to hers, alternately pleading and blowing breath into her silent mouth. Charlene, feeling the panic, frightened that her own life could go out as quickly, sneaked behind Everett.

Seeing Jerry's car keys on the chair, she reached for them and ran from the room. Racing through the coal basement, she smashed light bulbs as she passed beneath them, leaving the area in total darkness. She ran the length of the long underground passage and found her way out of the building. Rain had become torrential with lightning and thunder in sharp repetition. Charlene opened the car trunk lid.

"It's me, Jerry," she said reassuringly. He raised his head and then his body.

"It's okay. I'm all right. Jerry, Rhonda is dead. Everett shot her."

Jerry pulled himself out of the trunk and for a solid minute, they stood in the downpour, their arms locked around each other and neither one wanting to break their embrace. Charlene's eyes filled with tears and she cried loudly and unashamed. She fought herself to find words.

"I left Everett in the secret room with her," she managed to say. "She tried to defend me and he shot her," she stammered.

All at once, the glare of bright headlights caught them and they watched as a white Cadillac came along side and stopped a few feet away.

"I hate to interrupt you, Reverend," they heard. It was the recognizable voice of Walter Tompkins. Walter put an arm over Jerry's shoulder. "I'm so glad to see you two are all right. I hope you can forgive me, Jerry."

Jerry was ambivalent. If he only knew. In the headlights' reflective glare he saw the man's sad face. He reached for his arm.

"Walter, we need the police. Everett is in the church basement. There's an abandoned room below the manse. Mrs. Maefield is with him. She's dead. He shot her only minutes ago. We have reason to believe he may have murdered Doctor Maefield and also Detective Burroughs."

"I'll take care of him," Walter said. "But before I leave you I have to tell you there's more sad news. Michael Todd, my daughter's husband—he wrecked his pickup truck early this morning and was killed."

The harsh rain did not let up for sorrow. Lightning flashed close to them and the vibration from the thunder that followed shook them.

"No!" Jerry fumed. "No!" Walter's news was like the last drop in the cup of life. "This is a lot in one day, Walter. I'll call Madge as soon as I can. But let's contain Everett. And we need some medical assistance ourselves. He's down there armed. The police have to know how dangerous he is."

"I said I'd take care of him and I will," Walter retorted, his voice dropping to a less gentle cord.

Jerry and Charlene followed him to his car where he opened the back door, reached to the floor and came out with a long rifle. He quickly slipped it under his rain slicker.

"No, Walter! Let the police apprehend him. Stay out of this."

"He's family!" he shouted and shook off Jerry's attempt to restrain him.

"God forbid, Walter, there's been enough killing. Let me talk to him first."

"No!" Charlene screamed. "You've been close to death enough for one day. It's not our concern anymore."

Walter headed for the annex entrance. He had his key out and had the door locked behind him before Jerry could reach him.

"Quick, we'll go to the manse and call the police. The new manse key is with my car keys."

Charlene grabbed the keys from the lid lock. Jerry followed her into the car. They were as drenched as any two humans could be. She felt a chill in her bones as Jerry floored the Imperial and moved away from the Caddie. He was across the parking lot in seconds. They climbed the hill and unlocked the back door that led to the kitchen. A rancid odor fed their nostrils. Jerry snapped on the light switch, but there was no response. He repeated it, still nothing. He tried a lamp over the countertop next to the telephone, only there was no phone there. A flashlight beam came on, blinding him.

"I still have business with you two," Everett said, his voice low and clear, grave and hypnotic. "I knew you would come back here. You changed the locks, preacher. You made me waste a bullet on the front door, but no big loss. I have plenty more."

Vaguely, Jerry detected the outline of Everett's body during flashes of lightning.

"Put the gun down, Everett! Nothing can be accomplished now."

"If not for you and your Miss Dick, none of this would have happened. Rhonda wouldn't be dead. No one would know of our affair. I'd still have my little picture business. But you changed all that by snooping where you had no business."

"Please, Everett, at least, let Charlene go. I'll remain your hostage. Don't add more victims to your list."

"Shut up! You're already dead, preacher. It's her I want to keep alive a while longer."

"Well, here I am!" Charlene shouted as she stepped in front of Jerry to take the full beam of the flashlight. "Come on, Everett," she called, her voice seductive and enticing. She pushed Jerry back, slapped his hands in their continued effort to restrain her. "If I'm really all you want, come in close and stick it to me!" she beckoned, and took another step toward him. Raising her dress, her voice as sarcastic as she could make it, she exclaimed, "Now's the time to show me you're as good as you boast! Or, are you a fagot, who can't get it up for a woman?"

Training the flashlight on her midsection, Everett stepped forward. "I'll show you, Bitch!" he let fly and laid his gun on the countertop, then reached for her arm to swing her into possession. Too late, he saw the blade of a long kitchen knife. She thrust hard, catching him in the side, slitting his silk shirt just inside the lapel of his gaudy, silly jacket before slicing his flesh. But there she lost her grip, dropping her knife to the floor. Instant pain caused Everett to drop his flashlight, and to move back, where he grabbed his .45 handgun off the countertop. Jerry threw his weight into Charlene, pushing her ahead of him and around their stricken attacker. Together, they slammed their bodies to the floor and began to crawl out of sight. An instantaneous explosion from Everett's gun cracked the air, the bullet flying over their heads. Jerry found the flashlight and ditched the light, just before Everett blindly fired off another round, this one shattering the glass in the kitchen window.

Charlene and Jerry slithered across the dark floor, crawled out of the kitchen and into the sitting room, where they stumbled to their feet, slid open the deadbolt on the door to the cloister and ran outside. A loud burst from the .45 followed, the bullet pelting the ancient glass of the cloister door, then, ricocheting off the stone above their heads before chipping stone along the surface of the ceiling. Clinging to each other, they fled up the dimly lit cloister, desperate for a place to hide or a way to outlast their pursuer.

Jerry opened the gate to Shepherd House, but feared they would become open targets before they could reach the shelter. They looked back to see Everett staggering out of the manse. He fired at them, the bullet zipping above their heads, too close for comfort. They dashed ahead to try opening the door into the cathedral. Jerry pulled on the handle. The door moved in their direction. They slipped inside. Jerry slid the heavy plank lock forward. None too soon, they heard Everett pounding and kicking the door. For now, they were safe. The cathedral door had to be unbolted from inside. Charlene said their best hope was that someone had heard the gunshots and called the police. They needed time. Jerry knew Everett could find other ways into the cathedral. They ran up the dim stairway that opened to the narthex.

"We've got to hide," Jerry whispered as they limped into the great nave of the cathedral.

Only the tall, illuminated stained-glass windows and a dim spotlight over the altar lighted the sanctuary. This set a ghostly mood. Uneven shadows and darkness awaited them. Jerry turned on the flashlight. They started down the long center aisle.

"There's no chance. He'll be in here any minute."

They reversed themselves and returned to the narthex where they moved up the stairs to the balcony pews.

"I cut his gut," Charlene whispered. "Maybe he'll bleed to death before he gets in here." Suddenly Everett appeared from the door behind the choir pews.

"Fat chance," Jerry said as he took her hand.

Everett had no reason to be silent. "I'm going to get you! You're dead!" he bellowed, his rasping words echoing throughout the vaulted chamber.

They watched in the eerie light as Everett's bulky figure moved up the south aisle. He was holding his side and his pace appeared halting and tentative. He had another flashlight in his hand and he shined it inside and under the pews and then up on the balcony. Jerry took Charlene's arm and guided her to the back. He led the way to a door at the far end. It creaked as they

opened to a spiral stairway lit by dull light bulbs every ten steps
or so. Cautiously they ascended the steep, narrow, circling stairs
to a trap door giving access to the attic above the balcony. They
climbed into more darkness and crawled out onto a rough plank
floor. Jerry gently lowered the trap door and shined his flashlight
around an area contaminated by ages of dust and rat dung.

At the east side, they opened a door to the thin ledge circling
the cathedral nave, which Everett had used last Wednesday to
change light bulbs. Far below, they could make out the pews and
the low-lighted altar. Jerry silently closed the door and panned
his flashlight in the opposite direction; there a straight ladder
ascended to a ceiling panel.

"It must lead to the attic over the nave and to the bell tower,"
he whispered.

He motioned Charlene to start climbing. As she went up the
perilous hand-over-hand ladder, Jerry knelt by the trap door above
the stairs and listened, knowing he had heard Everett open the
creaky door below. Abruptly, the trap door sprung up, leaving
little time to react. Everett's big head rose above the floor, his
gun came to the fore. He was moving fast, Jerry swung the
flashlight, hitting Everett squarely in the nose. The Colt .45 fired.
Jerry fell over the trap door. He heard Everett squeal as the lid
crashed on his head. The bullet had missed Jerry's shoulder by
an inch and then chipped a hole out of a twelve-inch beam above.
Jerry headed for the ladder. Charlene had already pushed aside
the ceiling panel and boosted herself through the opening. She
took the flashlight from Jerry's hand as he passed above the
opening. They slid the panel into place.

"Maybe if we sit on it our combined weight will keep him
out," she suggested.

"No! I thought about that down below, but his bullets will
pass through. It's only plywood. Our best hope is time. He's hurt
bad. He's got to be tiring. We need to believe his injuries will
catch up with him. Let's go!"

Vented openings admitted a little outside light in the place
where they knelt. Scanning the darkness with the flashlight, they

saw the vast attic over the nave ceiling. Jerry panned the flashlight beam on electric wiring and hoists supporting the chandeliers. If they crawled that way, they would have to straddle a narrow catwalk. A slip either way and one or both could plummet through the thin plaster ceiling and fall to the nave floor.

To the west was an opening to the bell tower. Either way they faced a dead end, but Jerry reasoned they could buy more time climbing the tower. On hands and knees, crawling in that direction, they made their way over narrow planks. A near century of grime coated the rough wood boards. Rat dung, pigeon droppings and cobwebs were everywhere.

"Jerry, I hate to complain, but do you suppose on our next date you could take me someplace less dirty and where I won't have to skin my beautiful knees?"

"Hey, you said you wanted the whole tour, remember? Come on, crawl ahead of me . . . Point the flashlight."

Charlene led the way into the bell tower. It was not as dark here due to more venting in the tower walls. They stepped onto a solid floor grounding this level of the tower's interior. An electric motor, looking as ancient as the building itself, and serving as the clock for sounding the bell, took up part of the floor space. They heard a low whine as the mechanism moved clock hands high above. Without discussion, they climbed the narrow, steep stairs that circled the interior wall of the bell tower. A hundred steps above the machinery floor, they passed the giant clock bell, ten feet tall and twelve feet round, a stationary instrument, which sounded when hit by its outside clapper. Jerry showed his flashlight on the arrangement of steel cables and greased gears and where stone latticelike windows, which acted as primitive speakers, carrying the bell's sound to the outside, surrounded the scaffolding.

Out of breath, they took the last step on to a platform above the bell, seventeen stories high, inside a walled turret with narrow breaches looking out in all directions. A moist breeze greeted them and floodlights shown on the spire that was like a hat above them. They could go no higher unless they tried climbing the thirty-foot spire. Jerry shuttered at the thought. They looked out at a rain-soaked landscape. Lightning strikes etched the sky, but from the thunder that accompanied them, it seemed the heat of the storm had moved far off to the northeast. Below, they saw the streetlights of Tompkinsville, and for miles in all directions stretched the blank land of farms and pine forests. The bright glow of Atlantic City rested on the distant horizon and above the haze to the northwest, shown the glare of Philadelphia.

In the center of the platform, they looked down into a cutaway at the massive bell and the wood chamber that anchored it. Carefully, Jerry dangled his feet over the side and then twisted his body so that his stomach slid onto the bell's crown. The great bronze shell moved ever so slightly, a little give, so to speak, for when the clapper pounded its exterior lip. With nothing to hold on to, Jerry relied on his feet and the wide bell lip to stop his downward motion. From there, he twisted onto his back and then bridged his feet across the perilous emptiness. Pooling all his strength, he propelled his body forward into a confined space ten feet below the platform. Charlene followed him. Shorter and lighter, she put her back against the bell and began her slide to the edge. Sitting astride the frame, Jerry used his feet to stop her downward motion. She crouched as she put her hands in his and he pulled her into the constricted crevice. Quickly, she crawled behind him. Moving as far back in the scaffolding as they could, they positioned themselves on their sides. Charlene rested her chin against his back.

"We have to stop sleeping in places like this, Reverend," she said in a rueful tone.

"Quiet! Don't even breathe!" he whispered.

Below, they heard cautious footsteps stumbling up the tower stairs. The sound passed on the other side from where they hid. Then the bearer was on the platform above them. Now he circled the bell opening. He loitered for several minutes, puzzled by their disappearance. Could he believe they had outwitted him and had crawled instead into the attic over the nave? Jerry could only hope, but not for long.

"You're down there! I know you are! You couldn't hide anywhere else!"

They saw his feet dangle over the side and then his body struggling for a place on the side of the great bell. His weight was against him and his strength had greatly ebbed. But with no less courage, he edged onto the curved cast surface. Using his hands and feet to brake his decent, he got into position. The dim light and timbers around Jerry and Charlene were not enough to hide them. They watched as Everett fished his gun from his jacket pocket and slid closer to the edge. He stretched his feet across the three-foot divide to bridge his downward motion and brace himself. He had a clear shot and took aim.

Jerry shouted, "No!" and threw the flashlight, missing, but causing Everett to lose his balance and buying them time for the hammer of the great bell to begin tolling twelve midnight . . . vibrating its bronze canopy in the first move of its clapper, shattering the hollow silence with piercing, crushing, ringing, raging reverberation.

Jolted, Everett lost his footing and began to slide. As he fumbled to regain leverage, the clapper struck a second time for the bell's midnight call above the wide sea of city streets and country lanes. Leaning back and bracing his feet on the flange, he stopped his decent. But he was in a perilous state and unable to raise his handgun. So, frantically, as the bell hammered a third time, he dropped his feet over the bell-lip and squirmed on his back until his heels rose to bridge his body to the frame. A fourth time the bell shouted its call toward the midnight hour. He looked defiant, as if this would not out-do him. With untamed strength, he pushed with his feet and raised his body, his elbow off the surface to take careful aim at his caged targets. A confident smile creased his mouth. A fifth time the clapper brought the bell to life. And in that instant, he heard his name shouted from above, and looked up. As he stared, his smile faded. His eyes showed disbelief, and right away a different sound blasted with the sixth bell peel. Instantly, his face splattered. His gun dropped from his hand, clanked against the flange and fell into darkness.

His legs struggled to stop his decent and his hands waved violently, desperate for something to hold on to. The loud report of a second shot in unison with the seventh strike on the bell brought blood spurting from his chest. He fell to the side, his head hitting the forged lip before his whole body slipped away, falling into the dark abyss below.

Jerry and Charlene held their ears until the eerie silence after the twelfth toll. Charlene wanted to scream. She changed her mind when Jerry nudged her and playfully asked if she had any other ideas for a night on the town. She shivered against him.

"Give me a hand?" they heard above them—the voice of Walter suddenly the sweetest, kindest, most treasured voice either of them had ever heard. He assisted Charlene and then Jerry, raising them out of the bell housing.

Walter had shot Everett in the face and chest from less than ten feet. His bolt-action .8 mm deer rifle leaned against the tower wall, its barrel hot and smoking.

"He saw me," Walter said. "I wanted him to. He had to see me as his killer. God forgive me, Reverend, if I can't forgive myself."

From below, they heard police-cars sirens and looked over the side to see flashing lights of emergency vehicles. Cold and shaken, each one harboring thoughts about the events of this night, they began their descent to the nave and to the anxious questions of press and police.

PART II

YEAR'S END, 1962

CHAPTER 19

LOOKING BACK, LOOKING FORWARD

Summer Days

Ignoring his aches and pains, happy to have had Thursday for rest and a whole night's sleep, Jerry Flynn returned to work Friday to conduct the funeral service of Sam Hollister and to begin fielding the avalanche of sorrow and questions produced by the events of the last several days.

Detective John Burroughs was buried with full police honors on Saturday. St. Joseph's Catholic Church filled to capacity for a man greatly loved and respected. Charlene suffered through the mass more than Jerry did. She had met the detective and to her dying day, she believed she could not pardon herself for holding back information that could have put him on to Everett Wheeler sooner. Jerry tried to console her, but knew he needed consoling himself. In that moment bagpipers began *Amazing Grace*, his father's face and that of his mother weeping at his police funeral flashed before his eyes. Time doesn't heal everything. Like everyone else, Charlene and Jerry left the church with burning hearts and tearing eyes.

Jerry's ordination and installation service went on as scheduled Sunday afternoon. Meant as a service of celebration, in mourning for Michael Todd and Rhonda Maefield, and with news breaking about First Church's use by its custodian for pornography and murder, it was difficult for anyone to show a happy face. As Jerry knelt for the "laying on of hands" and promised, *"to be zealous and faithful in maintaining the truths of the Gospel,"* he understood as no one could the diversity of troubles planted in his office.

On Monday morning, he officiated at the funeral of Michael Todd.

Perhaps of all things memorable in that service, none touched people more than the procession of farm workers into the cathedral. Many men came dressed in white shirts and black pants, and women in black skirts and white blouses. Several men wore a red scarf tucked into their collar and some women had covered their heads with a red silk. Here and there, a man carried an ornate sombrero. All genuflected and took their places. "They have such respect for holy things," Jerry said afterwards, but most of all he saw how much they respected and cared for Madge Todd.

Nothing was more difficult for Jerry than Monday afternoon when he met a sobbing Marie Wheeler—under police guard—a half dozen people from First Church, and a few family members for a graveside service to lay Everett Wheeler to rest. To Jerry, the service represented the end of an angry, disturbed individual and the beginning of God's mercy. He had no answer for those who asked what had driven Everett to such torturous conclusions. But, with his prayer book in his hands, Jerry read the recommended prayers of assurance and promises of salvation. Without yet knowing of Marie's part in Everett's crimes, Jerry watched as sheriffs' deputies handcuffed her again and escorted her to a waiting van for transport back to the county jail.

On Tuesday, Jerry and Charlene attended a memorial service at Manhattan's Riverside Church for Rhonda Maefield. University faculty, law colleagues, neighbors from her apartment building and a number of friends from many years of friendship paid their respects. The church's pastor, who readily admitted not knowing her, drew upon verses from the Psalms and the Gospel of John for an inspiring message. Several people from First Church also attended. Neither Jerry nor Charlene missed that one of them was Madge Todd. They looked for her afterwards, but before they could reach her, she had hurried ahead and caught a taxi at curbside. Charlene alone understood the depth of Madge's double grief. She had promised herself never to reveal what she knew.

To Charlene's delight, her MG Midget had shown up at the Manhattan auto pound. Everett had apparently taken it from the parking garage and abandoned it under the FDR Drive. Left in a no parking zone, traffic police had towed it away. An hour after Rhonda's memorial service, Charlene and Jerry paid the fine and found the sports car amid the mass of other impounded vehicles. And what a convenient coincidence. Parked next to the MG, Jerry recognized Everett's brown pickup truck. Informed of the connection, New York police took it away for a thorough search. Among other stolen items, they found Charlene's wallet, address book, and all her identifying credentials. They discovered too a switchblade knife, which later became marked as the weapon used to murder Reverend Maefield.

In the weeks following, news media had a field day profiling the scandalous lives of Everett Wheeler and Rhonda Maefield. And First Church had to weather the storm of public scrutiny. Every day, Jerry answered reporters' questions and did his best to restore confidence in the church's leadership.

As it turned out, the District Attorney acted quickly to close his case against Everett Wheeler as the killer of Reverend Daniel Maefield and of Detective John Burroughs. The postmortem hearing included the cooperation of Marie Wheeler and Rhonda Maefield's taped recording. For motive, the District Attorney accused Wheeler of murdering Daniel Maefield in order to silence his threat to expose his licentious use of the hidden room, and also because Maefield had learned of Wheeler's affair with his wife, Rhonda. The State speculated that on the night of the murder an argument in the minister's study turned deadly. Wheeler, in a drunken rage, hit the minister with a coal shovel and then slit his throat. In an attempt to throw off investigators, Wheeler willfully brutalized the corpse and emptied Maefield's wallet, making the murder appear the work of a crazed intruder. In a further attempt to cover-up, the DA maintained that Wheeler burned his clothes in the church incinerator. Then, undaunted by his brutality, he met the unsuspecting Rhonda Maefield for sex in his secret studio. On the matter of pieces of black cloth found in the backyard fireplace at the Wheeler home, police lab tests identified these as fragments of wool from an English-tailored coat Reverend Maefield had put on to walk to Shepherd House hours before his murder. Rhonda had reported the coat missing. The DA offered this as further evidence of Wheeler's crime, saying Wheeler had put the coat over his own clothes after the murder to prevent traces of blood from inadvertently showing up during his flight to his basement studio. Fearing the coat too heavy to burn in the church incinerator, the prosecutor accused Everett of having hidden it until he could burn it in his backyard fireplace. As for the blindfolded male visitor Rhonda had spoken of in her taped recording, other than to present him as an illustration of the extreme hedonism practiced by the participants, the DA downplayed his significance.

On the matter of Detective John Burroughs, the DA surmised that the Chief of Homicide had acted more out of impulse than evidence, that he had gone to the Wheeler house to conduct an informal interview based on hearsay, and had instead become witness to a domestic dispute. Wheeler shot Burroughs as Burroughs attempted to stave off his violent assault on his wife, Marie. Detective Burroughs had acted as a brave policeman who had died in the line of duty.

Regarding Rhonda Maefield, the DA attached no culpability to her in the murder of her husband. He had found no proof linking her as a conspirator, either before or after the murder, and judged her a sad victim of her childhood past. While she had harbored the murderer, she had done so without knowledge of his felonious act. With Charlene Cunningham testifying as a witness, the presiding judge ruled Rhonda's death involuntary manslaughter. The Medical Examiner also pointed out that Mrs.

Maefield had an inordinate amount of hallucinogen medication in her blood at the time of her death.

A will prepared weeks prior to Rhonda's end had left her entire estate, including the anticipated million dollar insurance settlement on her husband, to organizations throughout the world dedicated to the resettlement and education of orphans of war. After cremation, Rhonda's relatives had her ashes interred with those of her father at a cemetery in West Berlin. Her lawyer friends, the Collins's, had seen to her funeral arrangements as well as her legal needs.

For his part, Walter Tompkins became a celebrated hero. News accounts dramatized his last minute rush to the aid of First Church's pastor and girlfriend as they hid in the church belfry. At the Everett Wheeler inquest, Walter testified that the sound of gunfire and prayer had led him to the tower platform of the cathedral. He had shot his nephew, Everett, he stated, "to defend against the murders of Flynn and Cunningham."

Jerry and Charlene were happy to have Walter's story overshadow their own. Except to say Everett Wheeler had held them hostage, they kept details of their Wednesday ordeal to themselves. Other than to the police, Charlene never spoke about her Tuesday abduction and Jerry never reported to anyone Walter and Jorge assaulting him. No bones were broken, cuts and bruises healed, exhaustion and fear faded into the past.

* * *

Charlene Cunningham remained the only person with doubts that Everett Wheeler killed Daniel Maefield. She based her skepticism more on gut feelings than on any hard evidence. Nor did she put much trust in the Maefield winter coat evidence. It made no sense that Everett would burn the heavy coat in his backyard fireplace when everything else of significance he destroyed with no trace in the church incinerator. And how could he have possibly gotten into a coat four sizes smaller than his frame? Furthermore, had he wanted to lead police on a hunt for a random intruder, instead of laughing that he had looked like Santa Clause, why not give an apt description of the man who had hung out at the church just before the murder, the man Charlene believed was the special visitor Rhonda had had sex with and had spoken about in her recorded testimony? But the DA countered that he could not prove a connection. And even if they were the same individual, for Everett, an arrest would have meant revealing his pornography at the church, and, as already shown, he was willing to murder the church's minister to keep his studio a secret. On the matter of the coat, the DA said Wheeler simply used the coat to cloak his clothes, so he didn't have to put his hands through the sleeves. And as far as using the outside fireplace at home instead of the church furnace to burn evidence, the DA would not try to explain the rationalizations of a deranged killer.

Throughout the hearing, Charlene had a gut feeling Marie Wheeler knew much more than she volunteered. Upon visiting her in prison, she was certain.

After Everett's post mortem judgment, Charlene met Marie in the privileged prisoner section of the New Jersey State Penitentiary for Women, a block of cells and visitors' lounge for cooperative witnesses in exceptional murder cases, the killing of a policeman being such a case. Charlene had asked for the meeting more out of curiosity than need for anything new to add to her final report.

Especially troubling, Charlene now knew that Marie was the person Everett had telephoned from the farm shed. Less than twenty seconds into the call, not enough time to trace it, he hung up. He had gone long enough to say, "Bring your car," when Marie had interrupted him to ask if he knew what time it was. Hardly relevant, Charlene theorized. In asking the question, had Marie passed a secret signal alerting Everett that police were listening in on their conversation? Charlene suspected she had. Like Rhonda, whether out of fear or love, Marie had sought to protect Everett to the bitter end. When Charlene asked, Marie denied the time question as a signal. Police had cautioned her to speak calm and natural and that the question, as heard in the tone of her voice, had reflected her usual temper when Everett called late at night.

The most significant insight to Marie's culpability, the whole time she and Charlene talked Marie chain-smoked Chesterfield cigarettes, each one stained by her pink-coated lips. A woman's curiosity allowed Charlene to inquire about this "mod" lipstick shade. Marie smiled proudly and showed her a Royal DuBarry lipstick, one of the luxuries, she commented, prison guards allowed her.

Connecting the cigarette and lipstick brands, Charlene asked Marie about her relationship with Reverend Maefield. Had she seen the minister the Sunday afternoon before the murder? Marie looked surprised and then offended. She replied that she had spent that Sunday in bed suffering from the flu. "How preposterous," she laughed, "that you would consider me visiting Shepherd House that day."

"I just thought I would ask. No harm in that," Charlene responded, her eyes never leaving the woman's lips. "Detective Burroughs collected evidence from the minister's desk indicating he had had a female visitor who smoked Chesterfields, your brand, and wore pink DuBarry lipstick."

"So do thousands of women," Marie snapped and crushed her cigarette as if it contained poison. "As sick as I was, what reason would I have to visit the minister on such a nasty afternoon?"

This time Marie did not look at Charlene. Instead, she pushed back her chair and showed impatience to get the interview behind her. Charlene was curt.

"Oh, I can think of lots of reasons, but I won't trouble your head with them."

Marie stared back with a poker player look. "If you're finished Miss Cunningham, I have an AA meeting to attend."

"I'm finished. Thank you for your time and good luck at your trial."

Charlene watched Marie pick up her cigarette pack and, without reply or change of face, leave the visitors' room.

Charlene could hardly blame Marie for hiding the whole truth. In spite of her privileged status, the charge against her was accessory after the fact in the murder of a policeman and she faced a sentence of life in prison. Her best defense would center on a perception of innocence respecting Everett's pornography and a jury sympathetic to her as one more example of Everett's abused victims. It was to her benefit now to show no remorse for Everett. Just look at the burn mark on her thigh. Her husband did that to her, she claimed, because she refused to hand over the incriminating photos of him with Rhonda. And cooperating with the DA, she had now admitted lying about Everett at home with her at the time of Maefield's murder, and so many other times she had fibbed for him. As things stood, Marie would plead guilty to a lesser charge. In less than three years, she would be a free woman and a very rich one. Why jeopardize that?

"There is nothing to gain in defending Everett Wheeler," Charlene said to herself as she walked off the prison grounds, "unless, of course, the killer of Reverend Maefield still walks the streets of Tompkinsville."

*   *   *

With Michael Todd's death, everyone assumed Madge's tears were for him. But a look into her mind would reveal that Ronda Maefield prompted greater grief.

People loved and respected Michael. They remembered him as a man of good moral character, a devoted father, *"a leader who stood strong for God and country,"* the mayor of Tompkinsville had eulogized at Michael's funeral. And what could Madge say? There was a time when she had seen him that way, and even now, when she knew better, she could not say anything that would destroy Michael's reputation. For the sake of his and her parents, for Dudley and Chip and for T&T Produce, Madge smiled and accepted everyone's platitudes and kind tributes. During the day, she collected them like medals. But alone at night, she gritted her teeth and recalled how she had suffered from Michael's verbal and sexual abuse.

But she realized too that death has a remedial affect. For her this was freedom to build her life on her own merits. Madge had inherited all that had belonged to Michael, including what now gave her a controlling interest in the T&T Produce Company. Within days of Michael's funeral, she had the directors elect her president (a formality) and announced management plans. In this, she showed a side of her personality people had missed—a tough, assertive, reform-minded businesswoman.

She acted on her new authority with a vengeance. She made Jorge Garcia an offer and he retired. Manuel quit. She hired a new field manager and new managers at the canning and frozen food factories. Within weeks of taking over, she reorganized her marketing department to give T&T national and worldwide exposure. Concurrently, she initiated a plan to build a new dormitory for seasonal male workers and for improving the cottages of families. She mandated portable chemical toilets in every working field. She intended to lead the way in pushing the local school board to improve on a state plan for public education of farm workers' children. Perhaps her most radical reform, last week at a grower's association meeting she presented a health plan for field workers. She knew the idea faced a long, uphill battle; however, she planned for T&T to lead the way.

As in the past, work agreed with her. Long hours tired her out, but gave her a grand sense of accomplishment. She accepted frequent squabbles with her father and T&T "advisory" directors as par for the course. None could argue her down. And when they saw business profits increase, they began coming to her side. Even her father swallowed his pride and complemented her progressive management style.

But before the end of July, Michael's behavior came back to haunt her.

When first informed that a twenty-one year old female had died with Michael, Madge had appeared unruffled. In public, she accepted the face-saving version: Michael had done a favor for a former T&T Produce employee, intending to take the young lady home, when the unfortunate accident had occurred. But Madge knew better. She anticipated that eventually the "dirty" truth about the accident would hit her hard. Only she hadn't counted on it happening with such ruining potential.

That July morning a lawyer called to ask for the name of the law firm representing her and T&T Produce Company. He gave his name as William Albert Smith, attorney for the mother of Margo Rasmeyer, "the young girl killed with your husband." Madge told him the name of the company lawyer, but—puzzled by Smith's inquiry—she added that she had already provided information about insurance to Mrs. Rasmeyer. William Albert Smith chuckled and then dropped the bombshell that Margo Rasmeyer's mother was planning a wrongful death and negligence lawsuit against the deceased Mr. Todd's T&T Company to the tune of five million dollars. Madge said, "Yes, you do want to speak to our attorney."

Soon after Madge met with David Eagleton, a specialty lawyer hired by T&T to represent Madge and the company's financial interests. Eagleton, with years of experience defending people of wealth against the prying hands of those who believed they could cut a better deal through threat of civil litigation, was up front and honest with Madge. He informed her that the lawsuit was not frivolous and she had to take it seriously. He outlined the case against them.

Michael had been on company business, driving in a company owned vehicle at seventy-five miles an hour in a forty-speed construction zone when he struck the pine tree. "And that was after grazing the guardrail, which had slowed him down considerably," Eagleton mused. An autopsy on Michael had turned up a blood alcohol level of 3.1, "So drunk," Eagleton gasped, "the man should have been unconscious before he got in his truck." The lawyer also informed Madge that lab tests on semen and vaginal samples had confirmed that Michael, age thirty-two, and Miss Rasmeyer, twenty-one, had engaged in intercourse "more likely than not with each other less than an hour before the accident. In addition, there was evidence of other body fluid exchange," Eagleton declared.

"Save me the details," Madge asserted.

Eagleton smiled, but said if the case went to trial, Madge would hear a lot more.

"How much does Mrs. Rasmeyer want?" Madge asked.

"Are you prepared to make a private offer?"

"If it will pacify Mrs. Rasmeyer, keep this from going to court and avoid juice for scandal hungry newspaper reporters? Yes!"

"People will always talk, Mrs. Todd," Eagleton said respectfully, "we can, however, avoid speaking their minds in court where it becomes public record, and Mrs. Rasmeyer would have to agree not to sue, or disclose details of any agreed settlement. I trust a reasonable offer will save the anxiety of preparing for trial.

In the end, on behalf of T&T Produce, Madge offered a hundred thousand dollars, plus all legal fees. She knew no amount of money could compensate a mother for the loss of her daughter; however, in an ordinary claim, at most, Margo's mother would have received no more than the auto insurance maximum of ten thousand dollars. In some ways, she wished she had fought her to the bitter end, dirt for dirt. As Eagleton had pointed out—he had plenty of fodder he could throw discrediting Margo. But Madge was in a hurry. She did not want a public fight.

Friday, August 31, late in the morning, Madge received word from Eagleton that Mrs. Rasmeyer had accepted and signed on to the settlement. Madge put down the phone, glad to have Michael's "last entertainment" behind her. That said she left her office and drove home where she changed into shorts and a men's t-shirt. The fact that the temperature had soared into the nineties and the humidity equally high, deterred her not a second. She needed a brisk run. Nothing freed her mind more.

After two miles at a modest pace, she changed stride to a brisk walk. Along the way, her fingers fiddled with her earlobes, or, more accurately, the diamond earrings Rhonda Maefield had attached. As she toyed, she felt chills race up her spine and her skin tingle. Lowering her hands to her sides, she changed stride again, this time fixing her run at top speed. For the next mile, she sprinted over a dirt path through fields of corn ready for late harvest. Suddenly, she was out of the cornfield and into a thick stand of old forest shading Tompkins' property on its western extremity. In less than five minutes, the scenery changed once more when she raced into a grassy clearing that led to the river where her father had built a boathouse many years ago. This was always such a peaceful place, she thought, as their old swimming hole came into view, its manmade sandy beach a much loved spot. She could remember learning how to swim here, family picnics and fireworks every Fourth of July. Since one mile north, the river flowed over a stone bed, too craggy for anything less shallow than a canoe, this side of the river for five miles southeast was private to the Tompkins farm through which it passed.

Slowing only to kick off her running shoes, Madge ran the length of the dock and dove to swim the hundred feet or more to the opposite shore. She was as good a swimmer as she was a runner and had followed this exercise route many times in her life. But nothing about it was as exhilarating as this final trial in cool river currents. Still in water over her head, she touched the floating dock ten feet from shore, flipped below the surface and spun out in a rapid return. Only now, she directed herself to a landing two hundred yards down river from the Tompkins dock where a smooth, wide sheet of granite rose on a gradual plane inside an inlet hidden from the river's view by heavy brush, boulders and trees. Here she emerged in her sodden shorts and top and quickly did away with them, then stretched out on her back—the hard, warm surface an instant comfort, the hot sun mixing with river breezes drying and tanning her naked body. This was Madge's very own private time and place.

A year ago on a weather day much like this she had come here with Rhonda.

How surprised she had been that August morning when Ronda showed up to run with her. She hadn't thought the dowdy woman athletic, much less a jogger or a swimmer, though, everyone knew she sprinted early mornings around the church grounds. Seeing her in colorful shorts and halter, her hair down and those ugly glasses off, was an added surprise. And soon enough, Madge learned how much in shape the older woman was—running and swimming to equal her speed and endurance.

As Madge thought about that day, once again she caught herself fiddling with her earrings. They were the only items she had that once belonged to Rhonda and since her funeral she had worn them every day.

*   *   *

When Madge first heard of Rhonda's death, she thought for sure it was a lie. Two o'clock in the morning, helping clean up in the kitchen of her parents' home after the constant flow of visitors mourning the death of Michael, she had overheard agitated voices in the parlor. Going there, she saw her father all hunched over and shielding his face with his hands. Again, he repeated how he had shot Everett dead in the church bell tower. He had had no choice. Everett was about to kill the minister and "his lady-friend" after having just killed Rhonda Maefield. Dad wasn't lying. Madge screamed, "Has the world gone absolutely crazy?" She ran from her parents' home, racing on foot to her own bedroom where she threw herself on the bed and sobbed it seemed until dawn. All time and death itself were dead, she believed, dead because of her sins, dead because of her pride, and dead because life wasn't worth living anymore. "And, O my God," she had cried, "I wouldn't give her the only thing she wanted from me, my forgiveness."

Over the years, their friendship had grown from simple sensitivity to complex involvement.

When Rhonda came to First Church as the new minister's wife, Madge had gone out of her way to show kindness and to make the timid woman feel welcome. Rhonda had appeared such a forlorn person. She had the look of boredom and a woman in another age, thus the buttress of many underhanded comments.

Madge saw her dress and manner as indications of unhappiness and so had gone out of her way to cheer her up. She gave her little gifts, greeted her with hugs and kissed her on the cheek. Madge was like that. She never thought anyone, especially another woman, would view such affection as sexually motivated. But then, she supposed, she should have seen the writing on the wall. For in recent years, it seemed Madge couldn't begin a conversation with Rhonda without it ending about sex, and always Madge was the one doing the talking. She was the one telling "tales out of school."

A good listener, Madge answered Rhonda's probing questions about Michael in bed, how and why she hated sex with him, her fear of pregnancy and her suspicions about Michael being unfaithful. She told Rhoda her dreams and her fantasies and even described her summer-college romance in Ethiopia with a boy from California. Nor did such inquisitiveness stop when Rhonda began attending Columbia law school. Letters and occasional phone calls kept them on cordial terms. And when Rhonda came home to visit, it seemed they always got together at one or the other's kitchen table.

*   *   *

"I went too far to please her," Madge whispered amid nature's summer sounds and the gentle flow of the river inches from her toes. "I wanted so much for her to trust me. What happened a year ago seemed so natural on this stone bed, the two of us stripped to nothing, stretched out, side-by-side."

Madge recalled how she had not objected when Rhonda pressed over her, their first intimate kiss, followed by arresting hand and body stimulation. While swimming back to the dock, floating their clothes behind them, they clung to each other. In a love letter a day later, Madge recalled writing, "*I imagined us akin to fish joined in deep water, lost in time and space, alone in safe passage and driven by forces innate in our very natures.*"

But within weeks, disillusionment and guilt dispelled those pure thoughts. Rhonda, busy with her law studies, had little patience with Madge's second thoughts. She told Madge her fears were foolish and she should stop reasoning like a schoolgirl. What they had done was a natural act, the fact they had done it as women had only enhanced its pleasure, and Madge should feel proud for having responded so freely. Back and forth letters refused to let the affair die.

In New York on business in November, Madge—feeling a need to explain in person what her correspondence had failed to do—made a luncheon date with Rhonda. They met at the "Oyster Bar" restaurant in Grand Central Terminal. Rhonda wore a fashionable Ole Borden dress and jacket. Its murky ink-blue and gold colors, inspired by a Persian print, were simple and subtle, so right for her tall, slim figure. She had let down her hair from its usual bun, combed its shinning black waves into a single strand, which she had tied with a dress-matching ribbon before it fell below her shoulders. She had traded her black horn rimmed glasses for a softer pair, which she only used for reading the menu. Her smile beamed genuine and her manner was cheerful and hopeful. In dress and personality that day, Madge saw Rhonda as a youthful woman of affluence, charm and—as at the river—seductive beauty.

Their lunch ended without Madge broaching the matter that so troubled her. With Rhonda insisting Madge see her little off campus apartment on 47th Street, Madge thought she would raise the issue there. She should have known better. Before the door closed behind them, they were in each other's arms. But when their passion paused, Madge's conscience took over and, after less than an hour in Rhonda's bed, she bolted, saying she had to catch a late afternoon train, leaving Rhonda, who had planned on her staying the night, angry and frustrated. Letters and repeated phone calls between them did nothing to change the uneasiness Madge felt. *Why does sex have to be part of our friendship?* Madge had written through tearing eyes. *I don't understand why I have to go so far to show I love you."*

Yet, horrifying as the truth was, and, as Rhonda had made clear, the sex was good. Madge had to admit, her conscience had always suffered a delayed reaction. "*Why not accept sex as a gift one lover gives another?*" Rhonda had written back. But Madge wondered if for Rhonda, love was inconsequential when it came to sex. Madge decided, sexual feelings aside, she had to take her stand.

Then came Sunday, January 21. Madge knew Rhonda was home for the weekend. She had to face her, had to confront her and once and for all explain her position. If it meant an end to their friendship, so be it. She would not trade her body again. And the manse seemed a safe haven to have it out with Rhonda. With Reverend Maefield in residence, surely, nothing, however tempting, could happen there. Having already made an appointment to see the minister at Shepherd House about Sunday school matters that afternoon, Madge decided to first drop in on Rhonda.

* * *

It was snowing lightly when Madge arrived at the manse and a glum Rhonda Maefield answered the bell. She looked in a worse than usual unfriendly mood as she greeted her in the dress and personality of her old, classic self. Without inviting Madge in, she asked, "Why are you here?" Impersonal and abrupt, she further acted out her annoyance with a facial expression drawn into a frown, and with arms folded tightly across her chest.

Madge thought—she's still brooding because I wouldn't stay the night with her.

At the last minute, before leaving her home, Madge had decided to return the long overdue books Reverend Maefield had loaned her in the belief that they were instructive for couples dealing with—as he called it—"sexual misinformation in marriage." The books contained text, photos and illustrations that left nothing to the imagination regarding the kinds of sexual acts consenting adults could perform. Because of their explicit nature, Madge had kept them in a brown paper bag and hidden. Today, she had tied them as a package with a kite string. As she answered Rhonda's curt question, she showed Rhonda a bashful smile and held out her package. "I have these books to return. They didn't help my marriage, but then, you already know that. I have no use for them and I don't want them in my house."

Ronda grabbed the package. "Why not drop them where you got them, at Shepherd House?" Rhonda asked with irritation and turned from left to right looking for somewhere out of the way to lay them. Unresolved, she clutched them to her chest and stared with steal eyes at the face of her caller.

"Also, I have an appointment to see the reverend at three-thirty. He said for me to meet him here and we would walk over to Shepherd House. But I came early specifically because I have matters you and I have to discuss."

Rhonda's face loosened a little. "Well, come in then!" she called, stepping from the open doorway. "Close the door quick!" she commanded. "I don't have to tell you how cold it is," she continued and showed Madge her back as she strode through the foyer. "You can take off your boots and leave them there," she said harshly, and turned to point her long finger to the matted floor. "You don't mind doing that, do you?"

"Not at all," Madge replied as she stepped onto the mat. Reaching down, with one foot up, she slipped off her left winter boot and then the other.

"I can loan you slippers if you don't like walking in your stockings."

"No, I'm fine. I'm really a barefoot farm girl, you know."

"Then maybe you should remove your stockings as well."

Madge let the suggestion pass. She knew the woman as a scoundrel when it came to cleanliness and neatness. Nothing in her house could be out of place. Madge appreciated that the minister showed much less grace. Rhonda must have a fit when she comes home after long absences to find the manse strung and messy. Just look at her, Madge thought, she wouldn't even put the books on a table, but on the floor against a table leg.

Madge handed over her parka. As she did, she took out of the pocket a tiny box, neatly gift-wrapped. Rhonda shook out the coat of the little snow that sill clung and put it on a hanger, which she then hung on a coat tree.

"And this is for you," Madge said, handing the present to Rhonda. "Congratulations on your law degree and finishing your bar exams."

She should have expected it. Only Madge would be so thoughtful.

Suddenly Rhonda's face lost its bitterness. "I don't deserve this," she protested, but then eagerly unwrapped it to reveal a set of silver strung pearl earrings. There was no question of their authenticity. The packaging showed Madge had purchased them in one of Philadelphia's upscale jewelry stores. "You are too generous. They are lovely," Rhonda said and, with Madge assisting her, she detached what she had on and put on the new. She pecked Madge on the cheek. "Here, you must accept these as my gift," she said softly. Ignoring protest, Rhonda undid Madge's dime-store pieces, commenting that they had "no class," were "cheap imitations" and fastened her diamond studs into Madge's earlobes. "Aren't you glad now you let me pierce your ears?" she asked in a proud voice. "Very European! Diamonds characterize you. Always wear the very best, Madge, especially with this short hair style."

Madge dropped the replaced earrings into the pocket of her skirt. She had not thought of their value when she had put them on. To her, it was wasteful to spend a lot of money on clothes and jewelry, unless as gifts. And since most of what she wore she purchased locally at Sears and Roebuck or Penny's, to Rhonda, who shopped Park Avenue and the likes, anything else was cheap and cheapened the buyer as well. Thus, while Rhonda's exchange flattered Madge, she also felt devalued by it. But she kept her hurt feeling hidden beneath her pert smile and quiet disposition. And Rhonda took up again her strict appeal.

"This house is very drafty today," she said, taking Madge's hand and leading her into the large, Victorian decorated living room. "You may want to borrow a sweater." Madge wore a sleeveless blouse and she did feel the chill. She was about to accept the offer when Rhonda cut her off. "I can offer you a drink if you like . . . coffee or tea . . . a brandy, perhaps?"

"No, thank you. I apologize for disturbing you. I suppose I could have waited outside Shepherd House."

"You do not disturb me. You should know that by now. As for pastor, he never told me he expected you this afternoon. He has too many ideas on his mind these days. Sit in his chair," she said, pointing to an old and worn recliner that looked out of place in the resplendent room. "If he doesn't return in ten minutes, I shall telephone him. Now, bring me up-to-date. When we talked at the Oyster Bar you hoped to go back to school for another post-graduate degree. I want to hear all about that. Sit!" she commanded.

Madge dutifully took a chair, but one close to her. At Rhonda's side was an end table holding an opened book, a decanter of brandy, and a near empty glass. Madge knew then she had indeed interrupted the woman's Sunday afternoon leisure. The thought hardly passed before Rhonda surprised her by complementing her on her long, bright green, flare skirt with its white hand-embroidered sketches of reindeer flying over trees and housetops. Holding the skirt out to admire its figures, Rhonda turned her gaze to Madge's cherry-red velvet blouse that created a snug fit across her bust. Letting go of the skirt, she leaned way forward to smooth her hand over the blouse. "That's got a nice feel."

Madge offered that she had last worn the outfit to a company party a few days before Christmas and had enjoyed the complements it had motivated from both men and women.

"How nice," Rhonda said, releasing the material and leaning back in her lounge chair. "I can see you spent a lot of time stitching the skirt figures. You have much talent, Madge." Then, looking up, she frowned and added, "But don't you know, dear, Christmas is over? You make too much of a good thing. Your red blouse would look better this time of year if you wore it with a short black skirt. You should show off your pretty legs. Why hide them under a long skirt, or as I see you so often, in those ugly men's field pants?"

"Oh, I like to dress comfortable, I guess," was all Madge could think to say and hold her tongue. But beneath her smile, she considered how Rhonda loves to raise her up only to put her down. And she should be critical of a long skirt, while sitting here like old "Mother Hubbard." But Madge swallowed her pride. If she had come to impress the lady with her cheerful, colorful outfit, she knew she had failed. She might just as well have arrived in, yes, bib overalls and a well-worn flannel shirt. And besides, Madge had serious things on her mind and she wanted to get them out of the way before Reverend Maefield interrupted them. Rhonda had to understand how conflicted she was. She had to know that their caressing ways had crossed the line and made her sick with worry about herself. But if not that, Rhonda could certainly appreciate how living and working in Tompkinsville was a whole lot different from New York, where it was easier to have a private life.

"Tell me," Rhonda asked, taking Madge back to where their conversation had begun, "Have you decided to go ahead with graduate school?"

"Yes, I want to. I am filling out application forms for postgraduate business courses at Rutgers. It helps that I already have my CPA license."

"Wonderful. I am very happy for you. Beautiful girls like you with a head for business are in much demand. You have the combination for success."

"Well, as you know, I have dire personal problems to solve. I appreciate your confidence in me, but I'm unsure whether to start school while my marriage is in such disarray. I have to get that together, Rhonda, and you're not helping me." Madge began to sob. "Please don't get upset again. You have to hear me out. I want to put our personal times behind me. I know you think what we do is all right, but I'll say it again, I can't live in two worlds. And I'm unprepared for the consequences of such a relationship. You thrill me Rhonda, you really do, and I count our together-hours as special. But no more. It makes me too uncomfortable."

Rhonda's face had remained cold. She tasted her brandy and lightly patted her mouth with a linen napkin. In her silence, she stared long and hard at Madge's uncommonly sad face.

"You can have it both ways," she said, an unfamiliar smile brightening her eyes. "I have for years. Living in Tompkinsville never stopped me."

"I've made my decision," Madge continued, tears running down her cheeks. "If we can't just be friends . . . well . . . you think about it! I have to go. Please tell the reverend I can come back another time." She stood to show she meant it.

"Nonsense," Rhonda growled. "Sit down!" she commanded as she got to her feet. "I will take you over to Shepherd House. First, I will call and tell him we are on our way."

Rhonda went to the kitchen, where she dialed an inside line connecting her to the minister's study. Madge overheard a little of what she said, enough to know that Reverend Maefield had indeed forgotten his appointment. She listened as Rhonda switched from English to German. From the tone of Rhonda's voice, she knew the woman was very upset, increasing Madge's anxiety. The urge to flee ignited her and she started toward the door. Just then, Rhonda returned to the living room. Apologizing for her husband's forgetfulness and explaining that someone had unexpectedly come by to see him, she then objected vigorously to Madge's second attempt to leave.

"You're right. We must talk about your concerns," Rhonda said sympathetically. "We can do so as we walk to Shepherd House. We'll use the underground passage. You won't need your coat."

Without waiting for an answer, Rhonda got a pair of slippers out of the foyer closet. "Here, put these on. The basement floor is filthy." She then picked up the bundle of books and handed it to Madge.

They descended the stairs to the basement, but were no farther than Reverend Maefield's wine cellar when Rhonda insisted Madge see the "private" apartment she kept, a complete surprise, and led her through the dark and cluttered storage room, commenting on the "absurdity" of the government, and how they should give these beds to the poor as her husband wanted. "It's a lot of nothing so civil defense workers can look busy," she scoffed.

Madge had little time to appraise the mess. Hurrying her along, Rhonda escorted her to the west end of the room where heavy double size mattresses in several side-by-side rows reached close to the ceiling. With Madge clutching her books, Rhonda cuddled in behind her and reached both hands forward. Little effort was required to push the heavy mattress bundle.

In the almost dark of the sheltered hall, Rhonda turned a key in the doorknob and prodded Madge into the studio. There, she switched on the floodlights dramatically illuminating the bed and other furnishings.

"Many years ago," Rhonda explained, "this corner of the basement had an outside entrance and was occupied by a resident housekeeper. The trustees changed that when they added the apartment upstairs and sealed this room. I have had it restored for my personal use. I trust you to keep this our little secret. Here, I'll take that package from you," Rhonda offered.

Preoccupied by what she saw, Madge handed her the wrapped books.

"We can talk in confidence here. No one will interrupt us," Rhonda said softly, leaving Madge to take her time looking over the room's inordinate features.

In the interim, Rhonda pulled away the kite string securing the package, tore off the brown paper and laid the three volumes on a table situated in front of a wall mirror. Attending a "Life" size picture volume, she turned the pages. "Graphic, aren't they? I can see why these pictures offended your puritan conscience, Madge. But you told me they aroused you as well. You said they made you feel 'nasty'. Isn't 'nasty' the word you used? And how I love you when you're nasty," she said. But Madge ignored her and concentrated instead on a modernist painting of a nude woman holding her breasts. "Daniel purchased these English language editions in Paris years ago. We were lucky to get them through customs. Americans are such prudes. Daniel has smuggled in other banned books."

Madge hadn't seen the hidden room then as a studio, but had thought it odd, scurrilous, the mirrors and all, debasing. Nor had she any idea that this was really Everett's secret den, that high tech cameras stood behind the mirrored glass, or that Everett and Rhonda used the room for their common pleasure. These things, and so much more, Madge would learn with the rest of the Tompkinsville community after Rhonda and Everett's deaths.

Instead, these moments passed half listening to Rhonda, and with some amusement as she eyed the exotic wall decorations and then the suggestive bedding. But looking up at her mirrored image, seeing Rhonda approach, Madge knew for sure why Rhonda had shown her in here. Nude to the waist, unzipping and dropping her skirt, Rhonda folded her arms around her.

"I'm sorry I was rude to you," Rhonda said as she hugged her back, her voice calm and unusually childlike. "I love your gift. You are such a friend to have thought of me."

Madge felt Rhonda's breath on her neck, her hands move up her velvet blouse where they pressed on her breasts. She had feared their detour would come to this. No, she couldn't allow it, and for long, she resisted.

Hands flew and words argued. Then, in one pawing incident, Rhonda's ring finger unintentionally nicked the corner of Madge's lip and drew a spit of blood. In the mix of apology and tears that followed, Rhonda cradled Madge down on to the bed, holding her there until Madge could no longer imprison her ignoble desires and, stripped to her nakedness, she responded in kind to her tempter's arousal.

*   *   *

What shocked Madge back to reality that afternoon was hearing a door slam. Suddenly, extreme sex turned to extreme fear and revulsion. She bolted, freeing herself from their embrace. No platitudes or assurances to the contrary forestalled her flight.

"Don't act so ashamed," Rhonda admonished. "Nothing done here was against your will, unless you let it become that way. You took love and you gave love."

"It wasn't love!" Madge shot back. "I don't understand why you pursued me."

"Stop! You are pitiful. You enjoyed what happened. You only fight me to suave your conscience."

"I didn't!" Madge yelled, and hurried around the room retrieving her clothes, then run into the bathroom to splash cold water on her face and gargle repeatedly with Listerine. She dressed where she stood. She could not find her panties, but she wasn't about to go back looking for them.

When she came out, Rhonda was waiting, tall and once more ugly in her stiff, charcoal-gray suit, her hair up in its usual bun and her black framed glasses on her face. When Rhonda tried to kiss her, Madge drove her off with warlike hands.

A hurt look on her face, Rhonda said, "Madge, if you prefer, you can believe today and every other time our bodies met never happened. I won't tempt you again. That's a promise. If there is a next time, it shall have to come at your invitation. Our affair is our secret. You tell no one about this room and no one will ever know we made love here. You have my word."

Rhonda unlocked the door. In dismal silence, Madge followed her through the storage room and up the manse staircase. As they emerged on the ground floor landing, Reverend Maefield greeted them. Cheery and gallant, he roared, "Madge, my lovely young friend! Where have you been? I waited for you at Shepherd House. Rhonda," he chirped, "you said you would personally escort Madge to my study."

"Your door was closed when we arrived," Rhonda fibbed, "so we did not disturb you. We went to the church parlor and made tea, gabbed for over an hour and then you were gone."

Madge's face remained ghost pale. Mayfield quickly turned nervous and hyper.

"I am so sorry," he purred, apologetic. "Shall we set another time?

Madge ignored him and brushed by. He followed her into the foyer. Snatching her parka from the coat tree, he held it open. She began to put her arm through the sleeve when he uttered, "Those books you borrowed, Madge? I wasn't looking for you to return them today."

Madge quit what she was doing and turned to stare at him. She had had the books with her in the secret room. How does he know?

"No!" she screamed. "How do you know I came here with your books?"

Madge thought he had taken on the look of a hunter caught in his own trap and trying now to wiggle out of it.

"I didn't say you had," Maefield stammered. "I only meant to remind you of them."

Her hands shook as she fished her boots out of the closet. It occurred to her then, how could he not know about that room? How could Rhonda have created such a scene without his help and permission? Was there a way to see through those walls, the mirrors?

Finishing putting on her boots, she looked up to see Maefield staring at Rhonda, as though she could save him. But Rhonda acted indifferent and shrugged her shoulder. "I know nothing about any books!" she asserted and walked away. Still holding Madge's parka to his chest, Maefield spoke over the bunched-up hood, "Madge, I'm sorry. I don't understand why my chance remark should upset you so. I meant only—

She grabbed her parka from his hands and, unassisted, she struggled into it. He tried to assist her, but she shook him off, ignored his plea to explain her anger. Unlatching the door, she swung it open and darted onto the open porch, the wind immediately catching her as it howled and blew falling snow into her face. Reverend Maefield stood behind. Trying to be conciliatory, he shouted, "You should have Michael come get you, Madge!" He took her arm and sought to hold her. She pulled away and raced off the porch steps, snow above her ankles. With Maefield walking behind, she buttoned her coat and tightened the hood over her head. "Don't drive in weather like this, Madge," she heard. "Your car is not equipped for snow and ice," he yelled through the densely falling snow. "The roads are too hazardous. Wait while I call Michael!"

"No, Reverend Maefield—please! Don't say anything more. Michael can't help me. No one can. Leave me be!"

Again, he reached for her. "Your father, then! Walter will be upset with me if I let you drive home in weather like this!"

She fended him off, this time swinging and pushing. Spinning forward, she ran through the raging blizzard to her station wagon parked two hundred feet down Cathedral Drive. Fortunately, the wind had kept her windshield clear. She squirmed inside and the car started on the first turn of the ignition. With wipers waving and headlights on, she shot forward. Rounding the curve past the manse, she saw the bespectacled minister hatless and coatless running to intercept her slow progress. He tried to tell her something she would not linger to hear. She would have run him over had he gotten in her way. Then she saw his sullen, shameless wife standing on the porch at the opened door, her arms folded across her chest, her face as cold and merciless as the weather striking it. "How could I allow her into my life," she wailed. Nausea seized her. At the exit from Cathedral Drive, she vomited the contents of her stomach. Without stopping to tend herself, she sped off and drove home.

Monday morning, news exploded throughout the city of Tompkinsville, and afternoon headlines told the story, **MINISTER MURDERED! Savage killing in church study**.

Madge lived in virtual isolation for almost a week. Contact between her and Rhonda appeared to have expired. But in March, Madge had finally wrestled her conscience clear to write a letter of condolence and to express how the murder of Reverend Maefield had only added to her guilt and fears. There was no reply until, two days following Rhonda's own death, Madge received Rhonda's tearful love letter. *"I fear I shall not see you again,"* Rhonda had written. *"But of all things I live for, it is for you to tell me to my face you can forgive me."*

*   *   *

The quiet lap of the river against the stone incline where Madge rested had pacified her. Eyes shut—feeling protected by the heavy foliage around her—Madge missed almost too late the purr of an outboard engine. She opened her eyes just before the boat's approach broke the peace. She stood out of sight to look up river at a familiar skiff approaching. Grabbing up her damp clothes she scurried into the brush where she watched as the little boat turned and headed for her inlet. Quickly, she got into her duds and fled deeper into the woods. Looking back, she recognized Bob, her sister, and her "new" boyfriend, a kid just graduated from high school. "Oh my God," Madge stammered as the teenagers pulled and pushed their boat onto the shallow stone shelf, and then laid out a blanket before it.

Madge debated whether to make her presence known or leave and brave the woods to the boathouse. But without shoes or long pants, the briar bushes and biting insects would murder her. She was about to yell, 'Boo!' and surprise them, when Bob and Cid— Madge thought that was his name—laid down on their blanket in a passionate embrace. Madge didn't know whether to laugh or cry as her kid sister suddenly sat up, stripped off the top of her bathing suit and helped the boyfriend out of his bottoms. In seconds, they lay naked in perfect trust of each other. Madge hoped to God, Cid had a condom, but no, they seemed oblivious to any need for that.

How times have changed, Madge thought, thinking back to when she was Bob's age. Then, more tolerant of the scene playing in her presence, she wished, oh how she wished she could have another chance at such love.

CHAPTER 20

TO MURDER AGAIN

Saturday Evening, October 6

Jerry Flynn had begun believing his life had returned to normal.

He looked forward to a few days off next week, his first break since coming to First Church four months ago. He and Charlene planned a romantic rendezvous at a Pennsylvania resort in the Pocono Mountains. They had talked about hiking in the brisk autumn air and accommodations in an old, rustic hotel where wood-burning fireplaces heated bedrooms and hot water pools for body soaking came from deep thermal wells.

After their violent ordeal, they had doctored each other to recovery and become faithful lovers. While they were not planning marriage right away, Jerry thought this mini vacation might be the perfect opportunity to set a date.

Charlene had continued her employment with Jason, Dolby & Herzfeld of Philadelphia and Jerry had begun making sweeping changes as the popular pastor of First Church. When Charlene was not away on company business, she enjoyed her weekends at Jerry's side. She especially enjoyed church services and when in town shared the spotlight with him at church and community social functions. Remaining a daring dresser, delightful in personality and attractive beyond description, Charlene set the

pace in style and originality as a new kind of woman and future
minister's wife. Beneath this public persona, she saw Jerry as the
most handsome, most dashing, most adorable person in the world.
And on that account, she had to admit to a streak of jealousy.
For, if male heads turned to admire her, she saw female arms
reaching to arrest him. She hated to complain, but maybe he
shouldn't act so friendly, to which he had laughed, shrugged and
went right on to greet the next female worshiper with open arms.
That anguish set aside, they both hated their weekday separations,
but agreed this was a good arrangement. And because they had
publicly expressed plans to marry soon, Charlene believed most
people had stopped counting the hours she stayed with Jerry at
the manse. At least, no one had said anything officially, though
Jerry sensed it was on many minds.

Having grown up Roman Catholic, there were many things
about Presbyterianism Charlene did not grasp. Although she had
learned not to call the Presbyterian service "mass," for the life of
her, she could not understand why these people celebrated Holy
Communion so sparingly. Jerry replied he meant to change that.
He explained how the frequency of serving communion to the
congregation was a decision made by the ruling elders of each
Presbyterian Church. To his credit, they agreed to let him lead
an eight o'clock service every Sunday morning that included
Communion. At that early service, he had introduced the use of
guitars, a prayer book written for young people and religious
songs that were often new and upbeat. Because he did parts of
the service in Spanish, many field workers participated. He limited
his sermons to ten minutes. Folks came dressed in casual attire.
Clapping, hugs, holding hands in a circle while sharing joys and
sorrows, made this worship different from that which attended
people later that morning.

Charlene had never thought much about religion until her
recent brushes with death. In those awful hours, she had prayed
as never before. Like Jerry, she believed it a miracle that the
cloister door into the cathedral had opened for them as they fled.
Had the door been locked—as it always was that time of night—

Everett would have shot them dead then and there. Charlene believed an angel had led them to their hiding place in the bell tower. Jerry said he believed the angel was the ghost of Daniel Maefield. When Charlene looked askance at his explanation, he introduced her to Lillie Palmer, who explained all about ghosts that occupied First Church.

"Well, I hope Everett Wheeler isn't among them now," she responded and shivered at the thought.

The prospect of becoming a minister's wife gave Charlene many sleepless nights. She saw that a minister had to be extremely dedicated to his congregation. She had already observed how much time the church took Jerry away from her. She knew how much he loved his work. But was she wrong to ask him to love her more? Unless he got out of town, there was no such thing as a day off. Maybe this kind of married life wasn't right for her. They had to face the future, and—during their week away—she planned on asking Jerry to consider a different profession.

She worried too about her own career, which now offered a new opportunity.

Last week, she had received an acceptance letter from an investigative wing of the Justice Department. It wasn't FBI, but she knew this was as close as a woman could get to an official appointment, and it was a foot in that door. But it would also mean undercover work and high-security-type assignments. More than likely, she would live miles away from home and in isolation from her real identity for long periods. That was no way to start a marriage. Charlene had to decide whether to accept her appointment by the end of next week.

What if Jerry said no to either one of her concerns? At the least, she would ask him to look for another church to serve. He was free to answer a call anywhere in the United States. First Church scared her. Everything about it reminded her of terror and evil. She understood that the church had become a victim of human failures, but—still—there remained a self-righteous attitude, which she considered pervasive and demeaning. The officers of the church had closed their eyes and ignored warnings about Everett Wheeler. They had refused to take advice from their own denomination officials that would have protected them from such a repressive personality. In their indifference, they had granted Everett unlimited use and control of church property.

Jerry, of course, pinned his hopes for First Church on the future. He pointed to the early morning worship service as proof of that. He had won approval of other changes. The elders had reclaimed their rightful authority as the church's ruling body and now acted in their duel rolls as spiritual leaders and trustees. For the first time in its history, the congregation would elect women elders. Another first, Detective Chester Walsh, who had joined the church as a young man, would become the first Negro elected to the church's ruling body. Walter Tompkins, who had for so long served as President of the Board of Trustees, resigned. At the same time, he supported Jerry in his new worship plans, administrative reforms and had publicly asked for his forgiveness.

It happened in a very emotional moment one Sunday morning. Walter stood during the Prayer of Confession and, walking to the front of the congregation, he tearfully confessed his transgressions. He apologized to Jerry, who he had misjudged and had caused physical harm. It was a moment like none other experienced in a Presbyterian service. Jerry came down from the lectern to hold the kneeling man's hands and pronounce words of forgiveness.

Like everyone, Charlene had applauded Walter's changed views. But at the same time, she held suspicions about his motivation for shooting Everett. After all, he had confessed to Jerry and her that he had intended to kill Everett, that he had wanted to watch him die. Heroics aside, she wondered what Everett knew about Walter that had made him show no mercy. Then, too, Marie's countenance continued to bother her. She saw Everett's post-mortem conviction as a rush to judgment, a convenience, for dead men can't defend themselves. Jerry, however, did not want to hear her theory. Because they argued about it, she had decided to keep suspicions to herself. But somewhere out there a killer waited, a mean one, and the avenue to truth would end in the death of another innocent person.

For those suspicions alone, she faced the reality that she might not be the best kind of woman to meet Jerry's career needs. Ministry was a lonely vocation and, without an understanding and an equally dedicated companion, a minister could fail. And yet she loved him. For all her negatives, she played the part.

This afternoon was no exception. Jerry came home after visiting parents of four children. The oldest had just turned five and the woman was expecting again in a few months.

"I can't believe such stupidity," were the first words out of Jerry's mouth as he entered the kitchen at the manse. "That was the most awful, pathetic situation I have ever witnessed."

"So what happened?" Charlene asked as she kissed him solidly on the cheek, deliberately leaving lipstick there.

"Oh, it's a long story," he continued as she removed the linen handkerchief from his breast pocket and dabbed the spot. He dropped into the bench at the kitchen table. She moved in next to him. She had set out a meal of baked lasagna and a tossed salad. She passed him a bottle of vinegar and oil, into which she had added mustard and honey.

Charlene had made the lasagna from a cookbook recipe and was quite proud of her accomplishment. She had by now accepted the idea that Jerry thought this no big deal, that all women—like his mother—were natural-born cooks. He had no idea Charlene was not like that and what she had prepared was for her only a little less than building a stairway to heaven. He went right on with his harangue.

"The house was filthy. Pigs keep their pen cleaner. And those kids, one running around without his pants on, two of them had their faces smeared with grape jelly and this while mucus ran out their noses. God, it was awful."

"Jerry, what do you expect with that many children? I mean how much time can the woman have?"

"Yah, well, her husband could have helped out a little . . . Lester, I mean. He sits in the most comfortable chair in the room, the television blaring. I finally had to ask him if he would mind turning the thing down. I couldn't hear. I reached over and did it myself. His big fat ass probably only moves when he wants to catch her big fat ass to do you know what with."

"No, what?" she teased. She was baiting him, enjoying his perplexity. Still, he didn't miss a beat.

"What? That's the problem—they're oversexed!"

Charlene laughed. She kidded him, said he sounded like his old enemy in Catholic school, Sister Grace. "Jerry! You can't mean that. Anyway, why was it so important they see you on this beautiful fall Saturday afternoon?"

"Money! They think the church has money to help them. Lester has to have an operation. He may have lung cancer. He smokes like a fiend. That really bothered me. Why is it they have money for cigarettes? Yet, they can't afford vitamins she needs during her pregnancy. Both of them smoked the whole time I was there. Smell my jacket!"

Charlene leaned over and took a whiff.

"Pretty bad! Why don't you take it off?"

She helped him remove his English tweed jacket and at the same time dislodge the white plastic tab that fit into the collar pockets of his black clergy shirt.

"You look so distinguished, Father!" she said with a giggle.

"I forgot I had it on."

"Let's eat, Jerry, before the food gets cold."

Jerry cut into the large helping Charlene had scooped onto his plate.

"Hey, this lasagna is great," he said, suddenly acknowledging her accomplishment. "Wow, you are so terrific!"

Her face brightened, but she ignored his flattery. "So, what did you tell them? There must be ways to help them through their crisis."

Jerry sighed and said, "Yes, I told them we would help out as much we could. I have discretionary funds I can use and the deacons can add from their account. They'll need cash to pay medical expenses not covered by insurance—gas money to Philadelphia, medicine, special food. Because he works for T&T Canning, I assume his medical plan there will pay for the hospital and surgeon. I'll talk to Madge Todd about that. T&T can probably chip in with other expenses and guarantee his job after he recovers. Lester will be out of work for two months. It won't be easy and I do feel badly for him. The aftermath of such surgery is terribly unpleasant and quite frankly, medically speaking, there isn't a lot of hope for long-term survival."

Then Jerry started to laugh. He couldn't stop. Charlene had to poke him.

"I hope it's not my cooking," she countered, pretending offense.

"No, I already told you how great you are. You're so beautiful. You know, I said to this guy, Lester. 'Lester,' I said, 'I hope you won't be offended, but you and your wife should consider birth control. I mean these kids, they're beautiful,' I lied, 'but for their sake and yours, you should think about family planning.' And you know what he says, as if he read my mind? 'I tried those birth-control pills and they don't work.' I couldn't believe it."

Jerry put his fork down.

"He tried birth control pills and 'they didn't work,' he told me, straight face. I mean he really didn't know. I had all I could do to keep from laughing in his face, Charlene. I said, 'Lester, they haven't perfected birth control pills for men; your wife has to take them.' He says, 'Oh!' Like this is the revelation of the century. I mean, can't he read? He says 'she didn't like taking them, so I did it.'"

Charlene did not see this as especially humorous.

"What about a condom? Maybe you should have taken Lester aside and given him some friendly man-to-man advice. It's not just the woman's problem. You know those pills may not be as safe as they say they are. Give the man credit for thinking he should take responsibility for preventing pregnancy. Believe me Jerry no woman likes to gobble down a pill every morning of her fertile life. It's a much regimented order and you can't forget or go without for a while."

"I know, I know, and I shouldn't laugh, but how in the world did he ever get the idea that he was supposed to fill his stomach with them to keep her from getting pregnant? Wouldn't her gynecologist have explained this to her?"

"When you find out tell me."

They finished their meal and ate ice cream for dessert.

"Well, I have to get going, Jerry."

Charlene was planning to drive back to her Philadelphia apartment. She had a case report due and was anxious to get it behind her before their four days in the Pocono Mountains. She arose to take the dishes to the sink. Jerry followed and put his arms around her waist, pulling her against him. She wanted him right then and there, but knew it would have to wait. She dropped out of his grasp and threaded herself behind him to hold him the same way he had held her.

"Nice move!"

"We can't!" she said as she stood on tiptoes to rest her chin on his shoulder.

"You're right! Besides I didn't take my pill this morning," he joked.

She released him from her arms.

"For that remark, you do the dishes!"

"No problem! I want you to get started." He helped her with her coat. "I'll call you at eleven."

They kissed long and hard. The chemistry was building, but she stopped him and as hard as it was, she said goodbye at the front door. Already dusk, he switched on the outside lights, something new Walter Tompkins had insisted on installing around all the church buildings. They kissed again before she ducked into her Midget MG. He watched her drive into evening traffic.

He already missed her, but he conceded she distracted him from his work on Saturday night, when he needed time to prepare for Sunday's services.

So much had changed since becoming pastor. He once loved Saturday night as a time to date, go out dancing, or take in a late movie. He now found such activities almost impossible. Already Charlene had extolled him for not accommodating her social life. Last week, he had turned down an invitation to accompany her to a party with her friends. She had called him an "old fogy" and when she decided to go without him, they had had their first heated argument. Then, last night, because he had had a funeral (which had included this morning for the graveside service), it was noon today before they connected. Three hours later, he had run off to call on Lester. So, instead of spending Saturday afternoon together, she had stayed at the manse and prepared supper. Conforming to his hours was difficult for her and he worried how to bridge the gap. He recalled advice Frank Scarpelli had given him. *"Jerry, don't let the church become your mistress."* Yet, here he was doing exactly that.

He went to his bedroom to change, but then dismissed the idea, opting instead to stay with his English tweed jacket. He hadn't visited at the hospital since Thursday morning, had two patients to see, and decided to visit them before going to his study. So, he inserted the white plastic tab into his clergy shirt collar and put on his jacket. It was a comfortable outfit. He confessed he had fallen into a form of clergy dress he had once rudely protested. He liked the instant identity. It saved having to answer questions about why he was in the hospital after visiting hours and helped him conform to a role that he had felt destined to perform.

* * *

It was almost nine o'clock when Jerry arrived at Shepherd House. Darkness had fallen and the church buildings were unusually quiet for a Saturday evening. There were no banquets, basketball games or meetings taking place. With everything locked up tight, he believed he was alone on the church grounds.

He wouldn't complain. He had two hours of preparation ahead of him and he hated any interruption. He needed to put finishing touches on tomorrow's sermon. He also had to review the communion liturgy. Tomorrow's eleven o'clock service would entail his first "common time" to administer the Lord's Supper, so he had to rehearse the words and rubrics from the prayer book.

Lighting a lamp near the back bookshelves, he looked for the Presbyterian **Book of Common Worship**. He had left his own copy at the manse. He had planned on finding a copy among Maefield's collection. It should not be difficult to spot a quarter-page size dark green book. Jerry looked for it amid hymnbooks and a wide range of prayer books. Come to think of it, he didn't remember seeing it when he had organized his library. There was a good chance that the volume had found its way into the cathedral. Ministers often keep it handy on a pulpit shelf. He had to go in there anyway to check on whether the deacons had followed his instructions for setting up the communion elements. He could do it now instead of later.

He took the long way, which was through Miss Blatty's office, then into the annex. He entered the cathedral from the vestry behind the choir stalls. In the sanctuary, outside floodlights lit the stained glass showing the biblical scenes in a spectacular way and leaving the long nave dim and ghostly blue. Jerry shuddered every time he came alone at night, unable to forget the hour Everett Wheeler had searched for him and Charlene. It seemed such a chilling place in its shadowy and echoing depth, so empty and joyless without a crowd of people occupying the pews.

He found the electric light panel in the transept. He switched on the spotlights that lit the preaching and sacrament furnishings.

As he approached the communion table at the center of the upper chancel, he knelt a short distance up the steps, prayed for God's forgiveness and in soft tones recited the Lord's Prayer. This had become his personal ritual. It comforted him. He said a prayer for Everett, for Rhonda and for Daniel. All had died in a violent way on these hallowed church grounds. He prayed for the family of Detective John Burroughs. He rose to his feet. He was happy to see that the deacons had done as he had asked and had included on the table next to the chalice a round, fresh, uncut loaf of bread. He would use it to do something new for this church, breaking bread from a whole loaf instead of holding up a paper-thin wafer, which hardly symbolized bread or conveyed a sense of the body of Christ. He climbed the steps to the high pulpit.

Preachers have a habit of leaving things here, even a Sunday sermon or two. But all he found were musty hymnbooks and an assortment of bibles. He descended the pulpit and walked across the chancel to look in the lectern shelves. In divided chancels like the cathedral, the minister or assistant read scripture lessons as well as other parts of the service from this raised desk. As he did in the pulpit shelves, here too Jerry rearranged bibles and hymnals. He set to the side a filthy water glass, thumbed through a pile of old church bulletins, some of them dating back six years. He saw a stack of torn pieces of paper used to mark pages or to write out announcements and reminders. There was an opened box of cough drops and a half-empty box of Kleenex tissues. Dust and rolled up pieces of paper littered the lower shelf. Underneath this, he spotted the little green prayer book. As he opened it, a tightly folded insert fell out and floated to the floor. He followed the paper to its landing place. Sitting on the chancel steps, he unfolded a typewritten letter from Daniel Maefield.

> **January 21, 1962**
> **9:00 P.M.**
>
> **Dear Friend,**
> **Please know the depth of heartache with which I**
> **write . . .**

For several minutes, Jerry sat with his head bowed as he thought about what he had read. Nervous and unsure of himself, he folded the single sheet in the way he had found it and slipped it back into the prayer book, which he then fit snugly into the side pocket of his jacket.

As he got to his feet, he heard a resounding clap on the slate floor somewhere far back among the darkened pews. The noise shattered the stillness. He guessed a hymnbook had fallen. He tried shielding his eyes from the glare of the spotlights to see if a person sat there. He called but no one answered in kind.

Why did he feel uneasy? The revealing letter? Yet, what did it say that he didn't already know? That Reverend Maefield was by no means a saint. That he planned to resign as pastor, divorce his wife and ask forgiveness for his toleration of an abusive use of the church buildings. He had written the letter, he wrote . . . *out of fear that Everett Wheeler will kill me before I derive courage to testify about his misconduct.* On that statement alone, the letter confirmed Everett had indeed murdered him. But Maefield's letter gave new information . . . the promise of . . . *revealing secrets in a hidden box.* "Where does this all end?" Jerry asked in exasperation.

Another book-dropping noise echoed from the vicinity of the pews. Jerry felt the hair stand up on his head. Maybe he was overreacting. Old buildings like this creek and heavy books left precariously on wooden pews fall to the floor. Was his mind playing tricks on him? He didn't really believe Lilly Palmer's tales about ghosts.

He left the chancel lights on and ran at a full gallop the length of the south aisle, returning to his study by way of the cloister. Locking the heavy oak Shepherd Door behind him, he planted himself in the swivel chair behind his desk. He lit his desk lamp. He took the prayer book from his pocket, removed the folded letter and—after toying with it for a minute—he locked it in the top drawer of his desk. "Later tonight, I'll see if I can locate Everett Wheeler's hidden box," he whispered.

He turned the pages in the prayer book to the communion text. He stopped and looked up, stared into the distant shadow of his study. He was sure this time he felt a breeze. Or was it more nervous reaction to the letter and to the knowledge of the awful murder that had taken place in this very room? Then, far off, in Miss Blatty's office, he distinctly heard a door slam. He continued to stare and saw someone staring at him through the low light. He sensed a hostile presence.

"Father, can I use your bathroom?" he heard and watched the tall man step forward.

Jerry focused on a stranger. His face alone reflected the room light, a face that was pock marked and narrow with a wide, black mustache curled down at the edge of his upper lip and a short, jagged untamed beard protruding from his chin. As he came closer, Jerry saw he wore a long, brown army coat, a little early in the season for such a heavy garment. In his gloved hands, he held a white baseball cap. He took slow steps toward Jerry. Jerry now saw his coat was torn and lacked several buttons. When he turned slightly to the side to stare up at the disciple windows above the center table, Jerry saw his thick, black hair hanging straight down his back in the fashion of a hippie.

"How did you get in here?" Jerry responded, suspicious, the adrenaline rising with his heart beat.

"Oh, sorry! Did I scare you? I came in through the building behind this one. The door from the parking lot was unlocked. I know my way around pretty good. I'm looking for my old friend, Everett. Does he still work here?"

Jerry decided not to say anything. He didn't know whether the visitor was putting him on, or if he really didn't know about the death of Wheeler.

"The bathroom is behind you, the door on your left, facing. You can use it, but then you'll have to leave."

"Oh I know," he said smartly, and went inside and closed the door.

Jerry thought it wise to call the police. Ikeda Inoko, the new church custodian, was not in the habit of leaving doors unlocked. Regardless of how this man had gotten in, he was trespassing. Maybe better he call Chester Walsh at home. A friendly chat with the detective might be a better course of action. Jerry dialed the number and got a busy signal. He was about to try again when the man exited the bathroom.

"Hey, man, did you take over for the old priest who died here?"

Jerry's blood turned cold. Daniel Maefield was dressed in

clerical clothes at the time of his death. But he had consistently dressed in an old style, soft pontifical collar. Jerry thought to himself, this stranger knows about Doctor Maefield's death, but not about Wheeler's. Is that a coincidence? Or, is there more to this?

"I'm asking you to leave. You can use the door in the secretary's office," Jerry asserted.

"What's the big rush, Father? The priest who used to be here . . . was real nice to me. He let me hangout in one of the classrooms for a few nights. A super, good guy . . . too bad what happened to him."

The visitor moved to Jerry's desk and, without asking permission, he dropped into one of the wingback chairs that faced it. Jerry continued to stare at him.

"I came by to see if Everett had any women he needed servicing," he quipped, a low smile breaking out on his mouth. "I suppose you don't know nothing about that? Well, last time here, back in January, Everett showed me a good time. Wow, what a night! But he owes me a hundred bucks. That's really why I'm in the land of peas and beans." He paused, looking toward Jerry for uncommon approval of what he was about to say. "But I'll take a blow job instead, you know what I mean?"

Jerry broke his silence.

"I think the police would like to talk to you; that is, if you have information about what happened the? . . . "

"Police! Hey, man, I don't talk to no goddamn police. You tell me, no bullshit! Is Wheeler here or not?"

"No! Mr. Wheeler had an accident. He died a few months ago."

"No shit! Well, I'll be a fucking son of a bitch! You're not screwing with me now?"

Jerry stood up.

"I want you out of here! I didn't invite you in and I won't have you staying."

"I'll be going! Don't get excited! You know it's not nice to make a stranger unwelcome. You being a Father and all should know that."

Jerry didn't answer. The man stood up and walked off toward the fireplace. The light from the desk lamp and the floor lamp behind Jerry's desk were the only ones lighting the room. The dark visitor almost disappeared into the shadows. He then ambled to the side bookshelves, docked his hat on the oval table and took a book off a shelf. Nervous and mindless, he started thumbing through it. Then, as if angry with himself, he tossed the book into a chair. He approached Jerry again, who had remained standing behind his desk.

"You got some cash, Father? I'm broke. I lost my job and I got 'a catch a bus to Philadelphia. You got 'a help me."

"Sure!" Jerry said, thinking anything to get him out of his study, and took out his wallet. He handed the visitor a ten-dollar bill. "That's all I have."

"That's real Christian of you. The old priest helped me out, too. I guess you guys get hit up a lot," he said as he tucked the money into his pocket.

"But a church like this . . . you always got to have cash in the poor box. I'm poor. How 'bout a few more bucks, Father? I really don't think ten will go very far."

"I told you! That's all I have." Jerry scolded, his patience worn thin.

"That's all I have," the man said, mocking Jerry's words.

There was no time to prepare. The lanky man lunged across the desk, grabbed Jerry's lapel with his gloved hand and pulled him forward, his other gloved hand, a fist, simultaneously chopped toward the back of Jerry's neck. But the fabric slipped away as Jerry bolted and the blow missed its mark, grazing his forehead instead. Protected by the width of the desk, a second blow whipped air. Jerry saw the knife then, heard it click as the blade snapped out of its sheath. Jerry tensed as the man held it up and looked for an opportunity to move in close for a critical jab. Brazenly, he started around the desk. Jerry pushed his swivel desk chair into his attacker's knees, then with his foot he drove the chair hard, slowing and injuring the man, but not stopping him.

"Bastard!" he shouted as he stumbled. He grabbed the chair,

rolled it to the side, and swung his knife at Jerry, who sidestepped his attack. As the man fell away from him, Jerry grabbed his knife hand at the wrist and turned it up with all his strength. The quick move caught his attacker by surprise. Off balance, he lost momentum and, in quick order, his brain signaled pain. Jerry twisted and swung the arm hard, doubling it high against the intruder's shoulder, cracking his wrist, concurrently getting a choke hold around his neck and tightening his grip. The knife dropped. Jerry kicked it to the side. He followed the move with a kick behind the man's knees, dropping him face forward on to the floor, the intruder's free hand folding beneath, as Jerry fell on top. The fall stunned the man and, for a moment, he didn't move.

It seemed as though all of Jerry's anger, stored inside these last four months rushed to the surface. He perceived he was fighting again for his own life and that the man he had just disarmed was Maefield's real murderer. So, he didn't wait for him to recover. While he had him down, Jerry let go of his neck and pounded his fist against his right ear. The man screamed in pain and rolled over. Jerry grabbed him by his coat and raised him up to face him. He dropped him hard into the swivel desk chair and turned him around so that once more he could wrench his arm high and place his head in a chokehold.

"What happened? Tell me what happened in this room last January. Tell me! Tell me or I'll break your neck!"

Jerry's violent side had taken over. He increased his hold on the man's arm, straining it at the shoulder, until he heard it crack. Howling in pain, the man swore, pleaded for mercy. Jerry forced him forward and shouted in his ear that was red and swollen from his punch.

"Tell me what happened to Reverend Maefield, or so help me God, I'll . . . "

"Don't! God, please! Enough! Enough! I'll confess," the man screamed. "Really, I'm sorry about it! . . . I can tell you, seeing as how you're a priest! Right?"

Jerry wasn't feeling like a priest, pastor, Father, whatever the man thought he was. He had no thought of turning this struggle into a religious rite. He wanted to get the police in here. But if this man would talk to him, confess—as he understood his position—Jerry decided he would listen. He relaxed his hold.

"I'm waiting," Jerry replied. "Tell me what you know!"

He kept the stranger's arm folded to his collarbone, but released his chokehold.

"Start by telling me your name."

"Fuck you!" he hastily replied.

Jerry twisted his arm and raised it again. He couldn't believe this guy had forgotten pain so soon.

"Antonio Lopez!" Roberto Ramous shouted—his real name by now almost lost to his consciousness. "Please, please," he begged, as his arm moved higher. "Stop! I'll tell you everything you want to know. God, please, let go of my wrist!"

"All right Antonio, I'll ease up, but no tricks" Jerry let the man's arm drop a little, but continued his hold. "Go ahead, Antonio. When did you come to Tompkinsville?"

"I came north for the first time in sixty-one to pick strawberries and stayed through January, then I took a bus south to Florida. Last June I returned for strawberry picking, but stayed less than a week. I've been on Long Island since then. The cabbage and potato crops there dried up and they dropped me. I hitchhiked here last week for apple and pumpkin harvests. There ain't enough work here either. I've been looking all week, but nobody's hiring. I want to get back to Florida or maybe Texas before it gets too cold. So, I came in here looking for Everett. He owes me a hundred bucks."

"How did you meet Everett Wheeler?"

"I met him last January. I heard from a 'brother' the minister at this church helped people in need. So, one cold day, midweek, I stopped in. Sure enough, the priest let me bunk in a classroom made into a homeless shelter. I only had to clean up after me and don't cause no trouble. Father said I had to be out Saturday. He let me use the kitchen and brought me food. The gym has a locker room with showers and all, so this is a nice set up. Everything was good for three days, no problems, no complaints . . . Can you ease up on my arm? Oh shit, I can't think, I'm in so much pain."

Jerry released his wrist, but stood behind him, ready to pounce if necessary.

He moaned and breathed heavy as he brought his arm around to his lap. "Oh, God! I think my wrist is broken and you dislocated my shoulder," he said as he began massaging the wrist area.

"I'll get you help after you confess to what happened between you and Reverend Maefield."

"Where was I? I can't think."

"You were given the hospitality of the church education building. You had use of the shower room. Now, how did you meet Wheeler?"

"O Yah. Well, that's where I met Everett. Friday afternoon he walks in on me when I'm in the shower. I guess he'd been away and had just learned about me. I didn't know who the hell he was. He shuts off the water from outside. He rushes in like a madman and smacks me in the head. He starts shouting and shoving me. He calls me a spic, rat, and a fag and lots of other names, then threatens to throw me outside in the cold without my clothes. I tell him the priest gave me permission, and he calls the padre a sick bastard, says the old man has no authority to let me stay in the church building. Anyway, he lets me get dressed and I start to leave the building. He's behind me, pushing and shouting. Before I get out the door, the old priest charges down the hall. He scolds Everett, tells him I'm a 'guest of the King' and to take his hands off me. Everett stands there silent while the old guy lectures him on doing good. He should show kindness to the poor and homeless, the old guy scolds. I keep my mouth shut and take it all in. I can tell Wheeler's upset and pissing in his pants. Then the priest tells me I can stay one more night, but I have to leave in the morning. He's real sorry, he says in a pitiful voice, but Mr. Wheeler is right, the church has rules. He can't let me stay longer."

Roberto paused, not wanting to continue. Jerry slapped him on the shoulder and pushed him forward in the chair.

"Keep talking!"

"Well, after the old guy leaves, Wheeler lays off. He's got things to do and I don't see him again until Saturday afternoon. By then, I'm hoping he's forgotten me. But about three o'clock he catches me napping on a cot in the shelter. He's less threatening, but he won't relent to let me stay at the church another night. He tells me he's got a better place for me. He drives me a half-hour out of town to a shit-bag motel. He's got his own key and don't have to do no registering or anything. He leaves me with sandwiches and three quarts of beer. He tells me to stay put and leaves. At six o'clock Sunday morning, he wakes me up. Again, he's as nice as a man can be. He drives me a mile down the road to a diner and buys me breakfast. While I'm eating sausage and pancakes, he makes me a proposition.

He says he's in the film business, sells girlie pictures and makes skin flicks as a sideline. Would I be interested in having sex in front of a camera? He says he rents a studio in the basement of an old warehouse. To protect the privacy of the owner, he has to keep the place a secret. He tells me I have to wear a blindfold. It sounds weird, but when he offers me a hundred bucks, I'm okay. He tells me it'll be the best fuck I ever had."

Tired of standing, Jerry pulled a chair behind and sat down.

"He drives me back to the motel and tells me he'll come by after dark to get me. Once more, he leaves me beer and sandwiches. It starts snowing around three and the roads begin looking real bad. All afternoon I watch television and sleep. Around 8:30 Sunday night, Wheeler walks into my room. Considering the weather, I think he's crazy driving all the way out there. We're in the middle of a blizzard and there's no sign it's going to stop. He's so drunk he don't seem to notice. He says he has to blindfold and tie me up before we leave the room. At first, I protest. I don't like kinky stuff. He don't want to hear that and his whole attitude changes from Mr. Friendly to hard-ass. He smacks me in the stomach and says I'm dead if I don't do exactly what I'm told. I ask about the hundred and he says, 'after the performance'. If I do well, he'll consider it. This is no time to argue, so I let him tie my hands behind my back. He covers my whole head in a rubber mask and wraps a piece of cloth over my eyes. I tell him he better not be a homosexual; I hate homos. He just laughs. He drapes my coat over my shoulders and leads me through the snow to his truck.

"He drives while he drinks. I can hear and smell him. He circles around for a long time before I hear a garage door going up by remote control from inside his truck. He pulls me out of the truck and starts pushing me along. He must've thought I was real stupid. He ain't fooled me, 'cause I know where I am. I'd been wandering around this church building for three days; picked the locks of any room I wanted, walked down every hallway, up and down stairs. I had even gotten into the basement. Its smell and sound are all too familiar. I'm sure. Now I know why the blindfold and all the shit about protecting someone's reputation. Suddenly, he pulls a tight gag over my mouth. I hear doors open and shut. Next thing I know I'm on a bed. He yanks my pants to my ankles. Several minutes later, I hear a woman with a German accent. Wheeler removes my blindfold. I see this woman with a red scarf covering her eyes. I think maybe she's old, but I'm not sure. She wears a manlike suit jacket and a long black skirt. Wheeler stands behind her. He unties her hair and makes it fall along her face and down over her shoulders. As I watch, he undoes her jacket and throws it onto a chair. She leans against him while he unbuttons her shirt and opens it, so I can see her breasts spilling over her brazier. I change my mind about her looks and age. Her tits are big suckers, long and sharp as knives. Wheeler puts his hands on them and she starts purring like a pussycat. He unhooks her brazier and drops it over my 'big-Joe', which by now is standing straight as a telephone pole. He unzips her skirt and pushes it to the floor. She's wearing see-through panties and black stockings."

As Roberto (alias Antonio Lopez) said this, Jerry remembered when Rhonda had stretched in front of him on the bed at the motel. His attacker was telling no fib. He had described Rhonda's nakedness, her allure, her indiscretion.

"I hear her ask him if someone besides the two of them is in the room. He laughs louder than before, 'I thought you'd never ask', and 'don't ever say I don't give you big presents.' He pushes the scarf off her eyes. The motherfucker looks at me, but she don't laugh. She looks amused, but greedy. She leans over and takes off my gag. Then she kneels at my side and uses her brazier like a glove. But before I go off, she gets over me and fucks me till I hurt. She does me big-time and keeps doing me long after I shoot my jism.

"I'm fucked-up 'cause I can't touch her . . . you know what I mean, Reverend?" Roberto asked as if Jerry should understand. "I beg Wheeler untie my hands. He laughs at me and stands there watching. He don't take no pictures, just watches his lady take a wild ride on me. I think he came in his pants. Then he says, 'That's it!' and he blindfolds and gags me. I hear them whispering to each other. They hike up my pants and help me stand. Wheeler drapes my coat over my shoulders and buttons it up. He takes me to his truck. He runs it out of the garage into the snow, real fast, 'cause he don't want to get stuck. He don't really drive me anywhere, but is more crazy than earlier. I hear 'm slugging from his booze bottle and all night I don't think he knew his head from his ass; he's so soused. The truck brakes and slides to a stop. He removes the blindfold, gag and face mask. He shows me a knife, the same kind I carry, which I'm hoping is still in my coat pocket. He cuts the rope from my wrists. He opens the door, points to the bus station down the street, hands me fifteen bucks and pushes me out. I fall in a snow bank. He throws me my coat. I ask 'm where's the hundred he promised? That's when the bastard tells me we're even; the difference is for the motel and all the food. 'You lucky I don't cut your balls off,' he shouts and slams the truck door. I reach for my coat, and find my knife. But he drives away in a hurry. It's snowing hard, weather's more miserable than before. I know there ain't no busses running out o' town in this shit. I find my leather gloves and put 'm on. I'm really pissed off. The bastard! He promised me a hundred bucks. No one can fuck with me like that. I' want 'a kill 'm. I walk up the street and cross through the park. There's three-foot drifts and slow going, exhausting. I'd like to freeze to death. I see the church up on the hill. I hear the bell and count eleven clangs. I see lights on in one of the buildings. I hike up there and try several doors, all locked. I find my way to this door." Ramous nodded toward the Shepherd Door behind Jerry. "I see light shining out of this room, same as tonight. I turn the bell. A light comes on over me and I figure the old priest is staring at me through the little window. He recognizes me from when he let me stay here. He unlocks the door and invites me in. He says to take off my coat and gloves and warm myself by the fire. But I know he wants to lecture me like before and I'm in no mood for his preaching. I interrupt to tell him I got business with Everett. He says he's nowhere around and I get angry. I yell at him not to bullshit me. I ask him if he knows what's going on in his basement. He acts only half surprised, like he knows something, but don't want to let on. I tell him about Wheeler and his whore. He says I am mistaken. This is a church and I shouldn't tell lies. I say I'm not making up anything, that less than an hour ago a woman down there fucked me good while Wheeler watched. I wore a mask and there may be pictures. Now the old priest's mood turns ugly. He stands up and hits me on my shoulder, tells me I'm foul mouthed and he can't let me stay. I argue I got no place to go. He insists I go to the bus station and wait there until busses are moving again. He will buy me a ticket to Philadelphia. I get out of the chair and say 'okay'. I don't want to be where I'm not wanted. Then I see a picture on the mantle of a young woman. She's older now, but I recognize her. I say, 'Is this your daughter?' I tell him she's the whore with Everett, who just drove me wild. The old priest is really pissed off at me now. He gets out of his chair and slaps my face, screams at me to get out. He don't want to hear my foul language. He pushes and slaps me at the same time. I warn him. Stop hitting me. He don't listen and keeps it up. I lose my temper. I pick up a coal shovel by the fireplace and swing it, hitting him in the nose. His glasses fly across the room. I hit 'm a second time with the shovel. Blood splatters on the glass doors behind him. It spills out of his nose like from a faucet. I didn't mean to hit him that hard, I swear! I don't know why I had to swing a second time. He drops into his chair. His hands try to stop the blood. I pull him out of the chair and hold him up with one hand. He's light as a feather. I have my knife out and I stab him in the gut. He looks surprised, pathetic. He's hurting and I don't want him to hurt no more. He opens his mouth to scream and I don't want him bringing anyone in here. So, I slash his throat. It wouldn't have been easier if he'd been a chicken. His blood bubbles up over his collar, spills on to my hands, coat and feet. I drop 'm on the floor. He goes out flat on his back in front of the fireplace. I get down over him and I stab him. I don't stop until I'm tired. I drive the knife into his heart. The stupid, old jerk! He shouldn't have shoved me and preached at me. I can only take so much o' that . . . "

Sitting forward, Ramous supported his head in his uninjured hand. Jerry allowed him this momentary silence, a few seconds of grace after having relived the murder. Jerry took the opportunity to pull the phone from across the desk. He dialed Detective Walsh at his home. He and Walsh had become close friends. This time, Walsh answered on the second ring.

"Chester, this is Jerry. No time for small talk. You need to come over to Shepherd House right away. I've got a guy here who has confessed he murdered Reverend Maefield . . . . Yes . . . I'm okay! He's got some broken bones."

Jerry hung up. He waited a few seconds before begging a final question.

"Antonio, you were covered with blood. How did you get away without leaving a trail?"

"Yeah, there's blood all over the priest and me. I dig into his pocket for his wallet. I come out with mostly five and ten dollar bills. I'm careful not to leave fingerprints. The whole time, I never took off my gloves. I stick the bills down my pants. I didn't want no one tracking me so I take off my shoes, socks and coat. I carry them by way of the office. I make my way through the gym and into the shower room where I clean up in the dark. I don't turn on a light. It's amazing how much a man can see in the dark, something prison teaches you. The door into the clothes-collection room is unlocked and I find a suit to fit and another coat, even a pair of warm socks and shoes. I pack all my bloody things into an old suitcase that's there. I fill my pockets with Christmas candy and crackers, a bottle of peanut butter and a half dozen cans of tuna fish. I don't even think about catching a bus. I carry the suitcase and walk through the snow. No one is out in this weather, no one notices me. Two miles west of town are field-worker cottages closed up for the winter. I stayed in one before I came to the church midweek. There's no heat or light, but I can take it for a few days. Fortunately, I find a 'brother' hang 'en out there who owns a car. We wait it out until Tuesday. I pay him for a ride and he drops me off in Norfolk, Virginia where I catch a Greyhound bus to Jacksonville, Florida. I throw the suitcase packed with bloody clothes into a trash bin a few blocks from the bus station. A week later, I get a job with a Florida farm crew. I don't like Florida, especially with summer coming, so I work my way north. In Delaware, I seen a green and white T&T bus. I sign on for strawberry picking and that's how I get back here. What else you want to know, Father?"

Jerry sat on the edge of his desk watching the figure slumped forward in the swivel desk chair. Suddenly he sat up straight and spun around.

"You ain't turning me in, are you? I mean you're a priest. You heard my confession. You can't tell nobody except God! Right?"

"You attacked me! You tried to kill me in the same way you killed the other minister. You're going to tell the police what you told me."

The man stared back in disbelief; his black eyes appeared tortured as he counted the consequences of what he considered a betrayal. He turned away.

Jerry heard a siren, got out of his chair to unlatch Shepherd Door . . .

He should not have let his appearance of contrition, or his wounded condition fool him. He should not have turned his back and disregarded his earlier danger.

Ramous sprung to his feet. As before, he acted like a bolt of lightning. Before Jerry turned to see him, Ramous had picked up a heavy bookend from the desk in his left hand and swung, grazing Jerry's cheek. The bruising blow drove Jerry against Shepherd Door, a thrown bookend followed, missing Jerry's head by an inch. In the next sweep of his uninjured left hand, Ramous picked up the brass desk lamp and hit Jerry on the forehead. Jerry fell to the floor as blood gushed and he felt a swift kick knick his elbow, but in a second kick, Jerry grabbed the man's foot, pulled forward, tripping him. Roberto crashed against the typing table a foot from the desk. The desk lamp flew from his grip as he plummeted to the floor. In the fallen light of the lamp, the man's spotted his knife a few feet away and reached for it. Jerry saw his intention, bent over him and again pulled his foot, this time twisting and jerking it hard, holding him but not enough to keep him from retrieving his knife. Shaking lose, Ramous flipped on to his back, held the knife in his left hand and waved the blade furiously.

Blood down his front, Jerry staggered to the side. Picking up the desk chair, he dropped it with force on top of his attacker, crushing his stomach. Still, he clenched the knife, desperate, snaking his body out from under the chair and away from Jerry. But it was over for him. Jerry renewed his attack by kicking and connecting against the man's left wrist, snapping it and knocking the knife out of his hand. Lost in his anger, Jerry pounded his fists into the man's midsection. Roberto begged him to stop. But he kept it up until the fallen man coughed blood and his face turned blue.

Exhausted, Jerry moved off him, found the electric switch to the overhead lights and turned them on. Instantly the room lost all its shadows. He heard shouts from outside and in seconds, Shepherd Door flew open. Three policemen rushed in.

Jerry pulled his handkerchief from his breast pocket, the same linen cloth Charlene had used to dab away her lipstick. He held it against his bleeding head. He dropped into a chair behind the oval table eyeing his confessor as he squirmed in pain on the oak floor.

Chester Walsh rolled the fallen man on to his stomach. Paying no attention to his crying protests, he cuffed him, not that there was much need of it. Ramous cursed and yelled when they hiked him to his feet and walked him to a waiting police cruiser. Chester pulled a chair up next to Jerry, who was having his head wounds treated by one of the uniformed cops.

"Preacher," Chester said, grinning from ear to ear, "You just got to tone down those sermons!"

"Yes, I know! There must be a safer way to earn a living."

CHAPTER 21

LOVE ME!

Monday Morning, November 19

Madge Todd watched from her kitchen window through pouring rain for Jerry Flynn's black Imperial. Due at nine this morning, it was almost that now. He had agreed yesterday to meet at her house.

This was the best time of day. The children were in school. She had no plans to go to the office. She had told her staff she was taking the day off and to hold her calls. Her parents were away on a long-planned vacation. Curiously, her father had made her promise to confide in Jerry.

Madge recalled how she had lingered after yesterday's service of worship, the last person among the congregation to greet the pastor at the cathedral door. Her heart had pounded as she told him she needed advice on a new crisis in her personal life.

In the weeks after the funeral, she had leaned on Jerry Flynn a lot. His guidance, prayers, the interest he had shown in her children, for everything he had done and said, if she never knew him any other way she would love him for his pastoral care. And whereas she had not revealed any of her dark secrets, she meant to do so today. She had so much to tell him. She had asked him if he could spare the whole morning.

At first, he had responded with a broad smile and a friendly hug. Maybe she had read more into his embrace than she should have, but he seemed to hold on to her longer than in the past. Then his eyes became glassy and his smile vanished. His personality changed from friendly, polite and adoring to one who looked at her as if from a distance. He surprised her by saying he was planning to call on her anyway. He had personal and very private matters to tell her. There followed a long pause in which she had worried they were both going to cry. Coyly, he dropped his head and turned from her, then walked away, leaving her alone.

Why had he treated her so unkindly in the end? Had he tired of consoling her? Had Charlene put the brakes on his cordiality? She and Charlene had shared confidences and she thought an enduring friendship. Madge had wished them the best in marriage and thought of herself as free of jealousy. But she had not seen Charlene in many weeks. Maybe she was away on a case and Jerry was feeling lost without her. Still, there was no reason for him to show rudeness. His hasty retreat had hurt her. As late as midnight, she had thought about calling and canceling their appointment. But, no, she had promised her dad and she had promised herself.

$$* \quad * \quad *$$

In reality, Madge's latest personal crisis represented a new definition of the old: her harassing fear that her affair with Rhonda Maefield would become common knowledge and bring disgrace to her family. It attacked with new vengeance last Friday. That morning, as she prepared to make Michael's office her own, she had started by clearing out his desk drawers.

Madge had put off this task long after Chester Walsh tracked down Michael's car keys, which included the key to his desk. Like everything else of Michael's personal property she had dealt with, she feared what she would find. And whether sorting through his clothes or his office papers, her task had always seemed like an invasion of privacy, as if looking into the life of a stranger instead of a man she had known as her husband for almost ten years.

In the bottom drawer, Madge browsed through folders holding information on machinery, equipment warrantees and marketing reports. If a folder no longer applied, she promptly dumped it into a tall trashcan standing next to her. Toward the back, she took out a manila folder labeled **Madge**. Inside were birthday and Valentine Day cards she had sent him, notes of hers he had kept, photographs of them when they were high school sweethearts, memorabilia of their senior prom, a snapshot when they were seventeen as they waded out of the family swimming hole. She smiled as she recalled the day, the first time she had worn a two-piece bathing suit and how her mother had had a fit when she first saw her in it, saying the style was less than underwear and unsuitable in public. But she didn't forbid me, Madge remembered. Mom blushed for me but she understood.

Madge had no idea Michael kept such memorabilia but they were here, a whole collection of things from those beautiful years. The preserved past touched her deeply. Michael's thoughtfulness and love for her had once been genuine. She got up from her chair, and closed and latched the office door. She wanted no one interrupting her. She did not need staff people to see her crying.

Once more at the desk, she continued to browse. From the back of the drawer, she pulled out a crunched folder with no label. Her heart jumped a beat as she opened it to reveal a five-by-seven studio-portrait photo of Sarah Draper, something taken ten years ago, when the woman was promoting herself as a New York model. Its full meaning hit Madge like a bolt of lightning as she read, one after another, trashy letters Sarah had addressed to Michael. Also in the folder were cash receipts from stores selling jewelry, lingerie and other gifts. She read receipts for cash paid to hotels and restaurants from New York to Philadelphia and from motels close by with names she recognized. Michael never threw away a receipt, no matter how insignificant. Hurt turned to shock as she opened an envelope with several beach scene snapshots of a bare breasted Sarah. "How she loved to showoff her blossoms!" Madge jeered. Then, from inside another envelope, she slid out a photo showing more than she wanted to see of her husband's and Sarah's anatomy. In this picture, Sarah had her face covered by a cat mask and that was all she wore while saddled on Michael's back. No mask hid his face. He was supposed to be a dog, Madge assumed. A second photo showed more of the same.

"You think you know someone; you don't know anyone," Madge said in a frail voice. "Stupid me! I never considered Sarah as someone he would go to for sex." She studied the photos closely. Was kinky sex what Michael craved? To have a woman treat him like a dog? "I can't believe he would allow this," she said in soft tones mixed with gentle sobs. But who am I to judge? Who would believe odd things about me?"

Madge put them to the side and turned to a brown envelope with **Photo enclosed. Do not Bend** stamped on the outside. Her stomach turned sour as she read its **Special Delivery** postmark from Stone Harbor, New Jersey, including a receipt-notice stamp dated **Monday, June 11, 1962, 11:00 A.M.**, the day of Sarah's murder, forty hours before Michael's fatal car crash. "I hate to look."

She glided two five-by-seven glossy black-and-white prints from the envelope. Her heart leaped to her throat as shocking obscenity greeted her. Surely, this was not of her? Her face, breasts and tummy? And the naked woman kneeling in front of her? Rhonda?

Beads of sweat broke out. She felt lightheaded and her heart pounded. Her hand shook, as she looked at the second photo. More unnerving than the first, the photographer had caught her in her own act of cunnilingus. Both photographs left no doubt of her identity.

She did not think she would make it in time to the adjoining bathroom. Lifting the seat, crouching on her knees, she threw up several times. She heaved until there was nothing more to vomit and she still wretched. She dropped the photos and envelope on the floor. She took her time getting up. She flushed and flushed again. She put down the toilet lid and sat on it. Her face, drained of all its color, collapsed in her hands. Perspiration poured off her forehead, neck and arms. She put her head between her legs to keep from fainting. After a long wait, she looked between her fingers at the scenes staring up at her. She lifted the photos and studied them again. She slid a letter out of the envelope.

> *Michael—*
>
> *Don't ask how I came into possession of this picture. Now you know why Madge doesn't want your pecker. Hey, I told you so! Here's proof of the company your affectionate wife really enjoys. And think of it this way, Michael. Show Sweetpea this picture and she'll give you whatever you want: sex your way, divorce under your terms, outright ownership of the family business, whatever your little head desires. All can be yours.*
>
> *So, no more feeling guilty after we play our own dirty games. Right? And no more hanging up on me. I'll be the one who says when our fucking days are over.*
>
> *Now that I've got your attention—yes, there's more. You will want to see my snap shots of our cat and dog game last November. You look fucking great without a mask. But best of all—I have a second photo of darling Sweetpea that makes me want her. Come have a look!*
>
> *When you get this mail, you'll know where to find mze. Don't delay.*
>
> *From your one and only, who loves her honey on your pecker.*

Many minutes passed before Madge looked away from the letter. Terror gripped her mind as she realized Michael had gone to Sarah's beach house the day of her murder. Where else would he have gotten the second photo referred to in Sarah's letter? Then the sickening questions hit her: How many more photos are there? Who took them? Where are they now? Was Michael planning to use these pictures to guarantee his control of the business?

Sick and fearful, she acted for the moment in the only rational way she knew how. Using a match pack from the medicine cabinet, she put the photos to the flame, held each fast burning print over the toilet until the last second before dropping it. "If only the bad pictures on my mind could disappear this easy," she cried. She flushed the toilet. She repeated the action with the letter and with every item in the file folder. Returning the matches to the cabinet, she saw a single edged razor blade. She thought about it for several seconds, then slammed the cabinet door. "No, I won't answer my problems that way," she said and left the bathroom. She could not, however, continue her routine at the office and, pausing only long enough to lock her desk and pick up her purse, she marched through the main office and exited to the parking lot. Although everyone who saw her leave said she looked like a walking dead person, and wondered about the acid smoke enveloping her office, no one said anything. She managed to drive home. In the hours following, she remained active and deflected telephone calls from staff about her health by saying she was "fine" and had merely passed through a "little post-mortem depression." Her mom dropped in at noon with her sister, Bob. Bob offered to stay through the night and she welcomed it. Nights were her worst times anyway and for this one, she took two sleeping pills. In the morning, she came down the stairs to find Bob fixing breakfast for her children and couldn't believe how late it was.

But she looked her usual self—bright and cheerful, her resident smile winning everyone's confidence. When her parents telephoned to suggest they would change their vacation plans, she got mad at them and said she wouldn't hear of such silliness. She felt great, she told them, and they would hurt her more by doing such a foolish thing. As planned, she drove them to Newark Airport for their flight to Scotland.

Everything went well until just before boarding began. Once more, for reasons she did not understand, her deep-seated emotions surfaced and her eyes filled with tears. She explained this as "runaway happiness," that after these many years, her parents were leaving the farm for a vacation. If not for yesterday, they would have accepted her explanation. Instead, Walter threatened to cancel their trip. Her mother, who had wanted to stay at home anyway, started talking to the ticket agent about rescheduling. Only Madge's insistence that she would be all right prevented them from changing their plans. Walter took her aside.

"Madge, I know you are sick to death about yourself. I saw it in your face long before Michael's death. You must know your mother and I support you. We will not let you down. We love you with all the love we have."

"Can you forgive me if I disgrace you?" she asked, her speech faltering and low.

"You don't have to ask forgiveness, Madge, because there is nothing that needs forgiving! Now," he said, holding her firmly in his arms, "for us to go ahead with this vacation, you have to promise me you'll meet with Jerry Flynn. I want you to confide in him, Sweetpea! He has information that may ally your worst fears."

"Daddy wouldn't let me go until I promised," Madge recalled in a meek voice. "I saw his tears as he wiped away my own. As lost and confused as I feel, suicide is not the answer. I remain hopeful and . . . ," her mind in a state of pause, she dared to say it. "I am in love."

Just then, she saw Jerry's Imperial turn into the long driveway, watched as it splashed through rain puddles and bounced over ruts in the gravel surface to park on the concrete apron in front of the garage. She shivered in anticipation of what she would say . . . do!

*　　*　　*

Jerry Flynn saw Madge step on to the porch as he eased out of his car. Her black hair, which she had allowed to grow long, was whipping in the wind. She wore no coat in the cool November air and had her arms folded protectively beneath her breasts, a pinafore covering her turtleneck sweater, its hem lifting in the wind a little above her knees. He thought she looked especially pretty, but more, she looked alluring, exciting.

She smiled as he shook out his umbrella and dropped it onto one of the old rocking chairs. Cheerful, and friendly as ever, she politely pecked him on the cheek. She opened the screen door, but—exercising a gentleman's right—he held it for her and followed her inside.

The house was warm and smelled of lavender. She had decorated the sitting room, which adjoined the kitchen and dinning room, in a bright, country style. She took his black raincoat and hung it on a hanger, which she hooked on the inside of the hall closet door. He had dressed in a comfortable sweatshirt and blue jeans. She liked him this way. It better suited his informal personality, not to mention his attractive physique.

"I have coffee and sugar buns. Would you like to sit at the kitchen table?"

"Sure, that pleases me just fine. I'm not very good at balancing things on my knees . . . failed knee-balancing in seminary, you know," he joked.

She laughed and said she understood. He followed her into a kitchen that—like the rest of the house—was ideally practical, neat and comfortable. She poured perked coffee and set out hot buns laced with cinnamon, raisins and coated with melted sugar. The kitchen smelt from their baking.

She had spent time preparing for him. Everywhere, it was obvious. He liked it that she had greeted him in a dress and not the long shirt and overalls more common to her at home. He thought the fashion made her look delicate, innocent and pure.

"If you want I can fry, poach or boil eggs?" she asked.

"Oh no, this is already second breakfast for me," he said at the same moment pulling a bun away from the pack, "Thanks, but I'll be happy with what's here."

He bit off what he could and held the rest in limbo. "What about you? The baker has to sample her wares."

"No, she's already had her share," she replied.

"I know . . . you don't want to get your fingers gooey," he

asserted and broke off half of his. He reached across the table. "Take it! I don't always give this kind of service."

Madge frowned, but shyly accepted his offering. He made her smile. Then he reached with his napkin and brushed away a speck of melted sugar on her chin. If he had meant to put her at ease, he had succeeded.

"Hey, I miss your friendly dog. Where is the little tyrant?" Jerry asked.

"Uncle John took him! Casper went after one of the neighbor kids a week ago, nipped him on the leg. I felt so bad. No harm done, but I can't chance it again. Dad's promised the boys a Lab puppy when he and mom get back from Scotland. But I miss the killer."

"Yah, he certainly was that. Last time I was here I thought he would bite my leg off."

Madge laughed, watched him smile. She thought back to the incident, recalled how she had to put the growling dog in the cellar. "Yes, Casper does not like men or children."

They sat for a few moments in silence. He stirred sugar into his coffee. He contemplated what he needed to say. She seemed so fragile; he worried whether she was strong enough for his news.

He appeared a bit nervous and she decided to break into his thoughts.

"How is Charlene?" she asked. "I haven't seen her out to church for several weeks."

"Oh, she's well . . . " He took a sip of coffee. "Counting yesterday, it's been five!"

He hadn't looked at her when he said this. Only after he had raised the coffee mug to his lips a second time did she see his eyes. They were hard and flushed—reminders of how he had left her yesterday. His face had lost its smile. There was no sign that it would return.

"Madge, Charlene and I . . . We've agreed to give each other some space. I haven't told anyone about it, not even my parents, but . . . well, there's just too much to sort out. After all we went through together, we thought we were ideal for each other. Then, between her job and mine, we saw a great divide. We had to take a hard look at our future."

He thought he would leave it at that, yet, knew it wasn't the whole story. Madge looked stunned. He knew he owed her more.

"After my second near death at the church," he continued, "Charlene made clear that my life as a minister did not appeal to her. It wasn't the danger. She knew that was an anomaly. My time and commitment to others bothered her. My weekend obligations were out of sync with her weekend days off. My preparing for services on Saturday night butted with what she wanted to do. In the beginning, she liked what I did, even thought it exciting. But as I got busier, that changed. The idea of becoming a minister's wife became anathema to her. I never saw it coming and was surprised when she let me know. She wanted me to find another occupation. I told her the choice of career wasn't mine. I knew it sounded corny. I didn't know that it also hurt her deeply. She replied that as long as I felt that way, she wouldn't interfere, but that she chose not to participate. I could sacrifice my life, she told me, but I didn't have the right to offer up hers. And I had to agree. Considering where her career was taking her, I was no happier with her choices than she was with mine . . . She's taken a job in the Justice Department and has already moved to Washington."

Jerry's voice had gone silent. Madge looked up. How long had he watched her in her trance? He was waiting for a response to his news.

"I'm sorry, Jerry," she said. "You seemed so happy together," she managed. She wanted to say so much more, but she did not have the heart for it. She was in love with this man and suddenly that thought burned inside her. But how could he love her? "You don't have to say anymore."

For several seconds they sat in silence, the only noise from the wind-rattling shutters and the rain hitting the kitchen windows.

"Look, I'm sorry!" he said, his face brightening a little. "You didn't invite me here to talk about my problems. But I wanted you to know. You and Charlene got along real well. I know she liked you and she would do anything to help you. Whether you'll have a chance to see her again, I doubt it! I guess I have to admit, our relationship is over. There's nothing more we have to say to each other . . . " He stared at his hands resting on the table. "We were two ships that got their anchors entwined. We almost went to the grave together. But we survived and then separated. We have no plans to pass again."

"I understand, Jerry. But consider yourselves lucky you both saw ahead."

"Yah . . . that's true," he said, his voice halting as he lifted his cup to drink coffee again.

When he looked at her, she was staring at him. Her face was sad yet soft, and those eyes—bright, dark and tender, like the first time he had so boldly looked into them. Nor did she waver now, holding his eyes in hers, even as she interrupted the silence.

"I see the wounds have healed."

She brushed her finger lightly over his brow, as if by magic what little remained of a deep cut should disappear.

"Yes, I thought I would have to get a skin graft, but the doctor did a good job sewing me up. In time, the crease won't be noticeable. Mr. Roberto Ramous—He told me his name was Antonio—but whatever his name, he left a reminder, but the wounds inside will take forever to heal."

They discussed the strange turn of events since Roberto Ramous, alias Antonio Lopez, found his way into Shepherd House. The press had described Jerry as a hero. He was quick to say, *"It's hard to consider yourself a hero when you're fighting for your own life."* In recent weeks, however, he was looking more as if he was the bad guy. Ramous or his lawyers were claiming Ramous had become the victim, that Jerry had beaten him up and put words in his mouth. Because Jerry had heard the confession using duress, Jerry's testimony was inadmissible. Ramous now admitted only to entering Shepherd House after the minister was dead. All he did was pick the dead man's pocket. Thus far, the DA had not charged Ramous with the murder of Daniel Maefield. Nor had he shown any interest in changing conclusions that had convicted Everett Wheeler.

Jerry was dumbfounded. The audacity of the law shocked him. There was no doubt Wheeler had cut down Detective Burroughs and Rhonda Maefield. But Jerry believed Ramous had killed Daniel Maefield. He confided to Madge that Ramous would never face trial for that murder.

"It's not like he'll be set free. When New Jersey makes up its mind on what to do about Ramous, Missouri is waiting for him. And if that's not enough, they want him in Florida on suspicion of murder. Personally, I think Ramous should get the death penalty," Jerry said. "What hurts most: I have colleagues who look on me as a monster for what I did to homeless, indefensible Roberto Ramous that night."

"He would have killed you," Madge interrupted and just as suddenly, she broke out in tears. Jerry handed over his napkin. Her outburst surprised him. "I'm sorry, I can't help it. My father hurt you. He did something I don't know how you can forgive him for. I'm not sure I understand it."

"You can!" Jerry said. He took a deep breath. Now is the time, he thought. I have to tell her what I know. "Everett was blackmailing your father. Did you know that?"

"No!"

"He wanted your father to scare me off because I knew about his studio . . . Madge, Everett had pictures."

"O God, no, don't tell me that!" she exploded and panic rose instantly to the surface. She put her hands over her eyes. The fright she had felt earlier returned. Only now, she meant to run and never stop, run until dead. She trembled and tried to stand. But Jerry quickly reached over and folded his hands over her arms. "Everett, my own cousin took them?" she moaned and sobbed all at once. "I knew the man indecent and lurid, but to do this . . . "

She tried again to break away.

"Stop! Madge, listen to me! No running," he said sternly, gripping her wrists.

She struggled to push back from the table, but he held down her arms.

"Let me finish. Madge! You have nothing to fear from what I'm going to tell you. That evening before his death, Reverend Maefield wrote a letter. In part, the letter was a typed confession. I found it folded inside a prayer book on a shelf in the lectern of the cathedral less than an hour before my bout with Ramous. This was what the police were looking for all those weeks they spent going through Maefield's library books and papers. Chester Walsh has told me Burroughs knew Maefield had written something relevant to his own murder. Burroughs had the FBI lab run tests on the ribbon from Maefield's typewriter. Under a microscope, and using other tricks of their trade, analysts could decipher a date and time of last use. They encrypted other words indicating Maefield had typed out something personal hours before his death. Also, Burroughs found bits of paper that missed full incineration in the fireplace, more evidence that put him on to searching for whatever Maefield had finished writing and had stored somewhere. Unfortunately, the detective never searched the cathedral."

Madge held Jerry's hands as she rested her head over them. Her soft hair tickled his wrists. He could feel her tears wetting his knuckles.

"In his letter Maefield wrote about Everett's use of the basement room to take pornographic pictures . . . He also revealed he knew Everett and Rhonda were having an affair. He had seen them together in the hidden room. None of that is any longer a surprise, however, Maefield's rather lengthy epistle substantiates the DA's assumption of motive and reflects Maefield's fear of Everett if the man caught him spying. Maefield even states his initial reason for the letter as fear Everett would kill him before he had an opportunity to stop what was happening in the basement and he wanted to leave behind the truth. But the letter goes further. Writing with sadness, Maefield announces his plans to resign as pastor and to separate from his wife. He calls Rhonda a 'nymphomaniac' and blames her condition on her youth in a prison-school run by the Nazis, which conditioned young women to live their lives as bisexual predators.

"Why he left his letter inside a prayer book in the cathedral is anybody's guess. In my opinion, he saw this as a safe place to keep it until free of Everett. If anything happened to him, he counted on investigators searching the lectern.

"What was new in Maefield's letter, and what delayed me from passing it on to the DA, were Maefield's instructions on where to find a box Everett used to store his pictures, forty-five caliber bullets, and an extra key unlocking the door to the secret studio. Maefield had made a copy of that key for his key ring, the same ring given me by your father. Charlene and I happened by and found the door mistakenly unhidden. I went through the keys on my ring until I found one that fit. We were in.

"Burroughs' failure to search the cathedral, or to check Maefield's keys, lost him two opportunities to break the case wide open within weeks of the murder. Burroughs, Everett, and Rhonda would be alive today had Burroughs discovered the hidden studio. But I held the last chance to bring the studio to his attention. If I had reported the room within an hour of Charlene and my discovering it that Sunday, the story we tell today would be much different."

Jerry's remorse escaped to the surface. His hands trembled over Madge's, perspiration dripped from his grim face. Madge lifted her head and saw his pain, his tears.

"You're punishing yourself," she said, her voice cracking with stress.

"If I don't admit my own complicity in all this, I couldn't live with myself! I ignored Charlene's advice. And she let me have my way. She wanted me as much as I wanted her that night. We were frightened out of our wits less than an hour before, yet we cuddled in each other's arms like lost lambs. We turned on the light of passion and turned out the darkness of death. We made love when we should have followed other impulses. By Monday's dawn, Everett had completely emptied the hidden room of any clue to the way we had seen it. I still find it hard to believe he could have done all that labor in such a short time, but he did . . ."

Madge said nothing. She was suffering, but she was listening. After a slight pause, Jerry went on, his voice becoming more assertive and bold.

"To get back to the letter. I kept Maefield's letter locked in my desk drawer. I never mentioned it to anyone, not even Charlene. She and I went ahead with our mini vacation plans in the Pocono Mountains. By our second night, we had begun arguing and sulking. Everything we disliked about each other's job surfaced. She begged me to quit the ministry. I wasn't happy she was a cop and hated the idea of her joining some secret agency in the Justice Department. After a whole night of wrangling, we checked out of the hotel and faced the beginning of the end of our relationship. The whole time we were together that week, I never thought about Maefield's letter. When I got home, that hadn't changed. I was as down in the dumps as I've ever been. I was busy nursing my wounds, answering questions by police and reporters, facing law people who no longer wanted to believe my statement about Ramous. Then came the Cuban missile thing and darned if Civil Defense didn't show up to check out our 'bomb shelter'—as if the whole state of New Jersey was going to camp in the church basement while the Soviets launched a nuclear attack. Incredible! They poked the ceiling and counted beds. The contents of Maefield's letter suddenly shocked my mind. I knew I couldn't procrastinate any longer. I certainly wasn't ready to turn over Maefield's letter until I searched for the box myself. In my first try, I came out empty handed. There was nothing where Maefield had said it would be. I pretty much decided Everett had hidden it somewhere else, or destroyed it prior to his own death. Still, though wrong doing so, I kept the letter in my possession. Last Friday morning, I decided on another look. This time I used a search light and stood on a stepladder so I could see into the opening Maefield had described. And there, out of reach, I saw the corner of a green box. Using a long shepherd's crook, a Christmas pageant prop leaning against a nearby wall, I managed to hook the box and drag it close enough to get my hands on it."

Madge tried leaving the table and Jerry restrained her. "Not now, Madge! Don't change your mind! Trust me, please!"

"Yes, I want you to continue." she reminded herself. She clutched his hands and laid her head down as before. "I do trust you!"

"There were several envelopes filled with pictures, most of them taken on location in Everett's studio, but also photos of unsuspecting people. Everett must have had hidden a camera in the locker rooms. I won't say what I saw. There were pictures from other places, all of them intrusive, private and candid. Everett used advanced, sophisticated equipment, telephoto lenses that could photograph an ant climbing a fence five-hundred feet away. He dated and coded every envelope. A few went back ten years."

Madge's hands felt cold. She raised her head. Her face had lost all its color. She took her hands away to wipe her eyes. Jerry reached across the table with his handkerchief, using it to dab her cheeks and eyes. He gathered her hands in his once more and held them down on the tabletop.

"The date written on the thickest envelope in the box was a week after Maefield's murder and—in parenthesis—the Sunday of the murder," he continued. "Maefield was already dead when Everett put these pictures into his hidden box."

"Please, No!" she cried over Jerry's hands. He played with her hair.

"Madge, look at me!"

Gently, he raised her head, supported her chin in his hand. She focused on his eyes.

"The pictures and their negatives, and all the other pictures and negatives from that box, even an undeveloped roll, the box itself, the envelopes, I burned in the church incinerator. I did it within fifteen minutes of discovery. The unused box of bullets and brass key I gave to your father. I told your dad that I had found them in a box of pictures and negatives that had belonged to Everett, but the photo stuff I had incinerated. He said, he understood. To make sure I had destroyed all, I went back and raked the ashes, and burned cardboard and newspapers on top of them. I waited five hours before calling the prosecutor's office. I met him privately an hour later and handed him Maefield's letter. I lied to him, Madge! I told him I had found Maefield's letter two hours ago. He read the letter, asked if I had the box. 'No!' I lied. I had looked in the ceiling hole, but had seen nothing, I told him. 'Will you swear on a Bible to that, Reverend, in a court of law?' 'Yes,' I said, 'I will so swear!' When I returned to the church, investigators were already there with a search warrant and sledgehammers, crowbars, floodlights. They slashed open every mattress in the storage room, then had everything in that room hauled outside for closer examination. They proceeded to take the storage room apart, ripped the plaster ceiling off its lattice, paneling off the walls, opened the sub floor, searched the coal bins and passageway, the maintenance garage and now the cathedral. They had as many as twenty cops there all night Friday, all day Saturday and came back again yesterday. They found nothing. The D.A. dropped in to see me late last night to tell me he was satisfied. They had completed their search."

Jerry felt her hands relax a little. She lifted her head. "Thank you!" she said and lowered her head again. This time, he felt her lips touch his fingers.

"The District Attorney, of course, suspects me of evidence tampering. He believes I found Everett's box. He's threatening to prosecute me if I don't don't come clean. I doubt anything will come of it so long as I don't mess with his conclusions about Everett Wheeler. In truth, that's the deal.

"There was nothing in that box that would have shed any more light on that murder. It's ironic, isn't it? If the police had found Everett's box two weeks into their investigation, they would have compromised the privacy of a lot of innocent people."

She sat up, her face pained.

"You saw me with Rhonda?"

"Yes!"

"What about Doctor Maefield? I know he saw us, Jerry. After Rhonda and I emerged from the secret room, he met us on the stair landing. He looked and acted so guilty!"

"You think he took those pictures?

She dabbed her eyes. "I don't know what to think.

Maefield's letter makes no mention of you, Madge. He provides no clue when he first or last saw Rhonda with Everett."

"We'll never know who took those pictures, will we, Jerry? Yet, somehow, the film fell into Everett's hands. He must have set someone up with a camera that afternoon, maybe one of his models. There's no other explanation."

"Maybe so, Madge! Why not let it rest?"

She would if she could, she thought. She kept it to herself, but in her mind, Sarah Draper had taken the pictures. She was Everett's friend. Photography was her hobby. Sarah enjoyed inordinate sexual displays and her letter had hinted as much. Yes, Everett and Sarah were the perfect pair and Madge contented herself in the knowledge that both were dead.

Jerry looked at Madge from across the table—her eyes swollen, her cheeks grooved by rivers of tears, her face perspiring and pale. She wiped her eyes with his handkerchief.

"You know there's nothing wrong with you, Madge. You think there is because of what happened that afternoon. You were a victim!"

"If you say that," she replied without looking at him, "then you saw that Rhonda and I began with a struggle. I have gotten sick over it. You can't believe the guilt and the shame I have experienced. Part of the problem, however, is that I was not a victim for long, neither then or other times we made love. You must also have seen that." She looked down, unable to look him in the eyes, but also to see into her past and to reflect on its gnawing truths. "I can not deny how her love making made me feel. Everything she did to me, I enjoyed. Voluntarily, I conformed to her game rules. I derived pleasure and I returned pleasure. Yet, every intimate session ended in me questioning my motives and in conflict with my conscience, something Rhonda did not understand and thought of as foolish. But, in her last letter to me, she begged for my forgiveness. Perhaps in the end, she did understand; she looked to me to initiate the next move.

"Strange, until her death, I knew nothing personal about her. Her affair with Everett and—as alleged—the many men and women with whom she had cohabitated over the years, her experiences as a young teenager in Nazi Germany—all that became late breaking news to me. In the press, they portrayed her as a Jezebel and seductress. I suppose she was. Yet, I only know how she had made me feel, and how I wanted to be with her again."

"So, do you think that makes you a bad person? Hey, it happens. The body can play tricks on the mind and vice versa. You gave into your emotions, your passion. I expect you did it for self gratification, not for love."

"Yes! But I did love her, Jerry. In an odd way, I wanted to please her. And if that is what defines love, I fulfilled it."

"Okay. What happens now? Will you let misplaced pleasure ruin the rest of your life? Will you punish yourself? Will you take a vow of celibacy, or swear off men? Perhaps you want to bag yourself in a monastery and cry 'poor little me'?"

"Worse than any of those ideas, Jerry, I think about . . . ending my life. If not for the grief I fear this would cause my parents and children . . . " Her face once more showed hurt and sadness.

"Well, there are other choices! If Rhonda awoke new feelings in you, all the better! Why waste them? Why die with a broken heart? You can love another woman, if that's what you want. You can love another man. It doesn't matter as long as that is your choice and what pleases you, what you're comfortable with, what you can live with."

After he said this, he looked down at the back of his hands, at the lipstick smudges she had left there. And when he looked up, her eyes riveted on him.

"Oh, Jerry, do you really believe that?"

"Yes, I do! I just ask you to sort it out with a competent therapist. You have to pass through the darkness, examine all the reasons. Know yourself!"

He said this without deflecting from her fearful gaze and as their hands bound each other's wrists. He smiled some as some color returned to her face and her hands relaxed.

"Will you go with me?"

"You honor me just to invite me."

There was silence between them. He trembled in the steadily growing recognition that he loved her and wherever she was sexually, it made no difference to him. He wanted her without care or question about any person to whom she had once made love. In that very moment, he vowed to conscience that if she would have him, he would become one with her and no other. As he rubbed her hands in a gentle motion, he felt them turn warm. He leaned across the table and pecked her on her forehead. He could smell her now; the lavender was not so much in the house as it had bathed her body.

"I'm going to do okay," she said, sitting straight up and allowing her familiar smile to settle on her face. Then, her fingers entangled in his she started crying again. She looked away. "I'm sorry you had to see me in those pictures."

"I burned that box and its contents, Madge, because they were no one's business, including mine. I burned what I saw of you because I love you! And I have lied about my action for the same reason."

She withdrew her hands to wipe her eyes. Suddenly, she pulled away. He did not restrain her. She got up from the table and reached for a box of tissues on the kitchen counter. She blew her nose and washed her hands. She remained standing by the sink, her back to Jerry. She stared out the window into the gray day.

Jerry stayed seated. He searched his mind for something to say. He hated the silence. He made an asserted effort to console her.

"I don't have answers for why people behave as they do, Madge. I can't answer for myself. No one is perfect. We try to look like we are. We want others to see us at our best. We hide the truth because we are afraid others will judge us harshly for who we are, for what we think. We have reason to fear if they see one wart and believe our whole body is that way. How we think, what we fantasize, our style of sex, all those things are no one's business unless we choose to show them."

Jerry was remorseful now and tears flooded his eyes. He waited a moment more to catch his thoughts and then he began again. "There's a quotation I'm fond of from *A Tale of Two Cities*, a novel by Charles Dickens: **'A solemn consideration, when I enter a great city by night, that every one of those darkly clustered houses encloses its own secret . . . that every beating heart in the hundreds of thousands of breasts there, is, in some of its imaginings, a secret to the heart nearest it.'** Isn't that how we all are, Madge? Hearts beating with secrets?"

She turned to rest her hands on his shoulders and to lean close, her mouth inches from his ear, "I hide no secrets from you, except if you don't know how much I love you, Jerry Flynn. My love is for you here and now. Tarnished, sick, wounded— whatever my love is—I hold it for you!" she whispered. "Two years or twenty-two, I would have held you in my heart. If I live a hundred years I shall love you then as I love you now."

She put her lips on the crown of his head. She moved away, leaving him with her thoughts and alone. She required fresh air. Ignoring the cold and the steady rain, she walked onto the front porch where she pressed her waist against the railing. The rain pelted her, the wind blew her dress and the harsh November chill settled in her bones. She looked across the wayward fields where ice crystals danced as they struck, listened to their considerable pounding on the metal roof above her head. A minute passed before his arms surrounded and warmed her, his chin cushioned by her hair.

She turned to face him. Their eyes connected as they had on so many occasions, only now there was no shyness, no turning to some aside distraction and no readiness to question and withdraw. Instead, he kissed her flushed eyes, tasted the saltiness of her tears while warm in their birth and kissed again following their flow to where they turned cold at the tiny corners of her lips. How hard she breathes, he thought, as he sought to drink her breath with her tears, as he felt her breasts press against him and her mouth open to hold him inside. She was first to speak, her words tumbling out of her mouth like a gentle stream over soft earth: "I love you!"

"I love you, Madge," he whispered.

"Do you love me as I am?" she asked, her mouth over his, her lips nipping his, forbidding his lips from leaving her until he answered.

"I love you as you are."

"Love me whole!" she whispered.

Their kiss turned aggressive, unrelenting in its excitement. She paused to catch her breath and when she withdrew, she held him away from her. Now her eyes sparkled in the beauty of her surrounding face, which had lit to a smile as broad and pleasing as he had ever seen it. She dropped her arms from his neck and stepped to the side, a new picture—appealing, alluring, captivating. He watched her back away and step off the porch on to the front lawn, where she stood distant in the rain, stripping away her pinafore dress and tossing it into the wind, taking off her canvas shoes and throwing them at him.

"Well, what do you think?" she said, laughing as she raised her turtleneck sweater, her bra and panties scarcely containing her nakedness.

"I think you're going to freeze to death," he chuckled. Cheerful and playful, she ran to engage him, took hold of his sweatshirt, raised it over his head and ran off with it, dropped it as he chased her on to the lawn where she dodged him until he caught her and, holding her close, they kissed again. "God, what if someone sees us like this?" he paused to admonish, at which she stepped out of his reach. Beguiling and immodest, her hands reached behind her.

"Put this on," she laughed, throwing him her bra.

He stumbled and fell as he caught it. She roared in laughter as his knees sunk into the soft soil of the garden. Unable to stop laughing, she went to help him up, but slipped herself and sat down hard, splashing mud in his face. He reached to catch her, but missed her. She got up and began running before he got to his feet.

Yelling and screeching, she crossed the leaf-strewn lawn, skipped over puddles and raced past piles of wood crates and a tractor parked to the side of the driveway. He followed, collecting their clothes and bundling them in his arms, as she disappeared through the open door of the old packing barn—dry and scented because of its old boards and fresh hay; darkish because of a single window emitting the stormy daylight; creaking because of the wind and the rain that beat on its roof; comforting because of old blankets strewn about, left over from her children's play. He rolled the barn door shut behind him and saw her in the gray light, exposed in her nakedness, nesting on a blanket over loose straw, her arms open and beckoning him to know her.

Wet and cold, they warmed each other. Hungry for affection, they kissed and caressed each other. Gentle and deliberate, they rode each other. Rising and falling, they pleasured each other. It was as though time had stopped and there appeared no end to life, or limits to energy charging their bodies.

"Don't ever stop!" she breathed into his mouth. "Love me today and tomorrow, love me in the morning and late at night, love me when I cry and when I laugh, when I awake and when I die."

Madge was no longer afraid, ashamed or alone. Jerry Flynn was her fulfillment, her rebirth, her rest in eternity. THE END.